Vengeance

By the same author

Vengeance

Empire: Volume Twelve

Anthony Riches

HODDER &
STOUGHTON

First published in Great Britain in 2021 by Hodder & Stoughton
An Hachette UK company

I

Copyright © Anthony Riches 2021

The right of Anthony Riches to be identified as the
Author of the Work has been asserted by him in accordance
with the Copyright, Designs and Patents Act 1988.

Maps © Rodney Paull

A CIP catalogue record for this title
is available from the British Library

Hardback ISBN 978 1 473 62888 5
eBook ISBN 978 1 473 62890 6

Typeset in Plantin Light by Palimpsest Book Production Limited,
Falkirk, Stirlingshire

Printed and bound in Great Britain by Clays Ltd, Elcograf S.p.A.

Hodder & Stoughton policy is to use papers that are natural, renewable
and recyclable products and made from wood grown in sustainable forests.
The logging and manufacturing processes are expected to conform to the
environmental regulations of the country of origin.

Hodder & Stoughton Ltd
Carmelite House
50 Victoria Embankment
London EC4Y 0DZ

www.hodder.co.uk

For Helen

ACKNOWLEDGEMENTS

After twelve stories in the Empire series it would be easy to be blasé when it comes to acknowledging the roles of the key people who help me bring these stories to you, the reader. I am, however, as acutely aware as ever that I quite literally could not do this job without the assistance, guidance, cajoling and occasional hefty nudge from several people. My agent Robin Wade has been a tower of strength throughout the fourteen years of our association, and I will always be grateful to him for picking the series up in the first place, finding a publisher and issuing one inestimable piece of advice (not to give up the day job easily, which, as the market has contracted and the number of players has mushroomed, has proven ever more prophetic). My debt of gratitude to Robin is immense, and even though he's now passed me on to new representation as he starts to ease down to a lower operational tempo (and as my output turns at least in part to new genres), he remains firmly on my Christmas card list.

My editor Carolyn Caughey has been splendid writing company over much the same period, having presided over the publication of fifteen books (twelve in this series and the Centurions trilogy) with an ever-present calm and light-touch approach. Assistants and publicists have tended to come and go, as is the way in the industry, but the ever-present assistance and guidance of an experienced and cool-headed editor is a thing of great value, and my cap is, as always, doffed. It would also be remiss not to mention Sharona Shelby, whose copyediting is a thing of wonder in which examples as far back as book seven are quoted to the author's complete awe and amazement. A higher quality job it would be very hard to imagine, so thanks!

And lastly, The Boss. Every writer should have a partner in crime to nurture, encourage and occasionally put them under mild duress to get the damn book started/moving/finished, and after sixteen books it's fair to say that Helen is the mistress of that particular skill-set. Ever patient, only occasionally eye-rolling at either work rate undershoots (I blame YouTube) or ego containment breaches, and treating both triumph and disaster as the imposters they are ('That's very nice/oh dear', and 'Never mind, now get on with it' being the unspoken but ever-present mood music no matter what the circumstances). She's currently administering vaccines in her role as a member of the caring profession, and I cannot think of anyone that could do a better job of being the adult member of our life partnership.

Which just leaves you. Thanks, reader, whether you've been here since the start or just picked this book up to see if the cover reflects the contents. I really couldn't have done any of this without you to breathe the life of your imagination into my characters. Let's hope we've got a few more stories to share yet!

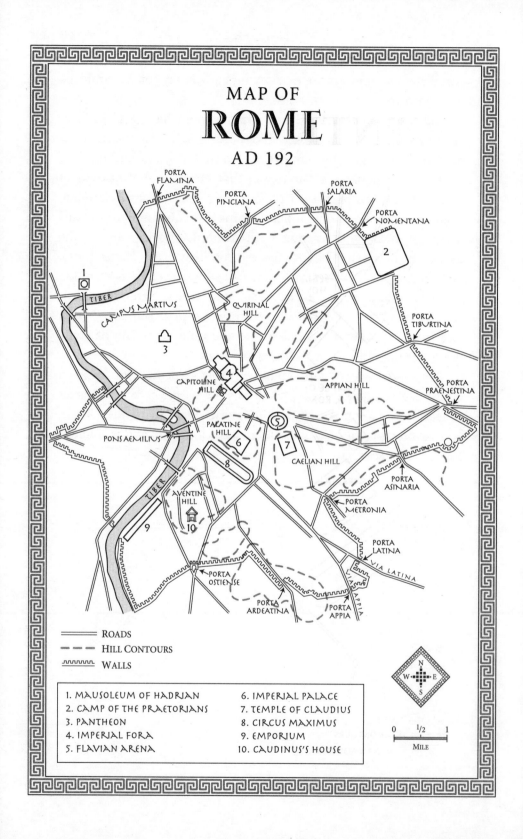

MAP OF
ROME
AD 192

PORTA FLAMINA
PORTA PINCIANA
PORTA SALARIA
PORTA NOMENTANA
PORTA TIBURTINA
PORTA PRAENESTINA
PORTA ASINARIA
PORTA METRONIA
PORTA LATINA
PORTA OSTIENSE
PORTA ARDEATINA
PORTA APPIA

TIBER
CAMPUS MARTIUS
QUIRINAL HILL
CAPITOLINE HILL
APPIAN HILL
PALATINE HILL
CAELIAN HILL
AVENTINE HILL
PONS AEMILIUS
VIA LATINA
VIA APPIA

1
2
3
4
5
6
7
8
9
10

——— ROADS
– – – HILL CONTOURS
〜〜〜 WALLS

1. MAUSOLEUM OF HADRIAN
2. CAMP OF THE PRAETORIANS
3. PANTHEON
4. IMPERIAL FORA
5. FLAVIAN ARENA
6. IMPERIAL PALACE
7. TEMPLE OF CLAUDIUS
8. CIRCUS MAXIMUS
9. EMPORIUM
10. CAUDINUS'S HOUSE

N W E S

0   1/2   1
MILE

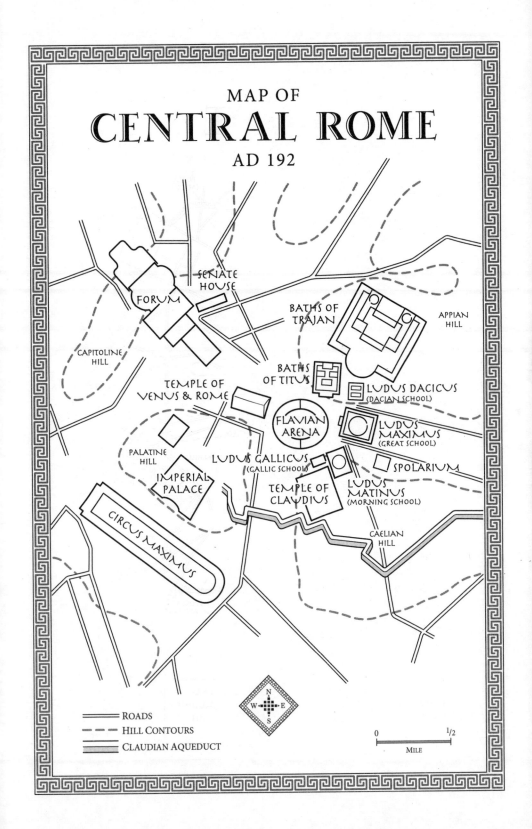

MAP OF
CENTRAL ROME
AD 192

SENATE HOUSE

FORUM

BATHS OF TRAJAN

APPIAN HILL

CAPITOLINE HILL

BATHS OF TITUS

LUDUS DACICUS
(DACIAN SCHOOL)

TEMPLE OF VENUS & ROME

FLAVIAN ARENA

LUDUS MAXIMUS
(GREAT SCHOOL)

PALATINE HILL

LUDUS GALLICUS
(GALLIC SCHOOL)

SPOLARIUM

IMPERIAL PALACE

TEMPLE OF CLAUDIUS

LUDUS MATINUS
(MORNING SCHOOL)

CIRCUS MAXIMUS

CAELIAN HILL

ROADS
HILL CONTOURS
CLAUDIAN AQUEDUCT

N
W E
S

0   1/2
MILE

Prologue

'What have I missed about Rome since the last time we were there? Absolutely *fucking* nothing!'

Gaius Rutilius Scaurus smiled to himself at the vehemence of the statement. He spoke without looking back down the party's line of mounted men, fifteen armed riders arrayed in front of and behind a pair of waggons on which several women and their children were being carried. Some of the riders were heavily built axemen, their weapons suspended from leather saddle-loops. Others, more slightly built, had bows strung across their shoulders and quivers of arrows at their sides.

They were riding along a road that was gradually rising towards the crest of a hill a mile ahead, forest on both sides forming a green tunnel through which the arrow-straight ribbon of cobbles was slowly climbing. Scaurus, a grey-eyed man in his late thirties, and one of only two male members of the party not heavily bearded, was riding at the small column's head next to the man to whom he was speaking, a heavily built former centurion whose hair and beard were shot through with grey.

'Come now, Julius, there must be something about the mother of the empire that you look forward to enjoying once again?'

'Let me think . . .' The big man riding beside him made a momentary show of thought. 'The constant smell of shit in the streets? Everyone I meet trying to gouge yet more coin out of my purse at every opportunity?' He gestured to the man riding beside Scaurus, the only other member of the party other than the tribune who was clean-shaven, and further distinguished by the two swords strapped to his body. 'Oh, yes, and the constant risk of Marcus being identified, and every single one of us being executed for harbouring an imperial fugitive?'

'That, and the fact that every time we go back to the bloody place we end up being sent away to the arse-end of nowhere, to defend Rome's interests against unpleasant men who want nothing more than to kill us.'

Julius looked over at the massively built and heavily bearded man riding a suitably powerful horse beside him and nodded approvingly.

'And, as Dubnus points out, there's the apparent inevitability of us forced to clean up yet another imperial fuck-up! Compared with all that, I'd say the life we've enjoyed for the last few years has been idyllic, as I suspect even you would be forced to agree.'

Scaurus conceded his points with a wave of his hand, but any more meaningful response was prevented by the sudden appearance of armed men on the road ahead of the party. One of them strode forward, raising his sword to halt their progress with a dozen men at his back. They appeared to be dressed in threadbare military tunics, and while their weapons were standard-issue infantry swords, and most of the bandits were equipped with curved rectangular legion shields, faded paint and rusted iron betrayed a lack of any recent maintenance.

The man with the sword, having apparently eschewed his shield, strolled easily to within a few paces of Scaurus's horse. His expression was one of complete confidence in both his own and his men's abilities, and when he spoke, his words carried a hint of boredom at a frequently repeated greeting.

'Stop where you are, friends! There are men behind you, and in the trees on either side too, more than twice as many swords as you can muster! And there's no way you can fight fifty of us!'

Julius barked a one-word order as he vaulted out of his horse's saddle.

'Dismount!'

The party's riders obeyed the command in one swift coordinated movement, every man drawing a sword, hefting an axe or nocking an arrow to a bow, clearly drilled for exactly such an eventuality. Dubnus pulled the long-handled axe from his horse's saddle and paced forward with the blade held down, taking a fighting stance alongside Scaurus and Marcus and shouting a challenge at the men blocking the road.

'It's not the number of swords you should be worried about, but the men behind them! Now get out of the fucking road before I'm forced to make you regret your choices in life!'

Scaurus moved to stand alongside him, raising a cautionary hand.

'There's no need for this to end in bloodshed.'

The bandit leader nodded, casting an anxious look at the axe and brandishing his own sword.

'Yes, you tell him to stand the fuck down before . . .'

He stopped talking as the Roman bared his teeth in a hard grin.

'I wasn't talking to him. I was talking to *you*.'

The robber shook his head in genuine puzzlement.

'What, you think you can fight off fifty men?'

Scaurus called back over his shoulder.

'Julius!'

'Tribune?'

Scaurus ignored the robbers' guffaws and looks of disbelief at his title.

'Man here wants to know if we can fight off fifty *men*. What do you think?'

The big man stalked forward, adding his sword to the line of weapons facing the bandits, cast a disparaging glance at the men blocking their way forward and then turned and looked back at the short column's rear, where another eight men stood, apparently ready to fight.

'What do I think? I think—'

The bandit leader shouted a distinctly irritated command at

them, the ragged edge of his frustration making his order sound petulant rather than authoritative.

'Put your fucking weapons down! I won't tell you again!'

Julius shook his head in evident amusement, tapping the blade of his drawn sword and raising an eyebrow.

'Didn't your mummy ever tell you it's rude to interrupt a man while he's talking? You do that again and it'll be the last thing you ever do.'

Another of the bandits bristled with anger, evidently graced with even less patience than his leader.

'You kill him, there's plenty more of us!'

Julius nodded.

'Noted. Dubnus. Kill *that* fool first.'

He turned back to Scaurus.

'So, what do I think? I think there's not even thirty of them, never mind fifty. I think they were stupid giving us time to dismount and air our iron, but then I doubt they've ever been offered a fight before. And look at them, not one of them with a scar on his pretty face. Whereas everyone knows that the spear you don't see coming usually leaves you with a permanent reminder, if it doesn't just kill you. And now I think they're shitting themselves at the idea of their first proper fight ever.'

He paused ostentatiously, tipping his head on one side as if to listen, waiting for the bandit leader to order an attack.

'Told you so. And I think even Lupus could have any one of them in a straight fight, never mind the rest of us.'

Scaurus shrugged at the bandit.

'Sorry, but there it is. This man has stood beside me on a dozen battlefields as we spilled the blood of Rome's enemies. So if he says you're bluffing, then I think you're bluffing.'

'We *will* fight you!'

The Roman nodded at the red-faced would-be robber.

'I know. You have no choice – you personally, I mean. After all, if you don't fight, then you all go hungry, and that would see you put at more risk than you could handle, wouldn't it? So yes, you'll fight. And you'll die. All of you.' He shot the man a calculating glance. 'It doesn't have to be that way though, and I could do without losing whichever of my people you get lucky enough to kill. So instead of that, how about we let our respective champions fight it out? If your man wins, we'll pay up fifty gold aureii and you'll let us pass. If your man loses, then you'll just let us pass, and you won't try to follow us. How does that sound?'

The bandit turned back to his men, and Scaurus knew all too well the look he was giving them. Julius stepped closer, his voice a quiet mutter.

'You do realise that whatever they agree to now, you've told them there's fifty in gold to be had. They'll follow us all the way to Rome if they have to, waiting for the chance to attack us in the middle of the night. We'd be better dealing with them now.'

'Clearly. Tell me, is Lupus actually ready for this?'

Julius raised an eyebrow at him.

'That was a figure of speech, nothing more. You actually want the boy to do this?'

'He's not a boy any longer. He's been training with Arminius every day for the last ten years, and practising serious blade-work with Marcus ever since we opted for the quiet life. And I'll remind you that he's already killed, and come to terms with taking that first life. So, do you think he's ready?'

Julius nodded slowly.

'Does he have the beating of any of this rabble? I'd hope so.'

'And that's good enough for me.'

Scaurus nodded decisively, raising his voice to get the bandits' attention.

'Come now, gentlemen, it's time to either piss or get off the pot. Either pick your champion, take the risk of offering us a proper fight or just back off and let us pass. And to make it easier for you to decide, we'll put up the youngest man among us as our champion.'

The bandit leader and the man who seemed to be his deputy exchanged glances that weren't hard to decode, and the former beckoned one of his men forward.

'Castus! Come and make yourself useful!'

The robber who strode forward was lanky and had a hard-edged look to him, handling his sword and shield with the sort of unconscious competence that could only result from years of training in the ranks of a legion or auxiliary cohort. He grinned in a clear attempt to unnerve Julius, revealing a mouthful of gapped and blackened teeth.

'Who wants killing then?'

Julius looked the legion deserter up and down.

'This is the best you've got?'

The bandit leader nodded, waving a hand at the waiting robber.

'He'll go through whoever you put up like shit through a goose. Get ready to pay up, *Tribune*, because he's a stone-cold killer.'

Julius turned away.

'Lupus!'

The young man came forward with a wary glance at the waiting ex-soldier, an infantry gladius in one hand and a dagger in the other. Julius shot a hard stare at his grandfather that kept Morban's mouth shut, although the older man's return stare was eloquent. Lupus, tall enough to look him straight in the eyes, and with muscles well defined from years of incessant sparring with anyone who would give him their time, was calmly sizing up his likely opponent, seemingly untroubled by the apparent fifteen-year difference in their ages.

'Julius.'

'See that?' He gestured to the waiting bandit, speaking quietly to avoid being overheard. 'Think you can beat him?'

The younger man shrugged, apparently unconcerned at the prospect.

'Only one way to find out.'

'You'll have to kill him.'

Lupus's expression remained emotionless.

'Kind of pointless fighting if we're not serious about it.'

Julius nodded, conceding the point with a frown at the younger man's lack of any concern.

'Right. But do it quickly. Nothing flashy, just stop his wind as quickly as you can. And when you've done him, step back sharply. No hanging around close enough to them for anyone to try to avenge him.'

'Kill him quick. Step back quick. Got it.'

Julius stared him in the eye for a moment longer, then turned back to the bandit leader.

'This is your last chance. Walk away now and you won't have to dig a hole for your man.'

The deserter looked Lupus up and down with a beaming grin.

'You really think that boy can handle a killer like Castus? Only in your dreams!'

Marcus, who had previously remained silent, stepped forward and handed Lupus the longer of his two swords, a cavalry spatha, the long sword used to reach down out of the saddle to kill infantry opponents.

'Use this. You know what to do. And do it your own way.'

The younger man sheathed his dagger and took the long sword in his right hand, transferring his gladius to his left, nodded at Marcus and stepped forward to face the waiting bandit. Castus grinned at him predatorily, supremely confident in his abilities.

'Ready to die, are you, youngster? And it's Lupus, is it? The wolf? You don't look much like a wolf, boy, you look more like a long streak of—'

The younger man fixed him with a level stare.

'Talkative, aren't you?'

The bandit frowned at the interruption, seemingly determined to go through a well-established routine.

'I like to describe a man to himself, sonny, before I stop his wind. Gives him one last chance to consider himself before he dies. Like you there, with your two swords. Everybody thinks a second sword'll make them look like a gladiator, but no bastard ever knows how to actually use—'

'Talkative, or just scared to fight?'

The deserter bridled, raising his sword blade threateningly.

'You cheeky cunt! You've got some front for a kid, I'll give you that, but that's all you are. A kid.' He grinned, believing himself re-established as the master of their interaction. 'I'll bet you haven't even had a woman yet, have you? Not unless one of those has taken pity on you!' He winked at the women watching impassively from their vantage point on the waggons. 'Is one of them your mother? Perhaps when I'm done with you, and your mates know they're beaten, I'll see if she fancies a proper length of cucumber!'

'Just scared then.' Lupus shrugged, crouching into a fighting stance and stepping forward, skimming his feet across the cobbles with a faint rattle of hobnails on stone. 'And I'm bored now. Let's get on with it.'

Castus came forward at him with a determined expression, one step at a time, edging towards the fight with his gladius arm cocked back so that the blade's point was level with the edge of his shield.

'Don't let him close . . .'

Marcus fixed Julius with a stare, shaking his head to silence his friend. Even as the big man nodded his understanding and pursed his lips, the bandit attacked, looking to take advantage of any resultant lapse in the younger man's concentration. Thrusting his sword blade in overhand, forcing Lupus to parry upwards with his gladius, he stepped in closer, swinging the weapon in low with all the speed and power he had, clearly hoping to distract the younger man from the threat of a punch with the boss of his shield.

His opponent took a swift step back, parrying again with the gladius in his left hand. But as the bandit stamped forward again, ready to punch, he stopped with a look of bafflement. Lupus's spatha, previously held low and with its tip withdrawn, had lanced in over the top of his shield so fast that he hadn't seen it coming, slicing a shallow gash in the side of his neck.

Stepping backwards a single pace, Castus looked down in consternation at the blood running down onto his left shoulder from the wound, while Lupus waited behind his raised blades with an unreadable expression.

'I told him not to waste any chance to make the kill!'

Marcus shook his head at Julius's concern.

'And I told him to fight in whatever way he felt right. So trust him.'

The deserter shot his comrades a swift glance but found no comfort in their shocked expressions. He shook his head in disbelief and then nodded at his opponent with a new, harder-faced expression.

'Fancy sword work, is it, you cocky young prick? Alright, let's see what good it does you against *this!*'

He advanced quickly in a legion-standard combat drill, punching out with his shield with every step forward, intent on getting to close quarters without risking a repeat of the attack that had wounded him. Lupus matched him, backing away step for step, watching his advance with narrowed eyes.

'Not so brave now, are you, eh wolf-boy?' The deserter advanced another step, his shield punching out again, but with each step forward the lower rim sank slightly closer to his leading foot than before, as the unaccustomed weight of the shield told on his poorly conditioned muscles. Lupus made to repeat his previous sword thrust at his opponent's exposed throat and shoulder, but as Castus raised his shield with a knowing grin, the younger man rolled his shoulder and turned the lunge into a lightning-fast stab that speared the sword's point down into the deserter's unprotected left foot. He twisted the blade, the men standing around them wincing at the click of breaking bones, then ripped it free and stepped back to leave his opponent staggering, his mouth opened wide with the agony of the wound, all thought of the fight momentarily forgotten.

Julius motioned Lupus forward impatiently.

'Finish him!'

The younger man ignored him, setting himself ready to fight again. After a moment the deserter remembered where he was, looking up from his ruined foot at the waiting Lupus. Hobbling on his good leg, with the other foot barely touching the bloodied cobbles, he held his sword and shield out on either side in an apparent signal of his surrender.

'I give up! You can't make me fight on like this!'

Lupus shook his head, still expressionless even as he refused any idea of mercy.

'And you'd have spared me, would you? We fight.'

'But—'

Castus yelped as his opponent stormed forward, hammering at his shield so hard with the spatha's evilly sharp blade that its iron rim sprang free with a soft twang, exposing the layered wood to his repeated chopping blows.

'Stop!'

The bandit leader attempted to intervene, jumping back as Lupus swung the spatha at his face with an easy grace, the blade's tip carving a bloody furrow into his cheek.

'You fucking—'

He fell silent as the long sword struck again and Castus's shield fell in two pieces from his battered hand, leaving the deserter both crippled and defenceless.

'Spare him! Let him live and we'll leave you alone!'

He took a step back as the twin blades swivelled to point at him. When he spoke, Lupus's words were as hard as the stare he was playing on the new target of his ire.

'You want to take his place?' He waited for an ostentatious moment before shaking his head. 'I thought not.'

He pivoted back towards the tottering Castus, his sword a bright arc of blurred steel as he chopped the blade's last foot of razor-edged steel through his opponent's neck, decapitating him with a single blow. The bandit's severed head fell to the cobbles and rolled down into the ditch, his headless corpse folding like a puppet with its strings cut. Ignoring Julius's instructions, Lupus stepped forward until he was within two paces of the horrified bandits, his face a blood-flecked mask of fury.

'Who's next? Come on, you cowards! All you have to do is put your hand to your iron and I'll know you want to dance!'

Faced with the immediate reality of their dead comrade, the would-be robbers raised their hands away from their weapons as one man, and Julius stepped forward to retake control of the situation.

'So your best man couldn't stand against the youngest among us? And now you're all flinching away from him like virgins in a whorehouse. I'd say this attempted robbery is over, wouldn't you? You, the so-called leader of this rabble, gather your men here where I can see them and disarm, before I lose what's left of my patience and tell my lads to paint themselves red with your blood. Come on, they're getting impatient!'

The robbers gathered and surrendered their swords, their faces mostly downcast, the few angry glances they dared met by the basilisk stares of the party's bowmen, their arrows nocked and ready to fly. Julius gestured to a solemn-faced Scaurus, who had placed a priest's veil over his head.

'The tribune is a priest in the cult of Mithras, which means that anything you say to him goes straight to the god's ear. So, here's what we're going to do. You fools are going to swear an oath to the Lightbringer that you're going to abandon this way of life. All of you, here and now. Which will make it an oath that you'll abandon at your peril. And any man that refuses to swear the oath will die, here and now, but slowly, roasted over a cooking fire by that big cannibal bastard.'

The humbled robbers looked at the indicated man in horror, blenching at the sight of him looming head and shoulders over his comrades, his hungry expression promising a painful passage from their lives. Julius indicated the spot where Scaurus was waiting.

'Get to it. Any man that refuses to swear will be that monster's dinner tonight.'

As the day slid towards dusk, the party gathered around a cooking fire over which a pair of soldiers were stewing the meat of a wild boar under the watchful eye of Julius's formidable wife Annia. The former centurion called Lupus over to join him, the younger man's expression just as imperturbable as before.

'You did well today. Risked your life, it has to be said, but—'

'Was *you* that risked my life.'

'He has a point, I'm forced to observe.' Marcus took a sip from his wine. 'We asked him to kill his opponent, so he did. You can't blame the man for choosing the way he went about it, can you?'

Julius nodded morosely, and Scaurus raised his cup in salute.

'You made a statement today, Lupus. And the Lightbringer will have heard that statement, you can be sure of that.'

Julius gave him an eloquent look, inspiring the former tribune to smile back at him.

'Go on, what's on your mind?'

'It occurred to me that what we did to Lupus today is pretty much what we're doing to ourselves in going back to Rome with you.'

'Picking a fight that we have no way of knowing whether we can win?'

'Picking a fight that by rights we should probably lose.'

Scaurus nodded.

'True. But as I told you when you took your sword down from over the fireplace of your house, it's not *your* fight.'

'And as I replied at the time, your fight *is* my fight. But Lupus has made an excellent point that you'd do well to be aware of.'

'Which is?'

Julius pointed over at Annia, who was holding her oldest child Victoria on her lap while her son Felix and Marcus's boy Appius played knucklebones on the grass at her feet.

'We also have a duty to those we love. Which means that we'll fight, but that the way we choose to do so might not be one you expect.'

Scaurus shrugged equably.

'We will all have our part to play in the salvation of our empire. What that part might be, I suspect none of us can predict. We can only offer our lives to the Lightbringer, and pray that he chooses to use them wisely.'

I

Rome, 28 December AD 192

Titus Menius Caudinus woke with a vague feeling of unease. His usual sentiment on waking was more one of smugness, as he once again rediscovered his happy situation in life. Tolerable wealth, a more than acceptable domicile, and the inestimable pleasure of having restored dignity, of a sort, to his family's name being his main sources of satisfaction. All of which had looked less than likely ten years before, when he had been forced to take menial service in the imperial palace as the alternative to being imprisoned for his debts. Debts which had been bequeathed to him by a spendthrift father, true enough, but binding all the same. Debts which had fortuitously, as it turned out, been purchased by an influential imperial freedman. Cleander had then put him to work as a scribe in his office, keeping back four-fifths of his income to pay off the debt at a dismayingly slow rate after the deduction of interest.

Fortuitously, however, because when Caudinus's new master had been elevated to the dizzy rank of imperial chamberlain, he had taken Caudinus with him. And a scribe in the chamberlain's office was a man in a powerful, if slightly precarious, position. He found himself increasingly trusted with state secrets, and privy to his master's business dealings. Dealings which were, as was to be expected, both somewhat dubious but highly profitable. And Caudinus's obvious lack of any moral compass beyond his own enrichment had made him an essential part of the great man's modus operandi. At first handsomely rewarded, and then freed from his debt, the role of scribe had been transformed into that of secretary. From which rank it had been a small step to confidant and intimately trusted assistant. By the end of the third year of his master's term of office, Caudinus had been moved from his secretarial role to the management of the chamberlain's personal trading operations. And, with the services of the praetorian fleets to command, what had started as a small-scale operation, with occasional opportunities for the clandestine shipment of low-volume and high-value consignments to the capital, had become routine. And larger in scale. Much larger.

So great had the profits from Caudinus's work become – and so much of a risk to his master's personal safety, were they to be revealed to an emperor famously jealous of his prerogatives – that he had become a man whose discretion was of vital importance. And, recognising the risk he would undoubtedly put himself in, were he to let slip any of the secrets he managed, he had resolved to remain silent at all times and on all subjects to anyone other than his master himself. And had been bounteously rewarded in consequence. Which was why he now enjoyed the ownership of a nice house, spacious in floor plan for Rome, set in the privacy of a walled garden high on the Aventine Hill. And why his banker was the custodian of enough gold to keep Caudinus in the style to which he had become accustomed, with fine food and wine and the regular company of attractive and compliant women, for the rest of his life. Even his master's downfall two years before hadn't been the disaster he might have feared. Contrary to Caudinus's expectations in a palace rife with corruption, the great man's successor, Eclectus, having unearthed the clandestine trading operation that bypassed imperial taxation, had chosen to lay the profits of the operation at the emperor's feet – and without naming Caudinus as part of the fraud, sparing him from almost certain execution for having facilitated Cleander's crimes. After which the single-minded Aegyptian had promptly put Caudinus back to work, his responsibilities unchanged other than there being a new beneficiary for the fruit of his talents.

All of which was usually grounds for a small glow of self-satisfaction on waking. But not, after a moment to regain some semblance of consciousness, on this occasion. There was something not right, and for a moment Caudinus struggled to work out what it was before realising, with something of a shock, that someone was sitting on his bed. Invisible in the darkness, but a distinct presence nonetheless, and a disturbing sensation of contact against his left leg.

'What—'

'Shh.'

If the unexpected presence was disturbing, being shushed like a naughty child was, under the circumstances, both absurd and terrifying. But hardly anywhere near as disturbing as what followed.

'He's awake.'

The gruff, matter-of-fact statement from whoever was sitting at the foot of the bed resulted in a prompt response. The bedroom door opened to reveal another man, this one carrying a lighted lamp whose tiny flame was just enough to dimly illuminate the intruders. Whose appearance was enough in itself to put the fear of any number of gods into Caudinus. The man at the end of the bed was eastern in appearance, and his accented speech was that of a cultured individual, but the expression on his face was at best daunting. The man . . . no, two men, Caudinus realised, who had entered the room at his command, were entirely another matter. Villainous, hard-faced and, fair to say, predatory in their aspect, both were staring down at him with expressions which were sadly lacking in any form of compassion. A hand patted his foot, then gripped his ankle with a vice-like hold, revealing the sort of strength that reinforced his initial impression that these men were professional ruffians.

'How—'

'Be quiet, Menius Caudinus. That's twice I have warned you to be silent. If I have to do so one more time I will invite these two to provide you with some motivation for there not to be a fourth. Saratos?'

The taller of the two men crouched at the foot of the bed, flicked away the covers to reveal Caudinus's feet and then, disturbingly, used his fingers to stroke the toes of his right foot.

'Good nails. Long enough for pliers. Perfect for being pulled out.'

'It seems your disregard for footcare provides us with an excellent opportunity. So if you utter one more word, other than when I invite you to speak, the result will be the removal of a toenail. You had best prepare the gag, Sanga, while your comrade prepares to remove a nail or two as an object lesson in how screaming one's head off can help a man learn to keep quiet. I suspect that our new friend here will require a practical demonstration soon enough.'

The ruffian looked up at his companion holding the lamp.

'Give me the pliers, Sanga.'

'Pliers? I ain't got them. I was lamp man. You, Saratos, was the pliers man.'

Surreally, and enough to have made Caudinus laugh under other circumstances, the man called Saratos rolled his eyes.

'It is always the same. You want a job doing, you do it yourself. No matter.'

He drew a short knife from a sheath on his belt and put the point under the nail of the captive's big toe on his right foot. Pushing it far enough under the nail for a sudden sharp feeling of discomfort to completely dispel any amusement. The scribe stiffened and reflexively tried to rise, but a firm hand on his chest prevented him from doing so with disturbing ease. The man called Saratos, dark-featured and with jet-black hair, nodded at the easterner.

'I am ready.'

'Excellent. Sanga?'

The second ruffian approached Caudinus with a swift, completely unapologetic grin, raising a strip of revoltingly filthy cloth that was clearly a soldier's neck scarf which had travelled far and wide in the empire's service.

'You just say if I need to muffle him, Centurion.'

The man at the foot of the bed glanced upwards swiftly, as if consulting his gods.

'I was thinking that you might restrain him, Sanga, as we discussed, rather than poison him with that noisome piece of wool. We can gag him with his own pillow. But no matter, perhaps our host will have the good sense not to provoke us to unnecessary violence.' He turned back to Caudinus. 'So, shall I explain our presence here?'

Caudinus, no fool, nodded silently.

'Good. You are Titus Menius Caudinus, secretary to the former chamberlain, Cleander. That is not a question, and if you seek to deny it you will incur the penalty already made very clear.'

Caudinus nodded a second time.

'Sensible. And you were, for several years, the former chamberlain's closest confidant. A trusted executor of his private business dealings.'

He paused, raising an interrogatory eyebrow, and Caudinus nodded again.

'Now we're making progress, and without any unnecessary unpleasantness. Since the chamberlain's untimely death, you have continued to operate his clandestine trading network. Just under different ownership, and with the principal beneficiary none other than the emperor himself. There is no need to nod, we know all about you. We have travelled on the ships of the praetorian fleet more than once, and we're familiar with the fact that they frequently carry unofficial cargoes which avoid the scrutiny of the customs inspectors.'

Caudinus looked up at the inscrutable intruder, thinking furiously. He thought through the likely options as to who the mysterious intruders might be and came to a swift conclusion. The easterner smiled at him.

'And now I see you making connections. Have you worked it out yet?' Caudinus nodded warily. 'You may speak.'

'I think that you are comrades of the fugitive Marcus Valerius

Aquila, who uses the pseudonym Marcus Tribulus Corvus. You
are the Syrian centurion from Hama. Your name is . . .' He thought
for a moment. 'Qadir. And I believe this because you have been
transported by that fleet on more than one occasion. Am I right?'

'Right first time. You are clearly well informed, if a little too
inquisitive for your own good. But no matter, curiosity can be
tolerated if it is accompanied by complete obedience. And my
appearance, here and now, means what, do you think?'

Caudinus pondered the question. Working hard to find some
way to make the unexpected turn of events look more favourable
to his personal situation than currently appeared to be the case.

'You were in hiding, I take it?'

The easterner nodded.

'After we managed to defeat the latest in a series of enemies
served up for us by your former master, in a battle far to the
south of Aegyptus, the dominus of our familia called us together
to take stock of our position. We had triumphed over the army
of Kush by a combination of inspired strategy and, it was obvious
to all, the beneficial favour of Fortuna herself. And not for the
first time. In fact, it was favour that, we were all forced to agree,
we had stretched to the limits of the goddess's beneficent patience
over the previous few years. And it was equally apparent that,
were we to attempt to return to Rome, our deaths were the most
likely outcome. Our dominus believed that since he had called
the governor of Aegyptus out as part of your former master's
fraudulent trading network, Cleander would order him to arrest
us all at the first opportunity.'

He gestured to Caudinus, who realised he was being invited to
comment.

'You were right. When Praefectus Augustalis Faustinianus
reported the allegations made to him by your master Gaius Rutilius
Scaurus in Alexandria, Cleander's fury was uncontrollable. He
replied with orders for you to be returned to Rome in chains.
Proof of your deaths, even incontrovertible proof, was deemed
very much a second-best option. I am quite sure he wished to

witness your deaths in person. He was quite an uncivilised man, for a Greek.'

Qadir nodded.

'As expected. And so we spent a good deal of the gold remaining to us in covering our tracks when we left the province. We found a quiet place, far away enough from Rome to be safe, close enough that we could return within weeks, if needed. And so we settled down to wait, no longer at the chamberlain's mercy. Having taken the precaution of getting our comrades out of Rome at the same time we left the city, there was no way for Cleander to force us to come forth for execution.'

Caudinus recalled with perfect clarity his master's violent rage when it had been revealed that Valerius Aquila's son had been spirited out of the imperial palace along with those of his comrade, the auxiliary centurion Julius. The children's effective detention had been the threat that the chamberlain had counted on to bring their father to heel, after the completion of the mission at the far end of the Middle Sea. His fury had only worsened when the resulting searches had revealed neither where the boys might be hidden nor the whereabouts of their surrogate mother, who had been detained with them. The woman and children, her husband and all of his associates had been put on wanted lists across the empire, but none of them had ever come to light over the intervening years.

'And now, with Cleander dead, you have returned.' Qadir nodded, his face imperturbable. 'Although he died two years ago, which means that you must have a specific purpose in returning now. A purpose which requires something from me, perhaps?'

Caudinus looked around him. Wondering if it was the house or his life they had come for.

'You fear for your life. But we do not wish to kill you. You expect to be evicted, since Valerius Aquila has a legal claim on his dead wife's house. But we do not wish to deny you this dwelling. We do, however, have certain expectations of you. If you satisfy them, you will come through the next few weeks with your position in the imperial palace unaffected. Or at least unchanged by any direct action of ours.'

'And if I fail to satisfy them?'

Qadir smiled gently.

'I fail to see that as being in your interests. But let us discuss the terms of your survival. The house is, as I say, whether the authorities recognise it or not, still the property of Valerius Aquila's deceased wife. Which he therefore inherited when she died. You can buy it from us, for a sum well in excess of its real value. The gold will come in handy. And don't try to deny that you have the money, when I tell you how much you will have to pay to keep it. We have made it our business to get to know your banker, and he has chosen to be most cooperative. Is this accept- able, or do you choose to fall at the first hurdle?'

Caudinus nodded. Evidently unsurprised.

'I will purchase this house for whatever value you place upon it, if I can afford it. I have become attached to the place.'

'Whereas for Valerius Aquila, it is a constant reminder of his wife. I'm sure you know what happened to her?'

The scribe nodded. The story of her impregnation by the emperor, and her death in childbirth, had been one in which Cleander had taken disturbing pleasure.

'What more do you need from me?'

Qadir gestured to the two ruffians at the foot of the bed.

'These men have been schooled in a skill that I possess. I have taught them to track a man across the stone forest that is the city. They could be watching you on the street and you would never see them, because I have trained them to act as informers, and in doing so unlocked their considerable innate talent for skuldug- gery. And now I am recruiting you in much the same capacity. You will act as our eyes and ears inside the palace. Our conduit into the office of the chamberlain. And into other parts of the palace too. I'd imagine that a man in your position will be able to go pretty much anywhere he likes?'

Caudinus looked up at the easterner with a resigned expression.

'You realise that if I am caught in an act of informing for you, I will be tortured to death?'

Qadir nodded, untroubled.

'I also realise that in the event of that happening, you will undoubtedly tell your captors whatever they want to know. Even before they proceed to torture you to death to prove the truth of your initial statement. Especially as I need you to be more than just a reporter of events. I need you to influence them as well.'

'You want me to influence . . . *events?*'

'Yes. Your first task is small, but it is vital to our plans. I need you to find me a man.'

'Who?'

The Hamian shrugged.

'I have no idea. All I do know is which legion he currently serves with. He is a centurion with the Fifteenth Apollinaris, serving in Cappadocia. He was enlisted into the legion about ten years ago, by means of a direct recruitment into the centurionate rather than having come up through the ranks.'

He leaned closer to the helpless Caudinus.

'So, when you go into the palace later today, you will find an excuse to go to the imperial records building. To that part of the imperial records that details the legions' personnel. Once there you will use your status as the chamberlain's secretary to have the room cleared of all staff. I suggest you tell them that your master requires you to make a private enquiry into several senior officers' records. And that the matter is to remain utterly secret, to avoid word getting to the men in question before official action is taken. Perhaps you should dismiss the record keepers, on the grounds that were they to see the names you are investigating, then they might lay themselves open to serious charges, if those men manage by any artifice to avoid justice. However you manage it, you're going to need to be alone with the Fifteenth Legion's paperwork for long enough to both find me that man and then discern several very specific pieces of information regarding his life. Birthdate, birthplace, enlistment date, dates of any commendations, which century he commands—'

Caudinus shook his head in disbelief.

'What? You're expecting me to commit an act of informing against the imperium itself? And in the legion records of all places?'

The Hamian smiled tightly.

'Yes. What did you think the price of sparing you from death was going to be? An occasional report on the palace gossip? Details of what Commodus has for his breakfast?'

'But if I'm caught taking liberties with legion paperwork I'll be . . .'

He fell silent, and after a moment Qadir spoke, his voice hard and uncaring.

'As we agreed, you will be tortured, most likely. Your master the chamberlain will be eager to know why you took such a monstrous risk, and won't hesitate to have you interrogated by the most brutal methods. And you will tell them everything you know before the fun and games begins, of course, but since you know next to nothing, that isn't going to keep them from going to work on you for very long. You could, of course, choose not to carry out my request, in which case you will be denounced as an informer to the chamberlain by an anonymous message. Anonymous but highly convincing. Which will put you in the interrogation chair just as quickly, while our inconvenience at losing your services will be no more than that. An inconvenience. So, on the one hand you risk possible torture and execution, while on the other, those outcomes are a certainty if you decide to fail us. And so that is your choice. I can allow you a short time in which to make the decision. Just do so in the certain knowledge of what will befall you if I tell my associates that you've decided not to assist us.'

He fell silent, waiting for the functionary to reply.

'It seems you leave me without any choice.'

Qadir smiled, reaching out a hand to pat his cheek.

'As I expected. You are a man of quite unerring instinct when it comes to plotting the path to self-preservation.'

★

'Gaius, my boy! It's good to see you again! I was starting to wonder if you hadn't vanished for good this time?'

Scaurus bowed. The gesture of respect was deep enough to indicate his abiding respect for his host, but not so fulsome as to be obsequious. Angular of features, with grey eyes that cast a penetrating stare out at the world, he had the sinewy build of a soldier, if not overly muscled. His face was shaved, unusual in Rome in an era where all men of the ruling classes copied the emperor's tonsorial stylings for fear of being seen as lacking respect, exposing the sharp planes of his face in a forbidding appearance. But if his physical appearance was a little daunting to the chance observer, it was the veiled menace in his cold grey eyes that had encouraged the senator's other visitors to leave the house's entrance hall quite as speedily as they had, when bidden to return the next day due to his unexpected arrival. The unconsciously predatory stare of a dangerous animal, intimidating without effort, his gaze was that of a man so accustomed to dealing death that it had settled on him like a cloak he no longer knew he wore. When he spoke, however, his tone was light, edged with affection for the man before him.

'Should I address you as senator or consul, Helvius Pertinax?'

The older man strode forward and took him in a bear hug. Well built, and formally dressed, he was clearly still a vital man even well into his sixties, an age at which many of his peers were either in their dotage or already dead. Heavily bearded, his hair was iron grey, and his face ruddy from decades of campaigning as one of Rome's foremost generals.

'For a start you can lose the formality, you cheeky pup! You can either call me Publius or Uncle, unless you'd like to take a place in line to meet with "the senator". And I was starting to wonder if you would arrive in time.'

Scaurus held the hug for a moment and then stepped back, smiling broadly with the pleasure of seeing the man whom he considered the closest thing to a father he'd had since his birth father's death in Germania two decades before.

'In which case, greetings, Uncle! I came as quickly as I could, once your invitation to return to the city reached me. With the passes over the mountains closed, we were forced to take the longer route to the west through Gallia Narbonense, but I hoped we'd reach Rome before the turn of the year as you requested, and so it has proven.'

'And for that I'm grateful. I'll be happier with you and your familia at my back in the events that are soon to come. And you're just in time.'

Pertinax led Scaurus from the entry hall of his house through a magnificent atrium whose twenty-foot-long pool reflected the sky above.

'We can't talk here, it's far too public. Come on.' He gestured to his waiting secretary. 'We'll take wine in the garden. The good stuff, mind you, not that watery vinegar you palm off on my clients.'

He led his guest out into a magnificent garden, its ornate lawns, hedged formal areas and tree-shaded arbours palatial by the standards of the city. Scaurus took the seat indicated, looking appreciatively out over Rome.

'I never tire of this view.'

'As I recall, there was a time when you were a good deal keener on being out in those streets than looking down upon them. Until we managed to beat the urchin out of you and replace him with something closer to a Roman gentleman. Although I suspect we never quite managed to eradicate that urge to gamble. Did we?'

The younger man grinned back at him guilelessly.

'It's not gambling when you know what the outcome will be.'

Pertinax shook his head with a knowing expression.

'It *is* gambling when all you know is what the outcome *ought* to be *if* all goes well. There is a difference, you know. And I've been watching your military career with enough interest to know that you've pushed your luck right to the limits of Fortuna's favour on several occasions. Britannia, Dacia, Germania, Gallia, Parthia and Aegyptus. Every one of them a victory in the teeth of the odds stacked against you. And that's without getting into your boldness here in Rome itself, in pursuit of your protégé Valerius Aquila's enemies, isn't it?'

Scaurus smiled back at him, and both men fell silent as the wine was delivered and poured into thick-walled glass cups. The younger man took a sip, smiling beatifically.

'Oh yes. That *is* good.'

'Yes. Well, I don't suppose you went short in Helvetia, hidden away on the far side of the Alps with nothing to do but drink good wine and make little Romans.' Pertinax looked questioningly at his ward for a moment. 'Tell me, would you ever have come back if I hadn't asked you to do so?'

'Honestly?' Scaurus fixed him with a direct stare. 'No. We were comfortable there. The province is large enough to be properly civilised, and to hide in. My familia were nicely settled, with children to raise and a young man to educate into manhood. Clean air, far from the corruption of Rome, good food . . . as you say, good wine from Gallia . . .' He smiled at the memory. 'No, not even the death of the man we were hiding from was enough to tempt us back to this moral cesspit.'

'And yet you came back at my request? I'm truly honoured.'

The younger man nodded. His face remaining imperturbable as he responded.

'Yes, I suppose you are. But how could I have refused? You are, after all, the closest thing I've ever had to a father. And your invitation to return made it clear that you intend to do something about the moral hazard that has overtaken the city.'

'Indeed . . .' The senator thought for a moment before continuing. 'Although you should be clear that siding with me in this matter has every chance of resulting in your death. Yours, and everyone you hold dear, since I gather you chose to bring your women and children with you.'

Scaurus shrugged.

'Better that than having to split what strength remained to us if we'd had to leave half our strength behind, to guard them against the ever-present threat of bandits and roaming packs of deserters.'

His uncle nodded knowingly.

'The legacy of twenty-five years of the plague and a succession of wars, some with enemies we sought and some who came looking for us when we least expected it. And yes, better that your men aren't distracted by fears of what might be happening at home. But nevertheless, the threat to your familia is a real one. Be very certain that you want to gift them that risk before agreeing to join with us.'

'Us?'

'We should save that question for later. I can't burden you with that sort of knowledge until you know whether to—'

Scaurus raised a hand, respectful but firm in his interjection.

'Whatever it is you plan to do, we're with you.'

Pertinax raised an eyebrow at him in question.

'You're sure?'

'*We're* sure. I discussed this with my familia before we left the mountains. And they have chosen, as ever, to display a faith in my ability to make such a decision that I find a little humbling. And I, in turn, recognise that you are the best man I have ever known. And that the fate of the empire may now lie in your hands.'

The older man nodded.

'Very well. In that case I have my co-conspirators' agreement to brief you fully as to our plan. But before I do, indulge me while I provide you with a short recounting of recent events. The version you've heard might be incomplete, or might have omitted the smaller but no less important details.'

Scaurus took another sip of his wine.

'Please do. I'm no stranger to the ins and outs of imperial propaganda. Who knows what might have been omitted from the official accounts?'

Pertinax sat forward on his bench.

'You did well to hide your people from that Greek bastard Cleander. His rule as chamberlain didn't get any less venal or deadly after your disappearance. Of course the emperor couldn't see it – he was too busy with his own private distractions – and besides the man was married to one of his former concubines. And as long as he milked the empire for the gold needed to keep the army fed and the praetorians well bribed, nothing else mattered. But of course he was a past master at feathering both his master's nest and his own. The 943rd year of the city set a new and ignoble record in the realm of public affairs.'

'We heard, even as far away as Helvetia. Cleander sold no fewer than twenty-five consulships, rather than the usual two and a pair of suffect consuls as potential replacements, and to some deeply unpleasant members of our class. When men like Septimius Severus managed to put themselves on the list, it was clear to us that the city had hit a new low point.'

'Indeed.' The senator grimaced at the mention of his rival's name. 'But, as is so often the case, the height of Cleander's pride was also the moment of his undoing. The grain supply from Aegyptus failed . . .' He nodded sourly at Scaurus's knowing look. 'Yes, or rather it was *allowed* to fail. Grain became scarce, and combined with a fresh outbreak of the plague from the east, it looked as if the people might rise up. Cleander sought to blame Papirius Dionysius, the prefect of the Annona – not unreasonably, given he was indeed responsible for keeping Rome supplied with grain from Aegyptus and Africa. But Dionysius, being no fool, put the blame straight back on Cleander. He claimed that the shortage was all part of the chamberlain's plan to unseat the emperor. Which was an interesting mutual attempt by both men to have the other take the blame. Especially given Dionysius had until then been Cleander's man.'

'So what was the truth of it?'

'If you mean which one of them was at the root of the grain shortage, I'd say it was probably Dionysius. There's nowhere in either Ostia or Rome where that sort of tonnage of grain could be hidden from a hungry populace, so where could Cleander have secreted such a hoard? It's much more likely that Dionysius simply used his power to order the grain ships to stay in

Alexandria's harbour until he felt the time was right. It might have been deemed unwise of Dionysius to try to betray his former mentor, had it not been for the fact that he was, it seems, part of a wider conspiracy. A classic case of the biter being bitten.'

Scaurus smiled knowingly.

'You'd also have to say it was also downright incompetent of Cleander not to have a very close eye on his associate, given the power of his position?'

'Exactly. Both men were guilty of quite astonishing hubris. Things got so bad that there was a full-scale riot in the Circus Maximus, with the mob apparently intent on marching out to Commodus's summer palace on the Via Appia to demand he give them the chamberlain to tear to pieces. Cleander sent in the equites singulares augusti, which was predictable given he'd been careful to get himself awarded their command as part of his plan to control the empire.'

'A thousand bodyguard cavalrymen unleashed on the citizenry in their own streets? I doubt that ended well for either side.'

'Indeed not. The horsemen drove the mob back into the city easily enough, but then found themselves subject to a barrage of tiles and stones from the rooftops. On top of which some of the praetorians joined the fight on the mob's side, and as urban prefect at the time, I sent in my cohorts to support them. I could hardly just let Cleander's private army run amok among my people. You know what those animals are like when they get the smell of blood in their nostrils. And so the mob, reinforced well enough to brush what was left of the mounted bodyguard aside, pushed through them and resumed their march on the emperor in pursuit of Cleander, baying for blood. Never was it more apparent to me that Rome is only ever a day's food supply from an orgy of violence.'

'And so Commodus did the only thing he knew would stop the riot and prevent the mob from looting his palace.'

Pertinax grimaced.

'Yes. A series of very high-profile executions. First Cleander was beheaded for his crimes. After watching his son die, of course.

A nice touch, on the orders of Eclectus, his replacement as chamberlain. He's an Aegyptian and outstrips even his own people's propensity for brisk and decisive action when the necessity arises. Then Dionysius was put to death for his part of the whole sordid affair that had caused the problem in the first place. All of which was pretty much to be expected, given the times we live in. But that was not enough for Commodus. Nowhere close to enough. And so what followed those initial killings was, to say the least of it, nothing less than a bloodbath. Almost everyone closely linked to Cleander was murdered in their turn. And it apparently only ended when the emperor's mistress Marcia decided that her place in his favours was sufficiently secure and encouraged him to a kingly show of mercy.'

'He's come under the woman's spell?'

'So it would seem. He will never marry her, as she's of too lowly a birth, but he worships her and has even put her on the coinage as "his amazon". But worse was to follow. Much worse.'

Scaurus smiled, the twisted grimace of dark amusement.

'I think we got the gist of it via the official announcements. Commodus declared himself the new Romulus, and refounded Rome as Colonia Lucia Anna Commodiana. Then he changed the months of the calendar to the twelve names of his official title and renamed all the legions Commodianae. I know more than one legion first spear who will have been absolutely furious at the very idea of it. He took control of the grain fleet and renamed that for himself as well, I believe, and then retitled you and your august colleagues as the Commodian Fortunate Senate.'

'Indeed. Commodiana Senatus Felix.' Pertinax smiled at the memory. 'Mainly fortunate to be alive, we decided, and so we kept our mouths firmly shut no matter how outraged some of us were. After that he had the head of the Colossus of Nero next to the Flavian Amphitheatre replaced with a bust of himself, gave the statue a club rather than the rudder and globe it was built with, and put a bronze lion at "his" feet. The perfect representation of himself as Hercules, of course. You should go and see it, it's really quite imposing. Not to mention amusing. Just don't laugh anywhere near it, if you don't want the praetorians to take a close and personal interest in you, though. And if that weren't enough, he had the revised statue dedicated to himself as "the only left-handed fighter to conquer twelve times one thousand men". He's gone completely mad, it seems – but then all the greatest tyrants from the city's history have been insane, so at least he's keeping with tradition.'

The senator paused for a moment, taking a sip of wine.

'And so enough, we have decided, is enough.'

'We?'

Pertinax waved a hand at the city's vista laid out before them.

'Myself and some of the most senior and influential members of the senate, who have banded together under the title of "the Saviours". Men with famous names and ancestors whose names stretch back to the days of the republic, whose forefathers were genuinely considered as peers to the five wise emperors in Rome's golden age, now sadly turned first to iron and lately to rust. This is a familiar path to anyone who's read recent history, Gaius, as I'm sure you will recognise all too easily. The man's another Domitian. And we all know that matters will only get worse as his madness and paranoia deepen. I for one would rather die trying to unseat the monster than end up dead simply because I did nothing and he eventually got around to having me killed. There are already mutterings of another round of executions to remove all potential threats, probably at the end of Saturnalia with the turn of the year, only days from now. And who knows which names will be on Commodus's list this time? We, and some well-placed allies within the palace, can all see very clearly that Commodus must eventually turn on us all in our turn. And we know that our only hope is to strike first, before Commodus decides to have us all murdered and replaced in the senate by his placemen.'

'And you think this plot can succeed?'

Pertinax shrugged.

'We have all of the criteria in place that will be needed to achieve a successful transition of power from Commodus to a more worthy replacement. The senate will rejoice, the majority of them deeply relieved at the removal of his ever-present threat, while the men who Commodus has recently adlected into their seats from humble backgrounds will be wise to keep any protests to themselves, for fear of instant reprisal. The Saviours have selected a man of the right age and experience to play the part of a temporary replacement for the emperor, while someone more suitable for the long term is found and gains the approval of all parties.' He spread his hands in a mock-regal gesture. 'I have reluctantly accepted the thankless burden of filling that role, and will hold the throne until we find a better long-term solution. *If* we are successful, I am to be emperor, for a time at least.'

'Then you are to be congratulated, if this comes to pass. But *if?* Is "if" a sufficient basis for such a momentous act?'

'That's why I called you back from your self-imposed exile, Gaius. We have everything we need to make this plan a reality, it seems, but I am not completely convinced. It hinges on a particular set of circumstances, and I suspect that any deviation from that carefully plotted path might be the whole delicate plan's undoing. And so it is my opinion that for us to be certain of successfully assassinating Commodus, we're going to need a man in the inside. Someone with a burning loathing of the man. Someone unafraid to spend his own life to take Commodus's. We need an assassin – someone skilled, motivated and ruthless. Do you know such a man, Gaius?'

'He wants Marcus to go back into the arena? No disrespect to you, Tribune, but is your sponsor a fucking idiot?'

Scaurus smiled tolerantly at Julius, and raised a hand to forestall the protests he saw on the faces of several other members of his familia gathered around the table. They were sitting in the garden of the house which Pertinax had discreetly purchased for them in one of the city's more exclusive districts, allowing them to hide in plain sight by posing as a wealthy but reclusive man and his former comrades in arms. The truth, or some approximation of it, often being, as the senator had observed, the best way to hide in plain sight.

'I understand your reaction. But perhaps we might consider the facts, before jumping to any conclusions?'

The powerfully built ex-soldier leaned forward on his stone seat, the look on his face presaging further vigorous argument. A former auxiliary cohort first spear, he had found his abrupt and enforced retirement a difficult transition. The Tungrian auxiliary cohorts he had once commanded had marched back to Britannia years before, a source of grief to Julius that Scaurus knew still stung him with every fresh dawn he awoke without the prospect of a morning roll call of his centurions. There was no doubt in the Roman's mind that Julius still saw himself as the no-nonsense leader of men he had been before the loss of his command, which had been the price of his having joined them in the anonymity in Helvetia to protect his wife and daughter, and the son they had adopted after the death of his mother, Marcus's wife Felicia, in childbirth. Scaurus stood and started to walk around the garden's walled enclosure.

'Firstly, Senator Pertinax isn't asking anyone to go back into the arena. He has a more subtle plan which, if it works, will put whoever carries it through within a blade's reach of the emperor.'

'*If* it works? And what are the odds it *will* work?'

The Roman transferred his attention from Julius to his equally imposing comrade, another man who he knew constantly regretted turning his back on military life. Still heavily muscled from daily weightlifting sessions with Julius, and equally impressively bearded, his sense of mourning for lost comrades and his status as a warrior king was, if anything, even keener than that of the man whom he still considered his superior.

'The odds, Dubnus? I suppose it all depends who's wielding the sword. Were it to be you, I'd imagine that Commodus would reduce you to a small pile of minced meat in short order.' He smiled, rendering the blunt statement of reality more palatable to the proud Briton. 'Our colleague, on the other hand . . .'

Scaurus gestured to Marcus, who was sitting in silence between the familia's two barbarians on the other side of the rectangular ornamental pond from the two former centurions. It was the German Arminius who spoke first, interjecting with the confidence of a man who had long been freed of his original servitude to Scaurus, which in itself had never stopped him from speaking his mind even before his manumission.

'So if I understand this correctly, the idea is for Marcus to become Commodus's sparring partner?'

'Yes. Or one of them at least.'

'And exactly how is that different to him re-entering the arena?'

If Scaurus was irritated by his freedman's questioning tone of voice it didn't show on his face, but he was beaten to the reply by the Hamian Qadir.

'I can help you with that question, Arminius. The information I have received from the new chamberlain's right-hand man is most instructive. The emperor has taken to referring to himself as a gladiator. He even sleeps in a gladiator's cell when the urge takes him, in one of the training schools adjacent to the Flavian Arena. The centuries-long tradition of social disgrace for any man who takes the oath of gladiatorial service has been overthrown overnight, it seems. And now he fights in the arena on a regular basis. His opponents are carefully selected, men whose best days are behind them, or those too new to the sand to have developed the instinct for survival. And he beats them, each and every one. Not simply because he's one of the best men with a sword in Rome, although it would be a fool who would underestimate the skills born of twenty years' training. He has one all-important advantage in any fight, which is simply that of being an emperor. Those men he cannot overmatch in a straight fight are smart enough to let him cut them once or twice before throwing themselves on his mercy. Which is almost always granted, if they have made a decent show of fighting. The arena has become a place of disgrace and ridicule, it seems. But that is of little importance compared to what else Caudinus told us. After all, Commodus's addiction to arena fighting is hardly a secret.'

His gaze flicked from the German to Marcus, still inscrutably silent, before continuing.

'If Commodus is for the most part a model of restraint in the arena, this is not the case inside the walls of the Palatine Hill. The emperor has a private arena in the palace grounds, and he fights in it routinely. He calls for fighters from the various gladiatorial schools to be brought to face him in what he calls practice sessions, but there isn't anything restrained about them. He goes all out for the kill with every man that's put before him, fighting as dirty as he likes. And he kills almost all of them, because none of them have the nerve to face down an emperor even when faced with their imminent demise.'

The giant Briton Lugos, sitting on Marcus's other side, leaned forward, a frown creasing his face. Where five years before, his spoken Latin had been little better than functionally competent, his time studying under the scribe and former imperial secretary Ptolemy had improved it significantly.

'Perhaps I am stupid. But I do not understand. To go into the arena with the emperor is to risk a small wound and then be spared. But to enter his practice arena is to face death. And yet you wish to send Marcus to the palace, not to the arena?'

The men around the pond all stared at Scaurus expectantly. Ptolemy, an Aegyptian-born former member of the imperial household sitting quietly to one side with a scroll open on his lap, was the first to respond.

'It's obvious, isn't it?'

Julius snorted derisively.

'Obvious to you, perhaps, bookworm. Enlighten the rest of us, if you please?'

The scribe rolled the scroll closed and leaned forward.

'It is clearly a simple decision to make. The emperor fights the weaker gladiators in the arena, to make himself look like a champion. So if Valerius Aquila faces him in the arena and fails to put him down with his first attack, the men who protect Commodus will realise there's something not right. At which point the arena archers are likely to turn our colleague into a pin cushion. Whereas if he fights the emperor in the palace, they will be expecting someone more competent. And Commodus won't expect his opponent to come at him with everything he has, but to hold off like all the others, which will give a skilled fighter a moment of advantage. And, if he manages to resist the initial attacks, it's to be hoped Marcus will have a little more time to have another try before they kill him.'

'And that's all very well, Sparrow.' Dubnus was shaking his head with the expression of a man who knew he was going to be disappointed even before his disapproval was voiced. 'But your argument ignores the one hundred per cent certainty that even if he kills Commodus, he'll be dead alongside him a dozen heartbeats later. The praetorians would tear him to pieces for killing their master.'

Marcus shrugged, untroubled by the prospect.

'I have no expectation of survival. And my loss still requires vengeance. My *losses*. The death of my family at the hands of his killers. My wife's rape and effective murder.'

'Marcus. My brother . . .' Dubnus paused, searching for the right thing to say. 'Your children . . . ?'

He fell silent, realising his mistake as Marcus set his face hard against any attempt at reason.

'Child. I have *one* son. Appius is my blood, but Felix belongs to Julius and Annia. He will never know that Annia was not his mother, nor the fact that his real mother died in childbirth.'

'Or, most importantly, that he's the bastard son of an emperor.' Julius's tone hardened. 'Because if he finds out, there's no way it'll stay secret for very long. And then we'll have the bloody grain officers hunting for us, along with every fool with a knife who fancies the gold they think they'd get for taking his head to the palace.' He sighed, shaking his head in exasperation. 'So you're set on this?'

Marcus nodded grimly.

'It's been five years since we managed to hide ourselves away.

Nearly six. And when we made the decision to do so it was my most fervent hope that time might dull the pain of my losses. But it was not to be. In all that time there isn't a day that's passed without my thinking about Felicia. I swore to have my revenge on everyone that was involved in her death, and nothing that's happened in all those years has eased my commitment to that oath. And besides . . .' He looked squarely at Dubnus, his gaze unwavering. 'I know for a fact that if I die at the hands of Commodus's praetorians, whether I take him with me or not, I will be reunited with her in the underworld.'

An uncomfortable silence fell. The argument, as every man around the pond knew, was incontrovertible. A priestess in Germany had worked holy magic on their friend years before, seemingly pulling him back from the brink of suicide. In doing so she had seemingly brought him to the attention of a goddess whose favour had later been confirmed by a holy man in Aegyptus, and all were slightly in awe, convinced that their friend would indeed be welcomed into the afterlife just as he expected.

'So we'll have no more argument, eh, brother?' The words were soft, his rebuttal of the Briton's concern so gentle as to be almost fond. Only the hard gleam of his eyes belied the outward appearance of being a man at peace. 'If you want to be of assistance to me, why not come with me to the ludus in the morning? I expect that leathery old bastard Sannitus will be so delighted to see the pair of us again that he'll be a pushover when it comes to allowing me to face my destiny.'

2

The first pale light of dawn was barely evident on the city's tallest rooftops when Marcus's party set out for the Dacian Ludus, a gladiatorial school situated in the heart of Rome to the east of the massive Flavian Arena. The party was half a dozen strong, enough to deter the footpads who lurked in the shadows of every street, and led by a very determined Julius, whose size, aggressive demeanour and drawn knife were enough to make any man think twice. Padding through the darkened city, they ignored jibes and catcalls from frustrated would-be robbers waiting for their prey in the shadows, stepping carefully around the faeces and refuse of the city's streets, in silence for the most part, until a familiar voice piped up from the back of the group.

'So will there be any gambling on the result of your fight with the emperor, young Marcus?'

The stunned silence that followed the question lasted for no more than a heartbeat.

'Have you *no* scruples, Morban?'

The burly ex-soldier shrugged without any sign of guilt at Dubnus's acerbically phrased question. Reduced in bulk a little from the days when he routinely carried his own weight in armour, weapons and an imperial standard around the battlefield, he still retained the rolling swagger of his heyday as the Tungrian cohort's foremost oddsmaker and the terror of every gambling man's purse.

'Scruples, *Prince* Dubnus, are for those that can afford them. And I can barely—'

'Of course he has no shame. He lives for coin.'

Morban immediately raised a hand in denial, turning his head away.

'I hardly think that a barbarian is qualified to comment on such matters!'

The party stopped walking as the giant Lugos turned and squatted down on his haunches, putting his face on the same level as Morban's. The ex-soldier looked around at the other members of Marcus's escort indignantly, as poorly muffled titters and sniggers greeted the incongruous sight. The barbarian's voice was a bass growl from the depths of his barrel chest, but his words were soft and thoughtful.

'From the first day I met you, when I could barely speak your language, it was clear to me that I had little need of your language to converse with you. For you are a man for whom gold speaks loudest. You will bet on anything that might make you a profit from the man you challenge. And you do not need to pretend to be shocked by this either, for all men know that you glory in your reputation as the emptier of other men's purses.'

The former standard-bearer shrugged.

'Eloquently put. And as for you, giant . . .' He leaned forward and put his face an inch from the huge Briton's. 'The combination of your monstrous body and the education that bookworm Ptolemy has gifted you is truly a thing of wonder. I think it's time I collected on my wager with Julius.'

'And Julius thinks you can re-insert that idea where the sun will never shine.' The heavily muscled former first spear laughed derisively from the street's shadows. 'The bet, statue waver, was that I'd pay you out on the day our overgrown friend here reads the *Iliad* to me, from start to finish, translating from the original Greek. And while this monster might have become something of a new man under the sparrow's tuition, his interest in thousand-year-old Greek fairy tales is no stronger than it ever was. So until then you can just dream of fingering my gold.'

'Gentlemen?' They turned to Marcus, who was gesturing to

the street before them. 'Touching though it is to witness your mutual delight at being back in some semblance of your old roles, neither time nor lanistas wait for any man.'

They resumed their progress through the dark city, reaching the gates of the Ludus Dacchius as the first pale light of dawn caressed the higher rooftops.

'I see the usual collection of the desperate and dangerous has washed up for inspection.' Julius looked down his nose at the twenty-odd men waiting by the gladiatorial school's gates. 'You'd better go and get in line. Not *you*, Dubnus.'

His fellow former centurion scowled at him in disbelief.

'What do you mean, not me?'

Marcus turned back to him, shaking his head at the Briton's evident ire.

'He's saving your life, brother. Literally. If you come with me, there are two places you'll end up – either in the arena or face to face with Commodus in the palace. And either of those options will see you dead on the sand inside a week, I promise you.'

Dubnus leaned forward, scowling hard at his friend.

'Are you trying to say that I'm no longer good enough to fight alongside you?'

The Roman smiled wanly into his friend's shameless attempt to use feigned anger to browbeat him.

'I'll fight, and *die*, alongside you any day. But I won't throw your life away in the pursuit of my own revenge. If you or I were to face him in the arena, I fail to see how either of us could avoid going for his throat. And such an outright attack would see both of us killed where we stood by the archers who protect him. Dead, and to no end. Which is why I'm seeking the alternative, to be sent up to his private arena on the Palatine Hill. But that's a path I must take alone.'

Dubnus nodded his head slowly, and Marcus put a hand on his shoulder.

'If this is the last time we ever speak, then remember that I owe the last ten years of my life entirely to you. Along with this opportunity to avenge the crime that almost resulted in my death back then.'

The gate opened and a squat, heavily built man walked out, his rolling gait instantly recognisable to both men.

'Right, what delights have the sewers washed up for me this morning? Let's have a look at you animals and see if any of you look like you've got what it takes to enter the ludus.' He walked down the waiting line of men, making snap judgements as to their suitability based purely on what he saw of their bodies and in their eyes.

'No, too skinny . . . no, too fat . . . And you, Blondie, no! Just *no*, right? And stop wasting my time! This is the third time I've had to fuck you off, and there isn't going to be a fourth! You're boss-eyed and cack-handed, and you'd probably fall over your own feet! If I see you again, I'll have you beaten senseless by my lads just to teach you a lesson. Now where was I . . . ?' He resumed his inspection of the waiting candidates. 'Yes, you look worth a try. You, no . . . you, maybe, go and stand over there . . . you, no . . .' He stopped in front of a burly applicant and shook his head with a knowing expression. 'Is that you back *again*, Brutus? The first two times the big man retired you weren't enough?'

The man in question laughed, hard-edged humour in his reply.

'It's good money, Edius. And how many chances to fight an emperor does a man get in his life, eh? All you have to do is let the mad fucker cut you a couple of times and then go down. He spares you, you get sewn up, you collect the gold and everyone's happy!'

'Indeed. Except you're supposed to retire for good after he's shown you who's the master, in awe of his skills and with gratitude for his merciful nature. We only got away with it last time by putting a full-face helmet on you and pretending you were a Thracian. You insist on coming in here a third time, then the best I can do is send you to his practice arena. 'Cause if I put you in the Flavian, he'll most likely recognise you and have your liver out for disrespect. But be warned, he doesn't play nice behind his own walls.'

The former gladiator shrugged.

'His practice arena? A bit of rough and tumble so he can get a sweat on? How hard can that be? And I ain't ever been in the palace, so I'll have some of that!'

The lanista shrugged in his turn.

'It's your funeral. The good news is that you can face him this morning, if you insist, so get over there with the other yeses.' He turned back to the waiting line of men. 'You, no . . . you, *fuck* no . . . you, yes . . . you, no . . . you . . . maybe. Go and join the other one over there.'

When he reached the back of the line and came face to face with Marcus, he stopped and frowned. A combination of recognition and imperfect memory made him pause for a moment before the realisation dawned on him.

'Is that . . . *Corvus*?' He shot a glance at the men behind the Roman and then whooped a joyful laugh. 'And the Briton! Dubnus, wasn't it? What the *fuck* are you two . . .'

His initial exuberance at their unexpected appearance died swiftly as he took in the uncompromising expression on Marcus's face.

'Oh. Of course. You're not just here to say hello, are you?'

'No.'

Edius looked at him for another moment and then turned away and pointed at his assistant.

'All those men I said yes to, go with him. You two maybes can wait there, I'll get round to you unless you come to your senses and leg it. And if any of the noes are still here by the time I've counted to fifty, I'll let the inmates use you for morning blade practice. Fuck off!' He turned back to Marcus and his friends. 'You lot, stay here. Sannitus isn't going to believe this.'

He was gone for a while, presumably summoning his master from his breakfast. When the man who had previously been the ludus's lanista came through the gate, his eyebrows already raised in disbelief, it was evident from his clothing that he had risen in the world. He waited until the two 'maybes' had been taken away for further testing before speaking.

'Is that really *you*, Corvus? We thought you'd be in the under-world long before now, given the death wish you were so eager to indulge the last time we met.'

As the previous master trainer of the gladiatorial school housed within the walls behind him, Sannitus had been a rough and ready character. With a long scar running from one eyebrow to the opposite ear, the top of which had been sliced off by whatever had gouged the line across the top of his head, he was a forbidding prospect. Bluff and uncompromising, he had ruled the ludus without favour or compassion, producing a stream of champions to represent the Ludus Dacchius on the sand of the Flavian Arena in whose shadow it stood. But this was a different man to the harshly indifferent fighter who had accepted Marcus and Dubnus into his school years before. That he had been worn smoother by the years was obvious, some measure of the fire in his eyes replaced by the calculating stare of an older, wiser man, but to Marcus's eyes there were more obvious changes. The rough practice tunic he'd habitually worn years before had been replaced by fine dark blue wool, and his belt was thick and wide, its leather polished to a buttery shine, as were his impeccably clean boots. He stood before Marcus with a knowing half-smile, evidently as conscious of the change the years had wrought on him as the man standing before him in the dawn half-light.

'So here you are, back again after all these years. Corvus. The man who made me watch as he destroyed the two greatest champions the Ludus Dacchius had to offer.'

'In point of fact I only killed one of them.'

The school's former head trainer laughed bitterly.

'Yes. But wasn't it a pity that you got the wrong one? And an even greater shame that the greatest champion Rome has ever seen had to come out of retirement to take the punishment you deserved for that mistake, when his brother came after you?'

Marcus nodded.

'I would have fought him in an instant, if Flamma hadn't insisted on taking my place. And I would have put him down, just like I did his brother.'

Sannitus grunted dismissively.

'Perhaps you would. But it's academic, isn't it? And I didn't say you killed them both, just that you were the cause of their destruction. One of them by your blade, the other by a combination of being beaten half to death by your champion and his own idiocy. The idiot was dead inside a day of that last bout, killed before he had the chance to get his wits back from the beating he took in the arena from your stand-in. I told him not to go out in that state, but he was never one to listen. He said he was going to find you and take revenge for his brother on the streets. Instead of which some gutless bastard cut his throat from behind.'

He raised an eyebrow at Marcus, who shook his head in denial.

'So we heard, but it wasn't my doing. Perhaps he upset the wrong gambler by not defeating Flamma.'

'Perhaps he did.' Sannitus shrugged. 'I, on the other hand, profited from the whole sordid affair in ways I could never have predicted. As you can see.' He looked down at his fine clothing with a sardonic grimace. 'I was summoned to the palace and brought before the emperor. And I thought that was it for me, for allowing both my champions to be killed. Commodus was a fool for a master swordsman even then. But instead of having me put to death, he came down from the throne and put an arm around me and gave me a cup of wine. More like a bucket of wine, really, and oh, *such* wine. And then he sat me down and had me served with food from his own kitchen. Me, a street urchin from Ostia, eating food given to me by a bloody emperor! It was a masterstroke, he reckoned, to bring Flamma the Great back for one last fight. He'd watched the indestructible bastard fighting as a child, back when we all called him the flying bath-house for his size and speed. It was Flamma's example that made him decide he wanted to be a gladiator one day, he told me. And so my bringing his hero back to the sand one last time put him in my debt, it seemed, especially given the way the big man made his exit. Sentimentally touching for Commodus, and profitable to boot, it seems. Because, based on the inside knowledge of his chamberlain, he'd bet heavily enough to make a fortune from the oddsmakers. And it got better, or worse, depending on your point of view. My procurator, he told me, was an idiot. Fit only to scrape shit out of the latrines, and lacking in the sort of genius and influence that puts a former all-time champion back on the sand. And so he'd decided to promote me into his place, and send the poor fool off to manage the city's sewers. He made me a member of the equestrian class with the click of his fingers. I was to report directly to him, and not to the chamberlain's office, he told me. Cleander stood there and smiled, of course, but I could tell that he was raging inside.'

'Another source of gold closed off to him.'

'Yes. And in return all the emperor wanted to know was where Flamma was buried.'

'Which you told him.'

'Of course. Not to have done so would probably have seen me floating down the river face down inside the hour.'

Marcus nodded, conceding the point.

'And I see that worked well for you. If not for my wife.'

Sannitus looked at him blankly.

'Your wife?' The Roman fixed him with a level stare. Waiting in silence while the former lanista made the connection. 'Ah . . . gods below . . .'

'The gods had no part in it. Not unless you're fool enough to believe your new master when he tells you that he's the reincarnation of Hercules.'

'What did he . . .'

'He waited until we'd been sent away by Cleander to perform another impossible mission on the empire's borders. And then he came to visit Flamma's grave, whose location he'd learned from you. A grave I mistakenly placed in my wife's garden to salve my own guilt at his having died to save my life. And then, as I'm sure Cleander intended, having laid eyes on my wife, he raped her. Repeatedly over a period of months. Resulting in her death.'

Sannitus lowered his gaze and looked at his feet for a moment. Then he raised his head and met Marcus's stare head-on.

'I'm so sorry. If I'd known there was any risk involved, I would have suggested you buried him somewhere else.'

The Roman shrugged.

'I expect Cleander would have sent the bastard to her house in any case. Flamma's grave was a pretext.'

'But you're here looking for revenge all the same. And expecting me to help you take it. Which means that just when I've become more than I ever dreamed I might achieve, you're here to present me with an opportunity to take all that good fortune and shit all over it, aren't you?'

Marcus nodded.

'In a manner of speaking. But before you raise a fist and invite me to fuck all the way off, I have a question for you.'

Sannitus put his head on one side, his look part curiosity and part knowing.

'*There's* that ruthless bastard I thought had managed to get me condemned to death, before I realised that your games had won me more gold than I could ever spend in one lifetime. Back to ask me one question that'll turn my world upside down. Again. Go on then.'

The Roman looked at him with a grave expression.

'See a lot of the emperor, do you?'

The procurator laughed tersely.

'Do I see a lot of the emperor? An all-powerful ruler who doesn't just *think* he's a cross between a gladiator and a living god, he absolutely knows it? Yes, of course I see a lot of him.' The former lanista shook his head in confusion at the question's apparent banality. 'It seems like he's never out of the fucking ludus, since you mention it. He uses the tunnel from the Palatine Hill down to the Flavian Arena, then walks through to the underground corridors that lead to the various ludi. Including this one. He can be here in almost no time at all, when the fancy takes him. Sometimes he even sleeps here. It scares the shit out of the boys, what with praetorians skulking around the place with their spears all sharp and glinting, and Commodus looking around him with eyes every bit as deadly. He's picked more than one of my lads at random and murdered him on the spot, you know? Although he does most of his killing in his own private arena up on the Palatine Hill. He says it's more intimate. And that the spirits of the men he's killing can enjoy the glory of communing with those of the emperors who have gone before him.' He shot Marcus a penetrating glance. 'But you already knew all that, didn't you?'

'Yes.' Marcus nodded curtly. 'I've been well briefed as to your master's bloodlust.'

'So you just wanted to hear me say it, right?'

'Not quite. That wasn't actually the question.'

Sannitus raised an eyebrow.

'That was just the foreplay, was it? Just getting me warmed up before you fuck me good and proper, eh? Go on then, do your w—'

The Roman overrode him, with an edge to his voice that shredded Sannitus's attempt at black humour.

'So do you think you'll see another year in that fine tunic? After all, it's the end of Saturnalia in less than a week, and he has a reputation for making grand gestures with each new year.'

The other man frowned, taken aback by the vehemence of the question.

'*What?* Do I think I'll see another year?'

Marcus raised an eyebrow and pursed his lips, his expression something between irritation and hard-faced amusement.

'It's a simple question, Sannitus, and you were never lacking in intelligence, only polish. How long do you think you can survive repeated interaction with the most powerful lunatic in the world? How long before he has you fight Edius there to the death just because he's bored of killing ring-fodder and fancies some real sport? Or tells you to take up a pair of swords and face him across the sand? How long? A week? A month? And do you think you'll even get to the end of the year? It should be a safe bet, given we're past the birthday of the Unconquered Sun and only three days from the kalends of Januarius. But what do you think the odds are that you'll be there to watch Commodus receive the public vows for his well-being for another year? Because I think that every time you go up onto that hill, you roll the dice as to whether that's the day he turns on you.'

'Because I know it's inevitable, you mean?'

'Yes, that's exactly what I mean. Because you *know* he'll turn on you, sooner or later. And we both know that a journeyman fighter like you wouldn't stand a chance against him, not even in a fair fight and if you were in your prime.'

The procurator turned and walked away a few steps, shaking his head.

'You cunt. I should have you beaten half to death and dump you on the sand in front of him. How fucking dare you imagine that you can stroll back into my ludus and try that shit on with me?'

Marcus smiled without a trace of humour, showing his teeth as the older man turned to him with a face that was a mask of anger.

'You're taking offence because I've brought you face to face with the way you're going to die, unless you do something about it? Enjoy that sense of outrage, Sannitus! Make the most of it, and use it to distract you from the truth of where your life is headed! Perhaps it'll see you through to the moment he guts you on a whim! *Perhaps.* I was going to show you a different path, but if you're determined to die meaninglessly at the hands of an emperor, you just go ahead!' He stepped closer to the former lanista and softened his tone. 'And when you meet his dead eyes across the sand, and realise that all reason left him a long time ago, remember this moment. Remember the chance I was offering you.'

He turned away, waving a hand in dismissal at the procurator. 'Wait.'

'Wait?' Marcus kept walking. 'What for? Wait for the praetorians to arrive?'

'Wait!'

The half-shout, half-entreaty made the Roman stop and turn back to face Sannitus, raising an eyebrow in question. The procurator shook his head slowly, and when he spoke again his words were hesitant.

'If you want to know the truth of it, he scares the shit out of me. Every *fucking* day. Because every day I wake up wondering if today's the day he puts a blade through me. But . . .'

'But there's no way to escape? Because once you're in the inner circle there's no way to leave other than by ferry across the Styx?'

'Put bluntly? Yes.'

'And?'

'And *what*? There's my problem, right there. I've been made rich. But now I'm a prisoner in a cage with golden bars.'

Marcus nodded, his words not unsympathetic.

'Yes, you are. And one day soon you'll voluntarily make the short walk from that cage to a place of your own execution. Unless you put another swordsman in your place. Someone with the skills to put that madman to death so quickly that his praetorians have no time to intervene. Take me up onto the Palatine in your next batch of victims, and leave the killing to me. And the dying.'

Sannitus looked at him silently for a moment.

'You're here for *that*?'

Marcus spread his hands wide, palms upwards.

'Why else would I be here? What else did you think might have drawn me back here? He had my entire family slaughtered! And then he murdered my wife, effectively.' Marcus took a step closer, lowering his voice to a harsh whisper. 'But it isn't about *me*, Sannitus, I'm just the sword blade of Rome's salvation. There are men of honour still in this city, whether their presence is visible or not. Distinguished men, who grew up under the reign of a succession of decent emperors. Men who have spent most of their lives in a golden age, quite literally, with the empire buoyed up by a wave of gold from Dacia and ruled by emperors whose main concern was for the empire and not themselves. And they are deeply troubled by the direction the present emperor has chosen for us all. They see it as a path to ruin. So they intend to remove Commodus from the throne before it's too late.'

He fell silent and waited for the procurator to respond, seeing the doubt and uncertainty in the other man's eyes.

'If I help you get close to him and you fail . . . or even if you succeed, I could be killed out of hand without a moment's hesitation.'

'True. And if you do nothing to help, then the time will come when your death as one of his collaborators is equally swift. So take me up onto the Palatine, and the two of us can die making a difference, rather than just because our time ran out.'

'You really want to go up the hill to his practice ground?'

'Just that. Today.'

The procurator shook his head slowly.

'And you know he kills the men we send to spar with him? The praetorians have made a game of it. We send up three men as a rule, and they're escorted into his practice arena under armed guard. The first man goes in and is sent onto the sand with the emperor. The first thing is that he realises it's for real. You see it in their eyes, that arse-clencher of a moment. Some of them piss themselves. Some of them manage to hold it together. But the second thing is, all of them panic. All of them dither. All of them die. *All* of them.'

'Because you don't send anyone up there who might give him a proper fight.'

'No, I don't. My instructions from Cleander were very clear on that, before he managed to get himself executed. Victims only, no skilled fighters. And there's a standing order, left over from his day. If Commodus dies, I die.'

'So don't come up there with me.'

'What good will that do? Those praetorian bastards are like bureaucrats with weapons. They'll follow their orders, hunt me down and make sure I take my time dying.'

'Not if you're not here. The men who stand behind me can protect you.'

Sannitus shook his head.

'I have to be there, to escort my fighters up onto the hill. And you're not listening. Nothing stops the praetorians. But know this, before you volunteer to go up there and face him – Commodus doesn't give his victims any real chance to fight back. And they don't usually die from a single stroke. He likes to take his time with them, like a cat playing with a mouse. Which means that the other two men usually realise that they're up to their nostrils in the shit at just about the time he puts his blade into the first of them. And the praetorians, of course, have good sport with the men waiting their turn. Who then die at his hand in their turn. All of them. I've watched it play out a hundred times. Shouting encouragement to him, as all good members of his inner circle are careful to do. I've seen the moment the men we send up there realise they've been sent to their deaths. And to a man, no matter how good they might have been on the sands of the Flavian, the life goes out of them. They give up, effectively.'

'That won't happen to me.'

The procurator considered him for a moment.

'No? What makes you different?'

Marcus regarded him for a moment.

'How many times have you stared death in the face?' He raised a hand to forestall the response he could see in the other man's eyes. 'I don't mean fights in the arena. Not unless they were death matches that you won. I mean that good old-fashioned realisation that you could be dead before the sun touches the horizon.'

Sannitus pondered.

'Twice. Once in a gang fight in the back streets of Ostia. That was where I got the scar. And the first time I faced Flamma on the sand, when I realised he was so fast he could kill me without even meaning to, if I made the wrong move. You?'

'At least half a dozen times. Battles we had no right to win. Being captured by men who wouldn't have thought twice about cutting my throat. I've considered myself as good as dead enough times not to have any concern about it any more. And I know for a fact that my wife will be waiting for me.'

Sannitus's eyes narrowed.

'You know? How?'

'I know because a priestess in Germania told me so, and asked for the favour of her goddess. And it was her goddess who pulled me from the pit into which my thoughts had fallen.' The procurator's eyes narrowed, but Marcus raised a hand to forestall any comment. 'And I know this because a priest in Aegyptus saw her mark upon me. He gave the deity a different name, of course, but it seems to me that all men worship the same gods but do so under their own choice of names.'

The other man leaned forward, unable to disguise the fervour Marcus knew was gripping him. And which, with a cynicism he could recognise for what it was even while shamelessly exploiting it, he had already decided to use to its maximum effect.

'Which goddess?'

'Does it matter?'

Sannitus leaned closer, lowering his voice and growling the question with a softness that belied the hardness of his stare.

'*Which. Goddess?*'

'The German priestess was a follower of Hertha, goddess of fertility, nature and magic. And the change her goddess made to me, while I slept, was little short of magical.'

'And the Aegyptian?'

'The priest was a man of Kush, the mighty kingdom to the south of Aegyptus. He told me that I had been touched by Nephthys, the goddess he served. And that she was the goddess of mourning, the dead, protection . . . and magic.'

The procurator stared at him wide-eyed for a moment.

'You know that I am a priest of the gladiators' goddess Invidia, known to the Greeks as Nemesis?'

Marcus nodded.

'I do.'

'And you are telling me that you have been touched . . . healed . . . by a goddess whose influence on you was so strong that another holy man was able to detect what remained of her presence?'

'So it seems. I certainly recall her coming to me, while I was under the influence of the German woman's potion. She told me that there were wrongs to be righted, and justice to be delivered. And that I was the one who was to deliver her vengeance on the part of the innocent victims. My wife among them.'

Sannitus looked around at the other members of Scaurus's familia.

'This is true?'

Dubnus shrugged.

'It's the same story he's told from that day to this. And he's not a man to invent such a thing.'

The procurator fell silent, staring at the ground at his feet. When he spoke, his voice was a murmur.

'Then I have no choice but to assist you.' He looked up at Marcus with the light of certainty in his eye. 'And you knew that even before you asked. Didn't you?'

Marcus stared impassively at the former gladiator.

'Of course I did. The goddess knows that I have my part to play and you have yours. What matters now is not whether we live or die, but whether we deliver justice for those of his victims whose spirits have found balm in her blessing. So take me to the Palatine Hill, and I will show you a sacrifice to her name that will blaze in history for as long as the empire's history endures.'

'You mean to say that this champion of yours intends to strike Commodus down *today*?'

Pertinax nodded at the speaker, a fellow senator whose age-hunched frame was draped in a pristine white toga and who, like most of the men around the table – the self-pronounced 'Saviours' – had entered their meeting place through an artfully concealed back door. Leaning on a stout walking stick, he was playing gimlet-sharp eyes across the other conspirators, his demeanour akin to that of a snake tasting the air with its flickering tongue. His escort, a pair of formidable former soldiers, were waiting in the next room along with the other men's bodyguards, a palpable tension evident in their ranks at the risk their masters were taking were they even to be seen entering such a gathering. Pertinax nodded, untroubled by his ire.

'Yes, Acilius Glabrio. He should be on his way up onto the Palatine Hill even as we speak. If the plan we discussed is proceeding as we hoped it would.'

'You've put the plan into effect without consulting us?'

Glabrio's face was creased into an angry frown, as if he could hardly believe what he was hearing. Pertinax nodded expressionlessly.

'Yes. The opportunity arose, and I took it. We've all expressed our agreement that we need to act now, before it's too late. Why else would you have returned from your estate after so long in self-imposed exile for the sake of your own safety?'

He gestured to another member of the group, mature in years, if not quite so trodden down by them as Glabrio, his tone abruptly becoming a good deal more respectful.

'The same question could, of course, reasonably be asked of our esteemed colleague Tiberius Claudius Pompeianus. After ten years of wisely avoiding imperial scrutiny, having accepted isolation from everything he holds dearest, as the price of his wife and stepson's failure to kill Commodus, he has chosen to overjoy his friends with his presence. So when two august men like yourselves decide to accept such a risk, the rest of us know that the time for the reckoning has arrived. And so I have acted. Not informing you until it's too late for any of us to influence events was an understandable precaution, I'm sure you'll agree.'

Pompeianus leaned forward to speak, his tone soft.

'I will confess myself confused, Publius. The *agreed* plan was for our palace insiders to deal with the monster when the time is propitious. We agreed that we would need him to be drunk, and unsuspecting when our killer delivers the poison. It was our collective opinion that the guards on duty would also need to be intoxicated, so as not to notice the surreptitious removal of his corpse. And our collective strategy was for the praetorians to be scattered across the city in the final revels of Saturnalia, and in no position to resist us when we march on their fortress. All of which is what we have planned for. And now it seems that you have committed us to a course of action which flies in the face of all of those agreed stratagems. Either your man kills Commodus, and we must act immediately to secure the throne, without any such advantages, or he loses and there will be a purge the likes of which . . .' His eyes narrowed as he realised that Pertinax was smiling faintly. 'What?'

'A purge, colleague? What reason could Commodus possibly have for a purge? A lone gladiator trying to fight back when finding himself under mortal threat? I doubt it.' He gestured to an equally formally dressed figure standing behind him. 'And my associate Rutilius Scaurus here assures me that there is no risk of his man naming anyone, even in the unlikely event that he is captured in the act of attempting to kill the emperor. Unlikely in the extreme, because he has declared himself content with the prospect of suicide, if there is any attempt to take him alive.'

Pompeianus shook his head in bafflement.

'Publius, in all the years of our association, you have always been the master of both tactics and strategy. Belying your humble origins by the brilliance of your abilities both on campaign and in battle. Always the first to predict an enemy's next move, and with the means of nullifying their plans at your fingertips. It took you no more than five years to prove yourself the equal of any cohort or legion commander in the army, and another ten to prove yourself one of the last emperor's foremost legati. You made me proud to be your sponsor, and the man who introduced you to the empire's service. But this is . . . *rash*. What makes you think this roll of the dice can even succeed? Why should your man even be admitted to the emperor's presence? Surely the men who select Commodus's victims are wise to the risk of an assassin being infiltrated into their number?'

Pertinax acknowledged the question's validity with a respectful dip of his head.

'There are different types of assassins, my friend. You and I are both well aware that there are thousands of men who, under normal circumstances, would happily kill the emperor for a suffi-cient sum in gold. Although few of them are skilled enough to defeat him in one-to-one combat. And, as you imply, men with that sort of skill are almost certainly sufficiently well known that none of them could make such an approach without being iden-tified and apprehended. But the man we have recruited is the perfect combination of deadly skill and near perfect anonymity. Our assassin is a former gladiator, but his career, if stellar, was fleeting. A matter of days, rather even than weeks. Added to that, he has a very singular motivation for the role he has happily accepted. Which means, unlike almost any other hired killer, there is no risk that he will take our money and run. Because he is not being paid. Indeed, as an honourable man, he has refused to accept any payment.'

'I see.' Pompeianus leaned back in his chair, playing a calcu-lating look over the men around him. 'So this is personal for him. But what guarantee can you give us that he even has the ability to kill the emperor?'

A man who had been sitting quietly in the corner of the room stood up, walked to the window and looked out across the city. It was his house that was being used for the meeting, the conspir-ators having decided that as an outsider to their ranks, he was less likely to be under any form of surveillance.

'There is no guarantee. How could there be?' His voice was gruff and authoritative, lacking the smooth tones of the moneyed and educated men around the table, but freighted with a note of authority that marked him as their equal, in his own way. 'Only a fool would expect one. And if you *need* a guarantee to take part in this dirty business, then you should not be sitting at the table.' He looked about him, raising an eyebrow. 'If any of you isn't capable of dealing with a little uncertainty, I suggest you get up and leave now. Perhaps none of you has the balls for this sort of work; you all look as jittery as rats in a roasting pot.' He grinned at the unhappy reactions of some of the gathered senators. 'What, you boys don't like being told what to do by the likes of me? You stiff-necked aristos think you're so important you can ignore an authentic war hero like Rutilius Scaurus there, never mind a sewer rat like me.' He smirked at Pompeianus, nodding at the senator's discomfiture. Yes, when an emperor tells you to jump your only question is "how high, Your Imperial Excellence", but when it's a man like me talking to you, you all pull that face. You know the one, the "who does this gutter-born bastard think he is?" face. Well, let me dispel any doubts you might have: your shit stinks at least as strongly as mine, boys.'

He looked around the table, smirking at the purse-lipped expressions of disapproval he saw on almost every face.

'Look at you all, clenching your arses because someone without a purple edge to his tunic dares to tell you what he thinks of you. You think that this is your city, the possession and plaything of your families since before the Divine Julius, don't you? And you sit in the senate house and sulk – those of you with the balls to come anywhere near Commodus, that is – because he's packed it with men his inner circle have persuaded him to adlect. Promoted to the same position you were born to, purely on the grounds of their competency. As if such a thing as knowing what you're doing ever mattered in the glory days when the senate ruled Rome, eh? And so you want rid of him, and rid of them, so that you can go back to lording it over the plebs in the old-fashioned way.'

He played a knowing smile across the sea of disapproval facing him.

'But the plebs see through you more easily than you might think. Trust me, you'll get no support from them if you choose to go through with this. There'll be no grateful cheering on the streets, you can be sure of that. And there'll be no support from the praetorians or the army either. They all think the sun shines out of the emperor's arse. If you lot follow through with this plot to kill Commodus, you're going to find yourselves in a lonely place, you can trust me on that even if no one else will tell you that truth.'

'So why are you here with us?' Glabrio hammered the tip of his stick onto the floorboards with an angry bang. 'What common cause does an extortionist and pimp find with such despicable examples of the aristocracy?'

Petrus grinned ferociously at Glabrio.

'I'm here for my own advantage, Acilius Glabrio. And not for yours! When your man here takes the throne, I'll be the first in line, benefitting from his patronage in more ways than you can imagine, in your meaningless little world of men carrying rods and axes around before you, and pointless debates about nothing that really matters to the people you wish to rule. Oh, and Senator . . . ?'

He waited for the senator, who had turned away to express his outrage to his neighbour, to return his attention to their verbal tussle.

'I know all too well that any normal man giving it back to you like this would be beaten senseless by your boys, or perhaps even murdered if the disrespect was too large to go unpunished. But, as you know all too well, my boys are a lot more numerous than yours. Which only leaves you the option of a quiet murder. But before you give any thought to having me sent off down the Tiber for my insolence – at any point between now and the day that old age takes me down into the underworld – be warned. I know a good deal more about some of you than you might be happy with, if you knew the dirty little secrets I make it my business to discover. I know about your business dealings, I know who you're fucking,

I know who your wives are fucking, I know who your children are fucking and I know which of you are fucking each other. I know where you live, I know your guards – probably better than you do – and I know where you are and when. So treat me with the appropriate respect for a man with your collective balls in my hand, gentlemen, or I promise you'll come to regret it. Not just one or two of you, but *all* of you self-important cunts.'

Pertinax raised a hand to interject, and the gang leader's grimace smoothed away into a broad smile.

'I know, Senator, you think I should probably shut the fuck up. And I will, once I've been really clear with your friends. Yes, I was born to a whore in the Subura. Yes, I fought my way out of poverty, and killed a lot of people doing it – although I should point out that most of them were trying to do the same to me. So perhaps I'm not as well qualified to assess the risks of this little venture of ours as you all *think* you are. But so fucking what? Life's tough, boys, or at least it is where I come from, where no one has soft hands that have never done a day's real work or felt the slippery kiss of another man's blood on their knuckles. You've all chosen to take a risk, to free the empire from a tyrant. And to fill your own pockets with gold along the way, eh? Don't look so insulted, it's certainly what I'm here for. But if it goes wrong, you'll all be for the executioner. And you won't see me alongside you if that happens, because my escape route is very nicely set up, bought and paid for. So make your minds up. Are you in or out?'

Pertinax nodded his agreement.

'Our colleague Petrus is right, for all his bombast. My plan is already in train, so this is the time for everyone here to decide if they're committed or not. Anyone who doesn't think they can be a part of this should make that decision now. Raise a hand if you want no part of this. And then leave.'

Standing behind him, Scaurus swept the assembled nobility of Rome with a deceptively disinterested gaze. Anyone who chose to back away from the cabal would of course be detained until the plot had played out. Enough of Petrus's men were waiting elsewhere in the house to subdue every one of their bodyguards, if need be. But, after a long moment's thought, not one of them raised a hand.

'Very good. And we'll be staying here until word comes from the palace as to whether Commodus has been killed or not. Which means a probable wait of several hours. So make yourselves comfortable, gentlemen. Your men will be served refreshments shortly, as will we. In the meantime, shall we discuss the immediate actions needed from each of us, in the event of a successful attempt on the emperor's life?'

3

The emperor's three would-be training partners followed Sannitus through the underground tunnel that led from the Dacian Ludus into the subterranean levels of the Flavian Arena. Walking through the underground maze of beast cages, elevators and cooking facilities, still quiet on a non-fighting day, they came to a halt in front of a heavy, barred iron gate that blocked a passage leading uphill. Beyond the framework of thick iron bars, the tunnel climbed at a gentle angle, its walls brightly lit by a string of blazing torches. The gate had the solidity of a painstakingly constructed and well-nigh impassable barrier, and a party of praetorians stood guard on both sides of the ironwork.

An immaculately turned-out tribune was waiting for them, wearing a polished iron muscle cuirass over a white tunic edged with purple to denote his lofty status. A double row of white stiffened-linen pteruges with decorative silver weights hung from its hem down his thighs, which were covered down to the knee by white bracchae, and shorter versions protected his upper arms, while a snow-white cloak with the same purple edging hung over his back and left shoulder, leaving his sword arm unencumbered. Marcus, relieved not to recognise him from his service alongside the palace guard in Germania years before, watched from behind the other fighters as the gate was opened at his command. The officer ushered the party through, signalled for it to be closed and bolted again, then turned to Sannitus and held out his hand.

'Salve, Sannitus. Your letter of authority to enter the Palatine Hill complex.'

Sannitus handed over a scroll, its permission to gain access to the palace date-specific and limited to a set number of men. The praetorian held it up to the light.

'Today's date, two trainers and three fighters. Any weapons to declare?'

Sannitus raised his arms in readiness for the inevitable body search.

'No point. The emperor's toys are all much nicer than anything I could bring to the party.'

The tribune smiled thinly at what was clearly an old joke, then nodded to a waiting centurion, whose equipment was almost the match of his own for quality and polish.

'Have them searched, Centurion Tausius. Make it thorough.'

Marcus stood impassively at the rear of the line of three fighters while a soldier roughly patted him down, running expert hands across his body in search of hidden weapons. Tempted to ask what the point was, when they would be equipped to fight in full gladiatorial combat, Marcus decided not to draw attention to himself. Unlike the two-time arena returnee Brutus, standing behind Sannitus, who was clearly incensed by the intimate nature of the search.

'Oi! Keep your fucking hands away from my cucumber!'

Sannitus turned to remonstrate with him, but was beaten to the punch by the centurion. The guard officer stepped close to the would-be fighter's right ear and spoke in a matter-of-fact tone, sounding almost bored. Marcus noted the way his hand moved to the hilt of his dagger, the better weapon for a close-quarters fight, and decided that the man had probably risen to his exalted position the hard way, rather than as the result of a rank purchase.

'You will be searched. If you decline to be searched I will assume that you're hiding something, and I will *have* you searched. And if I have you searched, you may not be in any state to face the emperor by the time that search is done with. Understand?'

Even Brutus's apparent loud-mouthed bravado dried up in the face of that naked threat.

'Yes . . . sir.'

The praetorian sneered.

'You do not call me sir. You call me "Centurion". Got that?'

'Yes . . . Centurion.'

'Good.' The scowling officer turned to his waiting men. 'Search him. *Thoroughly.*'

Their inspection finished, the party was allowed to proceed, albeit under the tribune's close eye. The passage ran straight and level towards the Palatine Hill for two hundred paces, wide enough for two soldiers to walk side by side, then turned abruptly to the right, the slope becoming a long set of steps climbing, Marcus presumed, up the side of the hill. After a one-hundred-pace ascent, the stairway emerged into daylight, having passed beneath the palace walls and into the grounds behind them. The tribune held up a hand to halt their progress.

'From this point you are under military jurisdiction. I don't care whether the emperor has invited you here, you are now my responsibility, and under my command. If any of you disobeys an order I won't be asking you twice. And if anyone tries to slide away into the palace grounds, he won't need to get on the sand with the emperor to meet his end. You got that?'

He turned away and led them up the long stone stairway that led to the top of the hill, only to turn back with a furious expression as Brutus shouted at Sannitus's back.

'What does he fucking mean, *meet my end*? Have you been straight with us, Sannitus, you c—'

He staggered as the centurion pivoted and swung his vine stick to strike him across the thigh. The blow was delivered with enough violence to mark the skin with an angry red line, and the gladiator shouted loudly with the pain. Any further invective, however, was silenced by the threat of a repeat blow. The tribune bent close, whispering a vehement warning.

'Shut your mouth, and keep it shut! If you disturb the peace and quiet of the imperial gardens one more time, you won't even make it to the emperor's arena!'

Sannitus turned to face the staggering gladiator, his face set hard.

'*You* insisted on this, Brutus. Edius tried to warn you, but you were blinded by your expectation of easy money. And so here you are. You chose your bed, now you can lie in it. And you can believe the tribune when he says he'll have you killed. We're all subject to the praetorians once we're through that gate, and being a big-mouthed fool doesn't make you an exception.'

Marcus stood in impassive silence, watching as the colour leached from Brutus's face with the realisation of the trap he'd pushed his way into. The centurion pointed up the long stone stairway with his vine stick and Sannitus started walking again, leading his men up the hill without a backward glance. Marcus cast a surreptitious glance back at the two praetorian officers behind them, and found them conferring out of earshot, both men staring pointedly at the chastened gladiator with expressions that didn't bode well for him. At the top of the path they were led away to the left, into the hill's maze of gardens and palace buildings, and after a short walk reached a point that overlooked a long rectangular garden, surrounded on all sides by a two-storey-high construction in the familiar style, a colonnade walkway running around the garden's perimeter beneath the second storey. The garden itself was decorated with statues of the gods, a nine-foot-high image of Hercules wielding a club most prominent among them. At the northern end, almost beneath their vantage point, an archery target stood ready for practice use, while a thirty-pace-wide oval of sand inside a raised stone perimeter dominated the southern aspect, and the praetorians led the small group down three flights of steps and then down the stadium's length until they were at the arena's edge.

Inside the stone ellipse a summa rudis was waiting, holding the wooden staff that was his symbol of authority as the traditional arbiter of gladiatorial combat. Behind him a hooded figure stood motionless with a long-handled iron mallet resting on the sand beside him, confirming Marcus's expectation that the morning's fights would indeed be sine missione, without mercy. But all eyes were inevitably drawn to the imperious figure standing in the small arena's centre. Commodus was waiting for the party's arrival, dressed like a gladiator in the traditional garb of a Thracian fighter. He was tall, and with a heavy musculature that spoke of both inherited strength and frequent strenuous exertion. His right arm enjoyed the protection of a manica's sturdy iron sleeve, his leg was armoured below the knee by a heavy greave, while his stomach and lower chest were covered by an ornate balteus decorated with thick silver plate that reached up as far as his sternum. A crested galea helmet was tucked under one arm, while his bare head was tilted up towards the sky above, his eyes closed in a study of silent prayer. Behind him stood a rack of weapons, all with the look of having been recently and thoroughly sharpened – swords, spears, knives and even, fittingly, given the emperor's often-stated belief that he was the son of Zeus, a club. A palace servant walked towards the party, gesturing to benches set up to one side.

'Be seated, gentlemen, while Hercules communes with his father Zeus, as is his habit before combat.' He shot a warning look at the three gladiators, and the praetorian tribune tapped his sword's hilt silently, clearly warning them as to the likely penalty for any sign of amusement. 'The master of the world and son of the gods will announce his readiness to fight by opening his eyes and taking a weapon from the rack behind him. He may speak to you; he may remain silent. In either case you are to remain completely silent unless and until he invites you to speak. You will be issued with whatever feels most appropriate with which to defend yourselves in the light of his choice of weapons, and the first of you will enter the arena to offer battle to mighty Hercules. Do you understand?'

Sannitus put a finger to his lips, speaking softly.

'Say nothing. Face this test like men and I will personally ensure that you, if you survive – or your dependants, if you do not – receive the promised reward. Make any sort of commotion, or try to escape, and your ending will be both brutal *and* unrewarded.'

Behind him the emperor opened his eyes and lowered his gaze to look at the waiting gladiators. He rolled his head on a thick, muscular neck before speaking, and when he did speak he sounded, to Marcus's ear, amused at the men paraded before him.

'So these are my new opponents? My thanks, faithful Sannitus! You have, as always, delivered exactly what was needed!'

He walked back to the rack, running his fingers along the rows of blades with a lightness of touch that told Marcus they were sharpened to deadly edges. After a moment's thought he selected his weapons, and turned to reveal a surprising choice. In his hands were the hilts of a pair of rudes, wooden swords of the type usually used for practice, and to indicate freedom from the gladiatorial oath for the favoured few, as their reward for suitable valour in the arena. To the Roman's eye it appeared that while one of them had a rounded end, the other's was sharpened to an almost stake-like point.

'My brother gladiators!' Commodus's voice was clear, deep and masculine, still carrying a note of amusement at the entertainment to come. He raised the wooden blades, crossing them before him. 'Your traditional reward for an adequate number of victories in the arena is a wooden sword like these. The rudis was, before my reign, perhaps a little easily earned, but I have changed all that! These days, a gladiator must be victorious in single combat fifty times to earn his rudis. And I have gifted less than a dozen of them in all my years judging fights in the arena, which means that they have become a mark of excellence in our shared skills! Since you are all men of the Dacian Ludus, skilled with two swords, today we will fight with these practice weapons. And any of you who can defeat me will have both of your own swords as your reward! You will number among the rudiarii, men who have earned their wooden swords, and in your case, doubly so! And your fame will be unbounded, for you will have defeated Hercules himself! Who will be the first man to face me?'

Brutus got to his feet with a relieved expression and a muttered comment.

'Wooden swords? I'll have some of that.'

His smile faded as he found himself pushed back onto his stone bench by the tip of the centurion's vine stick. Tausius shook his head forbiddingly, beckoning the second man forward.

'You just stay there. Let's see if you're still looking happy when he's done with the first of you.'

The gladiator indicated shrugged and stepped forward, clearly equally untroubled at the thought of facing practice weapons. He took a pair of wooden swords from a waiting slave and walked onto the sand, stopping a respectful distance from the emperor. Commodus looked at him for a moment, almost hungrily to Marcus's eye, then pulled on his helmet and buckled the strap, swinging his arms in a series of loosening exercises. The summa rudis stepped forward, bowing respectfully to the emperor, then nodding.

'Fighters . . . ready!'

Both men nodded their readiness to fight, and the arbiter gestured to the centre of the small arena with his stick.

'Fighters . . . begin!'

The gladiator waited respectfully for the master of the civilised world to make the first move, and Marcus glanced at Sannitus to see his head shake, his expression resigned to what he clearly believed was about to happen. After a moment Commodus raised his swords, shot another calculating glance at the waiting gladiator and then stepped quickly forward, closing the distance between them in three brisk paces. From the first clash of the wooden swords, it was evident to Marcus that not only was the emperor's opponent hopelessly overmatched – Commodus's almost leisurely attack seemed to be that of a man fighting well within his capabilities – but that the emperor's wooden swords somehow carried more power than his opponent's. With each clash of their blades, the emperor's blows seemed to brush his opponent's aside, rendering any ability the gladiator might have had to give him a proper fight impotent. Gradually increasing the tempo of the fight, Commodus forced his hapless opponent into an increasingly frantic defensive posture. The gladiator barely managed to fend off his questing swords until, seeming to tire of the pretence, the emperor flashed the tip of a rudis through his opponent's flailing defence. The blade's blunt, rounded end stabbed into the gladiator's throat hard enough to drop him to his knees, choking loudly and struggling to breathe through his bruised windpipe.

'Victory!' The emperor raised his swords and turned in a circle, as if accepting the adulation of an imaginary audience. When he spoke again, his voice was raised, and pitched in the manner of an arena show's editor commentating for the crowd. 'And for the defeated man, will it be mercy or death?' He walked around behind the struggling gladiator, who was so wrapped up in his struggle for breath that he was completely unaware of the drama surrounding him. 'Will the fallen gladiator appeal for mercy, or by his silence will he accept his fate and go bravely to meet his ancestors?' He waited for a moment. 'Will there be no appeal?'

The stricken fighter looked up at him in anguish, barely able to breathe, much less speak, fighting to force out the words that he hoped might save his life. The sole result was a gargling cough, and Commodus pounced with a cold-eyed eagerness that chilled the watching men.

'What's that, my friend? You'd rather die than seek mercy? Well chosen! For you will be buried with the appropriate ceremony, as a fallen but honourable foe!'

He stepped back, took a moment to judge the killing blow, then swung a rudis in a flat arc to strike the base of the fallen man's neck, parting his spine with an audible crack. The gladiator's body pitched forward onto the sand and lay still, the summa rudis gesturing to the slave dressed in the black robes of Charon to deliver the customary blow with his heavy hammer, ensuring that the fallen man really was dead. Sannitus covered his head with a priest's shawl, and began to intone a prayer to Nemesis for the dead man's spirit, while two more slaves hurried forward and dragged his corpse away, the deformed head lolling at an unnatural angle. The emperor strolled forward to within a few paces of the remaining two men, his face creased in a wide grin of triumph.

'Don't react.' Sannitus's whisper was almost inaudible, the movement of his lips hidden by the priest's shawl and his lowered head. 'At these moments he is truly insane with the joy of the kill.'

'And there's the advantage of practice swords! Can you see it, my brothers in the gladiatorial arts?' Commodus raised his eyebrows as if in question, but allowed no time for any answer. 'No blood! There is no need for us to wait while the arena staff expunge bloodstains from the sand! So, who's next?'

The centurion pointed his vine stick at Brutus, who shot Sannitus a disbelieving look as he got reluctantly to his feet.

'You can't send me to face that f—'

The procurator spoke loudly enough for all present to hear him, his voice hard in the face of the gladiator's entreaty.

'Nemesis awaits you, Brutus! She will guide and succour you once you are across the great river, if you fight well in her name. Go now, and make a good account of yourself, so that you may win your freedom or, if you are defeated, earn her favour in the afterlife!'

'Well said, Sannitus!' Commodus was practising lunges, speaking without turning to look at the former lanista. 'Any man who can best me will earn his freedom, that much I guarantee. And if you lose, then death by the hand of a living god is surely more than you could ever have hoped for when you embarked on our mutual career of glory!'

He turned back to his white-faced opponent and gestured to the swords that had been discarded on the sand by the previous fighter.

'Shall we? Or would you rather give your place up to the last man? Of course if you do, I'll have to hand you over to my praetorians . . . won't I, Vorenus Sextus?'

The praetorian tribune grinned back at him, clearly complicit in the act that Commodus was putting on to force Brutus to fight.

'I wish more of these animals would turn you down, Hercules. My men make great sport with those cowards who refuse to face you, before we dispose of them.'

The doomed gladiator swallowed hard, then bent to take up the wooden swords. Sannitus commented again from beneath his veil, the words once again so quiet that Marcus could barely hear them.

'And what he'll do now is try to rush the emperor when he thinks he's not ready. He's not the first man to find himself in this position . . .'

The Roman watched Brutus as he squared up to his opponent, seeing from the set of his body that he was indeed on the verge of an attack. And it was evident that Commodus sensed it too, for even as he waited for the summa rudis to declare the fight as begun, he was watching Brutus intently from beneath the protective peak of his galea.

'Fighters . . .'

His desperate opponent stormed forward before the command to fight, swinging his swords in a furious attack, and for an instant Marcus wondered if the frantic nature of his gambit might overwhelm even the emperor's defence. But in his desperate haste Brutus overreached, lunging into empty air as Commodus deftly sidestepped away from his attack. Then, while the other man was floundering, off balance and overextended, the emperor did something that made the Roman's blood run cold. Pivoting, and with a berserk roar that shattered the quiet of the palace's hilltop gardens, he stabbed the sharpened point of his right-hand rudis through the wall of Brutus's stomach muscles and deep into his body, releasing the weapon's hilt and stepping away with a flourish, as if signalling his own virtuosity to an audience. The gladiator grunted with the impact, taking a second to realise that he was grievously wounded as he staggered backwards away from the grinning emperor. Putting a hand to his side, he explored the wooden blade protruding from his flesh for a moment, all the while staring at Commodus with an expression of disbelief as blood pumped from between his fingers.

'You *cunt* . . .'

His eyes rolled up, and he collapsed onto the sand, shaking convulsively as the massive damage done to his organs overwhelmed his ability to remain either erect or conscious. Commodus placed a booted foot on his chest, pulled his rudis free and then turned away with a dismissive shrug, disdaining any thought of a mercy stroke.

'Take him away. And make sure there's no respectful burial for that one, Sannitus, and no prayers either. Have him dumped in the waste pits for the dogs. And now' – he turned to face Marcus – 'for the last course in this somewhat disappointing feast. Will *you* be any better, I wonder . . . ?'

He fell silent, eyes narrowing as he looked at the Roman properly for the first time.

'I know you from somewhere. Your face is at once familiar and not quite as I might have remembered it.'

Sannitus muttered one final instruction from beneath his veil.

'Call him Hercules. He laps that shit up with a ladle.'

Vorenus turned to glare suspiciously at Marcus, snapping out an order.

'Answer the emperor! Who are you?'

Standing, the Roman bowed deeply.

'Majestic Hercules, I am Aquila.' He watched Commodus's face carefully, but if the emperor made any connection between the relatively common name and his fugitive status, it was not apparent. 'My brother fought in the arena for a short time, several years ago. His arena name was Corvus.'

Recognition dawned on the emperor's face, and Marcus realised that the memory of his time fighting for the Dacian Ludus in the Flavian Arena was still close to the surface of Commodus's mind.

'*Corvus!* Of course! What a stir he caused! And where is he now, that brother of yours?'

'He returned to my family's country estate in a state of grief, Hercules. Flamma's sacrifice in the arena saved his life, but the stigma of his mentor's death forever shamed him.'

'And now you are here . . . to what end?'

'Hercules, I came to Rome to seek an opportunity to restore the pride that he feels he has lost.'

Commodus shook his head.

'I'm not asking why you're in Rome. Why are you *here*? Why seek me out when you of all people must be well enough informed to know that there is no mercy for the weak in my arena. Sannitus is here solely to intercede with the goddess Nemesis on the behalf of all the men who fall here. So tell me, what drives you to such a suicidal course of action?'

Marcus looked at him with a faint smile.

'When the procurator offered me this opportunity, I knew my chance had come. I believe that with the favour of the Lightbringer, I have some small chance of matching you in battle, Hercules. And I hope – by achieving that honour in combat with a living god – to earn my freedom, and restore my family's lost pride.'

'Fool.'

He ignored the praetorian tribune, whose dismissive statement was followed by Tausius hawking and spitting onto the sand in wordless eloquence. Commodus nodded slowly.

'Brave of you, Aquila. Foolhardy even. You do know that I am the son of Zeus?'

Marcus played to the emperor's delusion shamelessly, knowing it was his only chance to gain an opportunity to take revenge on him.

'I am aware of your godlike abilities, Hercules. How else could you have had the strength to put a wooden sword through a man's flesh?'

Commodus preened, smiling at Marcus in pleasure at having his sense of self-worth buffed so readily.

'And why, tell me, do you go by the name Aquila?'

The Roman was quick to laugh, putting every effort into trying to sound self-deprecating.

'As a child my father made it clear to me that my older brother would be the one to inherit and run the family estate. I was destined for the legions, he told me, and he had a wooden eagle made for me to march around with. And so the nickname stuck – indeed it was the cause of my brother being called Corvus, for the dark moods that sometimes overcame him. Our father sought to make light of his affliction, not realising that his son would increasingly be prey to the darkness in his spirit that led him to fight in the arena.'

The emperor smiled a little sadly.

'And while I already like you, Aquila, brother of Corvus, I fear that you will meet your end here today, unless your father gifted you the same lightning speed and grace your brother once displayed in the arena. Prepare to fight!'

Marcus bowed again, and turned to find Sannitus at his shoulder with a fresh pair of wooden practice swords surreptitiously taken from the back of the sword rack.

'Take these. They're a speciality of the ludus. Drilled out and filled with lead, so they look innocent. He has the same weapons, so this levels the game, nothing more.' The Roman took the blades and hefted their unusual weight. 'And the only advice I can offer you is to watch his eyes, not his swords. His technique is every bit as good as it ought to be with all the practice he gets and being as strong as he is, but you'll always know what his next move will be if you pay attention to where he's looking.' He gave Marcus one last sad look. 'I'll ask Nemesis to rejoin you with your wife's spirit, when he kills you. Either him, or those praetorian animals in the unlikely event you manage to kill him, before they deal with you and come for me.'

Marcus cocked an eyebrow at him – more amused than angered at the procurator's lack of faith in his ability to defeat his imperial opponent – then turned to face Commodus. The summa rudis stepped forward and raised a hand, intoning the routine instruction in regal tones.

'Fighters, ready!'

The Roman stepped forward and raised the wooden swords, fixing his gaze on Commodus's face.

'Are you ready to match the strength of a god, mortal?'

Marcus mastered the urge to laugh aloud with an effort, and answered without taking his eyes off his opponent.

'I am prepared for whatever the gods decree, Hercules.'

'Fighters . . . begin!'

The emperor came forward light-footedly, gliding his feet across the sand rather than lifting them, his eyes fastened on Marcus's right-hand side. Attacking on the right made sense, Marcus realised, maximising the value of the right-sided body armour which the emperor possessed and he did not. Altering his pose subtly to angle both of the wooden swords to point at his opponent, Marcus stepped backwards a pace, and one to the left, showing Commodus more of the side of the body his opponent seemed fixed on. The emperor took another swift step forward and attacked without pausing, swinging his left-hand blade in a wide arc which Marcus guessed was intended to draw his own right-hand weapon in a block, while the sharpened tip of his right-hand blade drew back in readiness to stab through the gap that would open up. Rather than attempting to block, as the emperor clearly expected, he stepped in close, inside the swinging blade's arc, the speed of his unexpected attack making Commodus's eyes widen in surprise. Using his left-hand sword to block any attempt at a stabbing attack with Commodus's other weapon, he went body to body with the emperor, hooking the other man's right leg with his own and pushing him over it. Commodus sprawled across the sand, scuttling backwards away from the threat of Marcus's twin swords as his opponent came after him, looking for the opportunity to put the tip of a rudis into his enemy's throat hard enough to shatter his larynx and close his windpipe. Then, just as he was tensing to stab down at the emperor, seeing the opportunity to make the kill as his opponent's elbow slipped and dumped him back on the sand, he reeled from a blow that sent him sprawling face down onto the ground beside Commodus. Tensing in readiness to leap back to his feet, he froze where he lay; a prick of metal in the back of his neck told him that to move would be to die. Tribune Vorenus's harsh voice barked an order at him, reinforced by a push of the sword's blade to prick his skin.

'Stay where you lie, Gladiator!'

His eyes met with the emperor's as the other man got back to his feet, brushing away the hand extended by the praetorian tribune. There was a curious absence of any emotion in the other man's stare. No pain. No rage. No humiliation. Nothing. It was as if the emperor's fall had sent him into a state of denial that the whole thing had just happened. He picked up his wooden swords, then passed them to Sannitus, whose hasty glance at Marcus, still helpless on the sand, looked as confused as the Roman felt. The emperor turned and walked away, leaving the tribune with his sword poised, still ready to kill Marcus.

'Shall I dispose of this scum, Majesty?'

Before Commodus could answer, Marcus turned his head to look over his shoulder, meeting the praetorian's eye.

'Make it quick, coward.'

His eyes widening in fury, the officer tensed to drive the blade down for the kill, then froze as Commodus spun and barked an order at him.

'*Hold!*'

Conditioned to instant obedience, the soldier refrained from delivering the attack, his eyes blazing with anger at Marcus's slur. Commodus walked back towards the two men with a hand outstretched.

'Step back, Vorenus, and give me your sword.'

The officer nodded, happy to pass his weapon to the emperor for the expected purpose of exacting his revenge. Commodus hefted the blade, then lowered the point to within an inch of Marcus's neck.

'You insult my bodyguards in terms that would see you take a long time reaching the far side of the river, if you did so anywhere else within these walls. With what justification? Be warned, I might kill you myself, if I believe you are needlessly traducing them.'

The Roman shrugged.

'I have fought on a dozen battlefields for *you*, Hercules. And never once seen any man of the praetorian cohorts at my shoulder.'

Which, if not entirely true, seemed to hook the emperor's curiosity. Commodus raised an eyebrow.

'So not just a gladiator, but also a veteran of Rome's wars? And you have fought where for me, exactly?'

'Britannia, Gallia, Germania, Dacia and Parthia, Hercules.'

'I see. And you no longer serve in the legions because . . . ?'

'My father became ill and died, Hercules, and my brother was in no fit state to take responsibility for the estate. Being of the rank of centurion—'

The praetorian centurion laughed in disbelief, only to fall silent as the emperor turned on him.

'You dare to laugh at a man brave enough to face *me*, a living god, in the arena?'

The abashed praetorian saw the trap before him and raised his hands in denial.

'No, Hercules! I simply question the truth of this wild story!'

'If I might stand, Hercules?'

Commodus turned back to Marcus, waving a distracted hand.

'You may, Aquila. Can you gainsay my sceptical bodyguard?'

The Roman got to his feet, wondering if he could sidestep the sword's blade and hit the emperor in the throat hard enough to kill him, but was dissuaded from the attempt by Vorenus's proximity and evident readiness with the long-bladed dagger he had drawn to replace his sword, the pugio's point unwavering.

'I can, Hercules.' He raised his voice to make sure Sannitus could hear his words clearly. 'I left imperial service temporarily three months ago, with the blessing of my legatus, and travelled back to Italy, first to my father's house in the north, and then to Rome, with the intention of meeting with my father's debtors to ensure repayment of the money he lent them years ago. I left most of my equipment with my family, but carried a small part of it with me to disprove any such attempts to call me a fraud. My vitis and phalerae are both to be found in my lodgings, and I ask that if you choose to end my life here, you have me buried with them.'

'His vine stick and medals are no more proof of this claim than—'

The centurion found himself looking down the blade of his tribune's sword, a clearly incensed Commodus having turned on him with the speed of a striking snake. Behind the emperor the tribune was shaking his head in a clear signal, grimacing at the apparent danger that his officer was risking.

'One more word in disparagement of this man's obvious love for the empire, and for *me*, and you'll find out what your own guts smell like before you die, Centurion!' He turned back to Marcus, still enticingly close and yet out of striking distance. 'Tell me, Aquila, do you fight bare-handed?'

Marcus was taken aback for a moment before realising that the emperor was unwittingly offering him another chance to achieve his goal. He extemporised frantically, thinking on his feet to come up with a credible story.

'Yes, Hercules, I do. My legion has a reputation for ferocity in battle that is almost the match of the old Twenty-First Rapax. My first spear is a fearsome individual who the legionaries have nicknamed Ferrus Pugnus. And "Iron Fist" made us practise a variety of fighting methods in readiness for the day that we were reduced to empty-handed combat. Officers included.'

The emperor cocked his head, raising an eyebrow.

'We should speak more about this man "Iron Fist". Such men are the foundation of my army, and my empire's glory. But for now, perhaps you could demonstrate some of these fighting methods, as a demonstration to my praetorians that your words are true?'

Marcus nodded.

'Of course, Hercules. Should we perhaps use some form of padding on our fists?'

Commodus laughed tersely.

'Padding? You seem to have forgotten that you are fighting with a *god*! Prepare yourself, Centurion, and if you make a decent opponent I might just have a use for you!'

Marcus turned away, stripping off his tunic and handing it to Sannitus, who accepted the garment with a blank expression.

'He's fast. Defend your throat and eyes, he likes to go for disabling strikes. And don't hit him in the face, you don't want to leave a bruise that might turn him against you when he looks in the mirror.'

The Roman nodded, quickly seeing Sannitus's point. Any sign of damage from the fight might infuriate the emperor, giving the lie to his claims of divinity. He turned and walked back to face Commodus, who had removed his armour and clothing and stripped down to a loincloth. The summa rudis stepped forward and raised his wooden rod.

'Fighters, ready!'

Both men nodded, and the adjudicator stepped back, pointing to the sand between them.

'Fighters, begin!'

Marcus stepped forward with his left hand extended and open, the right clenched and held back by his ear as if he were pulling back an arrow.

'The Sagittarius stance, I see.' Commodus was stepping to left and right, moving Marcus around with the look of an experienced fighter, bouncing lightly on the balls of his feet. 'Is that what you were taught by this Iron Fist?'

'We were taught a great many things, Hercules. I simply chose this because—'

The emperor lunged forward, one hand raised to parry a counter, the other cocked to strike. Marcus ducked under a hastily delivered punch aimed at his head and counterpunched, jabbing a fist into the other man's stomach before dancing back and waiting for Commodus's reaction, and his chance to go for the killing blow. Barely troubled by a blow that would have winded a lesser man, but clearly enraged by being caught unawares, the emperor lunged forward and managed to take hold of a handful of the Roman's hair before sinking to the floor, dragging Marcus down with him. For an instant the Roman was fifteen again, lying on the sandy surface of his father's private arena with his arms pinioned by the man behind him, a discharged legionary centurion who had been employed, alongside a champion gladiator, to teach him how to fight. The ex-soldier had laughed in his ear, his breath hot on Marcus's skin, and then belched, the smell of the sausage he'd eaten for lunch making the younger man's stomach turn.

'And now you're here on the ground with me, what are you going to do about it?'

Cotta had taken him unawares from behind, wrapping him up in an arm and leg grip from which there was no escape, and thrown himself down onto the arena's fighting surface, taking his young pupil with him. Hitting the ground hard enough to expel the breath from his lungs, Marcus hadn't realised what the former soldier was doing until he'd laughed in his captive's ear.

'The thing is, down here there aren't any rules.'

'What, and there are up here?'

Both men had stared up at the gladiator as he'd loomed over them, a big man still blessed with the mesmerising speed and grace of a striking panther despite fifteen years fighting in the Flavian Arena.

'Fuck off, you oaf. This is where he learns how to deal with the sort of animal who'll strike from behind and try to bite his ears off.'

The fighter had shrugged at Cotta, winking reassuringly at Marcus.

'Suit yourself. I'm not sure this is what his father had in mind though. And be careful what you inspire him to do.'

And with that the gladiator had ambled off to make small talk with the prettiest kitchen maid, leaving Marcus very much on his own.

'That thing about biting ears off – that wasn't a joke, by the way.' As if to prove his point, Cotta had taken a mouthful of his pupil's ear and squeezed the skin between his teeth hard enough for the pain to be intense.

'Argh! Get *off* me!'

The soldier had simply laughed.

'That tends not to work on the sort of people I'm talking about. Got any better ideas?'

Marcus had writhed in his arms for a moment before giving up.

'No. Let me go. I'll tell—'

'Your father? Be my guest! I didn't ask for this job, and I'm only doing it for the money. Did you think it was for the love of the young master that I slog up here from the Capena gate three times a week?'

'He won't pay you!'

'I think he will, but so fucking what?' Cotta had laughed again. 'There's more to life than gold, you young idiot. And the sooner you learn that the better. So, wriggling a bit isn't going to free you, and neither are threats, because I'm not afraid of you, or your father's purse. And neither are the people who'll do this to you. So, now that you're down here, what do you *think* would get you free?'

Marcus had thought for a moment.

'Hurting you badly enough that you have to turn me loose. Which sounds like quite a good idea to me!'

'Oh really?' Cotta had laughed again, genuine amusement and a hint of encouragement. 'Excellent! So, any ideas?'

'If I had a dagger . . .'

'Not a bad idea, but unfortunately for the purposes of this exercise you've already left your dagger in another man's eye. Somewhat inconveniently. So . . . ?'

'I can't turn round. So all I have are my hands.'

'Which are pinioned.'

'How do I get them free?'

'*That's* the right question! Cross your wrists. Yes, like that. Now turn your hands over so that your palms are inwards. Clench your fists . . .'

Cotta hadn't been ready for what came next. Anticipating his tutor's next instruction, to drag the fists apart with enough force to break the hold, Marcus had ripped his way free of the ex-soldier's grip, half turned and shot an elbow into his face. And, by what Cotta had at the time put down to good fortune, the point of his pupil's elbow had struck his left eye socket, sending him rolling away, his blinking and head-shaking accompanied by the uproarious guffaws of the gladiator. It was a lesson, as Cotta had fully intended, that he'd never forgotten.

Commodus was roaring, clearly furious at having been struck, fighting to wrap an arm around Marcus's neck with the evident intention of strangling the life out of him.

'I'll rip your head off, *mortal*! I'll—'

Marcus didn't wait for the emperor to stop shouting and concentrate on the fight, barely resisting the urge to elbow him in the face, but instead cupped his right fist with his left hand for leverage before thrusting his arm back into his opponent's sternum, finally managing to do some damage. Rolling away as the other man whooped for breath, he wondered for a moment whether he could get close enough to hit Commodus in the throat and finish the job, only to find Vorenus within half a dozen paces, his sword still drawn and his expression foreboding. Glancing swiftly at the emperor, who was still struggling to breathe, the praetorian made an instantaneous decision and raised the sword, stepping forward with the clear intention of removing Marcus's threat to his master.

'*Hold!* . . . Step . . . away . . . Vorenus!'

The tribune shot his master a look of disbelief, but obeyed, gesturing to Marcus to step back and keeping his sword raised in naked threat. Calculating that there was no way for him to reach and kill Commodus without being hacked down by the furious officer, Marcus obeyed the command, waiting for the emperor to regain his breath and get back to his feet. Expecting that his opponent's fury would, if anything, be greater after a second humiliation, he exchanged an uneasy glance with Sannitus and tensed himself for the rage that seemed inevitable, only to see that Commodus was, almost unbelievably, grinning widely. Breathing hard, he gestured for the praetorian to back away.

'Well fought, Aquila! I allowed you an opening in order to find out if you were capable of standing your ground against a living god, and by my father Zeus himself, you didn't disappoint me!' He turned to Sannitus. 'Procurator, come to your master!'

Sannitus stood, a slightly dazed expression on his face, and walked across to the panting emperor, who flung his arms around the former gladiator and squeezed him in a bear hug while the hapless lanista stared in bafflement at Marcus over his shoulder.

'I thought you'd brought me the usual three hopeless losers, when I laid eyes on them! And even more so when I dispatched the first two, but this man . . .' He released the procurator and pointed at Marcus. '*This* man is something special! You must be rewarded for bringing him to me, Sannitus, and I have decided what that reward should be! Your sword, Vorenus Sextus!'

The praetorian stepped forward and handed his weapon to the emperor hilt first, drawing his dagger again with his other hand before Marcus had a chance to take advantage of his being disarmed. Sannitus visibly braced himself, but his slit-eyed grimace became an uncontrollable gape of astonishment as the emperor raised the weapon reverentially in both hands before him.

'This sword will be replicated for you by my own swordsmith, with fittings of gold and silver! It will be a reminder of the day when your choice of opponent showed me the respect of giving me a *proper* fight!'

He turned away, gesturing for his servants who, clearly practised at meeting his needs, came forward with wine and a robe. Sextus nodded to his waiting praetorians, who advanced smoothly into position to escort the emperor away into the palace.

'You, Aquila, must fetch whatever belongings you brought with you to Rome, and then return to the palace! Not your clothes, of course. I will have clothes made for you, garments fit for a man who can stand and fight with Hercules himself, heedless of the terrible danger in which you put yourself! But bring your personal possessions, and be ready to tell me all about your exploits in the empire's service! Present yourself to the guards at the main Palatine gate and tell them your name, and Tribune Vorenus will ensure that you are delivered to the palace.'

He turned and walked away, his entourage and bodyguards flowing in practised patterns around him as he vanished into the palace. The praetorian tribune gave Marcus one last hard stare before turning to follow them, but his centurion lingered a moment longer, his narrowed eyes sending a message whose clarity was absolute.

'By the goddess . . .' Sannitus was still looking at the crumpled bodies of the two men the emperor had killed, both with their heads deformed by the brisk application of 'Charon's' hammer. 'I'm not entirely sure why you're not lying there with these poor fools.'

Marcus blew out a long breath, releasing the tension pent up within him.

'It seems that Commodus is every bit as fickle as his reputation implies. And I am to be his sparring partner, it seems. The man who dared to challenge a living god.'

4

'Surely there's no way we can allow him to go back in there?'

Julius, sitting on the other side of the table with a pugio on the wooden surface before him, spread his hands wide in question. In his eyes was a clear need for some sign that Scaurus agreed with him, but if he hoped for support he was swiftly disappointed. The Roman simply shook his head.

'On the contrary, I'm afraid. Our friend has no choice but to return to the Palatine. Today. Now, in fact.'

Marcus had walked to the house on the Caelian Hill in a daze, oblivious to the city's bustle as he mulled the almost surreal nature of his encounter with Commodus in the Palatine stadium, and the perplexing turn of events that had balanced failure with survival, and a second chance at revenge.

'But—'

'If he goes back in there he'll be dead before the turn of the year?' Scaurus nodded. 'You're almost certainly correct in that assumption. Perhaps Commodus will tire of him, and have him executed without ever giving him another chance. Perhaps this praetorian tribune Vorenus Sextus will find a way to make him disappear. Or perhaps the emperor will simply prove too skilled for him, the next time they meet on the sand of his private arena. But it is a risk that has to be borne.'

'How can you be so matter-of-fact about that?'

'After all we've been through, you mean?'

Julius shrugged.

'If you put it like that? Yes. After all we've been through *together*.'

Scaurus smiled sadly.

'I understand the point you're making, Julius. And I sympathise with the spirit of comradeship that's making you say it. So, for the sake of argument, let's say we just put our heads down and hide. What if Marcus doesn't return to the palace? What do you think happens first?'

It was Marcus who answered the question.

'I've already worked that out. Whether or not Commodus even remembers me when he wakes up tomorrow, I'm now a person of interest. If I don't return, and promptly, the palace secretariat will take action to find me. No one survives hand-to-hand combat with the emperor and gets to escape back into obscurity. And the first person they'll go after is Sannitus. After all, it was him that took me up onto the Palatine.'

Scaurus nodded.

'And it'll take no more than an hour from the moment that the orders for him to be summoned are issued for the praetorians to knock on his door. An hour after that he'll be in an interview room. The questions that he will be asked will be short and to the point. "Who is this man Aquila?" "Where did you find him?" "Is he really the gladiator Corvus's brother?" And the inevitable follow-up will be, "What do you mean, *you don't know*?"' Julius listened, stone-faced. 'And the walk from interview room to interrogation chamber is conveniently short. I'd expect him to be talking before nightfall, if not the moment they get him through the gates. After all, we roped him into this, it was never his own doing.'

'So we kill him. Now.' Julius's face was set hard. 'I mean it. If he's the one man who can betray us, then we stop his wind and get out of the city. Live the rest of our lives somewhere quiet. Go back over the mountains to the north, perhaps, or to the southern coast of Gallia.'

The equestrian shrugged.

'It's an attractive idea. Which only ignores two problems.'

Julius shook his head and picked up the knife.

'I see no problems. I'll kill the bastard, right now, then we get out of here while we still can!'

Scaurus smiled indulgently.

'The difficulties I was describing weren't moral. Although your determination is both noted and respected. The main problem would be getting to the man, were we to resolve to kill him. He lives, in case the hard reality hasn't sunk in, in a ludus. A school for gladiators. And you can be assured that he will have predicted this discussion. He'll have gone back to the Dacian school without a backward glance, just as fast as he could while retaining the dignity of his position. And, having reached his own walls, he will have taken refuge deep inside the building, with enough fighting men around him to make it impossible for us to even get to within a blade's reach of him. If, that is, we could get through the gates in the first place.'

Julius nodded morosely. Scaurus, seeing that his first point had been accepted, continued.

'My second problem is somewhat less physical.'

'Let me guess.' The big man looked up at him knowingly. 'If not us, who?'

'Well put. And correct.'

'Whereas what I'd counter that one with is, "If not us, *who cares*?" We can still run and hide. If we leave now we could be so far beyond the city that an initial search would be too little, too late. We could find somewhere quiet and burrow into the landscape.'

'And just live our lives out in peace?'

'Of course! And why not?'

'Because, Centurion, just like you, I swore an oath to Rome when I joined the army.'

'An oath you've been quietly ignoring for most of the last five years.'

Scaurus nodded, conceding his comrade's point.

'For as long as returning would be our collective death warrant *and* without purpose, yes, I let my oath slide. But when I found out the risk my sponsor was about to take to free the empire, I had to return. I can't just sit back and watch Rome slide into chaos any longer. And neither can he.'

He gestured to Marcus, who nodded his agreement. Julius shook his head in disappointingly fulfilled expectation.

'And the rest of us? The children?'

'You're all free to leave.' Marcus stood, walking to the house's window. 'And it would be for the best if you did. We have a day or two to get you away, because it'll probably be that long before I face Commodus across the sand again. Who knows what madness might sweep the city if I manage to kill him?'

Julius shook his head in disbelief.

'Is that really all there is to your plan? To kill the man whose presence keeps the empire sane, even if he is a lunatic who thinks he's some sort of gladiator god? Because if that's the limit of your ambitions, it's a bit limited for me. Tearing down the throne and waiting to see what fills the space left where it used to be sounds like a recipe for disaster. What about all that history you're always quoting to us, Tribune? Didn't the Year of the Four Emperors start out in just the same way?'

Scaurus looked at the table for a moment.

'A penetrating insight, as ever, Julius. Although this time—'

'It's different?'

The equestrian nodded, meeting his comrade's hard gaze head-on.

'Yes. The list of men stacked up behind us, in this attempt to wrestle control of the empire away from a mad emperor and his power-hungry functionaries, is a roll call of the most powerful men in the world.'

'And this senator Pertinax, who these powerful men will put on the throne, given the chance . . .' Julius fixed Scaurus with a penetrating stare. 'Is he even fit to rule?'

Scaurus nodded.

'I believe so. I fervently hope so.'

'You *hope* so.' Julius leaned forward in his chair. 'I took the time to read the books you recommended to me. The ones about what happened after Nero's death a hundred years ago. It was hard going at first, but when I eventually got used to all the big words,

I managed to make sense of it, more or less. Allow me to summarise my understanding of what happened after powerful men – like those Pertinax is aligning himself with – managed to get the emperor to kill himself.'

He jabbed the table with a finger.

'At the start of the whole bloody mess, a man was put on the throne who was acceptable to all of the other interested parties. An old man, called Galba, without an heir, so that they could work out which of them was to take his place, without fear of his sons objecting to the idea with the army and the praetorians at their backs. And since Galba could actually remember the time of Augustus sixty years before, they knew he'd want to make the empire a lot more like it had been in those days. By which he meant honourable, virtuous and less corrupt. Whereas what they were hoping for was what their grandfathers had got from Augustus, a sniff of the real power and a show of respect, along with the chance to be as corrupt as they liked just as long as he didn't find out. Anyway, it all seems to have gone wrong when this idiot Galba totally refused to pay off the praetorians. Who – completely unexpectedly, it seems, to that fool – then stood aside when a handful of them decided to murder him. Which they did, unsurprisingly enough, after being bribed by a relative outsider who offered them a handsome pay-off for doing so, and making him emperor. After that there was a year of chaos. Two generals allowed their legions to dress them in purple, one of them beat the new emperor's army and took the throne, but then had his arse handed to him on the battlefield by the other. Who, mercifully, it seems, was a relatively down-to-earth sort of man who managed to put the whole thing more or less straight again.'

Scaurus spread his hands in a gesture of acceptance.

'That seems like a reasonable summary. Although you missed out that Vespasian's son Domitian was another dangerous lunatic who had to be murdered to put the empire's eventual saviour Nerva on the throne twenty years later.'

'I was getting to that. In *his* case, I will admit, a maniac's death resulted in five successive men who managed to keep control of the empire. But Nero's suicide led to a civil war that tore the empire in half, and killed hundreds of thousands of innocent people. And would you like to know the difference between Galba and your hero Nerva, as far as I can see?' The equestrian gestured for him to continue. 'It's blindingly obvious. Galba refused to pay off the praetorians, and they killed him for it. It didn't matter how many rich men were standing behind him keeping their gold in their purses, because they were never going to stand up to the palace guard. Whereas Nerva paid up, promptly and with a smile. Which bought enough time for an orderly succession to be sorted out. Do you see my point?'

Scaurus smiled.

'I do. And it is well made.' He stood up. 'Rest assured, Helvius Pertinax is no fool. He will do whatever is needed to stabilise the throne, and keep control of the empire. And he will do so with the intention of naming the most able man in the city as his heir, whoever that is deemed to be.'

Julius shrugged.

'It seems to me that once Commodus is dead, the conspirators behind your man Pertinax will start to jockey for position, all seeing themselves clad in purple. But it will be enough for me if their grubbing around for power stays in their own circle, and doesn't end up in another war for us to get caught up in. So, if you trust this man Pertinax, it seems that we have no choice.' He stood and walked over to Marcus, putting a hand on his friend's shoulder. 'I will pray to our god Cocidius for your survival, Marcus. And while I'm doing that, I suggest you do what you should have done last night, before you went to face your destiny. Go and write your son a letter explaining what it is you hope to achieve by seeking your death in this way. Because fifteen years from now he's going to want to know why you vanished from his life so suddenly.'

The sun was close to setting behind the western hills when Menius Caudinus left his office on the Palatine Hill. Making his way through the checkpoints that guarded first the chamberlain's office and then the palace complex's main entrance, perched high above the Circus Maximus, he descended the staircases that led to street level and joined the stream of imperial functionaries heading home for the night. With his mind already firmly focused on dinner, wine and the evening's planned diversions, he started when an unexpected and firm grip on his arm drew him into the shadow of one of the entrances on the racetrack's north side.

'What? Unhand me!'

'Now now, Menius Caudinus. Is that any way to talk to a friend?'

Resetting his expectations from casual robbery to something likely to prove much worse, Caudinus turned to find Qadir's smiling face inches from his own. The Hamian wrapped him in a hug, then held him out at arm's length in the manner of a long-lost friend making an unexpected reacquaintance.

'I suggest you demonstrate some recognition. Before the city watch decide one of us is up to no good. And I am forced to prove them right.'

Caudinus nodded, taking the other man's hand and shaking it half-heartedly.

'What is it that you want? I'm a busy man, and I have plans—'

'For the evening. We know.' Qadir pointed discreetly to the two men lurking on the road's other side, leaning against the palace's foundation wall in the manner of the street toughs to be found on every corner of the city's streets. 'We followed you when you left the house this morning, and witnessed your transaction with the crone that runs a string of expensive girls for hire by the hour, a transaction you completed before you went into the palace. It's a good thing we were able to reschedule for you.'

'Reschedule . . . ?'

'Indeed. How else are you going to perform the new request I have for you?'

Caudinus stared at him for a moment as the realisation of the reason for their unexpected meeting became clear.

'I see. And what is it that you would like me to do?'

The Hamian grinned wolfishly.

'Excellent! You're every bit as quick on your feet as I'd expect from a man in your position! Although it's more a matter of what you're *going* to do, rather than what I might like.'

Caudinus considered that for a moment before replying, unable to keep a tone of resentment out of his voice.

'Indeed. What was I thinking? And the woman . . . ?'

'Has been rebooked to a later time. She'll have been let into the house by now, and will be cooking your meal just as planned, just a little later. So you'd better get on with the job and get back there, or you might find your dinner in one of the neighbourhood strays.'

The secretary nodded resignedly.

'What is it that you want of me?'

Qadir took a scroll from his belt.

'You will recall that you have carried out an act of informing for me. I asked you to examine a specific legion's records, and to find me the name of a suitable man.'

'And I did what you asked.'

'You did. And to verify that name, I had you bring me all the information that could be gleaned from the records with regard to his service.'

'Again, a *request* which I completed. At considerable personal risk.'

'Indeed.' Qadir nodded solemn agreement. 'And we have used the information you provided as to that man's time with the Fifteenth to produce this rather well-forged additional entry to the legion's records. Which means that all you have to do is go back into the palace and make your way back to the imperial secretariat. Go to the military records section and tell the night clerk to make himself scarce. Insert it at the right place in the document sequence for it to be believable and then return the file to its place. Simple enough for a man of your abilities.'

Caudinus shook his head.

'That's impossible. All documents are logged into the files, in a record book that provides proof of their authenticity. And all military dispatches are transcribed from the original, which is then destroyed.'

Qadir smiled broadly, but his voice took on a warning note.

'As I keep being forced to point out to you, we know everything. We know that that *was* the procedure, until the great fire.' He waited for the secretary to reply, and when no response was forthcoming, continued in a chiding tone. 'You need to do away with this expectation that everyone who's not a senior palace official is a fool, Menius Caudinus. We know all too well what the procedure used to be, because one of our number used to work with you.'

Caudinus nodded.

'I remember him, and recall his excitement on being assigned to accompany your party to Aegyptus – and the fact that he disappeared with you, either dead or turned to your service. Apparently the latter. His name is Ptolemy. A small man with the mannerisms of a bird?'

'Yes. Although you might not recognise him quite so easily now. A small man he remains, but he is a good deal fiercer than ever he was before five years' exposure to the roughest of men, whose example he has attempted to copy. And, through him, we know the current position with record-keeping. We know that the great fire that started in the forum a year and a half ago gutted much of the palace. We know that Commodus had to go and live in the Vectilian villa for over a year, until the Domus Augustana was refurbished. And that the imperial archive was burned to ash in the space of less than an hour. Which meant that, with all those hugely detailed legion records destroyed, the secretariat was forced to send instructions for all remaining paperwork held by the legions to be copied and the originals dispatched to Rome. The originals, not the copies, to ensure their accuracy. Which means that the legions now hold tidily copied records, all in the handwriting of the same few scribes, whereas the originals, in a multiplicity of scripts from dozens of military scribes over the decades, have been brought here. And we know that they are still being logged and collated, in the usual tidy-minded and methodical manner, in numerical order. And lastly, we know that for the legion in question, which has a high number, there is no record book as yet.'

He fixed Caudinus with a hard stare.

'Which means that you can introduce one small document to that legion's archive without the addition being obvious. It was drawn up for us by a man who knows the military record-keeping style all too well, and therefore it is completely authentic. It has a forged authorisation stamp of excellent quality, and you can be assured that nobody will ever know the difference. And it has to be in the records within the hour.'

'And if I fail to do this for some reason?'

'I find it very hard to imagine such a reason being valid, when compared to the consequences. But, for the sake of discussion, were that to happen, a good friend of mine will probably be dead before dawn tomorrow. Which will mean that those two men, who I am leaving here to escort you home once the job is done to ensure that no harm comes to you, will come upon you when you least expect it. They will cripple you, by cutting all the tendons in your knees and ankles, and leave you helpless on the street. So take this' – he held out the scroll, with a look that brooked no refusal – 'and get it into the records immediately, unless you wish to be responsible for two deaths. One of them your own.'

'Aquila, is it? Let's have a look and see if you're on the list for admittance.'

The praetorian chosen man commanding the Palatine Hill's main gate ostentatiously opened his tablet, scanning the list of names on what, in less serious circumstances, might have been called the palace guest list. His breath smelt of fried onions and wine, and it was Marcus's guess that he'd eaten just before coming on duty. The guard post was situated within the gate's arch, with a guardroom built into the left side of the vaulted hall behind the gate. A heavy wooden door on the portal's other side, propped ajar, promised a corridor into the depths of the palace complex, probably part of the network used by the praetorians and palace servants to move around behind the scenes.

'Ah, here we are . . . Aquila. It says here that you're to be escorted to the imperial household.' The soldier looked him up and down. 'You can't be a new boyfriend, you're much too long in the tooth for his usual taste. So what are you . . .' He raised a hand. 'No, let me guess. You're a—'

He shut his mouth and snapped to attention, followed an instant later by the three other men of the guard detachment. Marcus turned to find Vorenus behind him, the tribune having emerged from the passageway behind the wooden door.

'Not really your place to speculate, is it, Chosen Man? And somewhat risky as well, especially as it smells like you had a better lunch than might have been wise?'

The object of Vorenus's derision avoided eye contact, his reply pitched somewhere between loud speech and a shout.

'No, Tribune, none of my business!'

'Good.' Vorenus leaned in and spoke quietly in the hapless soldier's ear, his voice both soft and menacing. 'So keep your stupid questions, your opinions and your jokes to yourself. Because if you manage to get up the wrong person's nose, they'll unleash a bucket of shit that will briefly reside with me before I pick it up and pour it over your centurion. Upon which event, I expect he will take the empty bucket and throw it at you hard enough to take your fucking head off. Literally. Understood?'

'Yes, Tribune! Completely understood!'

Instantly dismissed from his superior's attention, he slid away into the background while his superior turned to look at Marcus with a look of disgust.

'I didn't think you'd be back. In fact, I stayed on duty specifically to see if you had the balls to make a reappearance. I was convinced, and I still am, that your story about being a legion centurion is nothing but lies. So go on, show me what you've got to prove that you are what you say you are.'

Marcus unrolled the linen-wrapped package he'd brought with him from the villa. Inside were his vine stick and phalerae, the gilded silver discs that adorned his body harness, proofs of valour in battle whose metal was polished to a gleaming shine. Vorenus curled his lip, clearly unimpressed.

'Is that it? I could buy the same in any one of a dozen armouries in the city. Where's the diploma that proves your honourable discharge?'

'A diploma is only issued to non-citizens when they leave the service, Tribune, granting them citizen status. As a citizen I would never receive or need such a thing.' Marcus gave the tribune a look that told the other man his bluff had been called. 'I do have this, though.'

He handed over a scroll, waiting while the praetorian unrolled it and read.

'To whomever it may concern . . . granted leave of absence to return to his family's estate and deal with the matters arising from his father's death.'

He raised a sceptical eyebrow.

'Anyone could have written this. So how am I supposed to prove who you are, before I let you into the palace?'

'The message carries the stamp of the legion's camp prefect. He approved my leave of absence.'

Vorenus shrugged.

'But what would a man like you be doing wearing a centurion's helmet in the first place? Surely your father would have bought you a position as a tribune when you were younger, if he had the sort of estate you're talking about?'

Marcus rolled up the bundle, his reply that of a man used to answering the question.

'The Corvus that the emperor was talking about is my older brother. He's the one who inherited the land and the slaves to work it, and that was always going to be the case. Father spent the money he had getting him as far up the cursus honorum as he could, which meant that what was left to me was the army.

He spent some gold gaining me access to the centurionate, and after that it was all down to me to make a success of myself. Fortunately I took to the soldier's life well enough for it to be obvious it was what I was made to do in my life.'

He waited for Vorenus to react, nodding slowly as a cynical look of continued disbelief formed itself on the tribune's face.

'I can see you don't believe me. Not that it matters. I'll be dead inside a week, won't I?'

The praetorian shrugged at him, his eyes hard.

'Probably. But are you suggesting I go easy on you because he's going to kill you?'

Marcus shrugged back at him.

'No, Tribune. I'm suggesting that you and I are much the same, when our differences in status are stripped away. We're both soldiers. We've both had to fight our way to where we are, myself no less than you. But there is one difference between us – I already know that I'm dead. And so the gods know it makes no difference to me whether I die here and now, at your hand, or within an hour or so for killing you, or in a few days when Commodus gets bored of my presence. So you choose, because I'm bored of the subject. Either pull that dagger and let's have at it, or take me to the palace.' He looked straight back into the praetorian's hard-faced stare. 'Shall we dance?'

Vorenus stared at him for a moment longer and then barked out a laugh.

'You're offering to fight *me*? A tribune in the imperial body-guard? Here and now?'

The Roman shrugged.

'If you're a man who's risen from the ranks, you'll know which end of the dagger does the damage.' He smiled grimly. 'And if not, we'll have to hope you're a quick learner.'

The praetorian shook his head briskly.

'No. If it got back to my prefect that I'd been brawling with a palace guest like a common soldier, it might not go well for me. Doubly so if I kill the emperor's new temporary favourite. So you can come inside and take your place in his household. And watch my men smirking at you as you wait your turn to die.'

Marcus relaxed fractionally, but as the praetorian turned away, gesturing for him to follow as he stepped into the corridor's dimly lit mouth, he made a casual statement that was a death sentence in its own right.

'And while you wait for that, you can wonder whether your brother will get here in time to see you depart this life.'

'What?'

The enjoyment of dropping the news into conversation dripped from every one of Vorenus's words.

'You've not heard then? Commodus has ordered us to fetch your brother, the infamous Corvus, to join you here. For what purpose, he hasn't said. Although I can guess, and you'll find out soon enough. So while you're being measured for all that finery he's going to dress you in, you can provide me with the whereabouts of your father's house, and I'll get some messengers on the road to summon him. And he'll be here soon enough. Nobody refuses the summons of a living god.'

'This is the entrance to the imperial household.'

The praetorian led Marcus round a right-handed corner, designed to aid a defender, he guessed, and down a further short length of walkway to a guarded checkpoint. A pair of praetorians snapped to attention the moment they saw Vorenus coming, keeping their eyes locked on the walls behind him.

'Nobody comes through here in either direction unless they have the appropriate pass. Including me.' Vorenus raised his right wrist to display a leather thong strung with scarlet beads, each one embossed with a minute aquila inlaid with gold leaf. 'Red beads for us praetorians, who can go anywhere we like except into the emperor's cubiculum. There are blue beads for admittance to the service areas and slave quarters, purple beads for admittance to the emperor's private section of the palace, yellow for those few who attend him in the privacy of his bedchamber, and green beads for household members who have permission to come and go from the palace, given by and returned to the freedman responsible for the royal household. And very carefully checked in and out. You don't get one unless the maior domus agrees, and since he'll be instructed to ask me . . .'

He left the point hanging, and Marcus decided to play along with him.

'I don't get one?'

'Right first time, smart boy. You're now the emperor's guest, and that's going to be the case until he either gets bored and dismisses you – which is rare – or you're carried out feet first – which isn't.'

Sextus looked down the corridor's short remaining length into the imperial household's antechamber, and Marcus caught sight of a slight figure in the large anteroom beyond.

'Ah, there he is. Sporus!'

A slightly built man peered into the passageway, nodded and bustled briskly towards them, a tablet held open in one hand and a stylus in the other. A serious-faced child of ten or so was following him with his own tablet held in perfect mimicry of the adult, dressed identically in a white linen tunic. Marcus realised that he had to be the palace's maior domus, the manager of the imperial household, although the child's close attendance had no obvious rationale at first glimpse. When he spoke, his voice was at once authoritative and soft, more suited to a strong-minded woman than the man standing before them.

'Tribune. This must be the emperor's new practice partner.'

Sextus shook his head in amusement.

'If that's what we're calling him, then yes, he must be.'

Sporus consulted a writing tablet.

'One new gladiator, by the name of Aquila, to be bathed, dressed, and tonsured in readiness for the emperor. He's a dinner guest this evening.'

The tribune pulled a wry face.

'Oh, *lucky* you. You get to hear Commodus telling everyone about how he realised he was a living god.'

Marcus shot Sporus a glance, finding the freedman's face a mask of indifference, feigned or genuine.

'Indeed he does. And thank you, Tribune, I'll take him from here.'

The tribune nodded.

'Very well. I'll do the rounds of my men and make sure they know that he's not allowed to leave under any circumstances. Something you and your people would do well to note.'

He turned away, and Sporus beckoned to Marcus with a conspiratorial smile, leading him into the anteroom with the child in close attendance.

'Always full of himself, that one.' The maior domus sighed. 'Come on then, let's have a look at you.'

His appraisal was swift and expert, once again copied in every detail by the boy at his side.

'Hair needs a cut, no beard to trim . . . most unmanly . . . the boots need replacing and that tunic needs to be burned. But most of all you need a bath! Follow me.'

He led Marcus down another corridor, talking as he walked.

'This is the Domus Augustana. Unlike the Domus Flavia next door' – he waved a hand to his left – 'which is where all the emperor's public functions are held, these are his private quarters. And everything that happens inside this palace with regard to care of the imperial party gets done by my people, slaves and freedmen. We feed him, clothe him, bathe him and make sure that he has everything he wishes for.'

Marcus smiled at the other man's back, striding out to keep up with his bustling pace, while the boy was almost running behind them.

'That must be a heavy burden of responsibility.'

Sporus laughed lightly.

'Only to a man who's not strong-minded enough to carry it. Whereas I've been training for this my whole life. You see Alinus here?' He gestured to the child. 'He's following the same path I did. And in due course he'll be my replacement.'

'Is he thladiae or castrati?'

Sporus stopped and turned back to face him.

'Crushed or cut? That's a harsh question, Gladiator.'

Marcus nodded, happy to be establishing a persona early on in their short relationship.

'And do you think my life from here will be a thing of rose petals and honey cakes, Maior Domus? I'm sure you view me as little more than a commodity, something to be cleaned up and put in front of Commodus like a mouse thrown to a cat.'

The slight figure inclined his head in acceptance of the point and started walking again.

'Alinus is neither, since you ask. I was careful to seek a bright young child with a reasonably normal upbringing, as much as is possible here in the palace, and one who has been labelled as a spado from birth due to a deformity of the offending organs. In the child's case, they are so small as to be non-existent.'

'And therefore do not need to be removed or destroyed.'

'Exactly. Which, if you'd ever even witnessed such an act, never mind actually suffered it, you would never wish to see inflicted on any man. And here we are . . .'

He led Marcus into a miniature version of a bathhouse. A pair of attendants stood ready, and Sporus gestured them to start work.

'Get him sweated, cleaned and dried, then send him over to the tonstrina. I'll be back in an hour, make sure he's ready by then. Oh, and send his clothes to the furnace.'

Marcus submitted to the two men's ministrations, and was sweated, scraped and then doused in cold water in relatively swift succession before being wrapped in a thick cotton robe and escorted down the corridor to the barber.

'Sporus told me to make you presentable, but to make sure you still look like a gladiator when I'm done. Or as much like a gladiator as possible, given you lack any proper beard.' The waiting stylist pointed to the chair. 'Sit down, close your eyes and keep still.'

He worked quickly, snipping carefully at his client's hair and beard, standing back with a satisfied look just as Sporus and the child returned.

'Much better. And right on time, as if there was ever any doubt. Very well, come this way and we'll get you outfitted.'

In another room, on the other side of the entrance antechamber, Marcus was measured and then issued with a temporary tunic whose material was nevertheless of excellent quality. The tailor brought out a long strip of white cloth folded into a heavy bundle, unwrapping it to reveal the garment Marcus had been expecting.

'You do know how to wear a toga, I presume?' The heavy woollen garment was wrapped around his body, and Sporus stepped back with a look of calculation. 'Carried as if you were born to it. But there's something missing . . . ah, shoes!'

A pair of ankle boots were produced in the right size and placed on Marcus's feet, their soft leather gentle compared to the harsh grip of new military footwear, which was usually more likely to cut the recipient's feet to ribbons than to conform to their shape. But when the outfitter went to pick up his discarded hobnailed caligae, Marcus raised a hand in warning.

'Do not throw those away.'

'But—'

Sporus took the battered but functional footwear from the hand of the bemused slave.

'These caligae have some sentimental value? We can replace them a dozen times over, and with boots of considerably higher quality. And besides, you can't wear them in the imperial living quarters, their hobnails will damage the flooring.'

Marcus shook his head.

'I have no sentimental need for them, but they have been broken in to fit me perfectly by hundreds of miles of marching. And I will need them, when the time comes for me to dance for the emperor's pleasure in the arena.'

'Ah. I see. In that case . . .' Sporus turned to the child beside him, handing him the offending footwear. 'Have those cleaned to a shine and then take them to the room we have allocated to Aquila. After that, you can return to the slave quarters for the evening. My compliments to your mother.'

The maior domus watched while Marcus walked around in the new shoes, smiling at his expression of pleasure.

'Nice, aren't they? We have our own cobbler who makes shoes for the imperial household.' He looked at Marcus's look of bemusement. 'What, were you thinking that the master of the world, a god in his own right, is going to shop for shoes in the forum with the plebs?' He gestured to the barber. 'Get some scent on him and we'll be away. Not too much, we're trying to put him across as an elegant man of action, not a male harlot.'

'I have just the thing.' The barber uncorked a small bottle and expertly dabbed a little of the oil within onto Marcus's temples with a fingertip. 'Santalum oil, pressed from the wood of a tree grown in the east.'

Sporus led Marcus out, his previous bustle having been relaxed into the slow stroll of a man of leisure, inviting the household's newest member to match his pace.

'And now, before the time for dinner is upon us, let me show you around the household. Or at least those parts of it that you are allowed to see.'

They walked back down the corridor to the anteroom, and Sporus stopped, gesturing to the praetorians on either side of the gate that led back out into the city.

'Firstly, we've got strict orders that you're not to be allowed to leave the palace. We have no choice in the matter, and if you did manage to get out, we'd all be punished for allowing it to happen, even if we had nothing to do with it.'

He looked at Marcus appraisingly, and the Roman inclined his head in acceptance.

'I have no need to make any sort of escape. If this is where I spend the remainder of my days, then so be it.'

The maior domus nodded, then continued.

'The palace complex is all a bit confusing if you're new to it, so come with me and I'll explain the layout as much as I can without doing the full tour. As I said earlier, this is the Domus Augustana, the emperor's private residence. On the western side of this part of the palace complex is the Domus Flavia, which is kept for public occasions involving the senate and their equestrian colleagues, and to the east is the stadium, which—'

'I've already seen.'

Sporus looked sharply at Marcus, responding to the gently acerbic tone of his voice. He was, the Roman suspected, as much surprised at receiving a sardonic reply from a man he probably considered something of a subordinate as at the response itself.

'Ah, yes, I was forgetting your recent acquaintanceship with the emperor. So, let us have a look at that part of the palace that you're confined to, shall we? Although if this is confinement, it is something of a golden cage.'

Apparently happy at having made the nature of their relationship clear with his reminder of Marcus's effective imprisonment, he walked through the hallway and led Marcus out into the open air. They emerged into an unroofed courtyard, bounded on three sides by buildings and on the fourth by a thirty-foot-high wall with a doorway leading into a viewing area through which the city's skyline was clearly visible. The open space was dominated by the central pool, with water from an ornate fountain playing softly down the sides of its plinth; the overall effect was one of tranquil formality. Turning to look through the southern wall's opening, Marcus could see that they were looking south with the Circus Maximus in the foreground and the Aventine Hill beyond it, the city's sprawl lit a soft yellow by the setting sun.

'This is the palace's central peristilium.' Sporus pointed to the two-storey buildings surrounding them on three sides, a colonnaded peristyle supporting the portico roof that ran around the courtyard. 'The upper floor forms the emperor's private quarters, with access guarded by the praetorians at all times. There are some parts of the ground floor that are reserved for occasional private ceremonial duties, but most of it is used by my staff. Access to the emperor's private residence, his sanctum – apart from the emperor's bedchamber – is granted by the possession of one of these.' He raised his wrist, and Marcus saw that among the multicoloured assortment of bracelets was a string of purple beads, their gold embossing contrasting with the rich, glossy colour. 'If you don't have one of these, then you have to be escorted at all times when granted access to the sanctum. By a praetorian. And before you ask, the penalty for being found in the sanctum without permission or an escort is usually death. Come on.'

He led Marcus around the central pool, making for the private wing's arched entrance and greeting the guards on duty with an easy manner that contrasted their stiff formality and looks of suspicion directed at Marcus.

'Good afternoon, gentlemen. I'd like to take this new resident of the palace into the ceremonial rooms, if I might? He's invited for dinner later on, so it would be good if he were familiar with how it all works.'

The detachment commander gestured one of his men forward.

'You go with them. Make sure they know the rules, make sure they obey the rules, and make sure they know what'll happen if they don't.'

The praetorian, a man in his early thirties with the look of a man who'd seen just about everything there was to be seen, beckoned the two men to follow him, speaking over his shoulder as he led them into a magnificently appointed anteroom.

'Maior Domus Sporus has the purple beads. The purple beads mean that he is trusted to come and go from the imperial residence as necessary, and to approach the imperial party *if* permitted.'

'Our praetorian colleagues stand guard over the emperor night and day, unless he is inside his bedchamber. Any member of the household with these' – Sporus tapped the purple beads tied around his wrist – 'may approach him, but permission to address him must still be sought through the guards.'

'And if you don't have the beads you must always be accompanied by one of us. You must always follow our instructions. And if you fail to follow our instructions there will be no warnings. Just this.'

He tapped the pommel of his dagger, and Marcus shot him a look, finding the soldier's face set hard.

'That's clear. Thank you.'

'Don't thank me. Just do what I tell you. Right, Sporus, where do you want to take him?'

'Through into the public area. The audience chamber, the dining room, the music room—'

'One thing at a time. The audience chamber . . .'

The praetorian led them past one of his colleagues whose role was clearly to make sure that anyone admitted to the anteroom got no further without the right permissions, down a narrow corridor and through another doorway into a circular space that Marcus recognised all too well as the place where the first part of his plan for revenge on his father's killers had come to fruition.

'This is the audience chamber. When the emperor needs to meet discreetly with his advisors, or with foreign dignitaries in a less formal setting, he uses this smaller throne room, rather than the larger and more public chamber next door in the Domus Flavia. It is here that the master of the world makes many of the myriad decisions required to run the empire . . .'

The maior domus continued his explanation of the room's function, blissfully unaware that Marcus had already stood only a few paces from where they were years before, watching as a former praetorian prefect had died slowly and painfully at the emperor's hand.

'. . . and which also gives him the ability to meet with his closest advisers less formally.'

Sporus looked at Marcus questioningly, and the Roman guessed that he was expected to show some appreciation of the gravitas with which he was investing the glimpse behind the scenes. And an ally would be an important thing over the next few days.

'Most impressive.' He gestured to the throne on its dais. 'To think that the decisions that rule a hundred million imperial citizens are made here.'

'Quite so.' The palace official lowered his voice conspiratorially. 'And to see the emperor at work is a sight, I can tell you. He wastes no time making his views known to the men who enact his wishes, I can tell you.'

Marcus mused on that inwardly while keeping a straight face.

'I'm sure he does. And you're a fortunate man to have witnessed him deciding the course of events.'

Sporus nodded firmly, happy to have his biases confirmed.

'Yes. We are indeed lucky to have him in these difficult days of plague and fire.'

Marcus followed him back out into the corridor and through a series of corners, emerging into a much larger room set with several rows of couches around a central space. Its walls were decorated with frescoes depicting the gods in their various guises. Hercules, he noted, was prominent among them, clearly identifiable by his club, and with facial features clearly discernible as those of Commodus himself.

'This is the emperor's larger private dining room. When there is a need to entertain members of the senate or other distinguished guests without the formality of a state banquet, then they are escorted here to dine with our master.'

'They must be awed by the magnificent paintings.'

'Indeed. The emperor favours an artist whose ability to capture his nobility is second to none.'

The Roman realised that another expression of admiration was expected.

'Most life-like. And illustrative of the emperor's singular muscularity, it has to be said.'

'Quite so!'

Marcus could have sworn that Sporus simpered, and in an

instant the nature of his devotion to Commodus became clear. He was on the verge of asking what other parts of the sanctum he might see when the praetorian spoke behind them, breaking the tenuous spell.

'You have to leave now. The guard will change over shortly, and I must return to the fortress with my tent party.'

The Roman suspected that the statement was a pretext to bring the praetorian's involvement in the tour to an end, but Sporus was clearly in no position to gainsay the soldier. He nodded, and was gesturing to the dining room's exit with a resigned expression when a flurry of activity at the room's other end caught their attention. A pair of guardsmen stalked in through a door at the far end, positioning themselves on either side and glaring around in search of any source of danger. A moment later the party they were escorting swept in, another four soldiers arrayed around a couple. The praetorian standing behind Marcus and Sporus, realising just who had entered the room, barked an order.

'It's the emperor! Out of here, you two!'

But as Marcus turned to do as he was bidden, a shout from the dining room's far end stopped him in his tracks.

'It's Aquila! You, Guardsman, bring those two men here!'

The praetorian turned and glowered at them, clearly discomfited at being singled out by the emperor, then hissed an instruction.

'Walk slowly towards him! When I say stop, you *stop*!'

Marcus allowed Sporus to lead as they walked at a steady pace down the room's length towards the imperial party. Commodus was standing beside a statuesque woman dressed in sheer silk that clung to her body in a way that would have been considered scandalous in public, but all of his attention was fixed on the two men coming towards him. When they got within a dozen paces, it was apparent that the emperor could no longer control his excitement. He strode forward with a joyful cry.

'Here's my new sparring partner!'

He rushed forward, brushing a wilting Sporus aside and wrapping Marcus in a bear hug so strong and unexpected that he was completely unable to act on the fleeting opportunity to mount an attack. Then, momentarily holding the stunned Roman at arm's length, he delivered a hearty shoulder slap that unbalanced Marcus just as he was tensing to strike while the emperor's throat was still within reach. By the time he'd regained both his equilibrium and balance, the opportunity was gone, two praetorians having stepped forward to flank their master.

'Aquila, brother of the acclaimed Corvus! How I look forward to seeing the two of you reunited! Sextus told you that I've ordered your sibling to be summoned to Rome from wherever it is that you call home, I presume?'

Marcus bowed in feigned acquiescence.

'Yes, Hercules, he did. And I thank you for it, it will be good to see him again.'

Commodus sparkled at the praise.

'Won't it? We can match the pair of you up, and see which one of you would win in a straight fight! And the two of you can fight me together, to show you just how strong the blood of the gods is when it roars through my body and I choose not to fight as a mortal! See, Marcia?' He turned to the woman, who was appraising Marcus with a cool gaze. 'This is the only man to have provided me with a proper fight in months! What do you say to inviting him to live with us here in the inner sanctum?'

She looked him up and down again before replying.

'Why not, my love? Perhaps he will provide you with counsel that is as fearsomely honest as his apparent willingness to offer you some real opposition in your arena for a change.'

'Will you?' Marcus mastered his instinct to start as the emperor spun on his heel to look at him, barking the question. 'Will you be fearless in telling me your views?'

'Of course, Hercules.' Marcus bowed again, his fingers twitching with the urge to lunge at the other man's throat despite the proximity of his bodyguards. 'I will never hold back in sharing my opinions with you.'

'That's settled then! Maior Domus Sporus, you may allocate

my good friend Aquila a room in the guest wing of the sanctum. Oh, and have him issued with whatever colour beads are required for him not to have a soldier watching everything he does.'

'As you command, Caesar.'

Sporus bowed low again, and Commodus waved him away with another smile at Marcus.

'You'll join us for dinner, of course?'

'Yes, Caesar. It would be my greatest pleasure.'

The two men watched as the emperor walked away, Marcia shooting Marcus an unreadable look over her shoulder as she accompanied him through the chamber's doors into the courtyard garden.

'You are indeed blessed . . .'

He turned to find Sporus staring hungrily at the couple, his voice that of an awestruck teenager.

'. . . to be greeted by name by a living *god*.'

The Roman followed his stare, watching as Commodus walked out into the garden.

'Indeed, I am blessed. And I look forward to being that close to the emperor again.'

5

Julius walked out into the villa's garden as the sun was dipping, a jug and two cups in his hand, walking across the immaculately laid flagstones to where Scaurus was sitting with a book in his hands.

'I'll join you, if you're open to company?'

The younger man smiled at him, rolling up the scroll and putting it down at his feet.

'How could I decline, since you come bearing wine? And besides, a little of this man's writing goes a long way. I find his style somewhat indigestible, especially not having read any of his work for a decade. How did you find the patience to finish it?'

Julius smiled wryly, pouring the master of his familia a cup and passing it to him.

'The truth is that I didn't actually finish it. Indigestible isn't a strong enough word, I'm afraid.'

Scaurus's smile broadened.

'And yet you made an excellent case against the plan that our sponsor has determined will be the saving of Rome.'

'That wasn't all me. I've been talking to your sponsor's tame gang leader. He and I got on well enough the last time we were in Rome hunting Maternus, so I took the chance to see what his opinion was of this whole thing.'

The Roman's face slipped into the familiar lopsided smile he used when discovering something he felt he ought to have guessed.

'I see. Well, it could never be said that Petrus lacks intelligence.

But then I suppose that being the master of the gangs that infest the city is a selection process simply by its ruthless nature.'

'Yes. And he has a very clear opinion of this conspiracy we're part of.'

'I'm sure he does. Let me guess. I suppose he believes that the Saviours are all in this for their own interests?'

'Indeed he does.'

Scaurus shrugged.

'He's right, of course. With the possible exception of my uncle's former sponsor Tiberius Claudius Pompeianus, they seem to be something of a reptilian collection of men. Saviours? They're more like a gang of the richest thieves you'll ever meet.' He drank again, raising a hand to forestall his friend's baffled question. 'I know, if that's the way I feel, then why am I working in league with them? The answer to that one's simple. Because it has to be done, and no one else looks like doing it.'

He held the cup out for a refill with a smile of gratitude.

'The army and the people of the empire are completely in the emperor's thrall, the result of his non-stop efforts to portray himself as Hercules ever since he was forced to sacrifice Cleander to their demands for blood. The coinage constantly titles him as Hercules, he poses with a club and lion skin at public events, and he demands to be addressed as a god. He knows it alienates the senate, but he doesn't care, because the army and the populace love it. And that's a combination that's more than enough to keep him in power until the day he dies. And in any case he's packing the senate with more of his own people with every month, ad-lecting freedmen into the curia alongside the aristocrats. Who therefore feel increasingly isolated. Quite understandably, given that literally the only way for him to prop the treasury up is to pick them off for their money, either one or two at a time or all of them in one great big purge.'

'And who therefore want him dead when literally nobody else really cares who rules? Or have much of a problem with him picking off rich men, as long as it doesn't affect them?'

'That's it, pretty much.'

'But . . .'

'I know. There are so many questions about this plan that it's hard to know where to start. What if all that results is a new dictatorship, but this time with the Saviours holding the puppet's strings? What if the praetorians refuse to let Pertinax take the throne? What if he manages to persuade them, but then the army refuse to honour it and put one of their own men in purple, starting a civil war? And what, worst of all, if several potential emperors emerge from such chaos, one in Britannia, one in Germania, one from the legions along the Danubius and one in the east?'

'Exactly. It's not my place to question your decisions, Tribune, but—'

'I haven't been a tribune for years, Julius. You can call me by my name.'

Julius waved the protest away.

'You're still a tribune to me. And while it really isn't my place to argue with you, I can tell you what I think.'

'Which is?'

'I think that this plan of your friend Pertinax's is going to result in nothing but misery. Misery for us, because Marcus dies no matter what else happens. And misery for everyone else involved too. Because I think Petrus is absolutely of the right mind when he says he's got his escape route planned. All it'll take will be one miscalculation, one mistake, and your "Saviours" will be left with nothing better than a pile of ashes to rule. If the praetorians turn on their shiny new emperor and put him to death, who rules then? Because the army are too far away to have anything to do with that question in the short term, and the people of the city will run and hide the moment the praetorians put their full strength on the streets. Which means that it'll be them that decide who rules, and that means it'll be the highest bidder, doesn't it?'

Scaurus nodded soberly.

'I agree with everything you say. Which is why Pertinax's first step will be to make sure that the guard get a nice fat donative to keep them happy and content with his rule.' He grinned at Julius. 'Don't worry, we have every intention of making this succession as smooth as the one that Nerva and his allies achieved a hundred years ago. And nothing like the mess Galba made of it twenty years before that. All it takes is money, and these men aren't fools enough to skimp when it comes to safeguarding the future of the empire.'

Julius shrugged.

'Let's hope that's true. Although that will still leave Marcus in the deepest shit of his entire life.'

'Marcus? Don't forget that our friend has made it a habit to defy even our most optimistic predictions as to his ability to survive. Don't condemn him to death too quickly.'

'So tell me, Aquila, which legion did you serve with?'

The question that Marcus had been waiting for dropped into the dinner conversation like a rock into a pool, instantly silencing the other guests around the dozen closely set dining couches. The evening had been deceptively relaxed, with a continual stream of food and wine of the highest quality, and Marcus had been careful to eat and drink sparingly as he chatted about inconsequentials with his neighbours. Having been raised in a wealthy household, he was well equipped for the anodyne discussion that had resulted, with all parties being careful to say nothing that might be taken as any sort of insult to the listening emperor, but at length Commodus had seemingly lost patience with waiting for the conversation to take a turn he approved of. Marcus bowed his head respectfully before replying.

'I am proud to have marched with Apollo's Fifteenth, Hercules.'

A freedman who had been hovering in the background behind the couches on which Commodus and Marcia were lounging stepped forward and bent to the emperor's ear. Marcus had noted him earlier, as he had passed the emperor a small bottle from which Commodus had taken a sip before taking any of the food laid out before them. He muttered whatever it was that he knew about the legion in question more quietly than Marcus could hear and was then waved away by the emperor.

'Legio Quintadecima Apollinaris Pia Fidelis, named faithful and loyal by my father for remaining true to the throne when Avidius Cassius tried to claim the throne. And headquartered in Satala, at the very edge of our empire in Cappadocia. You have literally gone to the very boundary of Commodiana in defence of my imperial glory.' Marcus held his breath without realising it, waiting for someone to reveal their previous service with the legion and start asking difficult questions, then slowly exhaled as nobody spoke up. 'It is a proud legion, I expect. Although not one with recent battle honours.'

He nodded at Commodus's further comment.

'None worthy of your attention, Hercules. Although we are kept constantly busy by Parthia's incursions and provocations. I saw action more than once, the result of which you see on my face.'

He gestured to the scar across the bridge of his nose, knowing that it was compelling evidence of his service, albeit not with the legion he was claiming, which had been chosen by Qadir simply for its distance from Rome.

'And your legatus was happy to allow you to leave the legion?'

Marcus turned to address Lucius Calpurnius Proculus, a florid senator known to have made the decision that being close to the emperor was, for all of the risks involved, better than not being in his favour. The man had military service in his past, and had sought to impress his peerless understanding of the legions on Marcus in earlier conversation.

'Indeed so, Senator. I was fortunate in that he had served under my father in the Germanic wars, and had some sympathy with the story I told him of his death and my brother's malaise after his time in the arena. I was granted leave to return to Italy and resolve the matter.'

Looking across the room, he saw the imperial chamberlain, Eclectus, nod to the freedman standing behind Commodus. The chamberlain had joined the dinner party after the first poetry reading, slipping in through a side door and taking a couch in the second row of diners, clearly not wishing to disrupt his master's entertainment. The functionary, clearly understanding the unspoken instruction, bowed deeply and left the dining room. Commodus caught the signal and sighed.

'Still determined to check my new training partner's bona fides, are you, Eclectus?' He shrugged at Marcus. 'What can I say, Aquila? They're so mistrustful, the men who run the empire for me.' He took a sip from his glass cup, savouring the wine before continuing. 'I'm already confident that you are who you say you are, and a man can't rule Rome for more than a decade without developing strong instincts in matters like this. But then even a god has to humour his servants.'

Marcus inclined his head in gentlemanly acceptance of the inevitable.

'Quite so, Hercules!'

He looked up to find Vorenus the praetorian smirking at him from behind the emperor, clearly expecting him to be found out by the freedman's search through the legion records.

'So, tell me more of this centurion under whom you served, Ferrus Pugnus. I wish to understand what it must be like to serve such a demanding master.'

Marcus smiled, thinking back to the various first spears he had served under and with.

'The role of first spear, Caesar, is quite unlike any other in the army, or in Roman society in general. To be a first spear is to be a warrior king, a leader of men . . . the most powerful man in the legion, bar none. A legatus commands, of course, but the first spear is the man who takes his commands and turns them into the reality. The sometimes terrible reality . . .'

He fell silent, lost in his memories for a moment, but returned his attention to the room as he realised that Calpurnius Proculus was speaking again, a gently chiding note in his voice.

'Terrible, Centurion? Surely doing battle for the empire must be the pinnacle of a soldier's ambitions?'

Marcus looked over at the senator, resisting the temptation to sneer in his face.

'Which legion was it that you commanded, Senator?'

The older man's eyes narrowed, perhaps with the suspicion of where the conversation was headed.

'I had the honour, and indeed the privilege, of commanding the First Minervia.'

Marcus nodded, allowing himself the pleasure of a knowing expression.

'First Minervia? The legion is based on the Rhenus, is it not? A region that the emperor pacified over a decade ago. Your legion never saw action during your time in Germania, did it, Senator?'

The older man bridled, but before he could respond with some cutting put-down, Commodus was on him.

'No, *you* never fought, did you, Lucius? Whereas I accompanied my father on his tours of the German frontier throughout the last four years of his life, and commanded in my own right for an entire campaigning season after his death. Which means that both Aquila and I can tell you that a soldier's life in battle is grim enough, even with the right men to lead and inspire them!'

'Err . . .' Caught off guard, Marcus could tell that Proculus was struggling to avoid blurting out his certainty that Commodus had never actually experienced battle, knowing that the emperor's delusions were such that if he believed he had, it would take a suicidally brave man to challenge that belief. 'Of course, Hercules, and I appreciate you correcting me on the subject!'

Commodus wilted his attempt to strengthen the hesitant agreement with a manly stare by the simple expedient of fixing him with a glare, then turned to Marcus and waved a hand in an extravagant instruction to continue.

'Do tell us more of your experience of battle, Centurion?'

'Battle is . . .' He pondered for a moment, trying to find the right words. 'The worst of all experiences, and yet the most exhilarating. The fear that grips a man's heart when he faces his empire's enemy across a few paces of trampled, slippery mud. Knowing that one slip at the wrong moment can gift a foe the chance to reap his life before the battle is even begun. The terror that must be mastered when the enemy is stronger, and begins to force the line back through simple brute force, knowing that to run is to die on the lances of cavalrymen waiting for the chance to ride down a fleeing scatter of soldiers. The uncertainty as the battle rages backwards and forwards, with unexpected threats on either side, or even to the rear.'

'You make it all sound somewhat dismal, if you don't mind me—'

Marcus overrode Proculus as if he hadn't even heard the senator's words.

'The blood-boiling rage of a centurion leading his legionaries across a bloody field and challenging them to fight like men. The joy, the sheer mad delight as a thousand-strong cohort fights like one man, putting the enemy to the spear and sword and dagger. The wonder, the horror and the glorious, shameful moment of rapture as you put your iron through an enemy soldier's throat or into his guts and watch the light leave his eyes as you take his life. And the man who makes all this work isn't very likely to be someone who was raised in the comfort of an opulent Roman household. He will be older than his legatus, less well learned, less well equipped and less well spoken. And yet most legati instinctively know that *they* are the lesser mortals when the time comes for their first spear to throw the legion – whose leadership they share – into battle. Because the man who fights his way to the top of his legion is that legion's warrior king.'

'Quite right!' Commodus was clapping, beaming broadly. 'Warrior kings, and moulded in my own image! Couldn't have put it any better myself! How dare my staff sully your name by checking the details of your service! I'll have none of it! As far as I'm concerned, you are who and what you say you are, and that's an end to it!' He drained the contents of his glass and stood, Marcia getting dutifully to her feet alongside him. 'And your stirring words have given me an idea! Tomorrow morning, Aquila, you and I will relive those moments of terror and rage in my stadium! Good night!'

He walked from the room with an imperious wave of his hand in farewell, leaving the guests staring at each other in disappointment.

'When the emperor has completed his meal, then it is time for the guests to leave.' Proculus stood, taking a last drink of wine and consuming the pastry in his hand in two swift bites. 'And good night to you, Aquila. I doubt we'll meet again, knowing Commodus's predilection for killing his training partners.'

He stalked away with his partner trailing in his wake, and Marcus got off his couch as Sporus left the corner in which he had quietly been waiting and came across the room to collect him.

'He likes you, that would be clear to a blind man. I find myself more than a little jealous of you. I am instructed to show you to your room and to make sure that you have everything you need.'

'One moment, Sporus.'

The servant turned and bowed as Eclectus approached them. 'Chamberlain. Might I be of assistance?'

The chamberlain made a dismissive flicking gesture with his right hand.

'Go back over there and wait. I wish to speak with this man.'

Sporus bowed again and hurried away, Eclectus waiting until he was out of earshot before speaking again. To Marcus, familiar with the people of the province that fed Rome, it was obvious that he was from Aegyptus, but he was ill-prepared for the force of the man's personality.

'I know what you are, Aquila. And I know what you are *not*.'

'And those things are, and are not, Chamberlain?'

The other man smiled at him.

'Your feigned innocence doesn't work with me. I've made a career out of discerning the truth from the sea of lies it usually floats in. And I know a liar when I see one. I don't believe for one moment you ever served with the Fifteenth Legion. In fact, I think you chose it simply because of the distance that it is from Rome. Making any check on your claim a matter of weeks, even by fast courier. But you've reckoned without the imperial records.'

Marcus kept a straight face, hoping that Qadir had managed to insert the information that would save his life.

'Weren't they destroyed by fire, Chamberlain?'

'Yes. But they were replaced soon after. So we'll know the truth of it soon enough. Sporus!'

'Chamberlain?'

'Take this man away and afford him the emperor's hospitality. Tribune Vorenus!'

The praetorian walked forward with a smile.

'Eclectus?'

'Make sure you have a man posted on Aquila's bedroom. The emperor might have authorised him to move around the palace as he wishes, but I want you to have eyes on him at all times. Understood?'

The tribune bowed curtly.

'As you wish.'

Eclectus shot him a hard stare.

'Good. And have your centurion assign me the men you usually have sleeping on the benches in your guardhouse. I have a call to make in the city, and I might just need a few guardsmen to make a point to my host.'

He waited while Vorenus issued the order to his centurion, and left with the junior officer, leaving Marcus and Vorenus both looking at him as he stalked away. The praetorian rolled his eyes.

'As if I wasn't going to have you watched at all times.'

'You still don't trust me either?'

Vorenus barked a laugh.

'Trust you? Hardly! You tell a pretty enough story about the terror and wonder of battle, but whether all that was based on actual experience or just something you heard at the dinner table, I have no idea.'

The Roman fixed him with a level stare.

'Obviously.'

The tribune smiled slowly, shaking his head in amusement.

'Oh, very good. Trying to provoke my manly pride, are you?'

He spat on the pristine marble floor, smirking at Sporus's disgust.

'The problem with that is that I couldn't give a shit for all that warrior nonsense. The last time guard cohorts went to war, they got the fright of their lives, and were captured by a bunch of robbers to boot. They had to be rescued by some ragtag cohort of auxiliaries. We were shamed, and Commodus decided that we'll never be put in that position again for as long as he's emperor. So the risk of your glory and terror ever being a part of my life is pretty much zero. Either here or on some distant battlefield. Nice try, though.'

He raised his hand, opening the closed fist to reveal a purple-beaded thong.

'This is for you, as ordered by the big man. Don't get too excited, it's the only one you're getting. It means that you're allowed to stay in the emperor's private quarters without the constant supervision of a guardsman, although you can expect to have more than one man keeping an eye on you, beads or no beads. That's what it does allow you to do. What you can't do, on pain of instant execution, is attempt to leave this part of the palace, unless you're under escort. This, Aquila' – he dropped the beaded thong into Marcus's hand – 'is as effective an incarceration as anything you might suffer at the hands of the law. And it carries a death sentence when it eventually expires, sooner or later. Probably sooner.'

★

'Chamberlain!'

Pertinax's jovial air was an almost perfect facade, except for the slight note of irritation that Scaurus, listening from an adjoining room, was able to detect from long experience of the older man's moods.

'Consul. Or should I perhaps call you colleague? Or conspirator?'

The Aegyptian's tone was so marginally deferential that it was impossible to tell whether it was genuinely intended as respect or rather as a subtle indication of the chamberlain's superiority to a senate member under an emperor known for his depredation of the elite's wealth.

'Please forgive the lateness of the hour, Helvius Pertinax. I was forced to endure yet another of the emperor's interminable dinner parties before I could get out of the palace to come and see you. Hercules's conversation is of course sparkling, but some of his guests . . .'

Eclectus rolled his eyes, inviting his host to share his amusement. Pertinax smiled thinly.

'You'll have to forgive me, Chamberlain, but delightful though it is to see you, I do not recall—'

The chamberlain continued, ignoring Pertinax's inevitable bafflement at his arriving so late in the evening.

'One of those guests, however, was far more entertaining than the procession of dullards and arse-lickers we usually have to suffer. A gaunt-faced ghost of a man with a battle scar across the top of his nose, a self-proclaimed centurion who seems to have become the emperor's latest playmate in his garden arena. When questioned by Commodus' – he smiled wolfishly – 'I think we can dispense with the pretence that he's really the son of Zeus between the two of us, don't you? Anyway, when questioned, he identified himself as having recently served with the Fifteenth Apollinaris in Cappadocia. And between you and me, it didn't quite ring true. I'm sure you meet just as many liars as I do, and one does develop something of a nose for them. So I had one of my functionaries check the legion archive, and I'll admit that I was genuinely surprised when he came back with the proof that what the man was saying was documented. There is a record of such a man, a centurion, being granted permission to return home and put his family's affairs in order. And that, on the face of it, should be that. The emperor's judgement validated, and all that. But . . .'

He fell silent, apparently waiting for Pertinax to fill that silence.

'Where are my manners! Sextus, bring us a jug of the good wine we had with dinner. Do take a seat, Eclectus, and allow me to offer you a cup before you continue.'

The two men exchanged small talk until the wine arrived, Pertinax waving the servant away and pouring the wine himself, raising his own cup.

'To our collaboration.'

'Quite so.' The chamberlain drank. 'So, where was I?'

Pertinax smiled at him, knowing full well the game that the chamberlain was playing.

'This centurion of whom you were speaking?'

'Ah yes. He goes by the name of Aquila. His brother, it seems, performed spectacularly well in the arena a few years ago under the name Corvus. And it seems that they are so alike as to be almost indistinguishable. Corvus disappeared under mysterious circumstances at the time, it seems. Simply vanished from the city overnight. The rumours at the time, my informers tell me, were that he might have been a soldier returning to active duty, having carved his bloody way into the arena crowd's heart. And that, of course, set me to thinking. But before I continue, perhaps you should suggest to Gaius Rutilius Scaurus that he might join us?'

Pertinax laughed, shaking his head.

'You might as well come out, Gaius. When a man as sharp as Eclectus gets onto your trail, it's easier just to admit defeat, most of the time.'

Scaurus came out of the anteroom, and the chamberlain smiled at him without any change of expression other than the slight curve of his lips.

'Yes, there he is. There's that threat-laden stare he used to use on Cleander's clerks years ago. You won't remember me; I was one of his fixers in those days, and spent most of my time away making the things he wanted to happen come to pass. But I saw enough of you to know what sort of a man you were. I warned Cleander too, but he never saw you as the threat I did. And still do. So tell me, this Aquila, he *is* the fugitive Marcus Valerius Aquila, I presume?'

Scaurus nodded brusquely, and Eclectus smiled broadly.

'Good. It's so much better for us all to be reading from the same scroll, wouldn't you agree, Helvius Pertinax? And presumably Aquila used his old gladiatorial contacts to get himself into the palace in the hope of putting a sword between the emperor's shoulder blades?'

'That does seem to have been his intention.'

'Thank you, Helvius Pertinax, but my question was addressed to your attack dog. Well, Rutilius Scaurus? Was it your plan to have your tame assassin murder the emperor in his private arena?'

The senator stood.

'Leave him alone, Eclectus. For one thing, it was my idea and not his, and for another, if you push him hard enough you'll come to understand what happens when the master loses control of his attack dog.'

'Is that a threat?'

'No, you fool. Look at him. Aquila might be the assassin, but my nephew here is a far more dangerous man.'

Eclectus smiled knowingly.

'Oh, I know that. I heard all about what happened to Praetorian Prefect Perennis, on the night that Cleander rose to power. I know what an animal your nephew can be, which is why I took the precaution of bringing my insurance policy with me. There are four tent parties of praetorians outside, with instructions to go through this house and kill everyone, in the event that I fail to re-emerge. Everyone – man, woman and child. So I'd suggest you put Gnasher here back on his rope. After all, it's not me that's thrown a gladiator-sized cat into our very delicately prepared pigeons, is it?'

30 December AD 192

Marcus lay still in the room's darkness, uncertain for a moment what it was that had led to him waking. He listened to the almost imperceptible sounds of the palace, quickly realising that he was unlikely to fall asleep again. He rose, donned one of the fine linen tunics that had been waiting on the bed when Sporus showed him to the room, picked up his worn caligae and opened the bedroom's door to reveal the corridor, dimly lit by a single lamp. He padded barefoot out into the palace, but got no more than a dozen paces from his room, looking around for any hint of where to find some food, before a harsh, familiar voice greeted him.

'There he is. The great Aquila, supposed centurion, and apparent brother of Corvus.'

Vorenus strolled out of the shadows, as immaculately equipped as ever, one hand on the hilt of his dagger.

'Tribune. Do you actually lie down to sleep, or have you been there since I retired last night?'

'Not me. But someone like me. And while I normally take a while to wake up, I was like a small child on his birthday when I woke. Yes, I was full of excitement that today's the day Commodus will show you just how good he really is with a sword. A proper sword, not a rudis.'

Marcus raised a weary eyebrow.

'Quite possibly. In the meantime, perhaps you could do me the service of showing me where I can get some breakfast? Having some bread in my belly will help me make a proper fight of it, and provide you a sufficiently entertaining display before I go down swinging.'

The praetorian smirked.

'Follow me. You might as well get a decent last meal.'

He led Marcus past the guards on the staircase that led to the kitchens, hailing the head cook with the familiarity of an old sparring partner. A brief exchange of half-hearted insults saw the two men provided with bread, honey cakes and honeyed wine, the latter sufficiently watered-down as to present little threat to Marcus's sobriety.

'You might as well drink it and then get another cup and drink that too.' Vorenus leered over the brim of his cup as he took a long sip. 'You're going to need all the courage there is when Commodus gets started on you.' He watched Marcus intently, waiting for a reaction, and snorted derision when it failed to manifest. 'You don't believe me?'

Marcus shrugged.

'I'm not saying that the emperor isn't a fine swordsman.'

'But you're better? What do you base that on? He's been training for the last twenty years, every day without exception. The man practically sleeps with a sword in his hand, and as we all know, practice is at the root of perfection. Add to that the fact he's muscled like a prize bull, and just about the fastest man I've ever seen on the sand. And what do you have to offer by comparison?'

Marcus smiled slowly.

'Wait and see. You think I would have come back here if I lacked confidence in my abilities?'

Vorenus snorted laughter.

'No one denies Commodus what he wants. *No one*. Not me, and definitely not you. If you hadn't shown up when you did, he'd have had your friend Sannitus back up here double quick for a game of truth or consequences. We'd have known where you were staying inside the hour. So coming back wasn't you being a hard man, it was just self-preservation. At least this way he likes you enough to make it quick and clean, by his standards. Unless, that is, you manage to find some way to piss him off. And trust me, that's not exactly a hard thing to do; the man could start a fight just by looking in the mirror.' The tribune looked at him levelly for a moment. 'To tell you the truth, since I have a sneaking regard for the size of your balls, I thought you'd fucked yourself good and proper when you poked him in the breadbasket yesterday. On any other day, I swear he'd have had me and my centurion pinion you and then beheaded you himself, there and then, just for having the temerity to get a punch in. And when you put your elbow into him and had him at your mercy, I was so certain you were fucked I nearly just killed you myself. So when he made you part of the household and promised that poor stupid bastard Sannitus a golden sword, I was amazed. But . . .'

He leaned back, chewing a piece of bread with a broad grin.

'That was then. And this is now. Yesterday he was just about as mellow as I've ever seen him, but for every good day he has, there's always another where he wakes up with the need to kill someone . . . *anyone* . . . before he's even eaten breakfast. And those bad days? They usually follow the good ones like night follows sunset. It's like there's something not quite right with him, like he's two different people.' He laughed softly. 'You'll find out. Finish that bread; it's time you were on the sand waiting for him. Good day or bad, he never likes to be kept waiting when there's a fight to be had. And he likes to fight in the dawn, so that he can attend the morning salutatio without keeping the great and good of the city waiting for any longer than usual.'

He led Marcus through the palace's ground floor to the arming room for the garden arena. Sporus was waiting for them, the child Alinus alongside him, standing beside a pile of equipment that was immediately familiar to Marcus.

'The emperor issued instructions for you to be equipped in a manner that will be familiar to you. The armourer has provided these as the closest that we have to what you'd expect.'

The Roman surveyed the equipment that he would be expected to wear for the coming bout. Piled in the curved inside of a legion-issue curved rectangular shield were a cross-crested, military-issue centurion's helmet, a scale-armoured lorica squamata with its padded arming jacket, and a pair of gilded iron greaves. The scale armour would provide the same protection he'd worn during his service with the Tungrian cohort, while the sword and dagger were instantly familiar.

'I usually fight with the longer cavalry sword.'

The armourer walked away to the rack of weapons and returned with a spatha, a full foot longer than the usual gladius, looking doubtfully at Marcus.

'Takes an experienced swordsman to throw one of these around. And a lot of practice, with all that extra weight. Sure your wrists are up to it?'

Marcus drew the weapon and tossed the scabbard aside, wielding the blade in experimental arcs that had Sporus and the child backing away from its hissing silver blur.

'I think I'll manage.' He put the weapon aside. 'Lace me into the armour, please.'

Shod in his caligae and clad in the gilded scale armour, with the sword and dagger belted around his waist and over his shoulder, and the crested helmet on his head with its cheek guards laced tight, he stood still while the greaves were buckled to his legs, then picked up the heavy curved shield. Squaring his shoulders, he walked through the open archway into the private arena, finding it entirely empty. Pleased to have a little time to himself before the emperor made an appearance, he looked around, enjoying the momentary silence.

Without the sun to warm it, the garden was cold, a slight frost giving the statuary a silver sheen, and Marcus inhaled the cold air deeply, enjoying the moment of peace. Looking up, he saw that Vorenus had taken up a position on the far side of the arena from the palace archway, frowning as he realised that the praetorian tribune was grinning at him. Hearing the scrape of hobnails on stone, he turned his head to see what was happening, catching a flurry of movement in the corner of his eye, then reared back as the glinting head and wooden shaft of a thrown spear flicked past him in the blink of an eye. Commodus, it seemed, had somehow managed to enter the garden without being noticed. Having hurled the spear that had missed by the slimmest margin, he had hurdled the low arena wall and was sprinting towards him across the sand with his sword drawn, seemingly unencumbered by the most magnificently decorated armour and helmet Marcus had ever seen on any man.

Turning to face the threat, Marcus reflexively drew his spatha from its scabbard as he pivoted on his right foot, swinging the heavy shield around just as his unexpected assailant barrelled into him at a dead run. Almost knocked flying by the big man's shoulder charge, barely managing to stay on his feet, he lost his grip on the scutum's handle. The attack's unexpected speed and ferocity barely gave him time to register that the shield had fallen curved side up on the arena's sand, its handle facing down and therefore inaccessible, in the fleeting instant before Commodus attacked again. Making the swift decision to leave the shield where it lay, he whipped out his dagger with his left hand, readying himself as Commodus reset his stance and came forward again with a roared challenge. The emperor was leading with his own shield, clearly intending to use it in the time-honoured manner by smashing the iron boss into his opponent's face. Marcus waited, stepping back at the last moment as the emperor pounced on him, leaving him to assault empty air, then swung his sword in a vicious arc to hack at the extended scutum's iron-shod rim with all the strength he could muster.

With a metallic twang the thin iron sheathing parted, both ends springing loose to wobble uncontrollably with every movement the emperor made. Commodus slowed for a moment and shook the shield, trying to dislodge the distracting metal, but, as Marcus knew well, it was riveted in several places to avoid it being lost to wear and tear. While the emperor was distracted, Marcus stepped back in, knowing he only had a moment before the assault was renewed, and that without a shield he was terribly vulnerable, but also realising that he had to take the chance on offer. Swinging the spatha again, he hacked at the same part of the emperor's scutum, the sharp blade cleaving a foot deep into the shield's wooden boards and then, before Commodus had a chance to react, used the embedded sword to pull it out of his opponent's hand. Kicking the shield off the sword, he grinned at the discomfited emperor as Commodus drew his own dagger and slowly smiled back at him.

'Well now, Aquila, I see you're not to be thrown off guard by an ambush! I told Vorenus that you wouldn't be fooled, and by my father Zeus, you weren't! What instinct was it that made you pull your head back, if not that of a trained and experienced soldier, eh?' He shouted across the arena at the praetorian. 'I told you he wouldn't fall for it, didn't I?'

The tribune bowed.

'Hercules is, as ever, all-knowing.'

'Indeed I am! And as for you, Centurion, let's see how we dance without shields, shall we? Perhaps you'll be less familiar with this sort of fighting, eh?'

He advanced on Marcus with his sword raised; the Roman noticed that he too was equipped with the longer spatha, his intention having been to put Marcus on the sand with a shorter gladius and thereby at a fatal disadvantage. The emperor attacked and Marcus parried the blow, giving ground by a pace to absorb the big man's fearsome power, then counter-attacked with a swing of his own that Commodus did well to block, such was its speed. The two men went blade to blade, Commodus swinging around to Marcus's right and stabbing low with his dagger, an arena-conditioned reflex attempt to put the blade into his side that the Roman ignored, knowing that his scale armour would in all probability deflect the weapon's point. As the dagger's point rebounded from his armoured hip, he went high with his own pugio's blade, stabbing across his body with the aim of putting it into the emperor's throat, but Commodus ducked and turned his head away reflexively, the weapon's point punching a dimple in the gold-chased cheek guard of his helmet and knocking his head to one side. Both men pushed away at the same moment, both bouncing back onto the balls of their feet, ready to re-engage in the fight. Commodus's eyes were sparkling with the joy of combat and an opponent he couldn't slaughter in the first few moves of a fight.

'You're awake then, battle brother! Can you feel the blood rushing through you! I always find an early fight sets me up for the—'

The emperor fell silent as Marcus went after him with silent, deadly purpose, but the Roman quickly realised that for all his speed and skill, Commodus was defending himself with comparative ease. Seeming almost relaxed in his footwork and parrying off Marcus's strikes, he abruptly went back on the attack, hacking high and low with his spatha, then high and low again in a series of swiftly delivered strikes the Roman guessed were intended to set a pattern and lull his opponent into expecting the next blow to follow the pattern. But the fifth blow, rather than being the predictable hack at Marcus's head, was a lunge so fast that he was barely able to half turn his body, presenting the angled surface of his scale-armoured chest along whose tiered scales the sword's point skated with a squeal. He counter-attacked with his dagger, aiming for the emperor's sword hand, but in a flurry of motion Commodus had retreated, gathering himself ready to renew the fight as fast as any man Marcus had ever fought, his spatha held with the blade slanting down with a cocked arm and the pugio lurking at his waist for the close-in work. And then, inexplicably, he dropped his weapons to the floor and turned away, showing Marcus his back with the insouciance of a man truly untroubled by any fear.

Readying himself to take the kill, already mentally rehearsing the slashing sword blow that would hamstring his mortal enemy and drop him to the ground, helpless to defend himself from the pugio's swift slice across his throat, Marcus shot a swift glance across the arena at Vorenus to be sure the praetorian was too distant to interfere with the act of revenge. And then lowered his sword to the floor and placed the dagger alongside it. The tribune nodded his men forward to collect the weapons, all the time keeping Marcus fixed with an unblinking gaze down the shaft of the arrow strung to the war bow in his hands. Capable of putting its pointed armour-piercing head straight through his armour's iron plates at twenty paces, it was a promise of death that would be delivered so swiftly that the Roman had no counter. Commodus called over his shoulder as he walked away.

'Tomorrow we will fight again, Aquila! I'll come up with another game for us to play in the meantime! But for now I feel the need for food, a bath and the company of my amazon queen, before I go to my great hall for the salutatio, where I will be forced to listen to the usual litany of miserable requests from the city's so-called fathers! For now, you may take pride in the fact that we are once again honours even! I imagine you can scarcely believe it!'

He walked away through the arch and into the palace, leaving Marcus standing in the centre of the arena as Vorenus handed his bow to a slave and strolled across to join him.

'I saw you look over at me. And I saw what was in your eyes when he turned his back on you.' The tribune's expression was a hard, knowing grin. 'You actually want to kill him, don't you?'

Marcus shrugged.

'A fight's a fight. And fights aren't often won by the half-hearted.'

'I don't think that's it, though. I don't know why, but I think you've got a hard-on for him that would do credit to a prize bull. Which is why I'm going to have two men follow you at all times – *all* times – and make sure you don't try to stab him with a sharpened spoon over dinner. He'll think it's funny that he's exercising with a man so dangerous that I have you at the point of a spear in every moment of the day, and I'll be certain that I won't end up taking the blame for his death. The only loser, Aquila, or whatever your real name is, will be you.'

'What is it that you all think you're doing, exactly?'

The man standing at the foot of Pertinax's table hammered a

fist down onto the wood with a resounding bang that made some of the gathered senators start, although Pertinax himself merely raised an eyebrow.

'You seem to be somewhat disturbed, Aemilius Laetus. Perhaps you could take a seat, and raise whatever it is that's troubling you in terms that might lead to a constructive discussion? I'd imagine it must be of some importance, to judge from the fact that you've chosen to come here in uniform?'

The newcomer had arrived at the villa's front door shortly after noon, swaggeringly self-confident and wearing armour and weapons which were in themselves rare in a city where the carriage of swords was completely forbidden to all but the praetorians. On being granted the immediate audience he had demanded with the senator, he had been somewhat nonplussed to find the cream of Rome's aristocracy waiting for him, gathered to discuss Eclectus's visit the previous evening. His host gestured to a vacant chair set out for him, answering the question in a tone that made it clear he was far from being intimidated, despite his not completely unexpected guest's fury.

'As to what it is I think I'm doing, that's simple. I'm acting in the best interests of the empire. As, I thought, was our agreement?'

The praetorian prefect remained standing, shaking his head slowly and folding his arms across his armoured chest. His gaze flicked from Pertinax to the man waiting behind him with his hands behind his back.

'I should have known it. Gaius Rutilius Scaurus. Although I could hardly believe the nerve of your reappearance in Rome when Eclectus told me this morning.'

Scaurus inclined his head with a sardonic smile.

'Prefect. We haven't been formally introduced.'

'I do know exactly who *you* are, Rutilius Scaurus. And just how much trouble you've caused over the years. I was in the throne room when you provoked Commodus to kill my predecessor. Your presence here confirms to me exactly what's happening in the palace.' He turned back to Pertinax. 'You didn't think it would be a good idea to warn me that you had a killer in play?'

Scaurus was the first to answer him.

'I warned against it. Indeed, I made it a condition of my man going into the palace yesterday.'

Pertinax nodded his agreement.

'Rutilius Scaurus was of the view that if you were forewarned, you might well have chosen to have our man killed, quickly and quietly, to prevent him from getting in the way of your own plans.'

Laetus unbuckled his belt, dropping the sword and dagger onto the highly polished wood with an ostentatious crash, then pulled the chair before him out from beneath the table and took a seat.

'And Rutilius Scaurus was absolutely correct. Your man's presence endangers everything we've been preparing for! Twice now he's been within a gnat's-cock length of killing Commodus, and the only thing that stopped him from doing so this morning was the fact that one of my tribunes took the precaution of putting an arrow to one of the emperor's practice bows, and made it clear he was ready to shoot.'

Pertinax looked across the table at him with a narrow-eyed expression of disbelief.

'Your man stopped ours from making the kill?'

Laetus shook his head in apparent disbelief.

'Of course he fucking stopped him! And if the fool had tried to follow through, my tribune would have put the arrow through him, new imperial favourite or not. It's what my men are *supposed* to do! Your man feigned ignorance of any such intention, of course, but Vorenus isn't fooled. The only thing stopping him from killing your assassin is the likelihood that Commodus will have him hanging from a hook if he does so without any proof of his intent to murder the emperor. Who is this man? And don't try to tell me that he's a centurion by the name of Aquila, because I won't believe you, no matter what the legion records say. Vorenus tells me he's Commodus's match with sword and shield, which is unusual in itself, and that the more he sees of him, the less he believes that he was ever what he claims to be, a legion centurion.'

Scaurus shrugged.

'There's no harm in you knowing, not now he's part of the imperial household. He was in fact exactly what he's claiming, but more besides. Much more. His name, his real name, is Marcus Valerius—'

'Gods below! That Aquila?' Laetus's expression hardened. 'You've introduced a known fugitive and traitor into the palace? If this is discovered, there'll be a purge that will make the last one look like a child's birthday party!' He pointed at Pertinax with a look of disbelief. 'You, Helvius Pertinax – *all* of you fools – will suffer for days before he has you finished. The gods only know that Commodus is like a tightly wound bolt thrower at the best of times, but this . . .'

He fell silent as Scaurus walked away to look out of the room's window, talking over his shoulder.

'So he failed to land a killing blow yesterday, and was prevented from doing so again today. And now you're calculating the best thing to do before he gets another chance.' He turned back to the room, and moved to stand beside his sponsor's chair. 'Perhaps you're thinking that your interests might be best served by betraying Valerius Aquila, before he has that third opportunity to kill Commodus? That way you reinforce your bona fides with the emperor, and if the poison fails to take him tomorrow night, you'll be able to denounce your highly placed co-conspirators from a position of cast-iron trustworthiness.'

Laetus nodded.

'That's exactly what I'm thinking. After all, if your man does manage to kill the emperor before the feast tomorrow night, then surely all of our plans are rendered useless with the sweep of a blade? My praetorians won't be scattered across the city and deep in their cups. The guards on duty in the palace won't be sleepy with drink, and easily fooled when the time comes to remove the body. And our plan to muster our supporters in front of an empty praetorian fortress and demand the guard's support won't be ready to implement. So yes, I'm struggling to see what *I* have to lose from such a tactic, given that your reckless throw of the dice in putting Aquila into the palace seems to have failed.'

He stood, reaching for his weapons. Pertinax leaned back in his chair, apparently still untroubled by the turn of events.

'Do you recall what it was that inspired our original plan to act tomorrow night, Laetus? And how we managed to gather such an impressive number of the most important men to support us? Don't trouble yourself to answer, I can do so for you. We made our plan when it became obvious that Commodus plans a fresh purge on the first day of the new year. That he intends to announce the prosecution of dozens of prominent members of the senate on charges of majestas. Treason of the worst kind, a threat to the imperial family! Starting with his co-consuls, who happen to be two of the richest men in Rome. They are to be executed for treason against the empire, it seems. A crime whose penalty is both death and the confiscation of property by the imperium. The confiscation of everything that the accused man owns, with no bequests to his children allowed. Which means that Commodus can knock down two birds with the same stone. He can solve whatever shortfall the treasury might currently be struggling under, because there is enough gold to be had that way to last the treasury for years. And he can cement his hold on power for the rest of his life, because with the mob and the army already standing behind him, he can clear the way to adlect a fresh crop of commoners into the senate, therein to form an obedient chorus for everything he decrees without any dissenting voice. And Rome will have become the plaything of a dictator once again. So, what do you think will happen if you tell him that his new favourite is in truth an assassin?'

Laetus looked back at him in silence, and Pertinax theatrically waited for a moment before continuing.

'Exactly. You fail to answer because the answer is one that should terrify us all. If you tell him about Aquila, you can be assured that he will act immediately, fearing other plots and knowing that the men around this table are those whom he should fear the most. Men with the influence and money needed to mount such a conspiracy. Most of us will be in chains by night-fall, and it won't take long for our confessions to doom apparently loyal men like yourself. Whereas if our man Aquila manages to deal the death stroke to him between now and tomorrow night, we have all the influence and money we need to take control of the city sitting around this table.'

The praetorian prefect stared back at him bleakly.

'So what you're saying is that if I betray your killer to Commodus, then I'm condemning us all to death. Something you might have thought through more carefully before you sent him in there.'

Pertinax shrugged.

'Aquila will either succeed – and his subsequent death at your men's hands will remove any risk of him having the truth that links him back to us tortured out of him – or he'll fail, and nobody will ever even suspect that he was our man. If he succeeds, then the risk of any immediate move to purge the senate will be removed, and even if he fails, the other half of our plot will still have the chance to play out. So you'd better tell your co-conspirators in the palace to be ready, hadn't you? Because if Commodus isn't dead by sunrise of the first day of the new year, we'll all be dead, or as good as, before that sun sets again.'

Bathed and dressed, wearing one of the fine woollen tunics that had been tailored for him, Marcus made his way into the Domus Augustana's peristilium to find Sporus watching a group of slaves who were painstakingly collecting fallen leaves from around the pool that dominated the pristine courtyard. The maior domus bowed, smiling at the sight of the Roman's purple-beaded bracelet, casting a wry eye on the two soldiers accompanying him.

'I am delighted to see you so honoured, so quickly. You must truly count among our master's most favoured companions. Although not, to judge from your escort, much in the good graces of Tribune Vorenus?' He shrugged, gesturing to the gardeners.

'Nevertheless, for a gladiator – until now the lowest of the low, ranking as low as these men who labour for nothing more than the food they receive – to be favoured with entry to his sanctum . . . this is truly remarkable.'

Marcus inclined his head respectfully in reply.

'It is indeed a new age that the emperor has introduced to the city of Commodiana.' Sporus looked at him sharply, looking for signs of humour, but the Roman was careful to keep his features composed. 'But tell me, what are these men doing?'

The slaves were down on their hands and knees, working their way around the fountain's ornate pool in a line.

'Hercules, may his father Zeus protect him, has a dislike, verging on hatred, of any hint of untidiness. And so we endeavour to keep his environs as clean and tidy as is physically possible. If he drops a scroll, a slave immediately collects it and puts it away in the right place. If a drop of wine is spilled, a man will mop it from the floor the moment that the emperor's back is turned. And here, in the garden, we collect all fallen leaves and discarded petals, and tend to the trees and shrubs with small shears to ensure that the environment is constantly pristine, ready for him to take his pleasure as he wishes. And you are free to enjoy it as well, although I must warn you to avoid the small dell that has been created in that corner over there.'

Sporus pointed to the north-east quadrant of the peristilium, where a handful of small trees in pots had been artfully positioned to create a shaded area in which a soft couch and low table awaited use, with a small chair on the table's other side. A brazier filled with glowing coals was positioned to warm the couch's user, the rippling haze above it testament to the heat of its contents.

'That part of the courtyard is reserved for the lady Marcia. After so long in the palace, she enjoys having the ability to with-draw from royal life to some degree, and the only person allowed to interrupt her peace when she chooses to use this private enclave is the emperor himself. Indeed she—'

He fell silent as the emperor's concubine came out of the

sanctum. Wrapped in a heavy shawl against the day's chill and carrying a scroll, she stood waiting without actually acknowledging the presence of either the two men or the slaves, a female servant behind her carrying a small jug of wine and a single glass. Putting a silver whistle to his lips, the maior domus blew a short, soft note, at which cue the gardeners got to their feet as one man and retreated into the western side of the palace. Marcia nodded her thanks to him and strolled languidly around the pool, taking her place on the couch and unrolling the scroll while her maid poured her a glass of wine and then withdrew. Satisfied that all was well, Sporus looked about himself to ensure that no one remained within the courtyard, then gestured to the eastern peristyle from which the concubine had emerged, and the rooms beyond it.

'We should also leave, you and I. Might I recommend that you take refuge in the upstairs gallery overlooking the Circus Maximus? I can watch the view from those windows for hours without ever tiring of it.'

Marcus nodded his agreement, and turned to make his way back into the palace, only to have his progress arrested by a call from within the grove.

'You! Gladiator! Come here!'

He exchanged glances with Sporus, who shrugged with an equally nonplussed expression.

'It is most unusual for the lady Marcia to address any man other than the emperor directly, but that is no justification for you to ignore her. I will escort you, to save you the potential risk of being accused of intruding upon her privacy.'

The two men approached the artificial grove, closely followed by the praetorians set to watch Marcus, Sporus taking the lead and bowing deeply before addressing the emperor's concubine.

'Domina, I gather that you wish to address the gladiator Aquila? Perhaps I might act as an interlocutor, to avoid there being any concern with regard to the potential for a misinterpretation of—'

He fell silent immediately as Marcia raised her hand.

'Thank you, Sporus, but there is no risk of any such mistaken perception here in an open garden. You may leave us.' She raised her voice to a commanding tone. 'And you two guardsmen may also leave us. Tell your tribune I commanded it!'

The maior domus bowed and withdrew, giving Marcus a look that combined bafflement with an entreaty to caution, and after a moment the disconcerted praetorians followed his example. Marcia extended a hand to point at the artificial dell's other chair.

'You may sit, Aquila.'

The Roman hesitated.

'Surely that chair is intended for the emperor's use, *Domina*?'

'That chair, *Gladiator*, is intended for whoever I request – or require – to sit on it.'

Marcus bowed his head in submission, as her reference to his implied formal status being no better than that of a slave required of him.

'In truth I am no gladiator, Domina, having neither sworn the oath nor submitted to any lanista, but, at your command . . .'

He sat, awaiting whatever it was that the emperor's concubine required of him.

'Not a gladiator, you say. And yet here you are, very clearly the emperor's *favourite* gladiator. Installed in the heart of the palace, much to the concern of the praetorians. And how, I wonder, do you come to be here, at this time?'

'At *this* time, Domina?'

She smiled at him knowingly.

'I think you know what I mean. But if you wish to maintain a facade of ignorance, I am willing to play along with you. So, you have fought the emperor twice now.'

'Yes, Domina.'

'And in both of those fights, you have worked to engineer an opportunity to kill him, have you not?' The tension between them had become palpable, Marcia's tone abruptly harder and more interrogative. 'You do not need to deny what I'm saying for any pretence of modesty; I observed both bouts from a concealed vantage point. He makes me watch, says it arouses him to come to me after having killed his victims.'

He took a moment to digest that revelation before composing his thoughts to answer in as anodyne a manner as he could.

'I cannot deny that there have been fleeting moments when I might have done harm to the emperor, Domina. But as a loyal—'

'Don't bother. And you can drop the act, Valerius Aquila, the praetorian prefect told Eclectus who you are, and he told me. You no more need to call me "Domina" than Commodus does, other than for politeness, because I am a concubine, not an empress, even if he's kind enough to have me preceded by the imperial vexillia when I go out into the city – not that a piece of heraldry is going to change many minds as to my suitability for the empress's throne.' Her tone was unchanged, but she leaned forward with a hard smile that told him she knew exactly what his objective was. 'The first time you were on the point of putting a practice sword into his throat, prevented from doing so only by his loyal protector Vorenus knocking you to the floor. And this morning he saved the emperor's life again, didn't he? I saw you tensing yourself to attack him from behind, only to find that you were under the threat of the tribune's bow. Two attempts. Two opportunities. Two failures. Have you learned anything from this, Aquila?'

Marcus smiled at Marcia, unable to gainsay her accusation.

'I have learned to bide my time, Domina. There will be more practice bouts, I expect.'

She sniffed disdainfully.

'For you? Perhaps. Who knows when his humour will turn, perhaps from some imagined slight. Or perhaps just because of the monster that he is, seeming to combine two people into one body. One of them a bluff, if somewhat impulsive, devotee of the arena. The other . . .' She shuddered. 'I never know which of them will visit me, after he's torn through the usual trio of victims in his garden. The first of his personas is kind enough. Considerate even. The other treats me like a street whore, taking exactly what he wants, heedless of the damage he does. And yes, for you, perhaps, there will be other opportunities. But your presence in the palace presents a risk to me. One that the men behind you either failed to consider or simply ignored when they sent you in here.'

'A risk, Domina?'

She stared at him in exasperation for a moment before continuing.

'How very much like a man. None of you bastards have given the first thought to my position here, have you? You *must* know of the plan that I have formed with Eclectus, because the ultimate beneficiary is the man who has inexplicably sent you in here. Pertinax knows that my plan will come to fruition tomorrow night. And that it has been months in the making. And yet Pertinax is willing to throw away all that careful, patient preparation in return for an opportunity that you must be starting to realise does not exist! And which will never exist! You have little to no chance of taking the emperor off guard in combat, because he's simply too good. Even for a man as skilled as you so clearly are. And you won't be able to put a blade into his back, or cut his throat from behind, because he's too well protected. Vorenus already suspects you, and while he's not in a position to deal with you in the face of Commodus's professed love of a "fellow gladiator", he can stop you from taking those fleeting opportunities simply by being ready to kill you at all times.'

She fell silent for a moment, looking up through the branches at the cloudless blue sky above them, obviously close to tears.

'Can you not see that your very presence here risks everything I have planned!'

Marcus abandoned his pretence at innocence.

'How so, Domina? Surely our two approaches to this question can coexist? All that is required is for one of us to succeed, and surely the question of which of us that is cannot matter compared to the importance of one of us doing so?'

Marcia shook her head firmly.

'No. You are sadly mistaken. If your next attempt fails, and he realises that you were in the act of attempting to kill him, his rage will know no boundaries. None at all. I've seen this before, and from as close as anyone could without paying with their life. You know the name Marcus Ummidius Quadratus, I presume?' Marcus nodded. 'Then you'll know that he was part of the plot to murder Commodus on the streets of the city one night ten years ago. He was one of the men who sent that fool Claudius Pompeianus Quintianus to the Flavian Amphitheatre with a knife, to ambush Commodus and kill him. And if Quintianus hadn't stood there waving the knife about and prattling about the senate having sent him, he would probably have succeeded, having managed to jump out of his hiding place undetected by the praetorians. But what you probably don't know is that I was Quadratus's mistress at the time. I was arrested and brought to the palace, knowing that I was going to die' – she paused, smiling grimly – 'just not how or when.'

'And yet here you are.'

'And yet here I am.' Marcia's voice hardened, and in an instant Marcus knew that the emperor's concubine was capable of much more than just the use of her sex to gain the advantage over a man. 'Can you even start to imagine the way in which I managed not only to avoid execution, but soon became the first among the many women that "Hercules" favours?' She laughed at him. 'Of course I know what's in your mind now. I'm a woman, he's a man, the answer is simple and obvious. Except the answer is *so* much more complex than you can imagine. I pander to his need to constantly be showered with adoration. I accommodate the variations in his humour, as each of his two personalities comes and goes. I tolerate the things he wants from me, when the mood overtakes him. And I always manage to hide the disgust he frequently inspires in me. You have no idea of some of the horrors I have seen, or the way they come back to me in my sleep.'

Marcus inclined his head respectfully.

'I can only congratulate you on your continued survival,

Domina. And as to the question of why I am here in spite of your well-advanced plans, the answer seems simple enough. It is because your ability to murder Commodus must be as uncertain as my own.'

'You doubt my ability to administer the poison to him when the time comes?'

'No. But there must be some doubt as to whether it will actually kill him.'

Marcia shook her head in frustration.

'How can it not? It was tested on animals and slaves before being provided to me, and it killed them all, administered at the right dose.'

'Exactly. At the right dose. It won't have escaped your notice that Commodus is a large man, with a body that would be the envy of any gladiator. Are you sure that the dose that can kill that big a victim won't have to be so large as to be easily detectable? And aside from that, I saw him drink from a medicine bottle before touching his food last night. I presume it was an antidote?'

'He takes an herbal tincture that is prepared for him by his doctor, a man called Galen who has declared himself an expert in the application of all kinds of plant-based remedies. The main ingredient seems to be a root called mandrake, from the little I have overheard. But whatever it is won't protect him against the size of dose I plan to give him tomorrow night, on the eve of the new year. I'll put it into his wine without any water, once he's intoxicated, and he'll never even taste it.'

'And perhaps that will work. But it might not. And it might not be needed, if I can take him by surprise and kill him on the sand. Surely it will be better for you if Commodus dies unexpectedly on his training ground?'

She considered the point.

'Yes, perhaps it well might. Better to be the grief-stricken concubine than the person all fingers will be pointed at if he dies of poisoning. Although I am still considering whether to influence him against you, and have you arrested and tortured just to get you out of the way.'

Marcus stood.

'In which case, Domina, it seems to me that I have spent more than long enough in your presence for my own safety, were this to be reported to the emperor. I wish you a good day.'

He bowed deeply, turned and walked away into the palace, leaving Marcia looking after him with a thoughtful expression.

'More than long enough for your own safety? That's true, *Gladiator*.'

6

'This is more like it! Have you ever seen me fight in the arena, Aquila?'

'No, Hercules, I have not had that honour.'

'That's a shame!' Commodus was tapping his foot impatiently while a pair of the armourer's slaves buckled him into his equipment. 'You have missed a truly remarkable spectacle, even if I say so myself! There are no weaklings or half-wits put on the sand before me either, only men with proven abilities who can give me a proper fight!' He raised his right arm, allowing one of them to inspect the buckles securing the heavy manica whose segmented metal sleeve protected his sword arm to a harness that encompassed his bulky chest. 'I beat them all, one way or another, and then I put the sword to their throats and tell them whether they will live or die. If they have given me a proper fight, they live. But if they have failed to meet me in combat in the manner I expect from the men of our brotherhood, they leave the arena through the Gate of Death!'

The emperor fell silent, and Marcus's instincts told him that he was expected to fill the silence with something that Commodus could use to further aggrandise his own achievements.

'And do you always fight as a secutor, Hercules?'

Commodus submitted to having his heavy helmet lifted into place by a pair of slaves, and the two halves of the smooth, curved faceplate laced together. Only his eyes were visible through the two holes in its featureless metal plate, other than for the finely drilled pinholes for him to breathe through, and when he spoke again his words were dulled by the helmet and robbed of their bombast.

'Always! When I persuaded my father to allow me to train for the arena, despite his misgivings, he employed a champion gladiator to educate me in the craft! And it was natural for him to choose a fighting style that would afford a future emperor with the maximum possible protection, even if I was only sparring in those days, and so he chose to apprentice me to a secutor! And of course, just as a man's allegiance to his chariot team is decided by his first visit to the Circus Maximus as a boy, and the men he accompanies, I was a chaser from that moment onwards!'

He spread his arms wide, holding the heavy sword and shield at arm's length in what Marcus took to be an effective demonstration of his effortless strength.

'And besides, I was born to fight this way, was I not? The secutor needs such great power and stamina, with all this iron to carry, that as my body matured and I became the very Hercules you see before you, it was the natural choice!'

Marcus looked the emperor up and down, and found himself forced to admit that few men had ever looked more at home in the armour of what was one half of the Roman public's favourite gladiatorial double act. The heavy iron manica, inlaid with complex silver chasing, and decorated with gold edging on each of its segments, protected the length of his right arm from shoulder to wrist. The flexible iron sleeve was topped by an equally intricate galerus plate that not only protected his shoulder but also covered much of his chest and back on his right-hand side, sleeve and plate held in place by thick leather straps that ran across and around his barrel chest. An equally robust and beautifully worked ocrea, a greave with a large knee guard, protected his left leg, and his gold-sheathed helmet was – to judge from the thickness of the gold and iron plate displayed by the flaring flanges that protected his neck – easily robust enough to resist the worst that Marcus would be able to do to it with his trident.

'And you, my battle brother, have you ever fought as a retiarius before?'

'No, Hercules. Being a net man will be a new experience for me.'

And, as Marcus was inclined to believe was the intention, quite likely to be a short-lived experience too. He knew little more than the theory of the way in which the armoured secutor and lightly equipped retiarius were supposed to fight. The chaser slow, even ponderous, but well protected. The net man nimble, but needing all that agility to evade the secutor's deadly blade, all the while trying to snare his opponent with the net held in his right hand, secured to his belt by a length of thick cord. Commodus laughed, what might have been an expression of good-natured humour rendered menacingly inhuman both by the helmet's muffling effect and by its brevity. The emperor was breathing hard, his sentences short, with a deep breath between each one, a sure sign of his preparation to fight with the armour's weight to carry. The arena slaves bowed deeply and backed away, their work complete, but Marcus noted that the arbiter was still standing outside the arena, and showing no sign of entering the circle to control the fight. This, it was starting to become evident, would be a fight without rules.

'To fight as the most effeminate of the arena's combatants? Lacking even the gladius to grace you with the title "gladiator"? This will not just be a new experience, my friend! It might well be the very last thing you ever do!' He leaned forward, lowering his voice in a conspiratorial manner. 'Do you want some advice from a professional?'

'By all means, Hercules.'

Even as he replied, Marcus shifted his weight onto his back foot, certain that Commodus, his arming complete, had no intention of waiting for the arbiter to call on the two men to fight. The emperor took a step forward, raising his shield and rotating his sword hand so that the blade was facing inwards, across his body, and in an instant the Roman was sure that the fight was already on. Taking an initial large pace back, he danced swiftly away as his opponent stamped forward, the emperor advancing in swift lunges to keep his armoured left leg and shield foremost, to present an almost impenetrable defence. He shouted after Marcus, as the Roman skipped backwards and around him to his right, forcing him to reorient in defence against the trident's three-pronged threat.

'Come here and fight, you fucking coward!'

The Roman grinned at Commodus's frustration despite the gravity of his situation, knowing all too clearly that his chances in a close-quarters duel would be non-existent. Where his opponent was wearing a good forty pounds of armour, and had the advantageous reach of a cavalry-length spatha, Marcus was almost naked by comparison. Aside from a loincloth, his left arm and lower leg were granted a somewhat illusory degree of protection by his own manica, galerus and ocrea, all fitted to his left side. But where the emperor's armour was thick iron plate, Marcus's manica was made from dried and stiffened leather, and the metal of his galerus and ocrea were so thin that their protection was no better than illusory against a heavy sword swung with power.

Commodus readjusted his stance and rampaged forward again, matching Marcus's attempts to escape to right and left with further swift advances. Looking behind him, the Roman realised that he was perilously close to the raised stone bars that delineated the arena's limits, and that his opponent was backing him up against them in the expectation of coming to close quarters. The decision to step back over them took no effort whatsoever. The emperor raged at him, his iron-rimmed eyes wide with fury at being frustrated.

'Come back into the arena and fight like a man!'

Marcus shook his head, laughing despite the seriousness of the situation.

'Your arena is too small for a net man to be anything other than blade fodder, Hercules! I'll fight inside the circle of statues! Either that, or you can have your praetorian shoot me with his bow and never know whether you really had the beating of me!'

And that, he knew, would be the moment of truth. Flicking a glance at Vorenus, he saw the tribune lower his bow, his face creased in a disbelieving expression. After a moment Commodus laughed.

'Again, you stamp down where most others fear to put their feet! Very well, Aquila, prepare to be hunted down without mercy!'

He stepped out of the ring of sand, pushing through the barrier of a low hedge that Marcus had jumped over, without breaking stride. Seeing his eyes flick down to judge the obstacle, the Roman took his chance with the net balled in his right hand. His cast was inexpert, missing the emperor by an arm's length, and Commodus laughed again as he advanced on his intended victim.

'You throw like a tyro! This is going to be easy!'

Marcus hurried to his right, jerking the rope attached to his balteus to retrieve the net just before the emperor could put his boot on it, and force him to either stand and fight for it or cut the cord with his dagger and abandon the snare. He dodged through the statues, collecting the net back into a throwable ball, then turned to face the oncoming emperor.

'Tired of running, are you, Aquila? Thinking of having a poke at me with that trident?'

Allowing him to approach to within the long weapon's reach, the Roman decided to take back some of the fight's initiative, remembering the last pairing of a secutor with a retiarius he had witnessed in the arena, five years previously.

'The secret to fighting in this way, Hercules, is not to allow the chaser to hide behind all that armour!'

Marcus lunged in with the trident's vicious prongs, Commodus's instinctive reaction being to raise his scutum between them to frustrate his attack. Jabbing again, so fast there was no opportunity for a counterblow, he aimed the trident low, attempting to spear the emperor's foot, but the shield was down to block the strike so fast that his attack was again fruitless. Sensing that his opponent was about to renew his advance, having successfully fended off two attacks, he struck again with lightning speed, thrusting the trident high at Commodus's armoured head. Rather than take the trident's vicious prongs on his armour, the emperor raised his shield again to block the strike, and, seeing him unsighted, Marcus cast the net low to land at the emperor's feet and then stepped back behind his weapon's threat.

'A nice attempt, but you won't even scratch my armour like th—'

As Commodus stepped forward onto the net, unseen at his feet due to his helmet's restricted vision, Marcus stepped back again and twisted his body, wrenching at the cord so hard that blood beaded on his knuckles where the rough fibres tore into his skin, then lunged with the trident as Commodus fought to keep his balance. The weapon's right-hand tine struck his opponent's helmet, scoring a long scratch into the gold sheath and jolting the emperor's head. Abruptly unbalanced by the net's movement beneath his booted feet, and disoriented by the trident's impact, the emperor staggered backwards, only managing to stay on his feet by throwing out his shield arm to steady himself against the magnificent statue of his namesake Hercules. The scutum's iron boss smashed into the demi-god's torso, snapping off the statue's stone club, and Commodus turned to stare at the damage in horror. After a moment he swivelled back to face Marcus, pointed his sword at him and bellowed two words.

'*Seize him!*'

A pair of praetorians started forward, and for a moment Marcus entertained the fantasy of hurling his trident at Commodus before following up with his dagger, only to see Vorenus sprinting across the garden with his sword drawn. Knowing that his chances of getting to Commodus before the praetorians put him to the sword were non-existent, he dropped the trident and raised his hands away from the pugio on his belt. Abruptly and forcefully pinioned by the guardsmen, he found himself face to face with an enraged emperor, who had furiously ripped off his helmet and thrown it to the ground. Still holding his gladius, the weapon apparently forgotten, he turned and stared in dismay at the broken statue for a moment longer before returning a hate-filled gaze to the man who had until that moment been his new favourite. Vorenus arrived at his shoulder with his own sword drawn just as Commodus tossed away his own blade and punched Marcus in the face, following up with a fist sunk deep into his stomach that drove the air out of his lungs and left him helpless, hanging from the guardsmen's grip on his arms. Drawing his dagger, the emperor raised the blade and put its point in his victim's face, roaring his spittle-flecked anger at Marcus.

'I'll cut your fucking liver out and feed it to the birds for that!'

Fighting for breath, the Roman shook his head.

'Do . . . what you . . . must.' He struggled back into as upright a position as the pain in his body would allow. 'I can . . . only wish . . . that I had—'

Vorenus stepped forward and punched him in the head, dropping the hapless Roman onto the gravel path with his senses scrambled.

'You don't need to listen to the ramblings of a blasphemer, Caesar, or sully your blade with the blood of such an obvious coward! We'll lock him away and you can take your leisure deciding how he should die, rather than missing the opportunity to give the matter the full benefit of your ever-creative imagination.'

Commodus contemplated the long knife in his hand for a moment, then returned it to its scabbard with a sigh of regret.

'Quite right, Tribune, and you have my thanks for preventing my anger at such a horrific act from resulting in far too swift a death for this . . . *animal*. I'll have him executed on the first day of the new year, along with the other traitors who would betray the glorious city of Commodiana, and I'll make sure that he pays a high price for such wanton disrespect of my likeness!'

He turned away, calling out an instruction over his shoulder.

'Imprison him within the palace! He can reflect on his blasphemy while he waits for his inevitable and drawn-out death!'

★

'You look resplendent, Uncle.'

Pertinax looked himself up and down in the polished silver sheet that he was using to critically examine the state of his toga, looking for any sign of a mark or blemish that might be construed as lacking in the appropriate dignitas – or worse, respect – for the emperor who was hosting the evening's feast.

'Thank you, Gaius. One always finds dressing for dinner with the emperor something of a guessing game. Some nights he dresses suitably formally, others he will come to dinner wearing a tunic, while on one occasion he dressed up in a secutor's armour and teased the ladies that he was making them all wet.'

'And so all you can do is present yourself as smartly as possible.'

'Indeed. I expect to be back before midnight, as it's usual for Commodus to bid his guests farewell at around the middle of the second watch and repair to his own quarters with his concubine.'

'At which point we expect Marcia to dose him with the poison Eclectus procured for her.'

'Indeed. Which means that there will be a somewhat anxious wait to be endured, while a host of variables play themselves out.' Pertinax smiled at his nephew's raised eyebrow. 'Variables, Gaius. The various factors that will determine the success or failure of the whole risky enterprise. Will he even drink what she puts into his goblet? Will it be strong enough? Will he have some sort of antidote close to hand? Will the job have to be finished by the hand of a man, or will the poison be enough? Will it succeed, and deliver us a bright new dawn, or fail, and subject us to a bloody morning of retribution?'

'When you put it like that . . .'

Pertinax shrugged.

'I've lived my life, Gaius. Few men have better earned retirement, and yet here I am, planning to eat dinner with a man and then return to my house and await news of his life or death, knowing that no matter what the result is – the remainder of the time I have left may be brief, whether as a victim of his purge or the uneasy recipient of his throne.'

Scaurus shook his head.

'If you are raised to the throne, then my familia and I will do whatever is required to ensure that you live long enough to effect real change in the city, and go into the underworld with the thanks of your citizens ringing in your ears.'

The senator put a hand on his shoulder.

'And your protection might just be the difference between success and failure, my boy. Let us hope that we at least have the opportunity to find out either way. And now I must go to the Palatine Hill. Hercules does not respond well to being kept waiting.'

Marcus started from his doze as his cell door's bolts were pulled free of their keeps with the rasp of iron on stone. Without any window by which to gauge the hour it was impossible to know how long he had been asleep, or what passed for sleep chained to a cell wall, but clearly his earlier exertions and the stresses of his infiltration of the palace had caught up with him at some point in the day. Grimacing at the pain in his arms from their unnatural position, manacled at the wrist and chained to an iron loop set in the stone blocks, he blinked at the light of a torch burning on the corridor's wall as the door swung open. A figure stepped into the doorway and stood silhouetted against the glare, his identity impossible to discern. He spoke to someone in the corridor.

'You can leave me alone with him. I don't think he's going to be offering much resistance.'

'Vorenus?'

The praetorian stepped into the cell, his face barely visible with the torch's light behind him.

'Yes. I thought I'd come and see how you're doing, and offer my sympathy. After all, it was a brave effort, and you almost got away with it. I salute your courage. But now it's over.' He held something out to Marcus. 'Here, drink this.'

Marcus's fingers were so numb from the manacles that he was barely able to hold the metal water bottle, and the tribune took it from him before he dropped it, unstopped the neck and held it for him while Marcus drank. Reaching into a pouch, he handed over a piece of bread.

'This will keep you going for a while.'

The Roman took a mouthful and chewed, looking up at his captor with a thoughtful expression.

'Thank you. But why . . . ?'

Vorenus laughed tersely.

'The same reason that I didn't put an arrow in your back yesterday, when it would have been the easiest thing in the world just to release my grip on its shaft and let it fly. Because even chained up down here, in the darkest, foulest recesses of the palace, a place from which very few men ever come out alive, you give us options.'

Marcus stared back at him for a moment.

'*Us?*'

Vorenus shook his head in amusement.

'Open your eyes, Valerius Aquila.' He waited patiently while his captive absorbed the fact that his true identity was not the secret he had believed. 'Yes, I know who you are. I've known since Laetus came back from a meeting with his co-conspirators, the so-called "Saviours", yesterday. They told him who you really are, and of course he told me. You were Pertinax's cross between an alternative and an insurance policy, capable of killing Commodus without assistance if you got lucky, or just a good man to have in place inside the palace if Marcia and Eclectus make a mess of their plan. The problem is, the timing was always going to be wrong, because you weren't able to control when Commodus would offer you the chance to kill him. And if you had succeeded before Marcia had the chance to poison him tonight, the result would have been mayhem. For one thing, the guard would have been incensed. They'd have taken to the streets to demonstrate just how enraged they were, and it would most likely have ended in a bloodbath. Don't forget that Commodus gave them the right to bear axes so that they can batter down the gates and doors of those senators he decides to purge, and I can assure you that they'd have used them to take revenge on those among the conscript fathers they believed were responsible for their hero's death. It wouldn't have been the best circumstances for the Saviours to attempt to take power, and my colleagues would probably have been insistent on selling the throne to the highest bidder, rather than allowing Pertinax and his cronies anywhere near it.'

'But surely Pertinax and his colleagues would be ready for such an eventuality?'

Vorenus laughed softly.

'Do you imagine that the Saviours have all the answers? Those empty vessels have all the money in the world, but they've been denied any real power as a class for so many years that I doubt they'd know what to do with it if it fell into their laps.'

Marcus shook his head in confusion.

'But you're part of their plot? If you don't believe in them . . .'

The praetorian shrugged.

'I'm just a small, and hopefully anonymous, member of their cabal. I don't plan for my name to go down in history, not like those fools. Someone else can have that dubious honour. But when Commodus dies, I will be partially instrumental. And, more to the point, well enough rewarded that I can live the rest of my days in luxury, somewhere quiet where nobody knows who I am. Don't fool yourself that this is in any way about Rome's destiny; it's all about money. Money for the Saviours, that is, gold by the sackful, and since I'm going to be caught up in it anyway, I might as well have some small share in that reward. That, and seeing Commodus dead before he has me executed out of the blue one day, on a whim, or just kills me himself when one of his vicious rages overtakes him. And besides, if you'd stabbed him in the throat with a rudis, or cut his throat from behind with a dagger, there's only one man who would have got the blame for it.'

Marcus nodded, realising the tribune's self-interest.

'You?'

'Me. I would have been dead inside a day – either executed for failing in my duty, or as a means of making Laetus look like he knows what he's doing, or sacrificed to fend off the ire of his men, or just caught in the wave of violence I expect my men would have embarked on as a reaction. Either way I would have been just as dead as him. The way that this is going to be done, tonight, is going to be presented as the despairing act of a woman with nothing to lose, rather than a plot to assassinate the emperor. And no praetorians will get the blame, especially not *me*.'

'I see.' Marcus sat back on the cell's narrow stone bench. 'So what happens now?'

'Now?' Vorenus held out the water bottle again, and Marcus managed to drink from it while the tribune answered the question. 'It's getting dark up there. The new year festivities have already begun, and the imperial party are feasting with their inner circle. Your man Pertinax is up there right now, smiling and toasting with the best of them, while all the time he plans to be sitting in the big man's chair this time tomorrow. My men are being indulged with the usual treats of food and wine, and even more generously than usual, which means that they're already somewhat intoxicated. By the end of the evening they'll be asleep at their posts, or so drunk that a dead emperor being carried past them won't even register, especially when he's concealed in a laundry basket replacing some inconveniently soiled sheets. I'd imagine that he'll be ingesting a lethal dose of poison some time soon, and the rest, as we so often hear, will be history. So sleep well. With any luck, your man Pertinax will be emperor by this time tomorrow, you'll be freed, I'll be paid, and we'll both have what we want.'

'There's no word from the palace?'

Scaurus shook his head at Pertinax's question, the senator having returned from the Palatine Hill while the younger man had been engaged in an inspection of the men waiting to escort them through the city to the praetorian fortress.

'It's too early for your conspirators' plans to have fully played out. I think we can assume that Marcus wasn't successful, though, either because his chance failed to materialise or, put bluntly, because he tried and failed.'

The older man nodded solemnly.

'It is to be hoped that the young man in question isn't dead, but if he is, I'm sure you can intercede with the Lightbringer to see him across the great river. And our people, are they ready?'

'Ready and waiting. Two dozen messengers, all ready to run, and all sober despite the lateness of the hour. Every significant member of the aristocracy who has promised to support you and your colleagues in taking the throne will hear of the emperor's death within an hour of our receiving word from the palace.'

'Excellent. Here, join me in a cup . . . ?' Pertinax handed his protégé a glass of wine, raising his own in salute. 'To a successful outcome, with as little blood spilled as possible!'

They drank, the older man putting an affectionate hand on Scaurus's shoulder.

'Here's to a successful new year, for Rome and for us both as well. This great venture of ours might yet propel you to greater power than you ever thought possible, Gaius.'

'I will serve in whatever position you think fit, Uncle, although you know that I have never seen either power or wealth as any motivation in joining you to make this change of ruler happen.'

Pertinax nodded, refilling their glasses.

'I know that full well. You are that rarity, a throwback to a more innocent time! A man well suited to the exercise of power who has no desire to possess it. The sort of man who in the heyday of the republic would have led an army to victory and then returned to his plough, uninterested in the tedium and politics of government. If the city were better blessed with men like you, it would be in a better state, I judge. It's a pity that I won't be able to use your talents in the way they would be best deployed, at least not in the short term, as all the major offices of state will be used to placate my myriad of backers. You will be aware that most of them are men of much higher birth than I, all of whom want nothing more than magisterial roles, with lictors to walk ahead of them clearing their path, and preferably more lictors than their fellows.' He shook his head, raising his eyebrows in an invitation for the younger man to share his dark amusement. 'Every man in the senate who isn't a recent beneficiary of this emperor's novel practice of promoting men to high positions simply on the basis of ability believes he has a claim on the empire. They all want to be a consul, or a praetor, or an aedile, or to gain the genuine power of one of the great offices of the state, prefect of the city, or the praetorians or the Annona. And tell me, what do you think it was that brought my former sponsor Claudius Pompeianus back to the city from his exile in the country? Was it for the love of Rome, and a desire to see the empire freed from a tyrannical madman, do you think, or could it have been the fact that his son by Commodus's sister Lucilla is effectively heir to the throne?'

'His support is conditional, I presume.'

'But of course! They'll make me emperor, my good friend Pompeianus and his good friend Acilius Glabrio, who secretly sneers at him for lacking the nobilitas of a long-established family, and despises me for being Pompeianus's father's client and there-fore even lower down the social pecking order. But it will be a gift package with so many strings attached that I'll be emperor only in name as far as the senate is concerned. They intend to sit on the benches beside me in the curia, in a gesture of solidarity that will in reality be a very clear message that this will be a triumvirate in reality. And it was made very clear in our negotia-tions that my own son is to retire to the country, and to take no part in the government of the empire. Something which, given the risks of the next few months, I was happy to concede.'

He sipped his wine.

'I am to leave the way to the throne clear for young Aurelius Commodus Pompeianus, the fruit of his marriage to the emper-or's sister and therefore the rightful blood heir. And of course since I am his father's client, and owe my entire career to his support and favour, no one has any doubt that I will do what is required of me. In due course I will be expected to name the boy as my successor, and shortly thereafter to step down and leave father and son to rule. I am to be cast as a modern-day Nerva, of course, the perfect historical precedent, handing the burden to another Trajan, with my obeisance to the new order as the price for a nice quiet retirement somewhere warm and, of course, suitably well guarded. It's not completely cut and dried, of course. Glabrio might well resurrect his claim to the throne through Marcus Aurelius's cousin Faustina, but his bloodline claim is the weaker of the two, and so I suspect he'll bide his time and hope for a mishap of some nature to overtake the younger Pompeianus. Or perhaps he'll conjure up such a mishap, who knows? My point is that, between the two of them, they think they have the empire in the bag.'

He drained his wine and slammed the heavy-bottomed cup down hard enough to crack it in two.

'But they reckon without *me*, Gaius! They mistake me for nothing more than a bluff old soldier. The son of a freedman. I am little better than a slave to these men. They plan to use me as the acceptable face of their bid to retake power, and then to put me to one side when I have made their grip on that power secure.' His face hardened, and Scaurus saw the man he'd always known lurked under its usual imperturbable facade: a skilled brawler on the battlefield and in the senate. 'But their plans fail to account for the real Publius Helvius Pertinax! Governor of Moesia, Dacia, Syria, Britannia and Africa, and prefect of the city of Rome! They fail to see the man who was consul twice under two different emperors, and who led the senate until that bastard Perennis forced me out. They underestimate the sheer bloody-minded determination of the man who was beaten senseless by the mutinying legions of Britannia when he had me exiled there, but who lived to see every one of those bastards die in agony. And, most unwisely of all, they underestimate *you*!'

Scaurus frowned, his expression a study in incomprehension.

'*Me?* What part can I play in all this? If they see you as a bluff old soldier, then they'll have me down as nothing better than your bright-eyed, bloody-masked ferret, ready to be put down the next rabbit hole.'

Pertinax nodded with a smile.

'Indeed. And it's a reputation I've done everything in my power to encourage. You are my enforcer as far as the "great and the good" are concerned, and nothing more. Their calculations with regard to you will be limited to whether to retain you in their service when they inevitably take power, or to have you removed as too great a threat. They see you as a zealot, brutal in your loyalty, but in no way capable of aspiring to the throne.'

'The throne?' The younger man shook his head in even deeper confusion. 'What has the throne got to do with me . . .' He fell silent for a moment, and when he spoke again, his voice was little more than a shocked whisper. 'You cannot mean what your words imply. It is not *possible!*'

Pertinax nodded implacably.

'Yes, it is possible. And I *do* mean it. When the time comes for me to announce my successor, when all those fools expect me to gracefully cede the greatest empire the world has ever known to a weak-chinned boy, whose preparation has been learning how to wear a toga, orate well and speak Greek, I am going to give them all the shock of their lives. I'm going to nominate a man who has fought on every frontier for the empire. A man who has risked his own life on numerous occasions for the empire. A man who has defeated the tribes of Britannia and Dacia, who outsmarted the Parthian hordes, and defeated the mighty army of Kush for the empire. I am going to nominate *you*, Gaius Rutilius Scaurus! And you are going to be the man who succeeds me as emperor, and who will drag Rome out of the gutter and back to its pre-eminent position in the world!'

7

Marcus looked up at his cell's door, alerted by the metallic scrape of bolts.

'Get him unchained and bring him out!'

A pair of jailers came into the confined space, released him from the manacles and hauled him to his feet, hurrying him out of the cell and down the corridor past a dozen other similar doors. A man who had to be Vorenus was walking quickly in front of him, a supposition that was confirmed when he turned and looked back as the corridor reached a staircase that climbed back into the palace's cellars above the dungeons.

'Here.'

The tribune pointed at a door at the top of the stairs, and the praetorians holding his arms thrust Marcus through it, releasing him as they did so. Half expecting to find Commodus waiting for him, he was bemused to find a lamplit room, empty except for a table and chair, with a steaming bowl of something that smelt good and a spoon laid out on the flat surface, a jug of wine beside them. Vorenus was talking to the guards, his voice both urgent and commanding.

'Get back to your duties guarding the rest of them. And keep this to yourselves if you know what's good for you. Dismissed!'

The sound of their hobnails clattering down the stone steps was cut off as the tribune stepped into the room and shut the door.

'Eat. You're going to need your strength. And get a cup or two of the good stuff inside you too.'

'What . . . ?'

'Eat and I'll tell you what's happening. But get on with it, there isn't any time to be wasted.'

Still confused, Marcus sat and started to eat the stew, blowing on each spoonful to cool it. Vorenus poured him a cup of wine and pushed it at him.

'Drink it. Trust me, you'll thank me when the time comes.'

'When what time comes?'

'Shut up and eat. It's close to midnight, and the palace is for the most part inebriated, servants and guards alike. If Marcia was suffering from any last-minute uncertainty, her mind was changed when she was given a death list with her name on it. Seems that the child who follows Sporus around found it on Commodus's desk and ran to her with it. She got a good dose of the poison into Commodus's wine an hour or so ago. He drank it down in a single gulp, went white, started sweating, gave an almighty groan and then puked it back up all over himself. It seems he's only half-dead, and that half is slowly starting to recover.'

Marcus looked up at him and nodded, swallowing a mouthful of stew before replying.

'I warned her that the dose that would kill a slave might not do the job with a man that big, especially one who habitually drinks some sort of antidote mixture. And if the poison wasn't in him long enough, then he'll probably feel as sick as a shithouse rat for a while, but he'll also probably survive. And when he comes back to his senses . . .'

Vorenus nodded.

'I know. He'll go on the rampage. If he wasn't planning a new year purge before this, he will be now. Probably starting with Marcia, since she's the one who's been serving his wine all night. Then he'll have Laetus gutted for failing to see it coming, after which he'll just keep killing people until he's burned out.'

'Most likely including you.'

'Yes. And you.'

'True.' Marcus shrugged. 'Thanks for the last meal, if that's what this is.'

The praetorian shook his head, grimacing at the Roman.

'Don't be a fool. He's currently lying in his bathhouse, trying to sweat out whatever it is that afflicted him. Someone needs to finish him off, and the body needs to be viewable afterwards.'

'And you think that I'm the man?'

'What I think doesn't matter. The question is, do *you* think you're the man? You've risked your life three times in the hope of a fleeting chance to put a blade into him, now I'm offering you a cast-iron chance to finish him.'

Marcus spooned up the last of the stew and drained the wine.

'He'll see me coming. And I'd imagine I'm still very much on his mind, given he thinks it was my fault he broke his statue of Hercules.'

Vorenus shook his head.

'I looked in not long ago. He's lying in his bath facing the door, muttering and groaning to himself, but the slaves' entrance is behind him. A soft-footed man like you could be on him before he even knew you were there. If you're man enough for it.'

The Roman stood, stretching his back.

'Oh, I'm man enough for it. He could be on his feet and fully armed and armoured and I'd still be man enough for it, now that you're not around to get in the way. Show me the way to this bathhouse.'

'Surely you can't be serious? Putting to one side whether I either want or could ever even discharge the role of emperor, there's no way Pompeianus or Glabrio would ever allow you to do something as rash as to place a complete unknown on the throne. Not when they have so much at stake when it comes to replacing you.'

Pertinax smiled knowingly at Scaurus, sipping at his wine with a twinkle in his eye.

'And as I've already told you, they won't have the choice.' He leaned forward across the table. 'The mechanics of a transfer of imperial power are very simple, Gaius. There are three sources of power in Rome for an emperor, and they are, in order of increasing importance, the people, the imperial bureaucracy and the praetorian guard. The people alone mean little, unless they're willing to take to the streets in outright rebellion, which is unlikely to happen unless they're starving. Which is why the prefect of Aegyptus is always an equestrian reporting directly to the palace, to make sure the grain keeps flowing. And while the palace staff are of vital importance to the running of an empire, pandering to the emperor's needs and keeping the people fed, they don't carry swords. Which means that unless the people revolt, it's the praetorians who have the power to put a man on the throne. Or to take him off it, if their displeasure is strong enough. The army, of course, can have an influence in the longer term, if the legions are sufficiently disaffected or greedy enough to dress a legatus in purple and prance about telling each other that they're rich soldiers; that's clear. But there's a good reason why they're all based on the frontiers and therefore months away – and it's not just because that's where the external threats are. No emperor wants to hand the power of several legions to a potential usurper without knowing he can balance it off by giving the same power to that man's rival, and that he has the time needed for a march on Rome to organise an effective defence. And there's something of a code of conduct against that sort of thing, if the man on the throne is deemed strong enough to make an effective emperor. Do you see where I'm going with this?'

'The people are too passive, the bureaucracy is toothless, and the legions are too far away. It's the guard that matters above anything else.'

'Exactly. Which is why our first move tonight, once we know Commodus is dead, will be to the praetorian fortress. We need to get the men of the guard behind us and make sure they stay loyal. Mainly by means of paying them a significant donative, enough to soothe their anger at their beloved emperor's death. Twelve thousand sestertii ought to be enough. And once the dust has settled, I intend to engineer a reason to replace Laetus with another candidate. You.'

Scaurus frowned.

'Surely they'll take that as an insult?'

'Not if they're suitably bribed. It really is all about the praetorians, Gaius, and I'm telling you, all we have to do is keep them sweet for this to play out exactly as I plan it. Once they've settled down and adapted to the change of ruler, with any friction lubricated by their having been handsomely paid off, we'll slide Laetus out of his position and I'll promote you to command them.'

'Me? Praetorian prefect?'

'Why not? You're an equestrian, so you're qualified in terms of your status. You're known to more than a few of them as the man who gave them back their pride in that matter with Maternus. And you're a war hero! They'll take to you quickly enough, I'm sure of that.'

The younger man shook his head, thinking quickly.

'But surely your co-rulers will see what it is that you're trying to do?'

Pertinax smiled slowly.

'Pompeianus and Glabrio, and all their supporters, will be discovering the realities of imperial power. Which are that the man who commands the loyalty of the praetorians and the palace can afford to ignore the senate. Only when an emperor is fool enough to let the protection of the guard and his household slip away is he truly vulnerable. As, it is to be hoped, Commodus is just about to discover. The hard way.'

Eclectus and Marcia were waiting for them outside the bathhouse, a pair of slaves standing an appropriate distance behind them. The woman's hands were shaking as she pointed at the door, her face as white as a sheet.

'He's just in there. The last time I saw him he was lying in his bath, still vomiting.'

'The poison wasn't strong enough then?'

Eclectus shook his head impatiently.

'It wasn't in his stomach for long enough before he vomited it back up. Not long enough to kill a man that powerful.'

'And now you want me to go in there and kill him, before he recovers his wits and has you all executed for attempting to murder him. And after that?'

The chamberlain pointed to the waiting slaves.

'The official line until we have the guard on our side will be that Commodus died from natural causes. We can use the death list as our justification for the murder, as it includes the consuls who were to be sworn in tomorrow, but only once the guard are committed to our cause. So these two trusted men will take the body to the summer palace on the Via Appia, where it can be kept safely until the time comes for it to be displayed to quell any speculation. Which means it will need to be unmarked, or at least show no sign of anything worse than he might have incurred in a fall during his "seizure". Tribune Vorenus will make sure they get past the praetorians, although his men are all so drunk I doubt they'd notice. Now get on with what you're being paid for.'

Marcus narrowed his eyes and took a step forward to go face to face with the discomfited Aegyptian, his voice a low snarl.

'I'm not being paid. This is personal. So mind your words, because I'll happily see anyone who connived in his crimes dead alongside him. And just be clear that if the man who killed the emperor is named, that name isn't mine, or your life will be shorter and more interesting than you might find desirable.'

Vorenus stepped in, putting a hand on Marcus's shoulder and gesturing to the door.

'The last time I saw him he was almost prostrate with the agony. So all you have to do is stay quiet, creep up on him and finish him. Strangle him, drown him, whatever works.'

Marcus stared at the door Vorenus was indicating for a moment, summoning his hatred for the emperor from the place inside him where it waited, coiled and ready to rise. The praetorian smiled grimly.

'I know. It's not every day a man is called from a cell to murder an emperor. And it's easier to kill a man, any man, in hot blood rather than cold. But the longer you wait, the more chance there is of him having recovered enough to fight you off.'

The Roman shook his head.

'I don't care how that animal dies. And I've been waiting for this chance for over ten years. It's just . . .' He pondered for a moment. 'I suppose it comes down to not knowing what comes next, I suppose.'

Vorenus laughed softly.

'Welcome back to the real world, Aquila. Most of us would be happy just to know what we'll be eating in the evening when we wake up, never mind where life is taking us. And you know as well as I do the tricks that life can play on a man, and turn everything he's striven towards to ashes in his mouth.' He put a hand on Marcus's shoulder. 'So go and take your revenge, while it's still there to be had. As to what comes next, worry about that when you get there, eh?'

Marcus nodded, opened the door and slipped into the darkened room on its other side. The bathhouse was almost completely dark, a single lamp illuminating one corner in which a circular stone bath, fully twelve feet across and filled with gently steaming water, was dimly visible inside its circle of light. But where he was expecting to see the slumped form of Commodus, there was nothing.

'Who's that?'

The sudden challenge froze him where he stood, unable to see the speaker in the gloom. Commodus's voice was slurred, and edged with physical stress, as if the speaker was straining his muscles. 'Who is it? Show yourself!'

Marcus paused for a moment longer, thinking frantically, then took a step forward and spoke, pitching his voice a little higher than usual.

'Here I am, Hercules! I heard you were sick and needed help!'

The emperor grunted, then dry-heaved with a violently abrupt spasm, his body still in open revolt against the traces of the poison that it had expelled. When Commodus spoke again he was panting for breath.

'Sporus? I feel like I'm dying. Fetch help!'

As his eyes adapted, Marcus realised that the emperor was sitting on a bench next to the bath, hunched over with his head almost between his knees and a small pool of dark liquid at his feet. Even with his massive frame wracked by the poison's effects he was an imposing figure, his physique so well developed by years of exercise that every muscle and sinew seemed to be visible beneath his skin. Even as Marcus was calculating how to kill such a formidable opponent without a blade, Commodus heaved again, trailing another drool of bile into the puddle at his feet.

'Help me, for Zeus's sake! I'm dying here! Fetch my physician! Galen will know—'

Another spasm wracked his body, this time so violently that he fell from the bench onto his knees, and when he looked up at Marcus, the red rims of his tear-filled eyes confirmed what the Roman already suspected.

'I can't see a bloody thing, I'm puking so hard! Fetch Vorenus, he'll take me to safety! Anyone could blunder in here, and a limp pansy like you isn't going to protect me!'

Marcus stepped closer to the stricken emperor, deliberately stepping around to his right to stay out of the lamp's circle of illumination.

'Tribune Vorenus is waiting outside the bathhouse, Hercules. Even at times like these, he knows better than to enter—'

'Get me up, you fool! I can barely stand!'

Commodus held out a hand, and without time for conscious thought, Marcus stepped forward and took it, hauling the emperor onto his feet. Close up, his fetid, poisoned breath was enough to make Marcus recoil despite himself. The emperor stared in amazement through his slitted, tear-filled eyes at the Roman.

'*Aquila?* But—'

Marcus stepped forward, putting a foot behind his legs and pushing him over it with all his strength. Unable to resist in his weakened state, Commodus fell backwards, striking his head hard on the stone bench behind him. Dazed, he rolled sluggishly over and struggled onto his hands and knees, then collapsed onto the point of his chin as Marcus kicked his hands out from underneath him.

'Wha . . . ?'

The Roman went on one knee, taking a handful of the stunned emperor's hair and lifting his head.

'My name is more than just Aquila. I am Marcus Valerius Aquila.'

'Eh . . . ?' The emperor's eyes struggled to focus on his attacker. 'You . . . ?'

'Ten years ago you had my family slaughtered to steal my father's wealth!'

Gripping his semi-comatose victim by his hair, the Roman started dragging him towards the bath, but as he heaved the stuporous emperor forward, he realised that there was no way he was going to get such a dead weight over the bath's stone side. Commodus groaned and reached out a hand to grip Marcus's ankle, grunting in agony as the Roman stamped a hobnailed boot on his wrist, feeling the bones cracking under his heel. Releasing his grip, and allowing the emperor's prostrate figure to fall back onto the flagstones, he stepped astride the semi-conscious man and then lowered himself onto Commodus's back, muttering in his victim's ear as he wrapped an arm around his neck.

'You raped my wife on a whim, causing her death. Now you pay for your crimes!'

He flexed his arm to pinch the other man's throat shut, leaning back and tensing his body against the inevitable death struggle he knew must follow. A desperate burst of strength flooded through the other man's body, driven perhaps by the realisation somewhere in his reeling mind that he was in danger of losing his life, and Marcus clung on doggedly as the emperor summoned the strength to lift both his own weight and that of the man on his back off the ground, first to his knees and then, shaking with the effort, to his feet. Stabbing a knee forward into the back of Commodus's legs, he put the emperor off balance, but found himself pinned under his heavy weight as the struggling man fell sideways, taking them both to the stone floor. Something wet was soaking into his tunic, and he realised that the emperor had lost control of his bladder. Commodus's body was shaking uncontrollably as his guts spasmed again, ejecting yet more bile which, with no route of escape from his body, flooded into his lungs. He thrashed violently, making it all Marcus could do just to maintain his stranglehold, whatever instinct for self-preservation remained in him making one last frantic effort to escape impending death. And then, as if the candle of his spirit had been blown out, he subsided onto the floor and lay still. The Roman stayed where he was beneath what he presumed was the emperor's corpse, keeping his arm locked in place to prevent Commodus from breathing if he was attempting to feign death, but after another dozen breaths he realised that his revenge was complete. He pushed the dead man off him, stood up, and opened the door for Vorenus and the conspirators.

'He's dead.'

The tribune looked down at Commodus's body dispassionately, then turned back to Eclectus.

'Time for your part of this, Chamberlain.'

The Aegyptian nodded, beckoning the two slaves forward, each man carrying a heavy woollen blanket.

'Double-wrap him so that there's no chance of an arm or a leg coming loose and alerting the praetorians. Tribune Vorenus will escort you to the forum ramp; the cart that's waiting there will take you to the Villa of the Quintilii, on the Via Appia. When you get there, ask for Publius Livius Larensis, he's the procurator patrimonii who controls the summer palace and he'll be expecting you. He'll see that you are rewarded.'

Marcus watched while the two men wrapped the emperor's corpse in the blankets, then carried it away behind Vorenus, struggling with its weight. Taking off the noisome tunic, Marcus found a towel and used it to remove the worst of the bile and urine that had smeared his body while he had fought with Commodus, then washed the evil smell from his skin with water from the bath.

After a short time Vorenus returned, handing Marcus a clean tunic fetched from his room.

'The body is safely away, and the palace is quiet.' He shot a calculating glance at Marcia and Eclectus. 'You're ready for what happens next? The senate's unbridled joy, while every man looks at you and wonders why you should be allowed to live when you were his supporters for so long?'

Eclectus held up a writing tablet.

'They'll understand their close escape when they see this.'

The tribune took it from him and read what was scribed into the soft wax surface.

'This is genuine, or part of the plot?'

'It's nothing of my invention, I assure you.'

Vorenus whistled softly.

'The names on this list are some of the richest men in Rome . . .' He frowned, holding the tablet up to the torchlight. 'Including both of the men who were to be appointed consul in the morning. He was nothing if not ambitious. And' – he flicked a glance at Marcia – 'you're on here too!'

Eclectus nodded.

'He had his reasons. But we can worry about those later. For now, that's all the reason we could ever have needed for acting as we did. He left it by his bed, and the child Alinus found it.'

The praetorian nodded slowly.

'I saw him walking around with it, mimicking Sporus. And all the time he was holding an imperial death list?'

'He left it on a table, when he grew tired of the pretence.' Marcia's voice was hard, but her tear-misted eyes betrayed her true emotions. 'I picked it up, on a whim.'

Vorenus bowed.

'And I can only imagine your shock.'

He turned to Eclectus.

'Have you sent a message to Pertinax?'

The chamberlain nodded.

'The plan is in motion.'

'Very well. You, I presume, will now convince your chosen scapegoat that it's in his best interests to accept the blame for this, and to get himself as far as he can from Rome before the praetorians wake up to what's happened? And for me to go up to the fortress and play my part in handing over the city to the "Saviours".' He turned to Marcus. 'Will you come with me? The palace is probably not going to be a good place for the emperor's favourite gladiator once my men realise what's happened under their drunken noses!'

'Put these on.' Vorenus handed Marcus a bracelet of red praetorian beads and a hooded red cloak. 'Where's the fun in being the man with control of who comes and goes from the palace if I don't bend the rules a little every now and then?'

He led the Roman through the corridors that led to the palace's northern side, the two men emerging out into the gardens that overlooked the emperor's private stadium garden.

'The secret from now is for you to look less like a man who just killed an emperor, and more like an imperial functionary with a job to do. You're on imperial business and I am escorting you to make sure that nobody tries to rob you, right?'

He led the way down the stone staircase that Marcus had climbed almost three days before, turning left at the bottom and walking down the tunnel towards the iron gate that separated palace ground from the arena's underground precincts.

'I made sure that the men on duty here got a generous ration of wine even by tonight's standards. After all, who's going to try to break into the palace through a gate made of inch-thick iron bars? Now put your hood on, let's not take any unnecessary risks of you being recognised.'

Two of the four men on duty were rolled up in their cloaks and fast asleep, one of them snoring loudly enough to be heard from twenty paces, the other two coming to a dishevelled attention as the tribune approached.

'Good morning, Tribune, sir!'

Peering from beneath his cowl, Marcus realised that the breezy greeting from a slouching chosen man sounded familiar. Looking more closely, he realised that the man was the same praetorian who had admitted him to the palace two days before.

'Good morning, Chosen Man. I see you and your men have been making the most of the opportunity to be legitimately drunk on duty!'

Vorenus had moved to block off the soldier's view of Marcus, his tone light but still the voice of command. The praetorian soldier sounded a good deal more sober than Marcus would have expected, given the empty wine jugs that had been neatly lined up against the tunnel's wall.

'My lads have, thank you, sir! Given your comments the other day, and knowing you're on duty tonight, I decided it might be wise to limit my own consumption. We're going turn and turnabout on sleeping, just to give the lads a chance to recover enough not to puke their guts up on the way back to the fortress.'

'Very wise of you, Chosen, and gratifying to see my advice being taken seriously.' He thrust out his wrist to display his proof of authorisation, and Marcus copied the gesture to display his own beads. 'Two to leave the palace, both red bracelets.'

'Two to leave the palace it is, Tribune, and I verify that you have the appropriate authorisation. Get the gate open!'

Marcus relaxed slightly as the gate swung open, the chosen man calling out a cheery farewell.

'I wish you a good new year, Tribune, sir.' A slightly gleeful note crept into his voice as he added a second and final farewell. 'And you, Master Aquila.'

Both men stopped and turned to look at him, but the soldier's face was innocent of anything other than a hint of good humour. Vorenus stepped back up to the gate, fixing the man with a steady gaze.

'And how is it that you think you know this man's name, Chosen? After all, you can see that he's conducting imperial business and has sought to do so incognito.'

The soldier's face was knowing, his certainty apparent in the confidence with which he answered his superior's question.

'It's the boots, Tribune. Those are soldier's boots, hobnailed, which is a rarity around here unless you're one of us. Well worn, battered even, but still well polished just like a soldier would keep them, if he knew what was good for him. I made a note of them when he came through the main gate as being out of the ordinary. Oh, and the one on his right foot has a nick in the leather about a third the way up from his toes. Sir.'

Vorenus nodded his acceptance of the undeniable accuracy of his man's statement.

'Excellent observational skills, Chosen Man. We might just make a centurion out of you yet.'

The two men walked away, Vorenus swearing softly under his breath.

'Shit. So much for making a quiet and unnoticed exit from the palace. And there, if you ever needed it, is a demonstration of the law of unintended consequences. If only I hadn't kicked his arse for stinking of wine the last time I saw him, he might have been one of the men rolled up in a cloak.'

He led Marcus on a brisk walk through the arena's subterranean maze and up another staircase to the surface, exiting the huge building through the gate of death, close to the one-hundred-foot-high colossus that loomed above them, silhouetted against the stars. The praetorian looked up at it with a cynical grin.

'I wonder how long it'll take for that to be restored to its original condition?'

Marcus shrugged.

'All depends on whether they kept the original head, and the rudder and globe that Commodus had replaced with a club. But I'd imagine the next emperor will make that a priority, wouldn't you? Who wants the face of his predecessor staring down at him when he goes to the arena, and for it to be a constant reminder to the praetorians?'

They walked up through the Viminal Hill's moonlit streets in silence, Vorenus keeping a hand on his sword in case any of the city's robbers decided that two men walking alone were fair game. They were only halfway to the praetorian fortress when the sound of running feet became audible behind them.

'That's quick . . .'

They turned to look back down the hill, seeing a group of five men running along the same route they had followed from the Flavian Arena. At first glance they were racing each other, but as they drew closer it was apparent that they were in fact running together, pacing each other as they panted up the incline. One by one, runners split away from the group, diving into the maze of streets to the right and left.

'And so it begins.' The praetorian crossed his arms. 'Wait and listen.'

They waited for several long moments before hearing the first outburst of shouting, but from that instant the noise was constant, a distant racket of whistles, cheers and imprecations shouted at the stars, in an extravagant display of joy at the news that had been delivered by the runners. The cacophony grew louder as each of them reached their destination, and the messages they were carrying reached the ears that had been waiting for them. A moment later a mob started streaming around the corner of a street further down the hill, heading up the road towards them, easily two hundred men strong, their exultant shouts discernible now that they were close enough to be heard clearly.

> *'Drag his body in the dust!*
> *Throw his body to the dogs!*
> *Drag his body with a hook!*
> *Put his head upon a spear!'*

As the mob drew closer it was apparent that they were a mixed bag, with a small proportion of toga-clad patricians escorted by a larger contingent of respectable-looking working men, while the largest share of their numbers was marked as little better than vagabonds by their garb and demeanour. A dignified figure was proceeding serenely at their heart, his hands in the air to receive the adulation of the men around him. Vorenus shook his head, smiling sadly.

'And so it begins. The richest men of the senate, those who feared Commodus the most, are bringing their friends, their clients and the roughest of Rome's population out onto the street. The latter in return for gold. And now they've showed themselves, they know all too well that they have to make the loudest possible demonstration of joy, and cow the ordinary citizens into silence. Anyone trying to gainsay them tonight is likely to find themselves on the wrong end of a beating. Come on, we have to get to the fortress before the main body of the mob, or we'll never get through them to carry out Laetus's orders.'

They hurried up the hill ahead of the crowing crowd and his supporters, arriving at the praetorian fortress to find the massive stone edifice silent. Vorenus strode across the open space before it and hammered at a door set in the massive wooden gates.

'This is Tribune Vorenus! Open this bloody door!'

The vision slot set in the wooden door opened, a pair of eyes regarding the two men with disdain for an instant before the man behind the door realised who he was looking at. The door opened, and Vorenus pushed Marcus through it into the fortress before stepping inside and ordering it to be barred behind them.

'Fetch the duty centurion!' The soldier dithered, clearly the worse for wear, and Vorenus leaned closer to him, drawing breath to roar a single word. *'Now!'*

The hapless soldier scuttled unsteadily away, and Vorenus led Marcus up onto the fortress's walls to stare out over the parapet down into the city. The parade ground in front of the praetorian headquarters was starting to fill up, groups of chanting men converging on it from across the city in what had to be a carefully prepared plan. From their elevated vantage point, thirty feet above the ground, they could see the torches of dozens more groups making their way across the city to swell the mob to its maximum possible strength.

'This is the senate's great roll of the dice, or at least that part of the senate which Commodus didn't already own. Each one of those groups represents every man that each senator could bring out onto the streets to shout for their cause. And they're all coming here.'

There was a hint of sadness in his voice, and Marcus waited for him to continue, unwilling to intrude on his moment of personal conflict.

'In the normal run of events, these walls would be lined with men. Thousands of praetorians, champing at the bit to be launched into the crowd and put them to flight. Being a mob is all very well when you're kicking the shit out of some poor fool who chose the wrong moment to disagree with you, but it soon pales when the emperor's hunting dogs are turned loose. On any other day we'd chase those fools all the way to the Tiber – those we didn't spear in the back on the way – and watch them jump in the river and risk being washed out to sea with the rest of the city's shit just to get away from us.'

'But not today.'

'No.' Vorenus shook his head, looking down at his feet with a tone in his voice verging on self-disgust. 'Not today. The guard always was the key to the city, and Laetus has decided to turn that key in Pertinax's direction. He'll be out there with them, ready to sweep in here the moment the gates are opened, and start making promises of more money than any man in here could ever have expected when he woke up this morning. Which, of course, they will accept.'

The duty centurion strode down the wall towards them, and Marcus realised that it was Tausius, the brutal officer who had accompanied Vorenus on the day of his first bout with Commodus. He saluted the tribune crisply, without any sign of his having been overcome by alcohol, then narrowed his eyes as he realised who was standing alongside him.

'Tribune.'

Vorenus sketched a return salute, noting the direction of his subordinate's stare.

'Don't worry, he's with me. I brought him out of the palace to spare him from the madness that's about to overtake it.'

The other man nodded, turning to look at the swelling mob below them, a good proportion of them armed in contravention of the city's strict rules.

'Is it true, what they're shouting? Is the emperor dead?'

'Yes, it's true.'

The question came from between gritted teeth.

'How?'

The question hung in the air for a moment, the menace in it implicit. Vorenus shook his head, his pretence of sorrow consummate.

'I was told that he had a seizure in his bathhouse. Fell over, smashed his head on a stone bench and never woke up.'

The centurion shook his head.

'And you believe that?'

'I've seen his body. His head's a bloody mess.'

The junior officer shook his head obstinately.

'I'm not sure our boys are going to believe that, with all due respect, sir. Or at least not want to believe it. And the speed with which this lot have gathered doesn't exactly help make it look like it was an unexpected accident.'

'I know. And if they're suspicious already, those that aren't insensible with the drink, what I'm going to tell you to do next is going to make it worse. Much worse.'

'Go on . . . sir.'

Vorenus took a deep breath and blew it out, and Marcus reflected that planning to do something that would hand the city to the Saviours was very different from actually giving the order to make it happen.

'I am under orders from Prefect Laetus to open the gates of the fortress.'

The other man stared at him in disbelief.

'But . . .'

Vorenus overrode him, putting a note of certainty into his voice that Marcus suspected the tribune was far from feeling.

'But those men who aren't out in the city are barely capable of standing up? But we'll be allowing a mob largely composed of the city's scum to walk over us? But this means we'll be unable to put them down like we should? Yes to all that, Centurion. Now open the gate.'

'Tribune . . .' The centurion groped for a way to avoid insubordination while expressing his dismay. 'If I open the gates, this is *over*. We'll never be able to put that smoke back in the bottle. We should take the men that can put one foot in front of another and get into them with our swords. You *know* they'll run.'

'Yes. They would, were I to order it. And the man who I expect the senate will choose to be our next emperor is out there with them. If we give the city fathers a second corpse to wrap in purple, they'll disband the guard and split us up among the legions. And then select another puppet to do their bidding. This way we get paid a healthy donative for backing the new boy, keep our roles, keep our power . . . do I need to spell it out for you? And that's before I fall back on the fact that we're both sworn to do what the prefect tells us, *without* question.'

'Tribune.'

The centurion whipped his hand up in a punctilious salute and turned away barking orders, leaving the two men to stare out over the mob gathered below. Vorenus listened to their chant for a moment before speaking again.

'Hear that?'

The same few words were being shouted again, over and over, clearly orchestrated by the mob's cheerleaders from a predetermined script.

'Honour to the guiltless! Put his head upon a spear! Honour to the guiltless! Put his head upon a spear!'

'They're talking about the Saviours. The rich men who are about to take control of the empire again and take us back to the end days of the republic, when all that mattered was how much ambition a man had and how much gold he had to back it up with.'

Beneath them the fortress gates creaked open, and the mob surged forward with a cheer, pushing the guardsmen aside by the sheer weight of their numbers. Vorenus lowered his forehead onto the parapet's cold stone, his voice edged with anguish.

'I have obeyed my orders. And in doing so delivered the empire into the hands of men whose only desire is to enrich themselves at any cost. May the gods forgive me.'

1 Januarius AD 193

It was still two hours before dawn by the time Marcus and Vorenus arrived at the senate house, in the forum at the heart of the city. A huge crowd of senators and their torch-bearing supporters had gathered around the building, but the combination of insistent pushing and Vorenus's feared praetorian uniform cleared a path through the press of men until they reached the edge of a semi-circle that remained clear. A dozen of Petrus's men were keeping anyone without a role in the proceedings at bay, and their leader was lounging on the building's steps with the smug expression of a man who knew he was on the winning side. Spotting Marcus at the edge of the crowd of supporters and onlookers, he signalled to his men to allow the Roman through their cordon, and he pulled Vorenus along with him.

'Corvus . . .' Petrus grinned at him knowingly, raising his voice to be heard over the crowd's hubbub. 'Or is it Aquila these days? Whatever name you're going by now, well met. If my information is to be believed, then the Saviours, as they love to style themselves, have much to thank you for! Just don't expect to hear a word of those thanks anytime soon! And if you've got any sense, don't look for it either, but cherish your anonymity instead. The word on the street is that some idiot wrestler called Narcissus did the deed, and you'd be sensible to let that be the story that goes into the history books!'

He looked at Vorenus warily, taking in his praetorian finery.

'Who's the imperial enforcer?'

The tribune leaned forward, drawing alert gazes from the gang members closest to their leader.

'I'm the imperial enforcer who just handed this city to your "Saviours" on a plate, so a little respect wouldn't go amiss, given my actions have presumably fattened your purse considerably?'

Petrus laughed uproariously.

'I like your friend already, Aquila! And a little respect will indeed be given, Guardsman! I'd invite you into the curia, but it seems that the watchman legged it with the keys when this mob showed up. Wise of him too, I'd say. It's all too easy for an innocent to get himself kicked to death without any particular reason under these circumstances, unless of course he's got a few beefy friends along for the ride.' He winked, and tipped his head to the scarred and tattooed men standing around them. 'And since the senate house isn't accessible, our new emperor has vanished off towards the temple of Concord, with, I noted, those arseholes Glabrio and Pompeianus hot on his heels. Probably keen to make sure that the master of the world knows just who really holds the reins.'

'Petrus!'

He looked up, waving a hand at the gang member who'd hailed him from the crowd's edge, indicating a group of men who were instantly familiar.

'Let them in! Trust me, you don't want to be on their bad side!'

Scaurus and the rest of his familia came through the cordon, Lugos casting a contemptuous glance at the gang members scattering out of his path. Marcus went forward to meet them, grunting as Dubnus hurried forward and lifted him off his feet with the exuberance of his greeting.

'Put me down, you idiot!'

The Briton laughed and set him back on his feet only for Julius to wrap him up just as tightly a moment later. Scaurus patted him on the shoulder, looking about himself at the chaotic mob outside of the gang's cordon of muscle.

'We didn't think we'd see you again, so stop complaining and let your friends show you how pleased they are that you're still alive.' He turned to Vorenus and inclined his head in a gesture of respect. 'Well met, Tribune. Presumably the business of securing the guard's support wasn't too awkward?'

The praetorian shook his head.

'No, although my colleagues didn't have much choice once the gates were open and the mob were inside and shouting the odds. Especially since most of the guardsmen were still either inebriated from the Saturnalia celebrations or not even present, given that two thirds of the cohorts had permission to overnight in the city. Choosing this night for the coup was a masterstroke.'

'And Pertinax played his part?'

'He did well enough. The guard's resentment was somewhat assuaged by the promise of a donative of twelve thousand sesterces a head, but even then I wouldn't have described the atmosphere as jovial, never mind celebratory. Our new emperor is going to have to work a good deal harder than he might have hoped if he's to win them over.'

Scaurus shrugged, unsurprised.

'That's to be expected, I suppose, given the guard considered Commodus as their man, and were perfectly happy with his claim to be the son of Zeus since it added a shine to their authority. Ah, I see the night watchman has been found.'

A somewhat querulous old man was half escorted and half carried to the curia's door, and was still complaining as Petrus kindly but firmly helped him to insert and turn the all-important key. The senators left the safety of their supporters and streamed into the building, Pertinax sensibly waiting to make his reappearance until they were all inside. The emperor strolled down the steps from the temple of Concord and across the forum's open space accompanied by several of his most prominent colleagues and the chamberlain,

Eclectus clearly determined to present the world with a guarded expression that reflected his previous loyalty to Commodus while demonstrating his willingness to work with the new regime. Marcus was surprised not simply to see Marcia walking beside him, but that the chamberlain's behaviour towards her was solicitous and courtly, that of an intimate rather than simply gentlemanly. The group was preceded by the obligatory lictors bearing their bundles of rods, the imperial vexilla and the imperial fire, while an escort of disgruntled-looking praetorians led by a stone-faced Laetus pushed the crowd out of their path none too gently, brandishing their axes with meaningful looks in all directions. It was obvious enough from the close attendance of both Pompeianus and Glabrio on the new emperor that they were intent on keeping their new-found grip on power as tight as possible. Pertinax himself looked cheerful enough as he passed Scaurus, raising an imperious hand in salute before passing into the building, his escort deploying around the entrance and displacing Petrus's thugs with swift, authoritative commands. Scaurus tapped Marcus on the shoulder and gestured to the door.

'Shall we? I'm sure that Laetus will be happy enough to let us watch, if we promise to be discreet.'

The prefect waved them in with a jaundiced glance, and the two men entered the building's vaulted, torch-lit interior just in time to witness the senate members' greeting to the new emperor. Breaking into the same sort of rhythmic chanting that had been orchestrated to salute Commodus in the arena only days before, and marshalled by strategically placed cheerleaders, they poured their hatred for the dead emperor into a call and response tirade of abuse directed at the dead man and his supporters, the adlected freedmen who were grouped together nervously in one corner.

> *'Pertinax Caesar, you are safe!*
> *Pertinax Caesar, you have won!*
> *Pertinax Caesar, smash his statues!*
> *Pertinax Caesar, erase his memory!*

Pertinax Caesar, restore our honours!
Pertinax Caesar, make this right!'

Scaurus leaned over to mutter in Marcus's ear.

'Anyone would think they'd already put some thought into this.'

'He murdered innocents, drag him with the hook!
He stole inheritances, drag him with the hook!
The innocent were left unburied, drag him with the hook!
The innocent were disinterred, drag him with the hook!
To avenge the innocent, drag him with the hook!
Like a common criminal, drag him with the hook!'

Scaurus pointed to the minority group of recently appointed senators, clustered at one end of the curia's benches in a tight knot.

'If I were one of those recently adlected senators I would be feeling every bit as nervous as they look.'

'Pertinax Caesar, put it to the vote!
Call for justice, call for our vote!
He plundered temples, drag him with the hook!
Plundered the innocent, drag him with the hook!
Stole from the dead, drag him with the hook!
Erase his memory and drag him with the hook!
Put it to the vote, damnatio memoriae!'

After a good deal more chanting, and just as it seemed the assembled senators were starting to run out of energy, Pertinax raised a hand to call for silence. Nodding portentously to his main conspirators, he strode forward to address the ecstatic patricians.

'Conscript Fathers!' Smiling, he raised his hands to encompass them all. 'As you are aware, the emperor Commodus is dead!' He waited for their cheers to die away before continuing. 'He made the mistake of leaving a death list to be found! A death list containing several names from among this gathering, including, shockingly, this year's consuls, Gaius Julius Erucius Clarus Vibianus and Quintus Pompeius Sosius Falco, along with some from within his own household! And this list was discovered by a child in the imperial service, an innocent who had no idea as to its significance. By sheer chance, he left it where it was found by the emperor's companion, the lady Marcia, who determined that the only way to avert this slaughter of the innocent was his death.' He paused, allowing the dark mutterings aimed at the woman standing behind him alongside Eclectus to die away. 'And she poisoned him, my colleagues, with the assistance of the chamberlain and Praetorian Prefect Laetus. Both men abandoned their oaths of loyalty to save members of this house from his depredations.'

The senators were silent, contempt for the three counterbalanced by their escape from the emperor's planned purge, and Pertinax pressed on with his pre-prepared version of events.

'But, this being Commodus, the poison was not enough! He vomited it up and went to hide in his bathhouse, eager to recover and then embark on a frenzy of killing that might have seen us all dead inside the week! And the lady Marcia, knowing that she could not allow him to rise from his stupor, persuaded the emperor's wrestling partner, a man by the name of Narcissus, to go to Commodus and strangle him to death. But for her act, and her further intervention, he would now be standing before you with a bloody sword in his hand!'

Scaurus nudged Marcus.

'Remember that name. Narcissus has agreed to accept the responsibility in return for a hefty purse, and immediate departure from the city before the praetorians can lay hands on him, if he has any sense. You were never there.'

Pertinax continued, exhorting the gathered senators in an urgent tone.

'Now is a time for us to come together and speak as one! True, there are those among us who have been the most threatened by the previous emperor's rule, the best of men and yet the most traduced! Members of distinguished families, some with family links to the throne that have been grievously abused these last few years! Some of you trace your lines back to the glorious days of the republic, when our forefathers made Rome the ruler of the civilised world; others represent the more recently successful fresh blood, essential to the continued dynamism of the empire!'

He turned and made a small bow to Glabrio and Pompeianus, who inclined their heads gravely in reply.

'We are indeed fortunate that men like you have disdained personal risk and returned here in search of justice for the people and the senate of Rome!'

He paused, and the assembled senators took their cue to bestow a cascade of thunderous applause upon him – some of them even restarting their chanting – falling silent only when he raised a hand again.

'Noble friends, I come before you humbly, and with great respect! We have suffered together, you and I! And now we can celebrate together! Celebrate our new freedom from tyranny! Celebrate Rome's liberation from the tyrant! Celebrate a new start, and the re-establishment of a mutually beneficial relationship between the senate and the throne!'

Pertinax paused again, allowing time for another burst of applause.

'We come together, you and I, to plot out our way forward from this day! It is to be hoped that whatever decision we jointly agree to will be greeted favourably by our colleagues who command the empire's legions and provinces! And in order to encourage a decision that will be the most favourable for Rome, rather than for any individual, I intend returning here later today, to ask you for a vote on the matter of who should be emperor. No, Conscript Fathers!' He raised his hand to forestall another outburst. 'I will not allow you to vote now, and I beg your forgiveness in doing so. You need time to think, and to be sure as to this momentous decision, and in the meantime I will ascend the

Palatine Hill to discover the state of the imperial palaces, and see
to the preservation of the previous emperor's corpse.'

Scaurus shot Marcus a glance in the silence that followed, a
buzz of muttered dissent indicative of the senate's unhappiness
at Pertinax's words.

'What did they do with the body?'

'It was taken to the summer palace.'

'Sensible. He can't afford to let this lot drag it through the
streets with a hook if he's going to avoid provoking the praetorians
more than might be sensible.'

'What of his body!'

The shout had come from one of the oldest senators, a man
who Marcus knew had lost both of his sons to Commodus's
purges.

'His body, esteemed colleague, has been consigned to Livius
Larensis at the summer palace, and I have sent instructions to
him to provide it to Consul elect Fabius Cilo, who is to bury it
in the Mausoleum of Hadrian.'

A barrage of outraged shouting greeted his words, but the new
emperor stood his ground, barking a challenge back at the enraged
senators.

'Gentlemen!'

The harangue died away, and Pertinax lowered his voice to be
heard within the chamber but not by the soldiers standing guard
outside. He continued in a quieter tone, his words edged with an
urgency at odds with his previous emollience.

'Conscript Fathers, when we reconvene later today, I assure you
that I will ask you to vote upon a motion of damnatio memoriae
upon Commodus, for the traditional calendar to be restored, for
the city to revert to its thousand-year-old name, and all the other
measures required to remove the stain of the former emperor's
madness. And, if I have the chance to vote, in the event that you
select another man to be emperor, then I will vote in favour of
all of these measures. But I cannot . . . I *cannot* . . . allow the
desecration of his body. Are we not a body of honourable and

civilised men? And I tell you this . . .' He lowered his voice again, forcing the senators to cease their muttering in order to hear him. 'While you have the power to gainsay me in this matter, I will warn you that if you wish for the praetorians to revolt and put us all to the sword, then you only have to take a hook anywhere near that corpse! You may choose, but do so in the knowledge that you might all suffer prompt and violent deaths, and your families too, if you provoke such a reaction from men too recently stripped of their blasphemous "god" to think rationally.'

The senators renewed their unhappy muttering, but it was evident that the new emperor's words had sunk in with them, and there were no further demands for the corpse to be handed over for the sort of gleeful mutilation they clearly had in mind.

'And now, Conscript Fathers, I must leave you for a while. I shall make my way to the Palatine, and take stock of the imperial household and finances. Later today we will reconvene to consider the questions still left open with regard to the previous emperor, whose name I will no longer speak in anticipation of the votes I expect will be cast. In the meantime, I commend you all to return to your homes and enjoy the first day of a new era, one of peace and prosperity under the combined guidance of throne and senate!'

Still resentful at being denied their revenge on Commodus's corpse, the senators' farewell was a good deal less effusive than their greeting, but Pertinax managed to look cheerful enough as he passed Marcus and Scaurus. He gestured for them to accompany him.

'Walk with me, Gaius, and bring your man Aquila with you. I will feel a good deal more secure with you at my side. The palace, I feel, will not be a friendly place this morning.'

8

Night was giving way gradually to the dawn, but the palace was brightly lit, dozens of torches blazing in greeting for the new emperor as Prefect Laetus led Pertinax's entourage of a dozen of the most influential senators through the gate at the top of the zigzagging ramp that climbed up the hill from the forum. A crowd of supporters had waved laurel branches and shouted the same slogans that the senators had bombarded him with in the curia, and Scaurus had nudged Marcus with a knowing glance as Glabrio and Pompeianus waved their hands in salute alongside the emperor.

'Anyone would think we have three emperors.'

At the palace gates the praetorian duty tribune was waiting to salute the new emperor. But if the senior officer was crisply turned out and respectful, as Marcus would have expected of a man who, had his own fate been different, might have been his contemporary, his men were another matter. Still dishevelled from their rudely interrupted night of debauchery, the recall having gone out too late to prevent the humiliation of their fortress being invaded by the Saviours' mob, they were openly disgruntled at the loss of their beloved emperor.

'Caesar, welcome to the Palatine Hill and your new home!'

Pertinax ignored the angry looks that the tribune's men were giving him, taking comfort from the presence of Scaurus and Marcus at his sides.

'My thanks, Tribune. And although I will not be formally entitled to be called Caesar until the senate have made a formal decision as to who will ascend to the throne, I will allow its use in respect of the position I am temporarily occupying. And now, if you will lead the way, I must take the members of my consilium to confer within the palace.'

The officer bowed.

'Immediately, Caesar, although I must first ask you to grace us with your decision as to the day's watchword?'

The emperor smiled broadly.

'That is a duty which is nothing less than a pleasure, and takes me back to my legion command on the Danubius river. The watchword shall be "Let us be soldiers"!'

He gestured to the path leading into the palace complex, and the tribune turned and led them into the maze of buildings, although not without shooting a meaningful glance at Laetus first.

Alerted to the new emperor's arrival, Sporus was waiting inside the Domus Flavia's ornately decorated entrance hall with the look of a man who was still distraught at the loss of his beloved master. His greeting was less than effusive.

'Welcome, Caesar, to your new home.'

'This is Sporus, the palace's maior domus.' Eclectus had walked up onto the Palatine Hill in Pertinax's shadow, knowing that his best chance of surviving the hatred that the Saviours' supporters felt for him was to make himself indispensable to the new regime. 'He is responsible for the smooth operation of the royal palaces, both public and private, and there is no part of the Palatine that he does not know intimately, nor any service that he cannot provide. I commend him to you.'

Pertinax turned to the maior domus, nodding in reply to his fulsome bow.

'Thank you, Sporus. For now, all that I and my colleagues require is somewhere private in which to consider the work laid out before us.'

The head butler gestured through the entrance hall's inner archway.

'In which case, Caesar, follow me.' He led the group into the palace's inner peristilium and around its central fountain to the left, into the great Emperor's Hall. The party stopped for a moment to drink in the enormous room's majesty, the ceiling one hundred feet above them supported by thick columns of Phrygian purple marble and the eight colossal statues looking down at them from wall niches on either side, while the emperor's dais, built into a semi-circular apse on the southern wall, was flanked by towering green sandstone effigies of Hercules and Bacchus.

'Perhaps the hall is a little oversized for your immediate purposes, Caesar.'

Sporus led them through a doored archway to the left and into the smaller council chamber, only one third the width of the Emperor's Hall, gesturing to the table around which a dozen chairs were set.

'This is the room that the emperor . . . the previous emperor, that is . . . used to use for meetings with his consilium.'

'And this will serve admirably.' Glabrio shuffled into the room, looking around himself with a gleeful smile. 'To make decisions in the same room that the gladiator used to plan his excesses against the innocent is close to perfection.' He turned back to scowl at Scaurus. 'You may leave us.'

'On the contrary, Senator!' Pertinax put an arm around his nephew's shoulder. 'This hard-faced soldier is a man I treasure above all others. He will be my most intimate companion as we seek to arrest the empire's fall from its peak of perfection, both for his firm counsel and the strength of his sword arm. And while I recognise the need for us to govern together, you will not gainsay me in this decision.'

Claudius Pompeianus turned to face the emperor with a smile that still managed to express doubt.

'You wish to add a man of his tender years to your consilium, Caesar?'

'You make a good point, Claudius Pompeianus, I have neglected to mention the other role that Rutilius Scaurus will play.' Pertinax returned the smile. 'I will add him both to my council *and* my bodyguard. The praetorians will do their usual expert job of keeping the people at bay when I walk in public, and preventing unauthorised access to the Palatine, but my safety will be in the best possible hands with him and the members of his familia at my side. They will be equipped and ranked as praetorians – Rutilius Scaurus as a tribune and his closest comrades as centurions – but will live here in the palace at my side. I'm sure you can understand my need to have an inner ring of protection, given the circumstances of my accession to the throne?'

His former patron bowed, his smile, if anything, wider.

'As you wish, Caesar. This is of course *your* decision.'

The emperor turned to the gaggle of a dozen senators who had followed in the royal party's wake when he had left the senate, the immediate clients of the conspiracy's most powerful members.

'And now, I think, we'll clear the room. I wish to discuss matters of the highest sensitivity with my most intimate advisors. Acilius Glabrio, Claudius Pompeianus, Rutilius Scaurus, Chamberlain Eclectus and Prefect Laetus will remain. Aemilius Laetus, I would be grateful if your men could escort the senators to the gates. If their supporters are not waiting for them, please provide them with an escort to their houses to ensure their safety on this momentous morning.'

Laetus nodded to Vorenus, who shepherded the disgruntled men out of the room, their expressions showing their severe disappointment at being excluded from the emperor's inner council. Pertinax gestured to the table, indicating that the remaining men in the room should take a seat. Scaurus sat down, signalling Marcus to stand guard at the door, while Pertinax remained standing, looking across their faces for a moment before speaking.

'Well now, here we are. As successful as we could have hoped to be, wouldn't you agree, colleagues? Commodus is dead and the empire's governance can be recast in a manner that will ensure the old values are reintroduced.'

Pompeianus nodded gracefully, reaching into his toga.

'Indeed, Caesar. And the balance between throne and senate can be recast along with it. With the assistance of your former colleagues, you have the opportunity, and indeed the duty, to become a latter-day Augustus, the first man among equals rather than indulging the disgusting Hellenistic despotism to which the last emperor aspired. It's a wonder that he didn't have us all prostrating ourselves to him and kissing his blasted feet like the Persians. And here, as a reminder, is the list of changes to the fiscal regulations that we agreed when we first determined to become the empire's saviours.'

Pompeianus passed a scroll across the table, and Pertinax put it to one side, its seal unbroken.

'Thank you, Tiberius, I recall the changes that we agreed all too clearly. My prime interest now is to gain an understanding of the one key fact that I do *not* know. While the demands that will be made upon the imperial treasury are clear to me, its ability to match them is yet to be determined. Chamberlain Eclectus?'

'Caesar.'

The Aegyptian presented a brave face to the other members of the consilium, appearing both composed and resolute, but Marcus, with a clear view of the men around the table, could see that he was the focus of hatred from both of the senators, and of nothing better than ambivalence from Pertinax and Laetus.

'You have your finger on the empire's pulse, I have no doubt. Tell us, what is the state of affairs?'

'There are currently no serious threats to the empire's integrity, Caesar. The Britons, the Germans, the Dacians and the Parthians are all quiescent, and the distant empire of Kush, to the south of Aegyptus, has kept itself to itself ever since my predecessor sent an expeditionary force to deal with them.'

'So militarily we have no rivals. And financially?'

The chamberlain hesitated, and the men around the table seemed to lean towards him in their eagerness to know the facts he was about to impart to them.

'I was planning to brief you privately, Caesar. Such matters can be sensitive, and I—'

'Nonsense, Chamberlain!' Glabrio was shaking his head in vigorous negation of any suggestion that Pertinax might be the recipient of information that wasn't shared with his co-rulers. 'The state of Rome's treasury is surely a matter for the emperor's consilium, if anything is. Don't you agree, Caesar?'

Scaurus stared at his uncle, willing him to disagree, but Pertinax seemed oblivious to the warning that the chamberlain was giving him.

'I do, Acilius Glabrio. So then, Eclectus . . . ?'

The chamberlain took a deep breath.

'Very well, Caesar. The best word I can find to describe the state of the imperial treasury is, I am afraid to say . . . empty.'

'Empty?' Pompeianus spluttered in disbelief. 'With all the taxes that are levied upon the people?'

Marcus surmised from his tone that the word 'people' actually meant 'us'.

'Empty, Senator. Down to the last million sesterces, which is effectively the same thing.' He paused for a moment, pondering, perhaps, how to explain the facts of life to men who had never wanted for anything their entire lives. 'The business of empire is a costly one, and the current flow of gold into the treasury is not what it used to be. And when I say "what it used to be", I mean under the reign of the successive emperors who succeeded Trajan until about fifteen years ago.'

'By which you mean what, exactly?'

Eclectus turned to address Glabrio, whose face was still a study in denial.

'There is a commonly held view, if only quietly expressed among those conscript fathers who consider themselves to be historians, Senator, that there were five wise emperors from the accession of Trajan to the throne. The last of them being the previous emperor's father, Marcus Aurelius. The truth of it, which can be seen in the financial records of the last one hundred years, is that it was the first of the five who established the conditions for prosperity; the other four were fortunate enough to be able to take advantage of his most important decision.'

'You're speaking of Trajan's decision to invade and conquer Dacia?'

The chamberlain nodded at Scaurus.

'Indeed I am, Tribune. The mines of Dacia supplied enough gold to pave the road from that province to Rome with solid gold cobbles over the eighty years after they were captured. Although their output has slowly but surely declined, and we have been forced to dig ever deeper into the mountains to reach the seams of gold in the rocks. And we reached the point, a decade or so ago, where their output is no longer very much more than what is required to pay for the legions that hold the province. In consequence, the problem of the empire's expenditure outstripping its income has come to the fore. Which means that while you might have an expectation of reducing the empire's financial expectations of yourselves, as the richest men in our society, the reality is that if it is taxes that are to pay for its unavoidable costs, then they will need to increase.' He ignored the outraged expressions on the senators' faces. 'The imperial treasury has dwindled away, despite the increased dilution of the actual silver and gold going into the coinage, until we have reached the bottom of the barrel. Commodus did indeed plan a purge in the new year, with the sole intention of stripping the richest men in Rome of their wealth, under the cover of charges of majestas.'

'Us.'

The Aegyptian nodded at Glabrio's statement.

'Indeed, Senator. Both you and your august colleague Claudius Pompeianus were on that list. Your conspiracy was exceptionally well timed, it has to be said.'

'And I presume that the treasury's lack of funds can be put down to Commodus's profligate spending habits when it came to arena shows?'

Eclectus shook his head authoritatively.

'Not really. The games were a drop in the ocean when compared to the costs of rebuilding the city after the great fire two years ago, which is what has drained the treasury. That one-off cost has removed any surplus from the imperial purse, and the constant running costs of empire have prevented any financial recovery. The empire is effectively bankrupt.'

'But surely the provinces generate tax revenues that are remitted to Rome? All those customs charges on imports? And the taxation that we apply to the better off in the provinces?'

'Provincial tax revenues, Senator, barely cover the costs of provincial government. There also tends to be a degree of, shall we say, diversion of tax receipts?'

Pompeianus shook his head with a frown.

'If you're trying to say that our colleagues in the governor roles have sticky fingers, you might want to exercise a little caution outside of this room.'

Eclectus nodded knowingly.

'Indeed, I agree. I have no desire to be beaten to death by enraged senators. But within this room, since that's the rule you've set, I think we can agree that it's a rare governor who doesn't divert some proportion of the tax he collects into his own *private projects?*'

'So, gentlemen . . .' Pertinax retook control of the discussion. 'What matters is not why the treasury is empty, because we could argue over that for a week and make no difference to the under-lying condition. What matters is what we are to do about it! The praetorians were promised twelve thousand sesterces apiece, and with ten thousand of them holding out their hands, I calculate that we'll need one hundred and twenty million simply to get their threat off our backs.'

'*Our* backs, Caesar?' The question was asked in an innocent tone, but the look on Glabrio's face was all too clearly one of cunning. 'I don't believe I was in the praetorian fortress when you made that promise. It's my age, you see – it would have taken me all night to get up the Viminal Hill.'

The emperor stared at him for a moment.

'And I suppose that any suggestion that we step back from the commitments you made to the men of the senate who supported our actions would be unacceptable to all concerned?'

Pompeianus shook his head briskly.

'Such a change of heart would be most unfortunate, Caesar. So many men have had their expectations raised to such a degree that I am quite unable to predict how they might respond to such a retrograde step.'

'I see.' Pertinax looked around the table with an unforgiving expression. 'So to summarise, you have invited me to head a conspiracy whose reward is a bankrupt empire, whose taxation I must immediately further reduce to satisfy the senate, who do *not* have swords, rather than increasing the tax rate as might be more prudent. And furthermore, an empire whose short-term costs I must in fact significantly increase to satisfy the praetorians, who *do* have swords. You present me with quite a conundrum. And it may not come as a massive surprise to you to learn that I find the possession of swords, and an evident willingness to use them, as a strong influence on my thought processes.'

Pompeianus smiled at him, ignoring the acid tone in his voice.

'The senate, Caesar, might not have swords, but they do have something of a history when it comes to rulers whose decisions fail to accord with their own thinking. And they do have knives. Perhaps we should give some consideration as to how we might satisfy both parties?'

After another hour of discussion, Scaurus beckoned to Marcus, opening the door out into the Emperor's Hall. The two men stepped out of the consilium unnoticed, as Pertinax and his colleagues discussed the empire's financial situation in increasingly robust terms.

'We're going to be here for the rest of what's left of the night, and then back down to the curia in the morning to see if the senate want to make Helvius Pertinax's position permanent. Which they will, of course. Even if anyone in there was thinking about taking it from him before Eclectus shared his news, there's no way any of them will want to have responsibility for a bankrupt treasury, expectant praetorians and a demanding senate. Since we're going to be here for a few hours, see if you can get the palace staff to produce some food, will you? Oh, and take a word of advice, if you will?'

'What's that?'

'You're likely to meet men you know from your time in the palace. They will be sure that you killed Commodus, and they will say so. And your temptation will be to agree with them, and ram the glorious fact of your revenge down their throats. But that would be unwise. Doing so will not only name you as Commodus's killer, but it will also make you a target for every guardsman in the city. You, and since revenge for such acts is rarely restricted to the killer, everyone you love and all of your brothers in arms. So if you'll accept my advice, you'll go against every instinct in your body, and deny that you had anything to do with his death. Unless, of course, you want to die within the month and take us all down to the underworld with you.'

He went back into the consilium, closing the door behind himself, and Marcus looked around the Emperor's Hall to find it deserted, without even a praetorian to stand guard on the council chamber. The statues of the gods stared down at him gravely, but there was no sign of any human presence. Frowning, he walked through into the peristilium garden and on into the banqueting hall on its far side, finding both still illuminated by fresh torches but equally devoid of either servants or guards. He was about to call out to anyone within earshot when a small noise of leather on marble warned him that there was someone approaching him across the magnificently decorated floor.

'Aquila. This *is* an unexpected pleasure.'

Marcus turned to find Sporus behind him, the maior domus's stare unexpectedly hard. Keeping his face blank, and resisting the urge to pick the butler up by his tunic and shake some sense into him, he nodded fractionally.

'Sporus. I'm looking for someone to bring the emperor and

his guests something to eat and drink. And yes, isn't it strange
how fate can turn things around so unexpectedly.'

The freedman sneered back at him, any hint of their former
relationship completely abandoned.

'Indeed. Take yourself, for example. There was me thinking that
you were a plaything that had been put before the emperor, when
all the time you were so very much more than that. Weren't you?'

The Roman wasn't fooled by the deceptively light tone, or the
arch way in which the butler tilted his face up to look at him. He
leaned forward to speak in the other man's ear.

'Be warned, I'm a praetorian now, even if I'm not in uniform
yet. So whatever it is you're trying to say, in your simpering,
elliptical manner, might be better voiced directly? No man likes
to have his reputation traduced by innuendo.'

Sporus's eyes blazed with anger.

'But you're not *any* man, are you, Aquila? You're a man who
disappears as a gladiator, on the night that the emperor dies
mysteriously, and then reappears escorting his successor into the
palace. You killed him for Pertinax! Try to deny it!'

Marcus shrugged, remembering Scaurus's warning.

'And you can prove that? Tell me, have you seen Narcissus
since the emperor's untimely demise? You do know that he's
claimed responsibility for it? And you of all people should be
aware of what happened here last night. How the child who follows
you around found Commodus's death list, and then happened to
leave it where Marcia caught sight of it?'

'Only to see her own name upon it, or so the story goes.' The
butler pursed his lips disapprovingly. 'Utter rubbish. The emperor
loved her more dearly than anyone or anything. He even went so
far as to put her on the coinage! I've seen that death list and I
know for a fact it's a forgery! Some skilled clerk in the chamberlain's office most likely.'

Marcus fixed him with an impassive gaze.

'Or perhaps it's real. Commodus wouldn't have hesitated to
have her executed, if he'd discovered that she was conducting an

affair with his chamberlain? Something you knew about all too well, didn't you, Sporus? Perhaps it was you that tipped him off, or gave him some clue as to their clandestine meetings? After all, there's no one better placed to know all the secrets that the palace staff see in the course of their duties, and no one more likely to be offended by their betrayal of the man you were in love with. Perhaps it was your doing that she was on that list?'

Sporus shook his head furiously.

'I would never have acted so unprofessionally! And besides . . .'

He fell silent, and Marcus gave him a knowing look.

'And besides, he had a habit of killing the people who brought him bad news? Like the psychotic animal he was, something your love for him blinded you to.'

The other man glared at him.

'So if you didn't kill him, where *were* you at the time he died?'

'In the cells, where do you think? Waiting to be dragged before him and executed for the crime of defending myself against his attempt to slaughter me! Vorenus was good enough to have me released before his men had the chance to take their frustration out on me.'

Sporus stared at him in disbelief.

'As well they might have. And still might. No one's fooled by this talk of Narcissus having killed the emperor, even if he did confess to it with all the eagerness of a man with something to gain from doing so. He'll have to watch his back from now on, and so should you, because if I know the guard, they won't rest until the man that they believe killed their emperor pays the full price for that moment of glory. I'll fetch your food.'

He walked away, leaving Marcus staring after him.

'They won't rest until they have the killer? And neither, I suspect, will you, Maior Domus.'

'No, Primus Lictor, thank you, but I will not be preceded to the senate house by the imperial fire, or indeed by any regalia.' Pertinax raised a hand at the leader of the twelve men who were waiting to escort him back down the imperial ramp into the forum in the early morning's rosy light, a burly ex-soldier with the bearing and innate self-confidence of a centurion. 'I accepted all the pomp last night, to send a message of continuity, but today there is a choice to be made, and I will not be seen to be presumptuous. You lictors may walk before me, to clear the public from my path and reflect the dignitas expected from this role I am currently filling, but there must be no presumption that I am the right man to lead the empire into its new age.'

'You're not having second thoughts, perhaps, Caesar?' Glabrio stumped up to Pertinax, eyeing him without any regard to the niceties of his rank. 'You're not wondering whether some other man might be better placed to deal with the conundrum that faces you?'

The emperor bent to speak in his ear, and only Marcus, sharp of hearing and standing close by, heard his words.

'I'm wondering, Acilius Glabrio, whether an emperor would tolerate your continual pushing at the boundaries of acceptable behaviour towards Rome's first citizen. Perhaps it's as well that we both still have a short time to adjust to our respective places in the carefully rehearsed charade that we're about to play out? Your part is simple – to insist that I take the throne, despite my manifest unsuitability given my age and lack of social standing as the humble son of a freedman. Little better than a slave from your lofty and completely unearned perch, eh? My obvious unsuitability, about which I intend to be very clear with my senatorial colleagues. My part, if the assembled nobility decides to elect me to the role, will then be to thread a difficult path between an empty treasury and the immediate – and some might even say inappropriate – demands of my co-conspirators. So let us revisit this discussion when you have dragged me, against my will, to the imperial bench in the curia, and I have had the purple irrevocably forced upon me, shall we?'

Glabrio's eyes narrowed at the imputation of greed, but the emperor kept talking, giving him no chance for a rebuttal.

'Of course you might decide that another man will better fit the bill, but were you to do so – with my absolute blessing, I ought to say, given what I now know – then I suggest that you choose him with great care! Because I doubt there's another senator who'll be acceptable to enough of his colleagues to be selected in my place, and then your only alternative will be to bring our associate Pompeianus's son to Rome somewhat earlier than planned. And while you might be willing to risk his life in that way, given that you stand next in line if he dies prematurely, the praetorians could treat such impudence as the last straw. I realise that you probably see the young man in question as dispensable, but your colleague Pompeianus might well not be quite so keen to put his own flesh and blood at risk. Or, of course, we could just enjoy the comedy of you putting yourself up for consideration, and the looks on the faces of all those enemies you've made over the years through your unenviable sense of superiority?'

Glabrio shot him a malicious look, but the ex-soldier simply smiled in his face.

'Indeed, and as I thought, you have no alternative. So I suggest you concentrate on not tripping up and falling down the hill as we make our way to the curia, eh?' He raised his voice, turning back to the waiting escort party. 'After you, Primus Lictor. Let's not keep my august colleagues waiting!'

With a dozen lictors and twenty times as many praetorians to hold the crowds back, the party made smooth progress, walking across the forum watched by the city's populace, who seemed more bemused than in any way celebratory, apart from those men who Marcus presumed had been paid to shout the new emperor's name. Pertinax commented wryly to Scaurus on the crowd's silence, waving a patrician hand to nobody in particular as he walked past the temple of the Divine Julius and the slab of marble on which the great man's corpse had been burned.

'As I told you, Gaius, the people of the city felt no need for Commodus's removal, and neither do they understand what's happening now. We cannot hope for their support if the praetorians decide to turn against us.'

As the royal party entered the curia, the assembled senators gathered around their new emperor and burst into synchronised chanting.

'*Augustus! Augustus! Augustus!*'

Pertinax waved Glabrio and Pompeianus away to join their peers, raising both hands both to acknowledge the applause of his peers and to entreat them to allow him to speak, waiting until they had fallen quiet and he had complete silence in which to be heard.

'Esteemed Conscript Fathers!'

From Marcus's place by the door it seemed that the senate's mood towards their new emperor was almost completely favourable, Commodus's former rump of support having clearly decided overnight that their interests were indeed best served in getting behind Pertinax.

'I come before you with the sole intention of seeking your assistance to ensure that Rome is as well governed as possible. We are all aware that an unfortunate chain of events has resulted in the death of the previous ruler of the city . . .' He waited for the murmured comments to die away before continuing, 'And that as a consequence I have accepted the interim role of provisional ruler, to ensure continuity until we have the chance to select a longer-term replacement. And now comes that chance for your voices to be heard, my colleagues!'

A barrage of protests rained down on him from the assembled senators, protestations that they had already selected their emperor. Pertinax waited for a moment and then raised his hands again.

'Colleagues, *surely* a better candidate must be available? A man of my age and lack of nobility, a man without even a single ancestral death mask in his atrium, the son of a freed slave – *surely* I cannot be your first choice? Surely one of my more noble senior colleagues would be a better choice?' He approached Glabrio and Pompeianus, taking the former by the hand and attempting to pull him towards the imperial bench while the older man protested, and made a show of refusing. 'What, will nobody step forward to take on this monumental responsibility? Colleagues, I am surrounded by men of higher quality than myself! Will none of you make this ultimate sacrifice?'

The senators continued to refuse, and at length he made a show of graceful exasperation.

'Very well, if you will not listen to reason, then I suggest we consult with the most esteemed men within our number. At this point we must let the consuls be heard!'

One at a time, and with due ceremony, the men who had been allocated roles as Rome's chief magistrate for the coming year came forward, starting with the suffect consuls intended to substitute if one of the two office holders fell sick or died. All showered the new emperor with fresh praise, and all condemned the reign of Commodus, Pertinax answering each of them with gracious thanks and reciprocal praise. In due course, with all of the senior men among the suffects heard, only two men remained to speak, the consuls themselves.

'Colleagues, we have heard from all our esteemed suffect consuls. It remains only for Julius Erucius Clarus Vibianus and Quintus Pompeius Sosius Falco, ordinary consuls for the coming year, to take the floor!'

The older of the two came forward first, one of Rome's most powerful men, and Marcus watched from a position to one side as he looked down at the floor for a moment before speaking, as if composing himself.

'I can think of no man among us better suited to the role that you must now assume, colleague! And I wish only that you will be as good and wise an emperor as you were an imperial legatus augusti – firm, forthright and resolute! You have my vote!'

Pertinax returned his bow with a look of gratitude, returned the kind words and gestured to the other consul, Clarus Vibianus's brother-in-law. The younger man stood and paced forward, but where his relative in marriage had been respectful in his countenance, he fixed a baleful stare on Laetus, Eclectus and Marcia in their places behind the emperor.

'Helvius Pertinax, you have replied to our colleagues with praise for your actions of last night by suggesting that they extend the warmth of their approval to include other members of the imperial household. And I see behind you the three people who you propose to retain in your service despite their gross unsuitability.'

A growl of dissent from the assembly threatened to drown him out, but far from being cowed, he barked at the senators to either side and in front of him on the benches facing his place with all the arrogant confidence of his nobility.

'I am the descendant of a line that stretches back to the emperor Trajan, and I *will* be heard!' In the silence that followed he addressed his pointed remarks directly to the emperor with a hand pointing at the group behind him. 'Eclectus, chamberlain to Commodus and responsible for much of the gladiator's victimisation of, murder of and shameless robbery from, men within our ranks! Laetus, whose praetorians are such a blight upon the city, and who have victimised innocent members of this house! And Marcia, Commodus's concubine, the woman who encouraged him to fight in the arena and so debase his place in Roman society as to be no higher than a common slave! All three of them, my colleagues, are now known to have been complicit in his death, which, as we all now know, was no sort of accident! Their presence behind you points very clearly to the sort of emperor that you will be, Helvius Pertinax!'

He subsided into his seat with an angry glare, ignoring the outraged comments being made by the men around him. The emperor raised his hands to entreat the senators to silence.

'Every man among us has the right of an opinion, colleagues. We will not be censored, as in the worst days of the previous emperor's reign! My young friend Pompeius Sosius Falco has every right to air his views, although my response has to be this: you are indeed a young man, Consul, and perhaps you do not fully understand the necessity of obedience to the throne. These three obeyed Commodus, as was their duty, but when the opportunity presented itself, they were quick to show what had been their true desire, were they not? And in so doing, saved *you* from the fate that would otherwise have stalked down the forum ramp dressed as either god or gladiator to end your life this very morning. You owe these subjects of your derision your continued existence.'

He waited for the senators to respond, but the chorus of approval was muted by comparison with what had gone before, the senate's mood somewhat deflated. Pompeianus got to his feet and walked out to join Pertinax on the chamber's floor.

'Very well, my colleagues, you have all spoken. Will you have another emperor, or are you content with our most esteemed colleague Publius Helvius Pertinax, a man whose devotion to the empire is all too clear? All in favour of this man serving as our emperor until the time comes for him to nominate his successor, and take a graceful retirement to enjoy the gratitude of the senate and the people, say aye!'

The roared assent was close to unanimous, and Pertinax bowed his head in seemingly reluctant acceptance.

'Very well, honoured Senators, I accept your vote of confidence. But I will not rule entirely alone! In addition to the usual panoply of imperial titles, I will also be known as Princeps Senatus! Yes, Chief of the Senate, the first among equals! And to demonstrate that equality, I demand that Claudius Pompeianus and Acilius Glabrio join me on the imperial bench!'

The two men nodded their august acceptance of this newly proposed duty, both moving to the indicated bench from where Commodus had previously glowered at his enemies.

'And I further propose the following for ratification by this senate: I will swear an oath never to condemn a member of this house to death, unlike my predecessor! I will rescind the law of majestas under which so many good men were falsely accused of treason, and murdered for their wealth! And I will forbid the praetorians from carrying the axes which I know are such a provocation to you all, given their use of those weapons to batter their way into the houses of the unjustly accused!'

Loud praise was shouted by the senators, some whose friends had been killed by Commodus under the majestas law, holding out their hands to the emperor as if to embrace him.

'And I hereby invite the chief men among you, colleagues, to join me in a banquet to be held in the hall of Jupiter this evening! This practice, long since abandoned by Commodus, will once again become a regular part of the emperor's relationship with you, his most important and influential partners in ruling this mighty empire!'

The applause redoubled, and he waited for it to die away before speaking again.

'And now, Conscript Fathers, you must excuse me from your house! I will go from here to the temple of Jupiter, to make sacrifice and thereby gain the favour of the gods for this new stage of our imperial glory! But I will leave you with one command, which I expect you will be happy to accept and discharge!'

A hushed silence fell, all men present suspecting and praying for one instruction in particular.

'You must go forth from here and take up hammers, chisels and any such other tools that you see fit. And you must then throw down and destroy the statues of Commodus as Hercules! Simply behead the existing statues if you will, so that we can honour other good men with replacements, but wipe all trace of him from the city! Will you vote for his memory to be expunged from the record, and never to be spoken again?'

Pompeianus leapt to his feet.

'A vote! Damnatio memoriae for the gladiator! All in favour, say aye!'

The response was an immediate roar of approval, and Pertinax raised his hands to accept their applause before turning to leave. Scaurus and Marcus took their places beside him at the heart of his grim-faced praetorian escort, and walked back out into the forum, whose crowds' silence was at odds with the shouts of joy clearly audible from within the curia. The emperor called an instruction to Laetus in a commanding voice.

'We will go to the temple of Jupiter, Aemilius Laetus, there to dedicate ourselves to the empire's service!'

The prefect turned and saluted.

'As you wish, Caesar.'

Pertinax looked about him at the silent crowd, pursing his lips in grim amusement.

'The senate, the people, the army and the guard. The game every emperor has to master if he is to keep his head. Balancing one off against the other with enough subtlety for them not to realise they're being manipulated. And with an empty treasury.' He smiled at Scaurus wanly. 'A game I am left no choice but to play for all I'm worth. And so it begins.'

3 Januarius AD 193

'Impressive thing, isn't it?' Qadir leaned on the wall of the taverna from which he had purchased the lunch that he, his two soldiers, and the Aegyptian Ptolemy were eating, gesturing with his half-eaten pie to the towering edifice across the road. 'Thirty-foot-high walls, and big enough for there to be eight thousand of them in there at peak capacity, almost the strength of two legions. And when there are no legions in the vicinity, which is normal, they hold the city in their armoured fist.'

Ptolemy waved a hand at the walls, his voice taking on the lecturing tone that had the soldiers rolling their eyes at each other.

'It has been this way for two centuries, ever since the death of the blessed Augustus. We palace officials were always well aware of the praetorians' ambitions to turn their command of the city into gold on any suitable occasion.'

The two men beside him slouched listlessly, but their eyes were alert as they munched on the food, the Briton Sanga showering the disgusted scribe with crumbs as he spoke.

'It must be a mile around the walls, and you want us to keep an eye on the place? Two of us?'

Qadir bit off another mouthful and chewed it in a leisurely manner, at length swallowed, and only then replied.

'The thing is, these men think that they are the masters of the world. All-powerful, answering to no one other than the emperor, and even then that's their choice. In the case of Commodus, maddened by power until he believed he was the son of a god, they were happy enough to make him their man because of the power he conferred upon them.'

'Conferred?'

Saratos, still learning the finer points of Latin after almost ten years' service, gave Sanga a questioning look, but the Briton only grinned and shrugged, stuffing the remainder of his pie into his mouth and chewing so visibly that even his hardened comrade grimaced. Qadir averted his gaze, raising an eyebrow at the simultaneously revolted and mesmerised Ptolemy.

'Ignore him. Were his rudimentary skills not supplemented by a quite astonishing feral cunning, then you, Saratos, would be partnered by another man. When I say "conferred", I mean that he gave the praetorians a part of his power.'

'And axes.'

'And, as Sanga so helpfully reminds us, while providing a meal to any passing bird fast enough to catch the crumbs showering from his mouth, axes.' Qadir looked up at the fortress walls again, taking the measure of the men standing guard. 'He gave them axes with which to batter their way into the homes of those senators who were accused of majestas. It is like charging a man with treason, but with violent robbery, rape and murder thrown in for good measure. And they have developed a taste for it, it seems.'

'So they loved Commodus.'

Qadir nodded.

'After a fashion, yes, Saratos, they did. Because he gave them power. And now they despise his successor because he has taken it away from them.'

'And because he does not yet pay money he promised?'

'And because, as you say, he has discovered that the imperial cupboard is so bare he has no way to provide them with the donative that he promised them, back when he believed that the money would be readily available from the treasury. And because he has forbidden them to carry their axes. And because he treats them as if they are soldiers.'

The Dacian looked up at the wall guards in puzzlement.

'They look like soldiers. They have armour and spears. They stand guard on their fortress like soldiers.'

Sanga, having consumed his pie, was now casting envious looks at Ptolemy's meal.

'They're too good, right? Simple as that. And are you going to eat that, because if you ain't, I could easy finish it for you.'

The Aegyptian, having already transferred his food to his left hand, leaving the right free to fend off any attempt at impromptu redistribution, shook his head.

'They believe that they are too good. But they are no better than us. We are all simple soldiers.'

Qadir shrugged, ignoring the Briton's evident amusement at the diminutive scribe's inclusion of himself in the same category as his comrades.

'I am forced to conclude that Sanga actually has the right of it, astonishing though such a conclusion is to us both. They do, contrary to all logic, believe themselves to be head and shoulders better than us. For a start, they dominate Rome, and many of them actually live in the city, trusted to return each day to do their duty. The elite among them stand guard on the Palatine Hill, and see at close hand the way that the emperor and those around him live. And they reason, unsurprisingly, that if it's good for a man who was born the son of a freed slave, perhaps they should share in some of the same benefits. And they do not care whether the emperor's coffers are empty, because he made them a promise.'

'And half of them will already be drinking and gambling the money, the lucky bastards.'

Sanga scowled as Saratos turned ostentatiously away to take a mouthful of his pie, clearly pondering a lunge across Qadir, who froze him in his place with a baleful stare.

'It is more than that, although the point you make is clearly well informed from the shared perspective of the perpetual wastrel.' Sanga grunted non-committally, indicating his lack of understanding and equal failure to care very much. 'These are men who are, for the most part, married, or at least with women and children in the city. And most of them will have mentioned their expected windfall to those women who—'

'What sort of fool tells his woman he has money?'

'Who, Sanga, tending to be both wiser than their men where money is involved, and having many more commitments to deal with, will for the most part now be putting pressure on their men to deliver them some part of the money for the improvement of their circumstances.'

Saratos nodded his understanding, popping the rest of his pie into his mouth and smirking at Sanga.

'And you want us to do what about all this?'

Qadir sighed.

'Perhaps in another life I am not quite so burdened. It feels likely.' He fixed the Briton with a hard stare. 'What I want you to do about it is your usual. Not very much, in return for a disproportionate reward.'

'Dispro . . .'

'Undeserved.'

Qadir nodded at Ptolemy's swift translation.

'Undeserved, given that all you will be doing is squatting in the gutter and begging from the passers-by.'

'Who will be kicking us, for making them feel ashamed of their comparative wealth.'

The centurion cast an irritated glance at the Dacian, who shrugged.

'It is true. Rarely a day passes when we do this for you that we are not spat on and abused. Sometimes it is all I can do to prevent this animal—'

'Oi!'

'. . . from taking his dagger to a man.'

'The bloody women are worse, half the time! Anyway . . .' Sanga gave his officer a speculative glance. 'How much *undeserved* gold?'

'Who mentioned gold, you grasping British ingrate?'

Both soldiers smiled, one with avarice, the other simply knowingly.

'You wish for us to sit here, in the gutter, for days or even weeks at a time. Watching for the comings and goings of anyone out of the ordinary, am I right?'

Qadir nodded at Saratos as the Dacian went to the heart of what he wanted from them.

'Carry on.'

'You want us to stay here from dawn to dusk, waiting to see anything that looks out of the ordinary. A closed carriage, or a litter with the curtains drawn. Anyone coming into the fortress without wanting to be identified, perhaps?' The centurion nodded again. 'And then, of course, you will want us to follow them back to their house, when they leave, so that we can identify who is plotting with the men in there?'

'You have it.'

Saratos shrugged.

'Then Sanga, animal though he is, has it right. For some weeks of such thankless work the right colour must be gold.'

Qadir tapped the purse on his belt.

'Here's my offer. For the job you have described, a sestertius extra per day. For identifying a man of interest visiting the praetorians, a denarius, if he is genuinely of interest.' Qadir raised a hand. 'Men come to the camp seeking positions for their sons all the time. You follow one of them back to a modest dwelling and I'll be giving you the usual sestertius. What we're looking for here is any sign that one of a small number of men is in league with them. And' – he raised a hand to fend off Sanga's inevitable protest – 'if the man you follow home *proves* to be in league with the praetorians, a gold piece.'

'Each.'

Qadir shook his head at the Briton.

'Between you.'

'The money to be paid each day.'

'Paid on completion of the job. Consider it a savings policy, like the burial club.'

Sanga rolled his eyes.

'Fucking burial club? Good money I'll never see any benefit from, that's all that is. So, a bronze to sit here and get told to fuck off fifty times a day, a silver for a decent spot and a gold if we deliver some scheming bastard up. And a pie a day. This will be right hungry work.'

Qadir nodded wearily.

'Agreed.'

'Paid in advance.'

'Paid by the day. To be delivered by our colleague Ptolemy.'

'And I will receive some reward for my daily task, Centurion?'

'By the goddess . . .' The Hamian shook his head in disbelief. 'You have been around these men for too long, scribe. There will be a small coin every day for you . . .' He raised a hand to silence the question he saw on the Aegyptian's face. 'Copper, not brass.'

'The pie money. It starts now, right?'

'Of course.'

Sanga held out his hand, and Qadir ostentatiously looked down at it and then back at his face.

'What?'

'We'll be needing our first day's expenses, Centurion, or how else are we to eat? I'm starving!'

9

'Will I see *who?*'

The duty guard tribune looked down at his tablet.

'He claims to be a senator called . . .' The tribune consulted his tablet. 'Triarius Maternus Lascivius, Caesar. He arrived at the front gate a short time ago in something of a state of panic. And also in a state of undress. And smelling of plums. Caesar.'

Pertinax frowned in disbelief.

'Undress, Tribune? You mean he was naked?'

Apparently unperturbed, and exuding an air of unflappability, the praetorian nodded.

'Utterly, Caesar. And, as I say, smelling of plums. Reeking of them, in fact. He is demanding to be brought before the emperor, and says he has information regarding a plot against you. I had the maior domus find him a tunic and some shoes, and a bowl of water to wash his face in, in case you wish to see him?'

The emperor looked at Scaurus, who shrugged.

'Surely there can be no harm in meeting the man. Even if a coup plan three days into an emperor's reign would probably be some kind of record.'

'Very well, bring him in!'

The guards escorted a clearly terrified man into the room, one soldier on either side of him while the tribune walked behind. Escorting him to within a few paces of the waiting Pertinax, the more senior of the two soldiers put out a hand to stop him.

'Well now, Senator, I see that you are indeed who you claim

to be.' The emperor searched his memory for a moment. 'You were the ordinary consul about eight years ago, were you not? I seem to recall that it was during the period when I was temporarily forced out of public life by that animal Sextus Tigidius Perennis.' The newcomer remained silent, looking at the soldiers beside him with an expression of absolute terror. 'Come on, man, spit it out. What on earth possessed you to be running around the city stark naked and making yourself a figure of fun?'

'Caesar . . .' Lascivius was clearly close to being lost for words, so great was his fear. 'If we might speak privately?'

'Very well.' The emperor waved a hand to the praetorians. 'You may leave us, Tribune, and take these fine guardsmen of yours with you. I will be perfectly safe with Rutilius Scaurus and his men to protect me.'

The guardsmen withdrew, although not without pointed stares at Marcus and Julius, who were both now equipped as praetorian centurions, evidently disgusted at having their roles usurped. Pertinax gestured to a chair.

'Sit down, man, you look ready to drop. And tell me what it is that has you in such a state.'

The senator sat, visibly fighting to compose himself.

'Caesar . . . please understand, I had no part of this!' A tear trickled down his cheek as his composure started to collapse. 'I know that what they would have had me do carries a death sentence, but—'

'What *they* would have had you do? *Who* would have had you do *what*, Maternus Lascivius?'

The senator started back in his seat as Scaurus leaned forward and demanded the information. The emperor raised a hand as if to restrain his closest associate.

'Allow the senator to speak, Gaius. It seems he has suffered from some serious trauma.'

'Thank you, Caesar. And as to who . . .' The senator gathered his courage. 'It was the praetorians. They took me on the street.

Arrested me, without warning and without telling me on what charge I was detained. And they took me to their fortress.'

Pertinax shook his head, still not quite understanding what the senator was trying to tell him.

'But arresting a random senator on the street hardly equates to a plot against me, does it? And neither does it explain why you were . . .' He fell silent, his eyes narrowing as he started to make connections. 'Unless . . .'

'They said that I was going to be the next emperor, Caesar! They ordered me to remove my clothes, and provided me with imperial regalia! I was to dress in the purple and then present myself to them, so that they could acclaim me as their emperor and bring me here behind a wall of spears.'

'Gods below! The fucking impudence!'

Scaurus nodded, unperturbed by Pertinax's outburst.

'But you didn't put the garments they laid out for you on, did you?'

The senator looked from emperor to enforcer with wild, staring eyes.

'No! I kicked a window open and jumped out! Anything to avoid actually putting on the purple!'

'And it is to be assumed that you weren't several floors up in the fortress?'

Scaurus grinned at him, and Triarius was unable to prevent a giggle from escaping his lips.

'No, they were stupid enough to only have taken me up to the first floor, and in a room overlooking the street! And I landed on a fruit vendor's barrow as he was passing!'

'Which would explain the persistent aroma of plums?'

'Yes, the barrow collapsed under my weight and I managed to roll around in his stock while I was trying to get to my feet! I was slathered with the stuff!' The senator's fear of execution had transformed itself into something close to mania. 'He was really unhappy, until I promised to buy his entire stock in thanks for my avoiding a broken leg, or worse!'

Pertinax, having managed to reclaim control over his temper, raised a hand to re-enter the conversation.

'But why, Maternus Lascivius? Why *you*? Surely if the praetorians wanted a replacement for me, there must be other, better qualified candidates?'

'And so I would have assumed, Caesar!' Triarius was clearly desperate to be seen to be helpful, as he endeavoured to avoid being executed on a charge of majestas, something the situation absolutely allowed an emperor to enact, whether the formal law – employed by Commodus for the persecution of the rich – had been annulled or not. 'And I protested to that effect while they were dragging me bodily across the city! "Why?" I asked them! "Why me, when there are men of much closer blood to your beloved former emperor?"'

'And their answer?'

The senator shook his head as he recalled the praetorians' brutal honesty.

'They said that anyone would be better than you, Caesar, royal blood or not. And that they thought me well connected enough for my friends in the senate to rally round me, once they had me draped in a cloak of the imperial colour.'

Pertinax nodded slowly.

'That *is* perceptive. Someone has thought this through, I have to say. You are possessed of more than adequate nobilitas, for one thing, and your training in the law and practice as a iuridicus has equipped you with an excellent speaking voice and the confidence to perform in the curia. And that's before we get onto your connections. Your wife's family ranks among the most powerful in Rome, for one thing, and your sister married into the noble Erucii Clari, did she not? Between you, the pair of you must be related to what, three consuls?'

Triarius smiled, his pride winning the struggle with his fear.

'Four, Caesar, and a proconsul, and a serving legion legatus.'

'Yes . . .' Pertinax stood, walking away to the consilium's window. 'I can see why they might expect a good portion of the senate to back you, especially if I had been killed to remove any question of loyalty getting in the way. And, since Claudius Pompeianus's son is still safely tucked away on his estate out of harm's way, I'd imagine that they found themselves somewhat short of credible choices.'

Triarius, seeing what looked like a safe exit from the whole matter, kept his mouth shut and waited for the emperor to reach a decision.

'Very well, I have reached a decision. You, Triarius, are a fortunate man! Fortunate that the praetorians who planned this attempt to take the throne made such a mess of your conscription into their plan and allowed you to escape. Fortunate that your legally trained mind was sharp enough to do the only thing that could have saved you from execution, coming here and confessing the whole thing to me. Fortunate that the men on duty clearly had no knowledge of their colleagues' plan, and did not simply intercept you at the gate. And, most of all, fortunate that I am a beneficent ruler and can see that you had no part in their scheming. You are to be commended, and further, I hereby reward you by allowing you to gather your wife and family and leave the city immediately, rather than stay to give evidence against those who would have used you. Take up residence somewhere far away until this has all blown over and I expect that all will be well.'

He turned to Scaurus.

'Have your familia escort Triarius Maternus Lascivius to his house, will you, Gaius, and from there to the city gates and far enough down the Via Appia that he will be safe from reprisal?'

He gestured to the door, and Scaurus nodded to Marcus and Julius to accompany the senator.

'And now, I think, it's time for us to have a discussion of these events with the man I hold responsible for them. Tribune!'

The praetorian stepped back into the consilium from the great hall outside, snapping to attention.

'Caesar!'

'Send word to the praetorian prefect that I require him to attend upon me immediately! And send messengers to the other members of my inner consilium that they are requested to attend a meeting in the Domus Flavia. Immediately!'

Marcus and Julius escorted Lascivius out of the palace and through the forum's bustle, ignoring the curious stares on all sides at the sight of a pair of praetorians escorting a dishevelled-looking man whose hair was matted and sticky.

'I know you, Centurion.' The senator cast a sidelong look at Marcus as he walked, his face creased in a frown of half-recognition. 'But I do not know where from. Yours is a face I feel that I have seen before, and yet not at any point in the recent past.'

'Imperial ceremonies, perhaps.'

'No, that's not where I've seen you before.' Lascivius shook his head with pursed lips. 'I'm a lawyer, young man, and my mind is trained to recall the facts of hundreds of cases, precedents, and the great speeches of history. My memory is as sharp as that sword you bear, and I have seen you before, and on multiple occasions, but not recently . . .'

Marcus raised an eyebrow, and with a flash of insight Triarius made the connection.

'I have it! There's that look you used to give your father when one or other of his colleagues was talking nonsense. You're the Aquila boy, aren't you? Marcus Valerius Aquila! Appius Valerius Aquila used to bring you to the senate to watch us debate, and of course he would introduce you to those members who were his allies. As I recall, I was making my way up the higher rungs of the cursus honorem at the time, some five or six years before I was graced by being consul in the 938th year of the city. Your father was a strong supporter of fresh talent among our ranks, and he was particularly kind to me at a time when I needed support to stand out from the pack of ambitious men seeking positions. I recall him with great fondness.'

'As do I, Senator.'

'As you should. He was one of the best of us.' Triarius was

silent for a moment, perhaps considering his next words. 'When Commodus made him one of his first victims, murdered him and stripped him of his prodigious wealth, that was the moment that I and my colleagues should perhaps have seen the writing on the wall and decided to act, while we still had the time. But, of course, a single sheep being taken from the flock by a wolf excites little interest among those others whose sole interest is for themselves. And the emperor's wolves were particularly vicious under Perennis, and that's before we discuss the imperial assassins who were reputed to be doing his dirty work at the time. Better him than me, seemed to be the main reaction, and of course Commodus was placated for a while by your father's gold. So tell me, Valerius Aquila, where did you hide all these years?'

'He came to us.' Julius's answer to the senator's question was edged with pride. 'He ran to Britannia, and made his way to the northern frontier, as his father's last command. We hid him among us, made him one of our own, and were fortunate enough that a young tribune called Scaurus was appointed to lead our cohort. And for much of the last ten years we have fought the empire's battles wherever they were to be found, defeating every foe that we were thrown at.'

'And now you guard the new emperor against his enemies. A strange but nonetheless welcome reversal of your fortunes. But has it occurred to you that your troubles may not be at an end?'

'By which you mean what, exactly, Senator?'

'By which I mean that I have experienced something that you have not, for all your martial pride and obviously hard-won scars. I have been taken off the street and menaced by the praetorians, or more precisely, by their centurions. It was a half-dozen of them who came for me, all with the crested helmets and scale armour of their ranks, and they were not, I can assure you, minded for the taking of prisoners. They told me that I could either come quietly or they would come to my house and use their axes to put my door in.'

'And obviously you went with them rather than subject your family to such horror.'

'Indeed.' Lascivius gave Julius a knowing look. 'I know how that sort of man behaves once his blood is up. But you miss my point.'

Marcus shook his head.

'I think I know it, but please elucidate.'

'My point, Valerius Aquila, is that it is less than a week since our new emperor was unanimously acclaimed, or almost completely so, by the senate, the ruling body of the city which – at least in theory – is the arbiter of who rules. And yet the praetorian centurions who abducted me were clearly dead set on his removal from the throne he's barely had the time to warm with his backside.'

'You think they will try again?'

Triarius stopped by a high wooden gate, hammering at the knocker with the vigour of a man eager to be within his own walls.

'I *know* they will try again, and again, and as many times as it takes, until they have an emperor with more wit than to use the watchword "Let us be soldiers" with his bodyguard who, manifestly, are not soldiers and who see such a thing as a criticism. A man who pays up against his promises promptly, given they're waiting to receive the donative he swore to pay them. A man who will defy the senate and reverse the edict of damnatio memoriae against the emperor they more or less worshipped. In short, almost anyone other than Helvius Pertinax, who, they told me, they firmly believe was responsible for Commodus's death.'

The gate opened, and the servant on the other side gaped at his master's dishevelled state.

'Stop pulling faces, man, and fetch the butler. Run!'

He turned back to Marcus.

'To be perfectly blunt about it – while I am grateful to the emperor for being so gracious as to allow me to flee from the fate that would overtake me if I stayed in the city, I can be no more honest than to tell you that the man is a fool to think he can ride this angry horse. He'll get no loyalty from the mob, nothing but enmity from the guard, and that part of the senate who are using him for their own ends despise him behind his back. They laugh about the thin fare to be had at his banquets since he instituted the new standard of imperial frugality, and make arch comments with regard to his lack of nobilitas. In short, young man, they consider him an essential evil, required for the short term until things are calm enough for another man to mount the throne. He is a lightning conductor, nothing more, and they will dispense with him if the praetorians do not.'

An older servant came down the path from the house breathing hard.

'Dominus, what has—'

Lascivius raised a hand to silence his butler.

'There's no time! Gather the household, send a messenger to procure transport, and order the slaves and servants to pack only what they treasure the most, and no more than they can carry for a day on the road! We need to be gone from here within the hour, and preferably sooner than that!'

'But sir, your wife has friends gathered around her loom.'

The senator shot Marcus and Julius a knowing glance.

'In which case, what I must demand of her just got ten times as hard. Might I ask you gentlemen to stand guard until we leave? I promise not to waste a single moment of the time needed to put a safe distance between myself and this nest of vipers. Just remember my warning, and be ready to make yourselves scarce just as quickly when Pertinax's time comes. As – with all due respect to your martial abilities in his defence – it surely will!'

The two men waited, alert for any sign of praetorian retribution, but in the hour it took for Triarius to persuade and cajole his family and household onto the street and away, there was no sign of any backlash from the guard. They started walking back to the palace, both men reflecting on the senator's words.

'Well, that was . . .'

Marcus looked over at his friend.

'Illuminating?'

Julius shook his head gloomily.

'I was going to say predictable. Petrus is saying much the same as that poor bastard. And if the guard are unhappy that they've not had their twelve thousand apiece, he's raging that the treasury doesn't have the money to pay him the ten million he was promised.'

'You and he seem to have struck up quite a friendship.'

Julius nodded.

'We have, I suppose. He's a simple enough man, when you strip off all the tough talk he has to use to keep his men in line. And a lot of what he says is just common sense.'

'Go on then, what does a gang leader's common sense have to tell us about the state of Rome?'

'Well, for one thing, he's got a clearer understanding of the emperor's esteemed colleagues Pompeianus and Glabrio than Pertinax does. He was pointing out to me earlier that they're not spending any more time in the palace than they have to, and that both of them walk the streets, when they have to go out, with escorts of enough former soldiers and gladiators that it would take a dozen very determined praetorians to overcome them.'

Marcus nodded agreement.

'They don't seem very keen to be seen with the emperor, that's true enough.'

'Petrus thinks that's because they know just how badly pissed off the praetorians are, and neither of them want to find themselves trapped in the palace if the guard decide to run amok.'

'What other wisdom does he have to offer?'

'It's not so much anything else he knows, other than the fact that he's keeping his escape route from the city ready for use at a moment's notice, but something he said he suspected might be happening. And when he voiced that thought, it made such a lot of sense that I decided to have Qadir have our tame informers keep an eye on the situation. I expect they're already dunning him for gold just for having witnessed Lascivius jump out of a fortress window.'

Marcus smiled knowingly.

'What, you've sent those two out onto the streets of Rome unsupervised?'

His friend grinned back at him.

'Well, in point of fact, it was Qadir who made the final decision, once we'd agreed that there might be some value in putting eyes on the target. But yes, those two delicate flowers are once again inhabiting that level of society for which they are best suited.'

'The gutter?'

'Indeed.'

'I see.' Marcus pondered for a moment. 'Is that safe?'

Julius shrugged.

'It's a fair question. And yes, I think it's fair to say that the beggars and lowlifes of Rome might have a bit of an unpleasant surprise coming.'

By the time the two friends arrived back at the foot of the Palatine Hill, it was close to the beginning of the first watch, and darkness was falling across the city. The praetorians standing guard duty on the imperial ramp were more than usually terse with them, and Julius pointedly kept a hand on the handle of his pugio the entire time that he was within a blade's length of them. Walking up the ramp, and feeling the eyes of the men guarding the forum gate boring into their backs, he sent a last pointed stare back over his shoulder at them before shaking his head in disgust.

'Those bastards have a collective hard-on for us that would put a stud bull to shame.'

'It's hardly surprising, is it? The man they've been told killed Commodus is nowhere to be found, or they'd have cut his throat by now, and in his absence they'd be more than happy to take their anger out on us, since we're so clearly the new emperor's men.'

At the top of the ramp's zigzag course, both men raised their arms to display their scarlet beads, declining to stop as they barrelled through the guard post, leaving the incensed praetorians in their wake to consider Julius's suggestion that they might go and eat shit. Walking into the Emperor's Hall, they were intercepted by Sporus, who put up a hand in apparent challenge.

'The prefect said no one else was to be admitted.'

Marcus winked at Julius.

'You'd better stay out here and enforce that decision, hadn't you? I can't see the maior domus here having any ability to block the next pair of homicidal maniacs who come along, can you?'

Ignoring Sporus's outrage, he opened the council chamber's door and slipped inside unnoticed, all eyes being on Laetus. The prefect was standing in front of Pertinax with an expression somewhere between entreaty and protest.

'But Caesar, you know as well as I do that my guardsmen are a law unto themselves! I have no way to—'

'No!' The emperor raised a hand, demanding silence. 'I will not listen to you making such pathetic excuses for your inability to control your command.' He shot a glance at Scaurus. 'Perhaps the time has come for you to be removed from that post, Prefect, and another more capable man entrusted with that responsibility?'

He paused portentously, and the room went quiet as every man present waited for his decision, but it was Claudius Pompeianus who spoke first.

'Caesar, perhaps we might discuss this matter before you provide us with your decision?'

Apparently less surprised than Marcus might have expected, given he had been interrupted as he was on the point of revealing whatever it was that he intended to do about the threat to his rule, Pertinax nodded graciously at his former sponsor.

'As you suggest, Tiberius.'

The two men spoke in hushed tones for a moment, then Pertinax walked over to the side of the room and poured himself a cup of wine. Returning to the table, he took a seat and gestured for Laetus to do the same.

'My most trusted colleague Claudius Pompeianus has counselled me to show that I am capable of allowing the members of my consilium to learn from their mistakes, as an example to the senate. And so I have decided to be lenient with you, Prefect. It is my edict that you must make it clear to every man in your command, in person, that you do not expect any repeat of this rather weak attempt at undermining the rule of the emperor and senate. Address your guardsmen, Aemilius Laetus, and warn them that the consequences of another such failure will be fatal for any man whose involvement is proven. I will ring the praetorian camp with crosses, if that's what they provoke me to.' He pointed to the council chamber's door. 'You are dismissed. The rest of us will now consider the measures that will be announced to the senate tomorrow in the light of this outrage.'

Laetus left the room, clearly uncertain as to whether he should feel fury at his dismissal, and the way Pertinax had treated him, or gratitude at not being relieved of his post and further punished for his men's transgression.

'He looks as if he doesn't know whether to rage or run.'

Marcus nodded at Scaurus's wry observation, handing the tribune the glass of wine he had strolled across the room to collect, while Pertinax went into a huddle with Glabrio and Pompeianus.

'He knows that he could easily have been executed for what happened today. Indeed it was the emperor's firm intention to strip him of his rank, and appoint a new prefect, but politics have intervened, as they often do.'

'Politics? The guard were ready to unseat him; what possible cause can he have for not removing the man whose ineffectual lack of control over them is at the root of that attempt, and who knows how many more in the weeks and months to come?'

The tribune sipped at his wine, giving Marcus a knowing look over the glass's rim.

'My guess is that Pompeianus was reminding my uncle of the importance of remembering to consider the loyalty of the legati augusti who command the empire's armies. The decision to remove Laetus from his post would have been easy enough, were we only to be concerned with Rome and its environs. But there is, of course, a wider empire to be considered. Having control of the city counts for nothing if the armies do not swear their allegiance. And, as Pompeianus has, I suspect, reminded our master, there is no guarantee that they will.'

He took another sip, then raised his glass to indicate the map of the world painted on the wall on the council chamber's other side.

'Of the three major concentrations of military power, only the eastern legions are currently deemed anywhere close to being safe from the urge for their legatus augusti to wrap himself in purple and claim the throne. And you know as well as I do that there isn't one of them who doesn't have an appropriately coloured cloak in his campaign chest waiting for just such a moment. Our old enemy Clodius Albinus commands the three legions of Britannia, a functional and battle-hardened battlegroup in its own right, and he is a ruthlessly ambitious man. His rival Pescennius Niger, who has command of the east, with the potential to muster six legions, is, as we know well, a straightforward servant of the empire. But the most powerful of them all is Septimius Severus, legatus augusti of the Danubius battlegroup. His brother commands in Moesia Inferior, which means that they muster eleven legions between them, and the five legions based on the Rhenus to the north are more likely to throw in with him than to side with Albinus, given the constant exchange between them along the frontier. And sixteen legions is more than enough to hold the balance of power, even were Albinus and Niger to ally, which is obviously unlikely in itself at such a distance. Messengers have been sent to all three men, of course, explaining Commodus's untimely death, and stating that the senate has made its choice as to who rules, entreating all three men to join with their colleagues in acclaiming him as "their" emperor, and hail the beginning of a new golden age. Whether they will, or not, now depends on the calculations of Severus and Albinus as to their ability to wrest the prize from Pertinax's hands.'

Marcus nodded soberly.

'The legions of Britannia will be as hard as nails after so many years of facing down the tribes. Whereas Niger's strength, if twice that of Albinus's, is in men who are for the most part unblooded for over twenty-five years. There won't be many men left in their ranks who can recall the feel of blood on their faces, other than those we took into Parthia.'

Scaurus looked up at the map.

'And it was the legions on the Rhenus and the Danubius that took the brunt of the German wars, which only ended a decade or so ago. Their greybeards will know the face of battle, and will provide a firm backbone for the younger men if it comes to a fight. A combination of strength and experience that means that Severus must surely hold the balance of power. And Severus, as Pompeianus was quick to remind the emperor, was appointed to his role purely on the back of Aemilius Laetus's recommendation to Commodus. Severus and Laetus are amici, the closest of friends, it seems, which means that were he to discharge Laetus from the role of praetorian prefect, the emperor might be handing Severus a ready-made excuse to revolt.'

'All the reason he could ever need to claim the throne.'

'Yes. Which means that while the Saviours must now be firmly of the opinion that Laetus needs to be removed from his post, there's no way that they'll be brave enough to do so while Severus's loyalty remains undeclared.' Scaurus grinned at his friend, shaking his head ruefully. 'Which means that my uncle's desire to take him out of the position and appoint someone a good deal more trustworthy has run into the rocks of hard reality. What remains to be seen now is how many more compromises he'll be forced to make, as he endeavours to guide this leaking ship of state through all the other hazards that lie in its path.'

5 Januarius AD 193

'Conscript Fathers!'

The senate's buzz of discussion died away to a respectful silence at Pertinax's call to order. The curia was completely full, its doors open to allow a dozen or so latecomers to listen from their places clustered around the entrance. The emperor waited until the silence was total before continuing, being as aware as any man present of the need to match his performance to the high stakes involved.

'Conscript Fathers, I have requested your time today in order to put before you the facts of certain recent events – serious events, gentlemen – and to inform you of my intended response to these matters! I also plan to provide you with an update as to my plans for the treasury, and various financial regulations in which you will doubtless share a close interest!'

A silence so complete that the faintest rustlings of toga cloth could be heard descended upon the assembly.

'Firstly, it is my sad duty to confirm what some of you may already have heard, with regard to the abduction of one of our number!' An undercurrent of muttered comments greeted his words and Juventius Celsus, one of the older and deafer members of the house, barked out the word 'outrageous' somewhat louder and more querulously than might have been intended, the emperor nodding in reply. 'Indeed it is outrageous, for Triarius Maternus Lascivius to have been taken on the street and forced to accompany his kidnappers to the praetorian fort! Where they planned to dress him in the purple and then accompany him to the palace!' He paused, allowing the astonished comments to die away before continuing. 'With the obvious and quite astonishing intention, Conscript Fathers, of putting him on the throne!'

The emperor looked around at his audience, gauging their mood before continuing.

'Of course this violation of the senate's authority is a shameful matter for a number of reasons! The kidnapping itself, for one thing! Is no member of this house safe on the streets of our glorious city? And the plan to replace a serving emperor with the hapless victim of that kidnapping, for another! For it implies the murder of that emperor! And then, Conscript Fathers, consider what the guard might have insisted upon as the price of their "favour"? What would they have demanded of you, when they were standing behind your new emperor with their swords drawn and still dripping with the blood of his predecessor? A doubled donative, perhaps, when they already have the promise of twelve thousand sesterces?'

A rumble of disapproval from the benches on either side of the emperor told their own story as to the senate's willingness to gift yet more money to the praetorians. Pertinax nodded vigorously, making it clear that he shared their disquiet.

'Indeed so, Conscript Fathers, indeed so! The very idea of the whole matter is as unacceptable a thing as it is possible for me to imagine! It all reeks of a quite shocking failure of discipline! And, I am forced to observe, of leadership! Ordinarily I would have had the ringleaders executed immediately, but in this case there were no clear ringleaders to be dealt with, because no men were identified as having led the small group described by our colleague Lascivius! And so I have instructed the praetorian prefect . . .'

He paused, as if deliberately, and the senate, on cue, erupted into vocal condemnation of Aemilius Laetus, demanding his dismissal and, in the case of some of the more robust shouts, execution. He waited for the outcry to die away before continuing.

'And so I have therefore instructed the praetorian prefect to make it very clear to the guard, to every last one of them, that this matter must not be repeated, on pain of execution for anyone found to be involved in such an unacceptable crime against the very empire itself!'

'*Dismiss him! Punish him!*'

Pertinax raised his hands to quiet the baying pack of senators howling for the prefect's blood.

'We might do well to consider, Conscript Fathers, the close links between Aemilius Laetus and our most august colleague Septimius Severus, who, along with his brother Geta, commands almost two thirds of the empire's fighting men.' He paused, allowing, Marcus presumed, the thought of Severus to sink in. A new man, utterly lacking in nobilitas and with a brash and forceful manner, a man who many of the older families quite possibly held in even greater disdain than himself. 'If our esteemed colleague Severus deems his amicus Aemilius Laetus to be a solid member of our imperial governance, then perhaps we would do well to heed that opinion?'

'Clever, isn't he?' Scaurus's expression remained neutral in the momentary silence that followed, but in his voice Marcus detected more than a trace of cynicism. 'Of course it was Laetus who recommended Severus, but by turning that around, he gives the senators the chance to row back from their urge to see Laetus executed, and without making it explicit that he can't do as they wish for fear of Severus's vengeance.'

'Yes, Conscript Fathers!' Pertinax was nodding again. 'I see you understand my meaning! And so I have trusted the prefect to deliver my message to his men in the sternest manner possible! And to warn them that he will have no choice but to punish any man that steps over the line he is drawing before them in the most robust way possible! I trust that you will support me in the issuance of this final warning!'

The senate's assent was slightly grudging, and quickly fell away into silence. But it was clear to Marcus that the emperor's mention of Severus, implying the potential for the empire's strongest general to turn usurper, had their attention. Scaurus leaned closer and whispered in his ear.

'If Severus is "provoked" to revolt, he will of course have to do so as Commodus's avenger. And most of these men have been instrumental in demanding and then carrying out the sentence of damnatio memoriae. A decree that he would in turn be obliged to both reverse and penalise. No wonder they all look a bit grey all of a sudden.'

Pertinax continued, shooting his nephew a meaningful glance.

'And it seems to me that perhaps any restiveness on the part of the guard might best be resolved by the prompt payment of their donative, which I can assure both yourselves . . . and any other listener' – he paused, giving the curia's doorway a meaningful look – 'that I shall make a matter of high priority as soon as the monies with which to do so are available! Unless anyone here has any strong objections to raise, of course?'

Not a single man rose to argue against such a course of action, and Pertinax bowed as if accepting their unspoken acceptance.

'Very well! And now, Conscript Fathers, let us turn to other matters! Matters of imperial finance! Of revenues, and of taxation!'

The senators growled their approval, having reached that part of the session of which their expectations were high.

'We face problems of both a fiscal and an agricultural nature, my colleagues. The treasury is close to empty, and the demands of the state are never-ending. And in addition, as demonstrated by the bread riots that resulted in the death of the previous chamberlain, food production is not as high as it might be, were all the land available to us actually under cultivation. I intend to take action on both of these matters!'

The senators waited in silence, eager to hear what his remedies might be.

'It is my intention to boost the finances of the empire by means of a series of tax reductions!' And that, from the sudden outbreak of smiles all around him, was exactly what they had been waiting for. 'The duties that the previous emperor levied on river traffic, harbours and roads within the empire, which are currently collected at the frontiers, are hereby repealed! The tax levied upon this assembly's members by the previous emperor on the occasion of his birthday are hereby repealed! The state's habit of profiting from legal complications or confusion with wills is hereby repealed! Estates which were confiscated under the laws of majestas will be returned to their rightful owners, and those men will be compensated for any losses resulting, when the funds are available to do so!'

He paused, allowing time for individual senators, those with importing and trading businesses, and those whose inheritances had been stolen from them by the state on the execution of their fathers, to shout individual praise.

'To increase the amount of land under the plough and enable us to feed the people, all land which is not currently cultivated – whether belonging to private individuals or indeed to the state – may be claimed by any landowner with the ability to farm it! In addition, this newly cultivated land's produce will be exempt from any taxation for a period of ten years!'

It was the turn of the senate's landowners to cheer their praise of Pertinax, knowing that they would be able to turn their armies of slave workers to farming the land in question where less well-resourced men had been struggling for years to find affordable labour, the result of war and plague. Glabrio and Pompeianus looked especially smug, Marcus noted, having had sufficient fore-knowledge of the pronouncement to have their estate managers ready to pounce on the land they could easily assimilate into their own estates well in advance of any competitors. Pertinax acknowl-edged his audience's praise with a magisterial nod of his head before returning to his script.

'We must also deal with the needs of the state, Conscript Fathers! The treasury has been left almost empty, by the combi-nation of the previous emperor's spendthrift ways and the mismanagement resulting from the use of the *wonderful* class of freed slaves to run much of the imperial government!'

Scaurus gave Marcus a meaningful look, the two men knowing that the emperor was deliberately pandering to the senate's deeply ingrained biases against men lacking their rank being allowed any share in the empire's power.

'And so I plan to trim state expenditures! I shall undertake a review of all of the men employed by the imperial bureaucracy! And those freedmen deemed to be unproductive will be forced to seek employment elsewhere! Furthermore, I plan to cease all payments to our so-called allies on the far side of the northern frontier, on the Rhenus and the Danubius! Let them fend for themselves; our armies will ensure that they cannot ever again expect to extort gold from Rome by the threat of invasion! I have sent word to the convoy that left for the Danubius carrying the latest shipment of gold to the tribes to be turned back, and the tribal leaders informed that Rome no longer buys its friends, but chooses them on the basis of their loyalty!'

'I wonder how Septimius Severus will take that little gem?' Scaurus's smile was lopsided, a sure sign of his innate cynicism coming to the fore. 'It's not that long ago that I heard the mechanism of providing our allies with subsidies described as a good deal cheaper than going to war with them.'

Pertinax pushed on in the silence provoked by the last announcement, as the senators digested the potential for them to find themselves having to fight a potential rerun of the bloody German wars.

'And furthermore, I plan to enable the state to profit from the unbridled spending on luxury and frippery in which the previous emperor's freedman encouraged him!' Faces brightened, this being exactly the sort of thing the rich men of the senate were keen to hear from their new emperor. 'All manner of unnecessary items currently reside within the imperial palaces, both on the Palatine and the Via Appia! Clothing of a nature most unsuitable for the ruler of the civilised world to be seen in! Gladiatorial and chariot-racing equipment made with precious metals, and decorated with rare jewels, which will never again be used by any emperor with a scintilla of dignity! Swords engraved with the images of the god the previous emperor claimed to be, which would otherwise rust on their racks! And much more besides! I plan to auction these items in the following days, and I invite you all to come and bid for a piece of history to display in your atria, enabling one and all of us to point to them and tell ourselves that these are remnants of a disturbing time, a difficult time, and a time that is now dead and buried!'

He struck a patrician pose, head back, chest out, and waited for the applause that he knew must be coming. The senators leapt to their feet and cheered him to the rafters, delighted with the package of measures and talking animatedly to each other, probably, Marcus guessed, about the forthcoming auction of Commodus's finery. Scaurus shouted in his ear to be heard over the thunderous waves of clapping.

'It does seem a little counter-intuitive to be reducing taxes at a time when the treasury is bare! And I wonder how the various losers from these measures will react, both inside and outside the empire! But he does seem to have made this audience happy!'

Marcus nodded.

'Perhaps his sale of Commodus's trinkets will provide sufficient clear water to keep the empire off the rocks! I look forward to seeing how many of these men are willing to open their purses in return for a piece of that dark history.'

'You're sure that's the place?'

Julius eyed the shop that Sanga had indicated with an appraising eye, a butcher's emporium with a window stacked with meat and the organs of a recently slaughtered cow whose blood was still being washed and brushed into the gutter by a pinch-faced lad.

'Yes. I followed the bastards back here, after we kicked their arses for trying to shake us down.'

The big man looked at his comrade questioningly.

'What do you think?'

Dubnus grinned mirthlessly.

'What do I think?' His brother centurion rolled his head in a circle, hefting the heavy bag that hung from his right hand. 'I think we need to get in there and deal with them now, while they're still talking themselves up to do some violence. Before they come out here and gain the room to outflank us.'

'Outflank us, eh? Once a soldier, forever a soldier. Are we coming in with you then?'

The Aegyptian Ptolemy had accompanied the two men in the company of Lugos, Arminius being on duty in the palace with Scaurus and Marcus. All three men turned to look quizzically at him, provoking an outraged protest from the diminutive former clerk.

'I can handle myself, you know that! Five years training . . .' He ticked off the fingers of one hand, looking like a small child practising his numbers by comparison with the giant standing beside him. 'With the sword, with the knife, even with the axe!'

'And we know how that ended, with the axe.' Dubnus reached out and tapped the scribe's forehead, where the thick white line of a deep wound marked his once pristine skin. 'Although more than one unkind person is of the opinion that you did it to yourself to have a scar to match ours.'

'Yes, including you, you bast—'

'I suggest . . . ?' Lugos's bass rumble silenced the petulant protest, the barbarian being the only man who could placate him once he was roused, the result of both his terrifying size and the prodigious learning that the giant had crammed into his head over the years of his tuition by the Aegyptian. 'I suggest that we go around the back, you and I, to catch the little rabbits who try to bolt from the holes when the stoats enter their warren?'

Honour satisfied, the scribe accompanied him around the corner and up the narrow alley behind the row of shops, while the two former centurions made sure that the contents of their bags were ready to use.

'Come on then.' Julius led the way to the butcher's doorway. 'Let's go and see if these fools are ready for the second round yet.'

Sanga and Saratos had been in position on the street for a matter of days, posing as beggars while they watched the praetorian camp's main entrance, when the first attempt to rob them had materialised – much as was to be expected with new arrivals in any district of the city. A pair of men who clearly considered themselves the neighbourhood toughs, to judge from the way that the locals had stepped out of their path and avoided eye contact with them, had stopped in the street in front of them. Their disconcertion when the two men they considered beggars had jumped to their feet, knowing that in a fight a man sitting on the floor was likely to lose without ever throwing a punch, had quickly been overcome by their innate sense of superiority.

'You two are new.' The words had been a statement of fact, so Saratos had waited in silence while his British comrade had grinned, exposing an array of broken and missing teeth. 'You're here to beg off the guardsmen as they come and go, aincha? You look like a pair of broken-down soldiers, right, so you think they'll toss the occasional coin your way, eh? Fat fucking chance of that, I reckon, but just in case they do, we're going to tax you anyway.'

'Tax?'

The bigger of the two men had smiled evilly, nodding happily at getting a reaction.

''S'right. Tax. How it works is this.'

Reaching out a hand, he had put his finger squarely on Saratos's chest. The Dacian had looked down at it, then back at his face, waiting for him to take the hint. Instead of which the finger had prodded him, hard.

'You pay us for the—'

His scream had been as loud as it was abrupt, as his hand was grabbed, the palm bent back viciously to immobilise him, and the prodding finger snapped at the first knuckle in one swift movement. His mate had gone for the knife at his belt, getting as far as putting his hand on the hilt before Sanga had stepped forward and snapped the heel of his flat palm into his face, following up with the taverna brawler's go-to expedient, a swift kick that had doubled him over, clutching at his genitals in anguish. Saratos had spun the man whose hand he was still holding around, pulling the arm around and up his back towards his neck.

'We pay you nothing! You run away now, and we will allow you to leave while you can still walk!'

The two men had staggered off up the street, the bigger of them supporting the other, who had been barely capable of walking, while Saratos had turned to Sanga with a knowing look.

'You go and fetch the big men, I will watch these two and find where they live.'

It had taken an hour for Julius and Dubnus to change into their exercise tunics, gather their equipment and make their way up the hill, finding Saratos in the cover of a doorway from which he could see their objective.

'It's the butcher's shop. Fifteen people went in, six of them didn't come out. Add in the butcher and that makes seven.'

'Big lads?'

The Dacian had grinned, happy to have the burly ex-officers at his back.

'As you know very well, the size of the dog in the fight is not the important thing.'

Julius had snorted derisively.

'It's the size of the fight in the dog? That's all very well until you're confronted with a room full of big lads all waving butcher's knives around. Good thing we brought these with us.'

He had lifted his bag, identical to the one in Dubnus's left hand, hefting its weight with a bulging biceps.

'Come on then, let's go and hand out yet another life lesson.'

Inside the shop the two men found themselves in a grisly scene; the butcher, a man made grotesquely muscular by the incessant physicality of his work, was engaged in hacking slabs of meat off a cow's back leg which had already been expertly skinned, while his apprentices were brushing up the flecks of bone and offal that were all that remained of the beast. Blood had been liberally sprayed around by the death throes of so many hapless creatures that the plastered walls were the colour of mottled bruises, and in places the score marks of hoofs and horns had stripped the plaster back to the lath.

'Help you?'

The big man had looked up from his work with the cleaver

poised to strike again, and Julius walked a few steps closer, weighing him up. He dropped the long bag and put his hands on his hips.

'I'm looking for the leader of a gang that works out of this shop.'

'And you've found him.' The butcher straightened, hefting his blade and eyeing the distance between them. 'What do you want?'

Julius smiled.

'Just a friendly chat.'

The big man shook his head brusquely, allowing the leg to fall to the floor.

'Don't do friendly, me. And I'd say you're fucking brave, coming here without so much as a knife between you. What's in the bags?'

Julius nodded happily.

'Just something we brought with us to persuade you to see things our way, and leave our mates out on the street alone.'

'These two cunts that ran my lads off?' The big man laughed tersely, shaking his head. 'Not going to happen, *friend*.' He shrugged. 'There's a question of appearances. And respect.'

'Ah. Respect.'

'Yeah. Respect for me and mine. I let two arsehole ex-soldiers defy me, before you know it, the entire street's telling me to fuck off and get my money somewhere else.'

'Understood. Let me give you this anyway, as a token of *my* respect?'

Julius reached into the bag with both hands, the smile on his face so broad that the butcher wasted the last crucial moment in which he might have strode forward and swung the cleaver. He lifted an axe out of its concealment, one hand on the handle's knob, the other up under its head.

'What the fuck!'

The two ex-soldiers attacked, all restraint cast aside. Brutally smashing the closer of the two apprentices aside as he reached for a knife, putting his axe handle's knob into the boy's forehead hard enough to bounce him off the wall, already unconscious,

Julius squared off with the furious butcher while Dubnus poleaxed the other with a swing of his weapon's blade, reversed to strike him with the heavy butt, then kicked open the door that led into the shop's back room and stepped through it with a blood-curdling roar, his axe already swinging. The butcher waved his heavy knife, shouting a warning at his opponent.

'You're fucking dead! Nobody comes into my—'

Julius stepped forward, lunging expertly and punching the big man in his face with the axe handle's wooden eye to rock him back on his heels and then stepped back, judging his moment perfectly to loop the axe head up and down just as his opponent recovered and stepped back into the fight. The butcher looked at the stump of his right arm in confusion, seemingly unable to work out where the hand holding his cleaver had gone, then gaped almost sleepily as the heavy blade rose again, and slammed down into his head, wielded with all the speed and power of a man who had been practising with the weapon for the previous five years. His nerveless body swayed for a moment and then crumpled, five pounds of sharp iron buried so deeply that the two halves of his skull were parted by inches. Julius released his grip on the handle and pushed it away, leaving the corpse to crumple onto the shop's bloody floor, head dragged unnaturally to one side by the axe's weight, then reached into the bag for a dagger. Stepping into the back room, he winced at the bodies of two dead men, both with their heads distorted by what must have been fearsome impacts, witness to his comrade's penchant for fighting with the heavier end of the axe head rather than the blade.

'I've told you before, Dubnus, the blade is better than the butt!'

'We're out here!'

He walked through into the shop's meagre yard, nodding at Ptolemy who was busy posing by the rough wooden gate with his knife, the body of a dead gang member at his feet. The bodies of two other men were protruding from the offal bins, flies already busy exploring every available orifice.

'Are you telling me that this big bastard' – he shot a bemused glance at Lugos – 'who now seems to be reading a book, did all three of these while I was messing around with the butcher?'

'I know.' Dubnus shrugged. 'I got one of mine as I came through the door, then took down the hindmost as they bolted out here. But this bloody show-off did these three with his bare hands.'

'I killed one of them!'

Dubnus grinned at the scribe.

'You killed one of them, Sparrow, after Lugos had smashed his head flat against the wall. It was touch-and-go whether you got the knife in before his body realised that it was already dead. But fair respect' – he raised the hand that wasn't holding his axe to placate the peevish scribe – 'at least you had the nerve to put the blade in and make sure of him.'

Julius frowned at the scroll in Lugos's hands, his eyes narrowing. 'Is that . . . *Greek*?'

IO

'Centurion.'

Marcus turned to find Sporus standing beside him. He had been standing to one side of the crowd of the city's well-to-do citizens, keeping a quiet eye on the praetorians situated around the Emperor's Hall just as much as the imperious members of Rome's elite who were eyeing them with a combination of disdain and nervousness.

'Maior Domus.' The two men had reached an uneasy accommodation of their mutual disregard over the days that had followed Commodus's murder, and were at least able to converse politely. 'Perhaps you've come to bid on a small item from the previous emperor's wardrobe, as a keepsake?'

The head butler shook his head.

'I wouldn't stand a chance against these fine people in a bidding fight. And they look like they mean business.'

Marcus was forced to incline his head in silent agreement. In the week since the senate session in which Pertinax had declared his intention to auction off Commodus's possessions, interest in the mooted sale had grown from initially just being surprisingly vigorous, until not even the most bullish of the idea's proponents could quite believe the resulting fervour. The resulting crowd not only filled the Emperor's Hall, but had spilled out to fill the Domus Flavia's peristyle courtyard and even a part of the great dining hall beyond. The senators and their wives had been escorted through the crush to prime positions close to the emperor's dais in the apse between the two looming green statues of Hercules and Bacchus, from which Commodus had glowered down at them in the days before his death. Pertinax was escorted across the marble floor from the door that connected to the Domus Augustana, taking his place behind a rostrum and looking out at the eager crowd filling the audience chamber to its capacity with a delighted, almost gleeful expression.

'Senators, knights of the city, ladies, welcome to the Flavian Palace! Welcome to an event that can never be repeated! Unusual though it might be for your emperor to play the part of an auctioneer, I take the role in good spirit, as it means that I can make a material difference to the empire's fortunes this day! As can you!'

'Common little man.' The wife of the senator standing in front of Marcus and Sporus was speaking more loudly than she might have intended, perhaps as the result of what the centurion guessed from her red face was a liberal consumption of wine prior to their having walked up the ramp to the palace. 'The sooner your colleagues remove him from the throne and replace him with a man of the right breeding, the better! And what better breeding than the son of a queen?'

She realised that her voice was pitched a little too loudly and blushed, fixing her attention on Pertinax, who was laying out the auction rules.

'You will be expected to stand by any bid that results in a sale, gentlemen, no matter how much you might regret getting carried away in a bidding war for an intelligent slave, a fine sword or ornate piece of clothing! I will ask you for your name, confirm the price with you, by means of an intermediary if you are out of earshot, and from that moment the item is yours, to be claimed when you bring the requisite amount of money to the imperial secretariat! And now, if nobody has any questions, we have a great many lots to get through!'

He gestured to the back of the room, and the first of a procession of items was walked forward to his dais by a particularly tall palace slave who held it aloft for inspection.

'Lot number one is perhaps one of the most valuable and symbolic items in the auction, gentlemen!' The slave took his place on a podium below the dais, enabling him to hold the item up in Pertinax's eyeline. 'The previous emperor's golden helmet! Fashioned by a master armourer, and finished by a goldsmith of incomparable talent, this is the very secutor's helmet that he used to fight in both the arena and his own private stadium! It even bears the recent mark of a retarius's trident! Who will start me off with a bid of fifty thousand sesterces?'

A man standing close to the dais shouted a bid, several of those closer to Marcus whistling softly at its audacity.

'Five hundred thousand!'

Pertinax grinned in delight, gesturing to the bidder.

'Half a million sesterces from Quintus Servilius Silanus! Do I hear a higher bid!'

Shouts from around the room signalled a bidding war for the helmet far in excess of anything that Marcus had expected, but in Sporus's eyes the only expression was sorrow, tinged with anger.

'And so it begins, as I knew it would. These *bastards* make sport of his death.' He pointed to Silanus. 'A day of entertainment and competition for men like him, competing to be the one to spend the most of the gold they have recently been gifted by the emperor's tax cuts. And all to rip away the things that made him what he was, to display in their atria and dining rooms for sport, and to show how big their balls are.'

Marcus looked at Sporus with a new sympathy, seeing that he was clearly appalled.

'Perhaps you would be better not watching? It can't be easy . . .'

The maior domus sniffed eloquently.

'Like you, Centurion, I have my duty. And if you'll excuse me, I must be about it.'

He walked away without a backward glance, and when Marcus next caught sight of him through the crush of bodies, he was deep in discussion with a praetorian centurion who the Roman instantly recognised as Tausius.

'Strange bedfellows.'

'Who are?' Scaurus had joined him unnoticed, and was following his gaze to where the head butler and praetorian officer were talking, both men wearing serious expressions. 'Ah, your friend Sporus and a guard officer. What of it?'

'That guard officer would have cut my throat in an instant, if Commodus had allowed it, when I was in the palace under false pretences. So what he's doing so deep in discussion with a delicate flower like Sporus is beyond my comprehension.'

The tribune shrugged.

'Strange times make for strange allegiances. Keep an eye on him though, who knows what they might be cooking up together.'

At the end of the day, with the great hall illuminated by the light of dozens of torches brought forth by Sporus's slaves in a practised routine that transformed the gathering gloom into incandescent light in moments, the exhausted emperor sat back on his chair in the consilium and tapped the sheaf of paper on the table before him.

'Hundreds of millions, gentlemen! Did you see the way they were competing to own his possessions? When that necklace worn in the arena by Flamma the Great sold for two million, I knew we were on the way to a proper day's sales!'

Every item on the list had provoked fierce bidding, selling for five or ten times their actual worth, as Rome's wealthy had conducted a day-long squabble over the exotic luxuries accrued by the former emperor over a decade of unconstrained expenditure. Togas worn by famous gladiators, gladiatorial and chariot-racing equipment encrusted with gold and jewels, swords made with exotic metals from beyond the empire's boundaries. All had been fought over, bid to unreal prices and hard won by each item's victor, to be displayed for the aggrandisement of the rich in their unending competition to be the greatest of Rome's elite. Their women had been equally hard-eyed for the most part, urging their husbands to compete for the ownership of silk robes embroidered with gold, cloaks of fur from the lands beyond the

Danubius and various garments in the military style, made to be worn on campaign, but stylish and risqué nonetheless, when draped over the shoulders of a woman of the senatorial elite.

'This sale will net us enough gold to provide a period of grace before the pressures of the imperial budget trouble us again. I think we can consider this a day well conducted.'

'Indeed, Caesar, and your officiation was a thing I will recall to the day I die.'

Eclectus sounded genuinely respectful, reflecting on the emperor's day-long labour, snatching sips of watered wine between lots as he had encouraged, cajoled and exhorted the rich men of the city to reach just a little higher in order to triumph over their fellows, and carry away some trinket that, in the cold light of the next dawn, would probably provoke the remorse of the hasty bidder.

'However, I would be remiss were I not to sound a note of caution at this point.' The chamberlain looked around at the members of Pertinax's inner consilium. 'Before anyone around the table proposes ways in which the massive sum that we have earned for the empire today might be used to generate yet more rewards for your clients?'

Scaurus nudged Marcus, looking pointedly at Acilius Glabrio, whose face, set hard and unreadable, betrayed the strong likelihood that he had been about to make exactly such a proposal. Claudius Pompeianus, who had probably been of the same mind, presented with hundreds of millions of sesterces and, in Pertinax, the means of dispensing them, replied in a deceptively casual tone.

'We have earned a stupendous sum today, Chamberlain, have we not?'

Eclectus nodded, his own face set in similarly inscrutable lines to those of Pompeianus's amicus.

'Indeed so, Senator, if viewed in isolation.'

The patrician ignored the qualifying comment, realising that it was a hook into a line of discussion that would not help his cause.

'And the disbursement of a relatively small part of that magnificence, purely to defray the costs that we Saviours undertook in rescuing Rome from the monster, would appear to be a reasonable step, now that the treasury is suitably buoyed up on that wave of gold, would it not?'

Scaurus grinned, not caring that Glabrio was staring straight at him in disgust, and leaned close to Marcus's ear.

'Ah, I see their angle. Tax cuts for their clients in the senate, and a naked grab at the contents of the treasury for the men who have won themselves the keys. Let's see how the Aegyptian deals with this without getting himself into hot water.'

'It seems, Senators, and with the greatest of respect for both your nobilitas and the risks you took to rescue us all from the previous emperor's rule . . .' Eclectus's tone was mild, fulsome, even, but he shot a glance at Marcus that made the fact that it had primarily been their risk, and not that of the men around the table, abundantly plain, 'that I must once again make the treasury's position completely clear to you all.'

Pompeianus and Glabrio exchanged glances, and their intention to scoop a significant percentage of the auction funds became even more certain in Marcus's mind.

'Gentlemen, the great empires of the world have usually fallen as the result of internal pressures, as much as those from beyond their borders. And we are subject to the most grinding set of both internal and external pressures that our empire has ever faced.' The chamberlain pointed at the map of Rome's sprawl across the known world. 'In every province we have seen the depredations of the plague. Millions of dead, sapping both our ability to feed ourselves and the activity required to pay taxes. Taxes required both to satisfy the populace's desire for bread and circuses, and to feed, equip and pay the legions that defend our frontiers. On which borders we face dozens of hungry tribes, pushed at us by the tribes behind them in their hundreds, all competing for land on which to live. Never have we had more need of our legions, and quite possibly to put even more of them into the field than we have today. And yet never have we been less able to actually pay those soldiers. They are not slaves, gentlemen, and they do not fight solely for the empire's glory. They have to be *paid*.'

'We are not children, Chamberlain, we—'

Glabrio's eyes narrowed as Eclectus raised a hand to silence him.

'Forgive me, Senator, but I will continue to explain why there is no money with which you might recompense yourself for all the risks *you* took in the removal of the previous emperor. When I am done, you may decide to have me removed from my post, or even executed for my insolence, a mere freedman speaking to your exalted personages as I am. I care not. But make the decision with the full knowledge of what it is that you have seized control of?'

The senator's reply was icy.

'Do continue.'

'As I was saying, we are beset by the plague within and the barbarians without. Our tax revenues were already insufficient to pay for the upkeep of thirty legions, *and* all of their supporting auxiliary cohorts, *and* the reconstruction of the city after the great fire, *and* the maintenance of the imperial palaces and city facilities, even before Caesar's unavoidable decision to placate the senate with tax cuts intended to reward your clients for their support. And, I must remind you, that the treasury is *empty*!'

Pompeianus smiled broadly, pointing to the stack of paper in front of Pertinax.

'And yet there we have a sum of money promised that will net us perhaps two hundred and fifty million sesterces? The treasury is suddenly, miraculously, *not* empty!'

He turned a smug stare on the chamberlain, raising an eyebrow as if daring the freedman to gainsay him.

'Senator . . .' Eclectus's voice fell to an awed whisper, either a consummate act or just genuine astonishment in the face of his social superior's lack of ability to grasp the situation. 'Have you not been listening, these past few days?'

Pompeianus blazed with sudden fury, enraged at being spoken to with so little respect by a mere freedman.

'You impudent fucking—'

'Hear him out, Tiberius?' Both men looked at Pertinax, one grateful, the other in surprise. 'He may lack the honeyed words that you have become used to having dripped in your ear by those who seek to provide you with advice, or receive your favour, but I suspect that what he is trying to tell us, in his own rough way, deserves to be heard.'

'Thank you, Caesar.' The chamberlain stared levelly at the two senators facing him across the room. 'Gentlemen, forgive me my bluntness, if you will? I have spent most of my life in this place, working in an environment where only perfect is good enough. Emperors do not tend to suffer failure well, and so the men who work in the imperial bureaucracy tend to very quickly become fixated on success above all else. Which can sometimes make us a little intolerant of alternative views.'

The senator inclined his head gravely in acceptance of the apology, but his eyes remained hard and, from where Marcus was sitting, unforgiving.

'As you were about to say, Chamberlain?'

'I will try to be brief, Senator. It's been a long day and I'm sure we're all tired. The simple facts are these.' He raised a single finger. 'The auction we have held today did indeed raise just over two hundred and fifty million sesterces.' Another finger. 'Two, promises already made to the praetorians, and to the men of the city, will cost around two hundred million of that freshly gathered money, unless of course we choose to short pay either party in the short term.'

'Or both.'

'Or, as you say, both. If I then consider the gold that is required to complete the remaining reconstruction of damage inflicted by the great fire, the running costs for the palace and other public buildings, and the money already owed to a host of suppliers who we have been unable to pay for the last three months – and if I factor in a part payment to the city and the guard of, shall we say . . .' He thought for a moment. 'Forty per cent? Enough to be of some utility, not so little as to be insulting as an initial payment?'

Pompeianus nodded magisterially.

'Very good, I shall factor in a forty per cent payment of those promises. All of which means that by my very rough calculation, the amount we have left for any disbursement is . . .'

Glabrio leaned forward, eager to hear what pot of gold he might be about to take a share of.

'Nothing.'

'What? Surely all that money can't already be owed?'

Eclectus nodded solemnly.

'It can, Senator. And it is. Our room for manoeuvre is sadly limited by the actions of the emperor's predecessor. And I'm afraid that it can only get worse from here.'

'Worse?' Glabrio shook his head in disbelief. 'How can it get any worse? We have rescued the empire from the hands of a monster, only to discover that he has gifted us the legacy of an empty treasury and the threat of a city and a guard both seemingly intent on bankrupting us, if the bastards don't simply kill us all!'

'It will get worse, Senator, and it will do so quickly now. The problem lies in the sale that we have just completed. And in the nature of many of the men you decided to sell.'

'The slaves?' It was Pertinax's turn to be baffled. 'What possible bearing could slaves have on the imperial finances, Chamberlain? I made very sure not to sell any of the men or women that Maior Domus Sporus counselled me to keep.'

Eclectus nodded ruefully.

'Sporus was advising you from the perspective of his role. Which is to provide you, Caesar, with unceasing luxury. He was very careful not to lose any of his bath attendants, cooks, cleaners, gardeners and launderers. You still have a barber, a cobbler, several tailoring staff, and a hundred and more men and women with specialist abilities, all of whom who concentrate on making sure that you are perfectly presented to the world, and lack for nothing. My advice, you will recall, was not to sell any of the slaves he didn't nominate for retention without an examination of their roles and the likely impacts of their loss to the imperial bureaucracy.'

Pertinax shrugged.

'Indeed, I recall that advice, and the amount of time you indicated would be required for us to review each slave's role, which would have delayed the sale by more time than we could spare. So, what are the likely effects of their sale?'

Eclectus shook his head.

'I have asked the various men with responsibility for aspects of the imperial finances to make an assessment of the potential damage. Those we have not already sold are due to report back shortly, but I can promise you that the loss of the buyers who source the food and drink for the palace kitchens will be a painful one. The prices we pay will increase, and the quality of the goods we receive will suffer, because the men who step into their roles will be both overworked and led a merry dance by suppliers who have been made cynical by being forced to wait months for payment on several occasions. And that's just the running of the palace. The costs of losing so many of the men who were doing the work of running the empire may only become clear over several months.'

Pertinax glowered, unhappy at the inference that it was his impatience that had resulted in the problems that Eclectus was predicting.

'I see. Well, if the imperial budget is likely to suffer, then there is only one thing to do.' He fixed the chamberlain with an icy stare. 'Reduce the imperial budget. The slaves we sold were no drain on our finances, but the Palatine is still infested with the freedmen that Commodus seemed to think were the right men to run imperial affairs.'

Scaurus muttered a quiet aside to Marcus.

'Oh dear. I sense a return to a theme.'

'Caesar, I strongly advise against the loss of any more of the expertise that—'

Pertinax was visibly growing angrier as he spoke, his face reddening.

'No more discussion, Chamberlain. It is the previous emperor's freedmen whose pandering to his every whim led us to the absurd position of his fighting in the arena and adlecting anyone whose face fitted into the senate at the slightest excuse!'

'Caesar, I implore you, do not compound our problems by forcing me to remove the very men upon whom the empire depends?'

The emperor dismissed Eclectus's plea with a wave of his hand, looking away.

'Chamberlain, you are to reduce the Palatine Hill's complement of functionaries by half. You are to do so within two days. And you are to bring me the permissions that allow them to pass the guards every day as the proof that you have done so. If the cost of running the empire is too high, then this firm action will help you to reduce it!'

Pompeianus and Glabrio nodded their agreement, their faces still set in bitter lines at being denied what they deemed to be their fair share of the sale's proceeds. Eclectus looked around the council chamber with an almost haunted expression, then bowed his head in acceptance of the decision.

'As Caesar commands.'

Scaurus sat back against the wall behind him, his gaze locked on his uncle, his muttered comment to Marcus spoken in a grim tone.

'Oh dear. Until now I thought that my uncle was making the very best of this difficult situation that we have stepped into so unwittingly. But that gave every impression of having been a major misstep.'

'Can I help you, Centurion?'

Marcus turned to look at Sporus, who was standing in the doorway of the emperor's private lounge with a faintly aggrieved expression.

'Yes, you can, Maior Domus.' He gestured for the head butler to approach. 'Firstly you can take that "what are you doing in the emperor's private quarters" look and tuck it back up your backside.'

He waited impassively, watching an impotent fury wash across the other man's face, to be replaced by the vacuous urbanity that he recognised as a tortured soul's window for the world, presenting a smooth facade to anyone who might see through him to the vulnerability of his real personality.

'Ah, Aquila, *how* I've missed you.'

The Roman stared pitilessly down into his fixed smile.

'Oh, I very much doubt you miss a thing, do you?' He waited a moment before following up the seemingly offhand comment. 'You seem not to be accompanied on your rounds any more, Maior Domus. Tell me, what happened to the child that used to dog your footsteps?'

'As if you care, Centurion?'

'You'd be surprised how much I care when it comes to the innocent and the vulnerable. It's to be hoped that you simply returned the poor bastard to his mother?'

Sporus bristled.

'What are you trying—'

'Trying to say? I'm not trying to *say* anything, Sporus. I'm asking you whether you punished the poor little bastard for finding that death list?'

'How dare you? I—'

Drawing his dagger with the speed of long practice and muscle memory, Marcus grabbed a handful of the other man's tunic, lifting him onto his tiptoes and putting the weapon's point under his chin.

'Stop your bleating. Is. He. Alive? Yes or no, now, before I get bored and let you slip down into this knife?'

'Yes!' The head butler's body tensed with the need to stay on his toes, and Marcus began to reduce the effort going into keeping him off the dagger's blade. 'I sent him back into the slave pool, and your *bastard* emperor sold him to a man known for his taste in small boys! So who's the—'

'I see.' The Roman prodded him with the knife's point, forcing him back onto tiptoe. 'In which case, I'll trade you the boy's rescue from servitude for a little information, a rescue I will carry out when the time comes.'

'The time? What time?'

Marcus smiled knowingly.

'The time when your plot against Pertinax comes to fruition.'

'My plot . . . ?'

Abruptly released from the centurion's tight grip, Sporus tottered backwards.

'Your plot. The one you're formulating with that praetorian animal Tausius. Nothing I can prove, of course, but the time will come when the pair of you try to turn praetorian swords on the man they are supposed to protect. And when that time comes, if I don't just find and kill you both, I'll rescue the child from whoever bought him, and return him to you. All of which I will swear to, in return for a piece of information.'

Sporus cocked his head on one side.

'What could you possibly need from me, now that you're a praetorian yourself?'

'Something only you could know.' Marcus turned to look at the walls around them. 'And I think you already know what it is that I want to know. Don't you? Where is it?'

Early March AD 193

'I've seen that prick before.'

'I see many pricks. In fact, pricks is all I ever see, watching these bastards lording it over the rest of us. Of which prick do you speak?'

Sanga looked at his comrade with a disgusted expression. The two men had been watching the praetorian fortress for almost two months, day in, day out, and even their remarkable mutual patience was wearing somewhat thin.

'"Of which prick do I speak?" I liked you better when you could barely string three words together, you Dacian donkey-fucker. That prick there! The one in the blue tunic waiting to get let into the fortress.'

Saratos looked across the street, nodding when he found the waiting man.

'Not a praetorian? Makes a nice change.' He stared for a moment longer, appraising the subject of their discussion. 'Nice tunic too – fine wool, but undecorated. Soundly built boots too, but sturdy, not fancy. He is from a good house, but he is a slave.'

Sanga nodded his agreement, watching as the door opened, and a brief exchange of words ended with the centurion who had greeted him taking something from him and closing the door.

'Plus he's bowing and scraping like a good 'un too. He's a slave alright; look, they're leaving him out in the cold while they look at whatever it was he gave that crested cunt.'

The two men sat, exchanging the occasional greeting with the locals who passed them, and watched the slave stand patiently outside the fortress's main gate. They were heroes to the men and women who populated the street, since the gang that had taken over the territory from the dead butcher had, on discovering the dead bodies of their rivals, decided to tread decidedly lighter than their predecessors when it came to taking payment for their protection service.

'Interested in him, are you?'

The baker who routinely sold them their lunch sat down beside them, smiling as the two men stared at him suspiciously.

'Don't worry, if I was going to sell you out to the bastards in the red tunics, I'd have done it a month ago. We all know what you're doing, since none of us is stupid, but none of us is going to rat on the men who took that bastard of a butcher and split his head down the middle. So, what you watching for?'

Saratos and Sanga looked at each other, the Briton shrugging.

'Well, since you *all* know. We're watching the red tunic boys for any sign of another attempt to get rid of Pertinax. That a problem for you?'

The baker shook his head, albeit with a purse-lipped expression of disgust.

'Nah. Although you'd best keep quiet about who your boss is; the new emperor isn't all that well regarded round here. We were promised a hundred denarii apiece, and here we are two months later only paid out twenty-five? And those pricks in there are complaining that they only got half what he promised them? Greedy fuckers! So anyway, your man in the blue tunic . . . ?'

'Yes?'

'You know you pair buggered off at dusk last night?'

'Yes?'

Sanga's tone was making it clear that he was getting bored.

'Thing is, he was along about half an hour after you left, with a two-man escort to keep the robbers off him. Delivered a message, waited, took a message back.'

The two men exchanged glances.

'Any idea who he is?'

'No.' The baker grimaced at Saratos. 'You don't just wander up to someone waiting for a message outside the camp and ask them who they're running errands for. Not unless you want to get the shit kicked out of you. Oh look, that was quick!'

The slave had received a scroll, and turned away to head back down the hill at whose top the praetorian camp was positioned. Sanga nodded to Saratos, who got slowly to his feet and stretched his back, doing his best to look like a man getting ready to go for a stroll.

'Get after him, I'll stay here! We could be on for our gold piece here!'

'Gold, eh?' The baker looked down at Sanga speculatively as his partner in crime hurried away after the blue-tunicked messenger. 'Feel like sharing a little of that with the man who pointed him out to you?'

The Briton looked up at him for a moment, as if considering the question seriously, then shrugged.

'*Fuck* no.'

'It's a pleasure to get away from the palace. I know I shouldn't say such a thing, but between you and me, Gaius, I find the place stifling. And with a feeling of being . . . well . . .'

'Haunted by the spirits of past emperors?'

Pertinax shot his nephew a sideways glance, as if checking that he wasn't mocking him.

'You feel it too?'

Scaurus laughed softly.

'I'm not that sensitive, Caesar. All I see is stone, furniture and rebellious praetorians. But I know the feeling you're describing. That feeling that there are the spirits of a dozen men looking over your shoulder at everything you say and do. It goes with those stones, I suspect.'

They were riding west on the Via Ostiensis, making the twenty-mile journey from Rome to the port city that served it. Mindful of the events of two years before, at the height of the grain famine that had tipped the capital over into the chaos resulting in the death of Cleander and Commodus's last purge, Pertinax had resolved to ensure with his own eyes that the grain warehouses were both full and well maintained, and that the buildings were as proof against vermin as possible given the vital nature of their contents to the volatile populace.

'Yes.' He sighed, looking out over the fields on either side of the road, ignoring the shouting on the road ahead as his equites singulares ordered a convoy of waggons to make way for the imperial party to trot past them. 'And they're a critical set of bastards, in my imagination. Yes, I know, that's just me being self-critical, but it's hard to avoid the conclusion that this has been a somewhat less than stellar start to my rule.'

'There were factors that you could not have been aware of. The empty treasury, for one thing . . .'

'Indeed. If that fool Eclectus had chosen to share that fact with us before his woman murdered Commodus, I might have thought twice about agreeing to accept Pompeianus's invitation to be the man on whom the burden of the purple was placed.' He smiled ruefully at Scaurus. 'Yes, I know, it's hardly a burden to live in a palace in such luxury, but the role doesn't have a good record for its holders dying in their beds, much less enjoying a life of ease in their retirement. Look at Marcus Aurelius. Forced to contend with plague, famine, the revolt of his most trusted general at the behest of his wife . . . And he was supposed to have been one of the wise emperors, graced with the wit and judgement of the Caesars of old. One has to wonder what he would have made of all this.'

'You're making the best of a difficult situation, Uncle. The early emperors were able to expand the empire to restock their treasuries. Even a marginal province like Britannia was a ripe flower waiting to be plucked, once the moneylenders got to work on the tribal aristocracy and slowly but surely transferred their wealth to Rome. And then Trajan and all the men who followed him had the security of Dacian gold to enable them to abandon that expansion. Perhaps it was Commodus's misfortune to be the man on the throne when that source of wealth really started to dry up. And it's hardly your fault that a quarter of the city burned down two years ago, and has consumed so much of the available funds in rebuilding.'

Pertinax nodded ruefully.

'Indeed. But I have to tell you, this role is not what I expected. Far from being the commanding height of the empire, the Palatine Hill is more like a prison – for me, at least . . .' He paused again, looking across at Scaurus speculatively. 'Gaius, there's something we need to discuss, and where better than here, where the usual eager ears are far distant?'

'I know what it is, Uncle. You don't think you'll be able to deliver on your promises. And I understand.'

The emperor shook his head, raising his eyebrows in polite disbelief.

'You understand? I whip the promise of the throne off the table without so much as an apology and you're sanguine about the whole thing?'

Scaurus shrugged.

'You promised to make me praetorian prefect. To command a pack of gold-hungry so-called bodyguards who seem to have forgotten the meaning of the term loyalty, if indeed they ever knew it. Laetus has allowed them to abandon their oaths, and so they are surly and obstructive without ever going over the line into insubordination. While some among them plot to replace you with a man who will deliver them the gold you promised. To be clear, Uncle, if you made me their prefect, one of two things would happen in very short order: either I would be dead at their hands, or I would have thoroughly purged both their tribunes, who've lost all control of them, and the centurions who now seem to be in command, if anyone is. It would have to be done quickly, and with the maximum brutality, to put them on the back foot and make every one of them think twice about rebelling again. But, to be honest, with their anger having become as deep-seated as it seems to be, I can't see anything less than a complete change of personnel restoring their loyalty. And that would require the manpower of at least one legion, which is something we simply do not have.'

'No, or ever will have either. It's apparent that Niger, Albinus and Severus are waiting to see which way the dice land before deciding on their best course of action. Whatever happened to the empire's best men being solely concerned with its protection and continuation, I wonder?'

Scaurus shook his head.

'We know Niger and Albinus well enough. The former is a cautious man, and wants to see how your rule plays out. He'll know the financial difficulties involved. And Albinus always was an ambitious bastard, if something of a blowhard. But Severus . . . who knows . . . ?'

His musing was interrupted by the sounds of hoofs behind

them, a lone rider galloping his horse out from the city behind them at a pace which told Scaurus he was willing to exhaust the animal to deliver his message swiftly. Recognising the messenger's riding style, he turned his horse back to meet him.

'Qadir?'

The Hamian reined his beast in, snapping a swift salute to the two men. Walking his horse so close to Pertinax's that the mounted bodyguards put their hands to the hilts of their swords, he spoke quietly but urgently.

'Caesar, you must return to the city at once! And your safety demands that you leave your equites singulares here to await orders! They may be part of the plot!'

With his bodyguard reduced to Scaurus, Marcus, Dubnus and Qadir, the latter mounted on a fresh horse taken from a disgruntled member of the mounted bodyguard, Pertinax turned back to the east, and the city. Once they were out of earshot of the astonished horsemen, Pertinax asked the question that was on all of their lips.

'What plot? In the name of all the gods, Centurion, I demand that you—'

'Sosius Falco, Caesar! My informers who were set to watching the praetorian camp have evidence that he has been part of an exchange of messages with the guard!'

The emperor shook his head in confusion.

'What, *Falco*? You must be mistaken, Centurion! He's a nice enough young man; a bit headstrong and full of himself, but from a good family – one of the best as it happens, the Erucii Clari, and . . .'

He stopped talking, his eyes narrowing as he considered what he'd just said, and Qadir continued.

'Is he close to Gaius Julius Erucius Clarus Vibianus, Caesar? Because the messages that have been flowing to and from the praetorian camp originate in *his* house. Erucius sends a message to the praetorian camp, the praetorians reply, and the messenger takes that reply to Falco on his way back to Erucius.'

Pertinax looked up at the sky for a moment, shaking his head in disgust.

'Gods below! Now I see it! Our exiled friend Triarius Maternus Lascivius is the uncle of Gaius Julius Erucius Clarus Vibianus! And Sosius Falco is Clarus's fucking brother-in-law! The two of them were the consuls for this coming year, and they were both on Commodus's death list, ripe for plucking! So, unwitting victim or not, it seems that Lascivius was part of a bigger game. Doubtless if the praetorians had succeeded in putting him on the throne, the Erucii clan would have revealed their hands in good time! They are one of the most powerful and richest families in the city, and Falco's mother is Ceionia Fabia, the emperor Lucius Verus's sister. Which makes him part of the royal family, and gives him a decent enough claim to the throne. And there's enough nobilitas between the Erucii and the Sosii families to satisfy even the most demanding of examinations as to their fitness to rule! Doubtless the fucking praetorians would have found him a good deal more acceptable than a freed slave's son from Alba Pompeia! They would have put him on the throne while his brother-in-law stood behind it and pulled his strings!'

Scaurus nodded, thinking quickly.

'Which means that, far from being a spur-of-the-moment abduction from a city street when they took Lascivius and presented him with the purple, the bastards were acting on orders. Orders issued by someone who's in league with Clarus Vibianus. But who? Laetus?'

Pertinax spurred his horse to a fast trot.

'It's hard to see who else it could be! And if I get so much as a whiff of treason off that bastard I'll have his balls fed to the fucking lions while he's still attached to them! Come on, we need to get back to the Palatine!'

'I come to you today not as your colleague, Conscript Fathers, but as your emperor. Take note of that, and be careful how you respond to what I am about to tell you.'

Having waited in ostentatious silence, standing before them unspeaking until the senate had fallen silent without having to be bidden to do so, Pertinax made it clear from his first words that he was incandescently angry. Working hard to use his oratorical gifts to their best effect, he had pitched his opening comments in a conversational tone that had an already hushed senate subconsciously straining their ears to hear him.

'What did he say?'

Juventius Celsus's querulous question, pitched higher than the emperor's statement, was the opening Pertinax had been waiting for, and even as the aged senator's neighbours shushed him, Pertinax bellowed a reply at the startled assembly members.

'I said that I am your fucking *EMPEROR*! And that you would do well to remember that fact, whether you like it or *NOT*!'

The words crashed down on them with the impact of a thrown brick, but he had already turned away and was pacing across the curia's floor like a caged animal, looking around him with the alert expression and questing eyes of, to Marcus's mind, a beast searching for escape from its cage. He had dressed in his formal imperial finery in silence, and the descent down the ramp and into the forum had been conducted in the same manner, the emperor clearly still as furious as he had been as Qadir had laid out the evidence before him.

'I did not want this role, if you will recall, Conscript Fathers?' Having reached the far end of the building, he turned and leaned back against the wall in another symbolically powerful gesture. 'I begged you august gentlemen to find a man better suited to the requirements of the role! And in reply you shouted that you had found your emperor, and would have nobody else! You were unanimous in that opinion, it seemed!'

He shook his head and strolled back into the heart of the gathering.

'But now, it seems, I am plotted against for the second time in less than three months! Once again, my *loyal* praetorians have conspired with members of this house to have me replaced by one of my colleagues! Once again the plan was to have another man placed on the throne, and the current emperor, I imagine, quietly murdered! Except, gentlemen, I will not go quietly!'

He looked about him, fixing certain men with a hard stare from which there could be no flinching.

'Of course, the last time they tried the same trick, the conspiracy was not of the man in question's doing, and so I allowed him to leave Rome. Triarius Maternus Lascivius was kidnapped from the street and taken back to the praetorian camp, where imperial robes awaited him! Terror-stricken, he fled, and threw himself on my mercy! Which, being a reasonable man, I granted! And, putting the matter down to a few overeager praetorians, I had them warned what would befall them if it happened again and then, like the magnanimous man I always try to be, thought no more of it! Until today . . .'

He paced back to the chamber's other end, leaving the senators awaiting his next words and looking at each other in perplexity.

'But today, I learn, through the unceasing efforts of my true protectors, that there is another plot to take the throne! Another plan to murder me! Which, as you might imagine, would prove fatal to me, and very definitely have the potential to prove fatal to some of you! So would anyone here like to declare anything to their colleagues? Perhaps share their plan that has me unexpectedly in the mood for reinstating the majestas laws?' He cocked his head on one side, exaggerating for effect. 'Nobody? You're all as innocent as the driven snow, are you?' Another pause. 'Very well, it seems we must do this the hard way!'

He turned and nodded at Scaurus, who stepped forward with a hand on the hilt of his dagger, then swivelled back to face his audience, raising his voice in a clear command.

'Quintus Pompeius Sosius Falco, step forward!'

The astonished young man looked around him in confusion, his face flushing with the unexpected challenge.

'But . . . I . . .'

'Step! *Forward!*'

Pertinax's parade-ground roar shocked the swiftly growing mutters of disbelief back to absolute silence, and the man in question stepped out of the throng of his colleagues to face the emperor.'

'Caesar, I—'

'Silence! You will have your chance to speak before I decide what to do with you!' The emperor turned away. 'There was a plot, Sosius Falco, that was supposed to reach its fruition today. A plot discovered by the good offices of men reporting to Praetorian Tribune Scaurus. I will not tell you how I know this, but I know that messages have been exchanged between the praetorian camp and your own household!'

The younger man spread his arms beseechingly.

'Caesar, as the gods know, I am wholly innocent of . . .'

His protest tailed off as Pertinax raised a finger to silence him.

'All in good time. As I say, it is *known* that you have been involved in an exchange of messages with the praetorians! It is a *fact*! Praetorians who, incidentally, are now being investigated by their prefect with the most rigorous of methods! Any of them who are discovered to have conspired against me will be stripped of their citizenship, dismissed from their service, stripped, beaten, scourged and crucified in front of their fortress. My days of tiptoeing around while my own so-called *protectors*' – he spat the word out as if it were distasteful – 'and my so-called *colleagues*' – another pause – 'persist in their attempts to murder me, are *over*! I will have no more of it! If any of you have the courage, come at me now with your blades and we'll see just how brave you really are!'

Scaurus, standing behind him, raked the benches with the hard, cold eyes of a man looking for his next victim.

He turned a slow circle, raising his arms to demonstrate his perplexity with the situation.

'Nobody? Very well! I will assume that I have the backing of this august body of gentlemen! Although that leaves me with the difficult question of how to deal with the traitor Sosius Falco, does it not? Or rather it would, were he actually guilty of having led the plot against me!'

He raised a hand to quieten the perplexed Falco.

'Oh, there was a plot, of that much we are quite certain! But I do not believe that our young colleague here was its leader, any more than Triarius Maternus Lascivius was back in Januarius! I believe that we are looking at a greater conspiracy behind this innocent young man, whose only crime is that he was a prime target for my praetorians in their misguided urge to replace me with someone a little more compliant to their wishes! And so you, Sosius Falco, may step back into the welcoming press of your colleagues! And when this session is complete, my advice to you would be to leave Rome, today, and not to make a reappearance until expressly invited to do so by your emperor! Because to be seen on the streets of the city might just be sufficient provocation either for my erstwhile protectors to abduct you, as they did our colleague Lascivius, or for my real bodyguards to remove you as a threat to my reign! Do you understand me?'

Falco nodded hurriedly, and the emperor made a shooing gesture, ushering him back into the ranks of men behind him, those closest comically backing away and refusing him the comfort of the slightest comradely contact.

'And now . . . I have a message for the man who stands behind these two attempts to remove me from the throne! The man who, through his close connection to both of them, has revealed himself to be a plotter, and a schemer! A man who, if I so much as catch sight of him on the streets of the city – and believe me, I *will* be looking for him – *will* be charged with majestas, *will* be executed in very short order, and *will* have his entire fortune confiscated! *Without* the right of inheritance! His family will be cast out onto the streets, and no man will be allowed to lift a finger in their assistance! And with that, I will leave you to consider your behaviour! And to ponder your futures!'

He stared up at the top row of benches, apparently nodding his respects to one man in particular.

'Good day to you, Gaius Julius Erucius Clarus Vibianus. I wish you long life, and a more careful choice the next time you ponder whether to dabble in politics.'

'So, Prefect. Perhaps you might like to try explaining how it is that once again your men are implicated in an attempt to replace the emperor, while you claim to have no knowledge of the matter?'

Laetus leaned across the table, casting a nervous glance at Scaurus's familia in their places around the room.

'Do we have to discuss this matter in front of—'

'My bodyguards are the only reason that this latest attempt to remove and presumably kill me failed, Laetus. So yes, we have to discuss it in front of them, so that they can tell me when you deviate from the unhappy truths they have discovered, saving me from the unexpected arrival of Sosius Falco in the palace along with a pack of rabid praetorians!'

'Yes, Caesar . . .' Laetus swallowed. 'I have made my investigation, with Tribune Vorenus as my right-hand man. And we have discovered that the roots of the plot were shallow.'

'Shallow?' Pertinax raised a disbelieving eyebrow. 'Two of the oldest and richest families in the senate decide to collude with disaffected members of your command in a plot to replace me, which could only ever have resulted in my death, and you call that shallow? And how on earth could the entire guard not have known what was happening, even if only a few of them were conspiring against me? They live cheek by jowl in a fortress that's barely big enough for the number of cohorts the guard now has; so close that when one man farts, a thousand others know what he had for dinner the previous night.' He paused, staring hard at his prefect. 'Go on then, just how many men have you implicated in this plot?'

'Nine, Caesar.'

'Nine . . . *nine*?'

'Caesar, if you'll allow me to explain?'

Pertinax waved a hand, his expression stony.

'Please do. This I cannot wait to hear.'

'The principal leader was a centurion, by the name of—'

'*One* centurion? A plot is hatched to kill the emperor by a single centurion?'

'He confessed immediately, Caesar, without any coercion. And before we started the process of questioning the officers.'

'That's convenient.'

Laetus shot a hate-filled glance at Scaurus.

'Whether it is convenient or not, I have a confession. He named eight of his men, and they in turn have confessed, in return for clean executions.'

The emperor leaned forward.

'Say that last bit again? I could have sworn I heard you say that you had promised these men clean executions. Which of course could not be the case, because before I sent you up to the fortress, I most specifically ordered that the guilty men should be executed with the full force of the very worst fate that can befall a traitor. By what authority did you believe you had the right to gainsay that direct order, Prefect?'

'I knew that you would want a swift conclusion to the matter, Caesar. And so I decided to offer a swift death as the reward for confession.'

'And it didn't enter into your thinking that the conspirators might use that as their opportunity to force a few well-chosen outsiders to take the blame for them? Offer them money, safeguard their families' futures, and ultimately give them no choice?' Scaurus walked forward until he was looking down at the white-faced prefect. 'Because if I had a conspiracy to cover up, that's what I think I'd do. Tell a man who nobody cares for that he'll die, along with his family in the city, and badly, unless he accepts a helpfully merciful execution. With the promise of enough gold to set that family up in comfort for life, of course. And when will this sentence be carried out?'

Laetus returned his stare.

'The death sentence on the conspirators has already been

delivered, Caesar. I could hardly hold back, when the men in question had confessed their hatred for you so vehemently?'

Pertinax went deathly still.

'And this sentence of death. How was it delivered?'

'Exactly as you would have expected, Caesar. Revocation of their citizenship, scourging, and finally crucifixion.'

The emperor gave him a knowing look.

'Crucifixion? That's not all that "swift", is it? So they must still be hanging from the nails. Shall we take a walk up there, perhaps, and have a look at how well they're holding up? After all, it takes most men at least a day to die, even after a proper scourging.'

'That would usually be the case, Caesar, but the former comrades of the men in question took their spears to them in hatred of their disloyalty. They are all dead, and their bodies have been cast onto the waste pits outside the city.'

'I see.' Pertinax stared at him for a moment longer and then waved a hand. 'Dismissed, Prefect. I find your account of the roots of this latest attempt on the throne less than credible, but, as you are all too well aware, I am unable to remove you from your position for fear of inciting your clients, the Severus brothers, to revolt. It is your key advantage in this unhappy situation, but I fear will ultimately lead to your downfall. You may leave. Do not disgust me with your presence again without a specific order to do so.'

He waited until Laetus had scuttled from the room before turning back to the council table, addressing his next words to Pompeianus and Glabrio.

'You may, of course, feel that I was too harsh, colleagues. But then you both seem very relaxed about this matter. Neither of you twitched as much as an eyebrow in the senate, when I would have expected you both to be deeply perturbed as to the risk that the praetorians would have posed to you too. After all, if their motivation is to seek revenge for Commodus's death, then surely the two of you must be targets just as much as I?'

He waited for a moment, but neither man spoke.

'I see. An eloquent silence is to be my reply, is it?' The emperor walked to the table and sat down. 'Very well, let's get down to the meat of the matter, shall we? In you two men I see an interesting juxtaposition of the old and the new. You, Glabrio, have a respected name from the glory days of the republic. You are very much of the ruling clique, or rather what would be the ruling clique if such a thing could ever truly be said to exist. Which, of course, it does not, because there is no real power in this palace, or in the curia, while the praetorians are in their current state of mismanagement.'

'But surely we three are comrades in—'

Pertinax cut him off with a wave of his hand.

'We three *were* comrades in a seizure of power, Acilius Glabrio, until about an hour ago. Until I realised that that arsehole Clarus had conspired with the praetorians to have me murdered, to clear the way for his brother-in-law to don the purple and make him even richer than he already is. And until it occurred to me that you must both have been at the very least aware of it.'

He stared at the two men without blinking, Glabrio shaking his head and looking down while Pompeianus tried to meet his gaze.

'Helvius Pertinax, I—'

'Call me by the fucking title you persuaded me to take, Tiberius? At least grant me that dignity. And tell me, while you're at it, what was it that Clarus promised you? A father-and-son consulate, perhaps? After all, the most influential man in the senate had pulled your chain, had he not? I'd imagine any reasonably sized bauble would have been enough to save your face. Although I would have hoped that a new man like you would have had more sense than to fall for his bullshit. After all, you're no more to him than the dung on his sandals when he crosses the road, are you? But you fell on your back and opened your legs like that stupid old bastard beside you, didn't you?'

He looked at the two dumbfounded men with a look that made clear how much he despised them.

'Fuck the pair of you. If I had the loyalty of the praetorians, I'd have them batter your doors down and do to your families exactly what Clarus would have ordered them to do, once he had his arse parked firmly on the seat behind the throne, you idiots. And do you want to know why I don't order my own men to do just that?'

He gestured to Scaurus.

'It's because I don't want these men to be any more exposed to the revenge of my enemies, when they eventually take me down. And, you fools, because they're too decent to do any such thing, unlike almost any other man in the city, because they have already suffered exactly that fate. Now get out of my sight.'

When the two men had left, he looked up from the table at Scaurus apologetically.

'I'm sorry you had to see such a thing, Gaius. All my high ambitions for the resurrection of the empire lie shattered on these fine marble floors. All we can hope for now, I suppose, is that Severus decides to back my rule, and sends us enough soldiers to pacify the guard. Because if no assistance is forthcoming, it can only be a matter of time before they try again. And they only have to get lucky once.'

II

'You wish me to interrupt the emperor while he's dressing, Tribune?'

Scaurus looked at Sporus with an expression of increasing exasperation.

'Yes, Maior Domus. Now. Before it's too late, and—'

'You are aware, Tribune, that I do not hold the rank of cubicularius?' The head butler looked down his nose at his adversary with pity. 'If you understood the way the palace works, you would know that I cannot simply stroll into the imperial bedchamber and make free with the emperor? It is my master the chamberlain who is the companion of the emperor's bedchamber, not I.'

Scaurus stepped closer to him and took a handful of his tunic's thick wool, hoisting him onto his toes and snarling his response into the other man's terrified face.

'I understand that you have free run of the palace, Sporus! I understand that you go just about anywhere you wish, when you wish, only maintaining the fiction that you don't enter the emperor's living quarters for the sake of appearances!'

He pushed the maior domus away, smiling grimly as he barely kept his balance. Sporus's response was gabbled, made frantic by his sudden, terrified realisation that the emperor's attack dog had slipped his collar.

'That's true, but only when he is absent! And only because I need to ensure that our master's personal environment is kept perfectly clean and ordered for him! I would never—'

'Break the precedent set by your service to Commodus? Break it, Maior Domus. Break it *now*, because I don't intend waiting for Eclectus to make an appearance before bringing word of the latest plot against the emperor to his attention. Break it, before I find myself forced to perform an impromptu execution for the crime of failing to alert the emperor to an immediate and pressing threat to his life. *Your* execution! And when I've executed you, I'll be forced to break precedent and go in there anyway! So just fucking *do it!*'

Blanching at the naked threat, Sporus hurried away to summon Pertinax.

'You're harsher with him than I ever was.'

Scaurus replied to Vorenus's amused observation without turning to look at the man behind him.

'In the days that you were the emperor's closest protector, Sporus was little more than an annoyance, flitting around and making sure that the cushions were plumped up. Whereas now, he has entirely another aim in life. I no more trust him than—'

Pertinax came through the door to his private quarters dressed in a snowy white toga with a thick purple border around its hem. The tunic beneath it was equally pristine and lavishly decorated, while a cloak of an identical shade of purple was draped over his shoulders and fastened with a heavy, jewelled gold brooch. At his shoulder was his father-in-law Flavius Sulpicianus, wearing the official robes of his office as the urban prefect. The emperor smiled at Scaurus and Vorenus, gesturing to his feet.

'Purple shoes, gentlemen? Why in the world anyone ever thought it would be a good idea for the emperor to wear purple shoes, I genuinely have no—'

His nephew interrupted his light-hearted comments.

'Caesar, I have news from the praetorian camp.'

The emperor raised an eyebrow, abandoning his fine adjustment of the toga.

'*Caesar?* Coming from you, Gaius, that almost sounds as if something has you worried. And Sporus told me that you'd been quite unpleasant to him?'

'My apologies, Uncle, I don't persecute the foolish unless circumstances require me to do so. But I must brief you as to fresh intelligence that has emerged overnight. If we thought that the executions after the Falco plot's discovery would be enough to quieten the guard's dissent with your rule, we were mistaken. Elements of the garrison are planning to come for you today. To finish what they started.'

'They plan to "come for me". Are you saying that they mean to attack me, here in the palace?'

A fresh voice interjected from behind them.

'Yes, Caesar, we believe they do. And so, I suspect, does this man!'

Both men turned to look at Marcus, who had appeared in the doorway, one hand on his dagger's hilt, the other gripping a cringing Sporus by his upper arm.

'I found your maior domus lurking in the corridor, apparently very interested in your discussion.'

Pertinax raised an eyebrow at the cringing butler.

'I see. Perhaps he'll have a decent explanation for his unannounced presence? Come now, Sporus, why would you be eavesdropping on my conversation?'

Sporus gabbled his answer, shooting sideways glances at the implacable centurion beside him.

'I simply wished to know whether you still intend to grace the poetry reading at the Athenaeum with your presence, Caesar?'

The emperor gestured to Marcus.

'Thank you for your diligence, Valerius Aquila, you may release the maior domus; I very much doubt he poses any threat to me. And I believe we need Prefect Laetus to join us, if you could have him summoned, Gaius? He should be in the palace by now; I suggest you look to find him in his private office.'

Scaurus nodded to Marcus, who gathered Dubnus by eye. As they made to leave the room, Pertinax spoke again, his voice hard.

'Oh, and don't take no for an answer, eh, Centurion? Laetus is to attend upon me whether he wishes it or not. You are authorised to use whatever force is necessary.'

He turned back to Scaurus.

'You believe that there is a continuing conspiracy?'

'I believe that Tribune Vorenus understands the threat the best of all of us, Caesar.'

Vorenus stepped forward, saluting the emperor with grave formality.

'I do, Caesar. As to whether an attempt on your life will result from it, I cannot say. But what I do know is that the fortress has been alive with rumours and speculation all night. There is a hard core of the men who were not executed after the Falco debacle, my centurion Tausius among them, who intend one last roll of the dice. I spent the hours of darkness listening from the shadows as they drank themselves into a state of fury, vying to be the most vehement in condemnation of you and the senate.'

Pertinax smiled wanly.

'Which is rich in itself, given that the senate seems to be running out of patience with me too. How many are they?'

'Two hundred and fifty, perhaps a little more or less either way. They have elements of the equites singulares in league with them, from what I saw overnight.'

'So I am betrayed even by the most elite of my bodyguards.'

Scaurus shook his head in frustration.

'Two hundred and fifty of them? A battle-hardened infantry century could face down that many men who've never seen combat.'

Vorenus nodded grimly at Scaurus.

'If you have an infantry century up your sleeve, now would be an excellent time to reveal them. Because I can tell you what's going to happen next. They're sleeping off the wine right now, but by late morning they'll have roused themselves and made the decision. Either they'll sulk a while longer and wait to see if you come up with the rest of the gold you promised them, or they'll come down the Viminal Hill with murder on their minds. I'd bet on the latter. And if they talk each other up into making an attack, then I expect that the gate guards won't stand in their way, nor the palace servants. Their minds have been poisoned against you.' He turned a pitiless gaze on the maior domus. 'Haven't they, Sporus? You were lurking in the corridor listening, weren't you, eager to relay news of our discussion back to your co-conspirators!'

The maior domus was unable to meet his emperor's eye.

'Caesar, I . . . I was only hoping to be of service to you!'

The emperor shook his head in dark amusement.

'Almost perfect, Sporus, except you missed off the words "one last time".'

'Caesar?'

Pertinax laughed aloud, his laughter laced with a sardonic edge.

'Butter wouldn't melt in your mouth, would it, Sporus? And yet I see that hatred in your eyes every time you address me. Don't I?'

'I don't know what you m—'

'Yes, you do.' The emperor stepped forward. 'I saw you in the presence of Commodus on hundreds of occasions, and what I saw in your eyes was nothing short of love for the man. And you consider me responsible for his death. So now you're plotting with the praetorians.' He raised a hand to stop the head butler's denial. 'We both know it's true, so I suggest you make life easier on yourself by telling me what you know. And to make myself clear, Sporus, I find myself experiencing that sudden rush of clarity that often comes to a man who is faced with his own death. I can see very clearly how you, and Laetus, and those around you, intend to betray me to a handful of gold-crazed soldiers – Laetus because he is a coward, and you because you hate me. So here's your choice. You can either start talking, immediately, or you can die here. Because I'm not the sort of man to send a traitor down into the dungeons to meet his fate. For one thing, I'd rather be sure that you've paid the price for your disloyalty. So you'll die, here and now, unless you start behaving like the palace servant you're supposed to be. I'll spatter these ludicrous purple shoes with your blood and leave your corpse for your praetorian friends to discover, when they finally crawl from their beds and come to find me. *Talk!*'

Marcus and Dubnus paced through the palace in silence, half expecting to be challenged by the guards who should have been on duty throughout the complex, but the corridors were empty except for the occasional servant going about their duties, seemingly unaware of the tension surrounding them. Leading his friend into the Flavian wing of the palace, Marcus pointed to the rooms on the other side of the peristilium from the open archway that led out to the palace exit overlooking the forum.

'Laetus's offices are in there. Stay here for a moment, I want to see what's happening outside. And if he comes out, don't let him go anywhere.'

Leaving the Briton waiting beside the prefect's office door, he walked quietly through the courtyard, peering into both the dining hall and the emperor's audience chamber to find both eerily quiet, without any sign of the guards who would usually be on duty. Grateful for the near silent footfall granted to him by his nail-less palace boots, he padded through the entrance hall and flattened himself against the wall next to the archway, usually a praetorian checkpoint to prevent unauthorised entry to the Domus Flavia. Taking off his distinctive plumed helmet, he peeped momentarily around the arch's stone edge to find a group of twenty guardsmen gathered around the archway that controlled the path down into the forum. Some were sitting, others standing in listless postures around the gate, and one man was passing a wineskin to his comrade. Pulling back into the wall's cover, Marcus listened to their conversation for a moment, nodding grimly as Vorenus's intelligence was confirmed.

'Seems wrong, drinking on duty. What if Tausius finds us at it?'

A louder, more confident voice answered.

'Tausius? He's not around to catch us, he's up at the camp getting the Avengers ready. And besides, if it's alright us drinking when they want us drunk, so that they can murder an emperor and smuggle his corpse out without us knowing, it's alright now.'

'Avengers? They're really going to do it then?'

The brash praetorian laughed.

'Are they really going to do it, boys?' A chorus of laughter answered his rhetorical question. 'You wasn't in the camp last night, was you? You was on the nest with that little Phrygian sort you're seeing down in the Subura, wasn't you? So you didn't hear them shouting and screaming about vengeance, did you? But we did, and Tausius gave us our orders this morning, before we came down here. Nobody comes in, or out, except for him and his brothers. They're all centurions and chosen men, see, just about every bloody officer in the camp who doesn't wear bronze and talk like they're chewing on marbles. They've got tired of trying to find the right man to replace Soldier Boy in there, so now the plan is to get him sorted, pull back to the camp with enough blokes left here to keep any looters out, and wait for the rich bastards to come and make us their best offers.'

'We're going to sell the fucking palace?'

Marcus smiled grimly at the astonishment in the praetorian's voice, but the answer was both swift and dismissive of any hint of awe at what was proposed.

'No, friend, we're going to sell the fucking throne! Soldier Boy offered us twelve thousand sesterces, but never even delivered half that much, so the throne owes us seven thousand apiece at the least. But we reckon there's a lot more than that to be had. Tausius reckons the Saviours will dry up and blow away when their man's head is on a spear on our walls, which'll leave the way clear for anyone else with the money who fancies a go to come and bid.'

'Bid?'

'Yeah, bid. We'll be waiting for them in the camp, and they can come and pitch themselves to us. The one with the deepest pockets will be the one we escort back down to the palace.'

Putting his helmet back on, the Roman made his way quietly

back to the prefect's office, finding Dubnus waiting patiently with his sword drawn.

'Any sign of him?'

The big Briton shook his head.

'Not a sound. Perhaps he's not even in there?'

'We'll soon find out. Kick the door in and let's have a look.'

Dubnus sheathed his weapon and took aim, his first kick smashing the lock but failing to open the door.

'It's bolted on the inside. Someone's in there alright.'

He smashed his booted foot into the door's lowest portion, snapping the bolt that was holding it in place, then put his shoulder to the remnants and burst it open.

'Get back!'

Both men stepped back as Laetus came through the doorway with his sword drawn, his face screwed up in a snarl. Marcus stepped back, flashed out his twin blades and put their points in his face, settling into a combat stance.

'Do you know who I am, Aemilius Laetus?'

The prefect nodded, his eyes mesmerised by the double threat of the two swords' points.

'You're the emperor's assassin!'

'Oh, I'm much more than that.' Stepping forward a pace, Marcus put the tip of his spatha against the praetorian's sword point with a gentle scrape of steel. 'I'm the son of a man your predecessor murdered for his wealth. I'm a soldier who's spilled the blood of a hundred men and more, while men like you hid behind me and my comrades. And I'm the gladiator Corvus, the man who destroyed Velox and Mortiferum in the arena. I am *death*, Prefect! Cursed with the double-edged gift of a gods-given ability to kill and an unending succession of men who seem determined to die. And I will visit my curse on you, if you do not stand down *now*!'

The prefect recoiled physically, his sword's blade falling to point at the floor. Marcus brushed past them and stared around the room in which the prefect had been hiding.

'Did you think you could hide here forever? When your guardsmen storm in with the intention of killing Pertinax, they won't be satisfied with just his head. They're going to want yours too, because they see you as his co-conspirator.'

Laetus shook his head.

'I wasn't hiding here! I tried to leave but they wouldn't let me! Those bastards told me that if I tried to leave the palace again they'd kill me!'

Marcus nodded knowingly.

'Centurion Tausius's orders, I presume. We both know where the real power lies in your command right now. The wisest thing any emperor could do would be to disband your sad excuse for a bodyguard. Anyway, time's wasting. Sheathe that sword, it's time you stood up to be counted.'

Eclectus and Marcia had arrived in the emperor's private quarters by the time Marcus and Dubnus reached the spacious room, the couple having taken up a position by the windows that looked out over the Circus Maximus. They were standing hand in hand, and the woman's face was streaked with tears as she talked quietly with the stoical Aegyptian. Pertinax, having divested himself of his cloak, was deep in discussion with Scaurus, the two men looking up as the centurions shepherded Laetus through the door. Of Sporus there was no sign, and Marcus presumed he had been dismissed.

'Well now, it's the praetorian prefect!' Pertinax strolled across the room to confront his erstwhile protector with a hard smile. 'You look surprised to see me, Aemilius Laetus. Were you expecting me to have made a run for it, when I found out what your rabble were planning?'

The prefect rallied, attempting a show of bravado that was belied by his pale complexion.

'Not at all, Caesar! I was awaiting your instructions in my office.'

'His door was locked and bolted?' Pertinax looked quizzically at Marcus, who simply nodded. 'I thought that might be the case.

They wouldn't let you leave the palace, I presume. Tell me, what are they calling themselves?'

Laetus shot the emperor a disbelieving glance.

'Calling themselves?'

'I'll forgive you your omission of the customary honorific, Prefect. After all, I will very possibly be dead quite shortly, and you'll never have to call me Caesar again. Although I'm forced to observe in reply that you have been quite miserably lacking in competence by the standards expected of a man in your position. Haven't you?'

The prefect looked at his feet in silence.

'You've got nothing to say then? Presumably you can see my point. We've suffered one coup attempt after another, all backed by the guard for which you have responsibility, and yet with no one that mattered ever brought to justice.' He shook his head. 'No matter, it will all be meaningless soon enough, I expect. And the question I was asking you was this: have your men accorded themselves a collective name? After all, we had the hubris to call ourselves "the Saviours", why shouldn't they choose something equally self-justificatory?'

Seeing that Laetus had no answer, Marcus stepped forward.

'They're calling themselves the "Avengers", Caesar. And it seems they're mostly centurions and their deputies.'

The emperor shook his head.

'If ever there was a perversion of the sacred contract that the empire has with its centurionate . . .' He pondered for a moment. 'Very well, it seems that these "Avengers" will be stepping onto palace ground soon enough, so I suggest that we decide what's to be done.'

'What's to be done, Caesar?' Scaurus pointed at the Roman suburbs to the palace's south through the opened window. 'Surely the only answer is to leave this place and find somewhere safe, to give us time to ready a counter-attack? We can fight our way through the guards at any gate we choose and escape into the city, and I doubt the urban cohorts would prevent you leaving

Rome. If we divest you of all that purple, then I'd imagine that we could go unnoticed for long enough to escape all this, and only announce your presence once we've found some loyal soldiers to face down the praetorians.'

Pertinax shook his head with a composure that Marcus found admirable under the circumstances.

'I will not run. Not only does it not suit me to undermine the gravity of the office I hold, but all it could ever do is delay the inevitable. They would hunt us down like dogs, Gaius, and any troops we could reach before they caught us would most likely share their enmity, given the reactions of the legati augusti. No, I will remain here, and confront these gold-grubbing pigs with all the dignity of my rank. An emperor does not run when a fight presents itself.'

His nephew nodded determinedly.

'In which case we will defend you, Caesar. No man will approach you with a drawn blade as long as any of us remains alive.'

'No.'

'But—'

Pertinax raised a hand to silence Scaurus's perplexed reply. The tribune shook his head in confusion.

'But how can we *not* defend you, Caesar?'

His uncle raised questioning eyebrows.

'More blood? Is that the answer?'

'If we have to shed blood to defend the empire, we will!'

'Think for a moment, Gaius. There have been two attempts to unseat me. And there will be more, if this one fails. Worse than that: if it fails because of your defence of me, you too will become targets for the praetorians. You, *and* your families. Do you want them to die because you fought in a lost cause?'

'A lost cause?'

Pertinax smiled sadly at his nephew, placing a hand on his shoulder.

'Gaius. My dear boy, it has been lost from the moment that

we discovered just how empty the treasury was. My fool of a sponsor Claudius Pompeianus and that arse Acilius Glabrio might have been stupid enough to persist with the delusion that they could pilfer a few million sesterces on the back of my new-found power, but I never shared that delusion, from the moment that Eclectus told us just how desperate the state of the empire's finances was. Everything between then and now has been no better than the frantic bailing out of a sinking ship.'

'But you can't expect me to just walk away and leave you to the thuggery of those bastards?'

The emperor smiled.

'What I expect is for you to take your familia out of harm's way, and spare them the ignominy of being hunted down by men who wish to punish you for your part in the betrayal of their emperor.'

'But—'

'*Tribune!*'

Scaurus snapped to attention.

'Caesar.'

'That's better. I have grown unaccustomed to being argued with, these last ten years or so. I have one last order for you, and it is an order that you *will* obey.' Pertinax smiled wryly. 'You weren't there, in Britannia, when the mutineers from the Sixth Victrix ran amok, sacked my residence, murdered my bodyguard to the last man and left me for dead in their haste to loot my possessions. I had the ringleaders of that piece of stupidity stripped of their citizenship, whipped close to death and then crucified, and the legions they came from decimated. I didn't step back then, and I will not step back now! But neither will I allow you to die with me, if that is my fate!'

He placed a hand on his nephew's shoulder.

'And so my order is for you to withdraw from my presence. Contact Petrus, and have him get you out of the city by whatever route it is that he has planned for himself. Save your people, Gaius, and grant them their lives in my name?'

'Caesar.' Scaurus straightened and saluted. 'With a heavy heart, I will do as you ask.'

'Good. And thank you.' Pertinax turned to Eclectus and Marcia. 'Escape while you can, Chamberlain, and take your woman with you.'

'I cannot, Caesar.' The Aegyptian raised a hand to forestall his master's insistence. 'I have no family to rescue. I only have my duty to discharge.'

'Your duty. That's noble, Chamberlain. But are you an accomplished swordsman, Eclectus?'

'No, Caesar. Although I did train with the sword as a younger man. I will give a good enough account of myself, when the time comes, to find my place in the histories.'

'I see. And your woman?'

'Marcia will leave with Scaurus and his men. It is already agreed between us that there is no reason for her to die here.'

'As you wish, Chamberlain. And who knows, you might even be witness to an unexpected and perhaps even glorious defiance of all expectations!'

He smiled, turning to Laetus.

'And you, Prefect. Will you also stay to share my fate?'

'I . . . Caesar . . .'

Pertinax nodded knowingly, his smile sliding seamlessly into a sneer.

'Never fear, Prefect. I suggest that you go and wait for these "Avengers" and order them to stand down with all the authority of your honoured position? If that fails, you might still be able to persuade them to let you live.'

The prefect nodded, swallowing.

'Yes, Caesar, of course. Thank you, Caesar.'

He shot a venomous glance at Marcus, turned and left the room.

'You realise that he's going to save his own skin, without a thought for his duty?'

Pertinax nodded at Scaurus's bitter statement.

'Yes, Gaius, I do. Laetus has done nothing but manoeuvre in the pursuit of his own interests since the day we took power. But I also know that he's condemning himself to a longer and more difficult road to the same destination than if he simply gathered his courage and confronted his men. After all, what man can run forever? Whenever fate catches up with him – be it days, weeks or months from now – it will trip him up and leave him sprawled on the cobbles as his executioner looms over him.' The emperor waved a dismissive hand. 'Let him run; all he does is condemn himself to death. A death whose cold hand on his neck will be the thing of nightmares for him in the days before he is forced to confront it.'

Eclectus gestured to the window that overlooked the Circus Maximus.

'They're here. I can hear them mustering down there.'

Scaurus joined him, the two men looking down at the street below. In the deep shadow cast by the racetrack, armoured men were marching towards the staircase that led up to the palace complex's main gate. At a barked command their ranks broke up, centurions and chosen men ascending the steps in a flood of iron-clad bodies, pushing aside the waiting guards. Scaurus turned back to address the emperor, his tone softer than before.

'Caesar, the renegade praetorians are inside the palace. They will be here in your private quarters very soon now. Will you relent, and allow us to defend you, or better, take you to a place of safety?'

Pertinax shook his head resolutely.

'No, Gaius. You may watch me from here, while I go out to face my destiny. Either the historians will record that I defied the ire of the praetorians and tamed their revolt through the force of my willpower, or that I died like a true Roman, with dignity and facing my persecutors. Either would be better than postponing this moment through the deaths of you and yours. Will you join me, Chamberlain, since you seem determined to share my fate?'

The two men walked to the stairs, and descended to the peristilium below while Scaurus and his men moved to the windows overlooking the courtyard. The emperor strolled out into the garden with a studied nonchalance that was completely at odds with Eclectus's stiff-legged gait, the chamberlain's drawn sword contrasting with his master's open hands. He waited, composed and calm, the sounds of the praetorians' progress through the palace growing louder as they stormed from room to room, until the first armoured men burst into the colonnaded garden. Face to face with the man they were seeking, the leading centurions seemed uncertain. The men pushing in from the corridor behind them spilled out into the open space to either side until Pertinax and Eclectus were faced by well over a hundred armed and armoured officers with only a few paces between their drawn swords and the defenceless emperor. Marcus recognised Tausius in the front rank, a murderous stare locked onto the man he held responsible for the death of his master.

'Well now, gentlemen, I see you've decided to bring some grudge or complaint directly to me! Welcome to my home, although of course you are as familiar with it as I am.' Pertinax opened his hands in greeting, seemingly untroubled by the mob's drawn swords and hostile stares. 'And maybe it's for the best that we speak now, without an audience? What better way for an emperor to make peace with his bodyguard than to listen to their arguments, and then do whatever lies within his power to resolve those issues. Perhaps we can find a way to repair the relationship between the empire's absolute ruler and the men who wield the most power of any body in Rome? Or will you strike me down without ever doing me the honour of sharing what it is that has brought you here in such evident anxiety?'

He waited, apparently serene, while the praetorians looked at each other in a state of confusion.

'Much easier to strike down a man who flees, than stab him in the front when he confronts his enemies with reasoning and authority.'

Julius shot a surprised glance at the giant Lugos, who was looking down with a thoughtful expression.

'Reasoning and authority? Fucking hell. Perhaps I ought to pay out Morban after all . . .'

The emperor was speaking again.

'Come now, exalted comrades! Every one of you holds a rank within my praetorian guard that is the result of years of service, and striving to be the best men in a unit that is already numbered among the elite!'

Scaurus laughed softly in spite of the tension gripping them.

'Now he's laying it on a little thick even for me to swallow.'

But the emperor's words were clearly finding a willing audience among many of the men facing him.

'Comrades, you are the descendants of the men who escorted our greatest emperors, both on the battlefield and to protect them against domestic enemies. Augustus, Tiberius, Vespasian, Trajan, Hadrian, Marcus Aurelius . . . all had praetorians at their side every moment of their waking lives. Honoured for their battlefield ferocity; lauded for their dedication and unceasing vigilance in the city. Indeed, there may be men here who were instrumental in protecting the previous emperor from an assassin's blade ten years ago, when Claudius Pompeianus Quintianus made his suicidal attempt to upset the natural order of the world.'

'Say his name!'

The emperor looked straight at the man who had barked out the demand.

'Say his name? I will! You men protected Commodus from the assassin's knife, and gifted Rome ten more years of his reign! But you could not protect him from his fate, not when he lost control, driven half mad by the pressures of his position and the empty coffers that left him with no way to rule except through wholesale murder of Rome's conscript fathers! Commodus was forced to plan a purge the likes of which this city has never seen before, and in turn his own closest advisors were forced to take his life before that purge could consume them too! He was a victim, my friends, of the vice-like pressure that ruling an empire of a hundred million people exerts on the man who finds himself carrying that burden.'

Scaurus muttered quietly to himself.

'Does he have them . . . ?'

The praetorians' swords were now pointed at the stone beneath their feet for the most part, their expressions thoughtful rather than angry.

'Comrades, if you take my life now, you will begin a rule of violence and greed that will pitch our glorious empire into a civil war that might take years to play out. The city will be riven with dissent, and innocents will be the main victims. Innocents like your own flesh and blood, the wives and children we both know you support. Kill me, and *they* will be the victims. Kill me, and whoever comes to power after a long and bloody struggle will refuse to trust you. It is my prediction that your magnificent cohorts will be disbanded, and your vaunted strength will be shared out among the legions to make up their losses in that struggle. You know all too well that your families will struggle to survive, without you to provide for them and protect them. Will their neighbours stand by them, I wonder, or seek to exploit their vulnerability?' He waited for a moment, allowing the men facing him time to consider the question. 'So tell me, what will it be? Will you take your swords, sworn to my protection, and murder your emperor over a half-paid donative and a question of your honour? Or will you stand *with* your emperor, shoulder to shoulder against the men who seek to wrest the empire from his control, and return our city to the days when the rich ran roughshod over the ordinary citizens? You can either pitch the empire into a crisis which will leave no life unchanged, or be part of reconstructing it in the image of the days when great men lived on this hill and ruled wisely! Choose now, and live with your choice! I grow weary of waiting, here on the cusp of both life and death!'

He played a hard stare across the praetorians, and Marcus saw many of them look away, some in shame at being called to task, others still hating him but seeing the wisdom of his argument and their own self-interest. Blades were being sheathed, and the men at the back of the group were starting to turn away when Tausius stepped forward and then turned to face them.

'What, we should let him off the hook because he tells us that there is a greater enemy? The very "enemy" with whom he colluded in the death of the true emperor? And you fools are going to let him get away with it? Well, not me!'

He stepped forward, swinging his sword in an arc to strike Pertinax once across the top of his head in the classic killing stroke taught to every legionary. The emperor, struck down in the moment of his apparent triumph, fell to the ground and covered his head with the purple-edged toga, the copious flow of blood from the sword's deep cut into his scalp staining the pristine white wool with a swiftly spreading crimson. He cried out in his agony, his voice strident even through the toga's heavy material.

'You fools! May Jove the Avenger smite you from the heavens!'

In an instant the spell that had inhibited the praetorians was shattered. Drawing their swords, they set about the fallen emperor, half a dozen of them vying to hack and stab at his writhing, recumbent body. As the comrades watched in horror, Eclectus struck from where he had been standing unnoticed. He stormed into the unsuspecting centurions and put two of them down, one with his throat opened to the bone by his first wild hack, the other felled with a horrific slash wound across his face, and then fell under the combined attack of their fellow guardsmen, blood foaming in his mouth as he was run through by a pair of swords. The blood frenzy jolted Marcus out of his momentary shock at Pertinax's death.

'We have to leave! Now!'

Scaurus was still staring down at the dying emperor, his eyes wide with shock. Marcus turned to Julius, barking a command.

'Bring him! And follow me!'

Turning away from the view over the peristilium, where the praetorians had started to fan out across the courtyard and into the buildings on either side in search of loot, he led them away into the emperor's private apartment at a trot. Dubnus called out to him as he and Julius gathered Scaurus by his arms and half led, half dragged the horrified tribune with them.

'Why are you leading us into this dead end?'

Marcus spoke over his shoulder, heading for a point on the private dining room's far side.

'Because it's only a dead end if you don't know where the exit is!' He found the hinged panel that Sporus had revealed to him months before, the route by which Commodus had delivered him an almost fatal surprise by arriving in the stadium garden unheard and unannounced, and pushed, opening the hidden door wide to reveal the dark staircase. 'Get down to the bottom and wait for me! Use the handrail, and don't fall!'

Waiting until the last of them was past him, he eased the door shut again, plunging the stairwell into near darkness, pushing hard to ensure that there would be no sign of the hidden exit to the rampaging praetorians. Hurrying down the stairs, he emerged into the stadium's daylight to find his friends waiting, and pointed to the northern end of the walled garden.

'This way!'

The party hurried through the statues, climbing the staircase that led to the palace's higher level, the sounds of the rampaging mob of praetorians and the screams of the palace servants caught by their depredations dying away. At the top of the staircase, Scaurus shook himself free from the grip that Julius and Dubnus had on his arms.

'I can walk for myself, thank you, gentlemen! Which way now?'

Marcus led them around the deserted guard post that over-looked the stadium and into the garden between it and the temple of Apollo, pointing to the stairs that led to the steeply sloping tunnel. The party hurried down the steps and into the half-light, Marcus stopping them at the bottom of the long descent.

'Get into formation: two abreast, the tribune in the middle. With any luck they'll just wave us through the gates.'

Rounding the corner, they marched down the tunnel's incline

towards the guards standing around the heavy iron gates that separated palace ground from that of the arena above them.

'Four of them on this side of the gate, four on the other side.' Marcus spoke quietly to the men behind him, gauging the risk presented by the men on the other side of the barrier. 'Be ready to deal with the rest of them, if it comes to knife work, or they'll spear whoever's trying to unlock it once we have the keys.'

Marcus led the party up to the security point, noting that the guards were grinning at them broadly, clearly mistaking them for members of the praetorian mob that had stormed the palace. Two of them were carrying the forbidden axes over their shoulders, having clearly decided that Pertinax's death would remove the prohibition on their use in the city. The Roman growled a warning at the men behind him.

'Be ready. But smile. So much the better if we can get out without fighting.'

One of the guards stepped forward, eager for news.

'Did you find the old bastard, or had he run away?'

'We found him alright. And now we're taking the news back to the camp.'

'Alright!'

The guardsmen were celebrating, clapping each other's armoured backs. The detachment's leader turned to the gate, but as he turned the key to open it, one of his men frowned at Dubnus.

'Hang on! Ain't you one of those—'

The words died in his throat as the big Briton pulled his dagger and stabbed its long blade up into the soft skin beneath his jaw. Taking the dying man's axe from his nerveless fingers, he shoulder-barged his victim into the man behind him and swung the heavy weapon's evilly sharp blade at the watch officer's hand as he started to close the gate. The praetorian screamed in agony, staring at the stumps of his fingers as he staggered back from the barrier, then died on Marcus's gladius as the party's other members stepped into the fight. Lugos reached over their heads and flicked the gate inwards to his left with a flex of his massive arm, the iron bars smashing the two men on their left into the tunnel wall behind them, both unconscious from the hammer blow, while Dubnus stepped through the opening and rampaged into the men on the arena side of the barrier.

Unable to swing the axe's heavy blade high in the confines of the tunnel, he lunged at the closest of them, smashing the butt into the gap between his helmet's cheek guards and sending him reeling away with blood pouring from his ruined face. Gripping the weapon two-handed, he rounded on the others, who were already flinching back from his unexpected onslaught. He pivoted to deliver a crunching blow with the handle's wooden knob to one of the two men facing him, bouncing him off the tunnel wall, then ripped out the other's throat with a surgically precise flick of the blade's beard, the triangular iron point tearing out the hapless praetorian's windpipe. Turning to deal with the last of them, he saw the man fall with an arrow in his throat, shot by Qadir through the gate's bars. Marcus came through the open gate with a piece of wool cut from one of the fallen praetorians' cloaks, holding it out to his friend with a grim smile.

'You've got blood on your armour. Let's not give the arena guards any reason to delay us.'

Scaurus came through the gate with a face like thunder, the shock of having seen his uncle murdered no longer paralysing his mind.

'Julius, take the familia back to the house. Find Petrus and tell him that we all need to use his escape route, including him if he's got any sense!'

The burly centurion shot him a concerned look.

'And you?'

The tribune pointed to the stairway that led up to the colossus.

'I plan to go the praetorian camp. I have revenge on my mind!'

With the sun long since set, the praetorian camp was brightly lit, as if in celebration, torches along its walls casting their illumination into the street below. In the middle of the wall, above the fortress's main gate, a spear had been set up with what appeared to be a bloodied and battered man's head on its long blade, its features almost unrecognisable. Scaurus and Marcus waited in a side alley out of view, their red praetorian uniform tunics fading to black in the shadows, the two men having decided to take advantage of the fear their uniforms inspired in the citizenry. A large detachment of guardsmen had marched from the fortress an hour previously, presumably to replace the men who had been guarding the empty palace since Pertinax's death, the men they had been sent to relieve marching back up the hill under the stern eye of their officers sometime later. The two men had shrunk back into the shadows as the returning guards had passed them, watching around the alley's corner as the red-tunicked soldiers had marched through the gates, which closed behind them to leave the dark street silent.

'So, what happens now?'

Scaurus shook his head at Marcus's question.

'I have no idea. What *ought* to happen is for the senate to meet and choose a replacement from among their best men. Perhaps with an eye to Commodus's bloodline, in which case it would probably have been Pompeianus's son, as Commodus's nephew. But now . . . ?' He laughed bitterly. 'The irony is that Pertinax originally intended making me praetorian prefect, before he actually took the throne and discovered that it was Laetus who'd recommended Commodus to appoint Septimius Severus to command the Danubius legions, and his brother Geta to command in Moesia. Which made him unsackable, if a prompt revolt by the pair of them and all of their legions was to be avoided. And his ultimate aim was to name me as his successor, which was something I would have detested, but borne for the good of the empire. Whereas now . . .'

'Do you think Sulpicianus is still in there?'

'It's likely. He certainly hasn't come out. And he's a decent enough man, and untainted by any participation in Commodus's death, even if he was Pertinax's father-in-law. Perhaps we can still hope that . . .'

He turned to look down the hill.

'Who's this then?'

A party of half a dozen toga-wearing men was walking up the hill, a number of rough-looking escorts with knives on their belts going before them to ensure their path was clear.

'Hang on . . .' Marcus stared hard at the advancing bodyguards. 'I recognise those thugs. They're Petrus's men!'

The two friends stepped out and waited for the escort to reach them, raising their empty hands to signal their lack of any intent on the party walking behind them. The man who was evidently their leader turned back, looking to his master for instructions, and Petrus waved a hand for him to keep walking up the hill.

'Let them through! That's my friend Corvus and his dominus Scaurus!'

They waited for the gang leader to reach them and fell into step with him, Scaurus looking back at the party walking twenty paces behind.

'I presume you're escorting them to the praetorian camp?'

'You presume correctly, Rutilius Scaurus. My commiserations on the death of your uncle, by the way. He was a good man, if not entirely suited to the role he found himself in. And as to what I'm doing here, take a wild guess. That's Marcus Didius Severus Julianus behind me, by the way. He turned up at my door about an hour ago, clearly half pissed, and told me that his wife and daughter had persuaded him to come up here and bid for the empire in the course of a dinner party! And did I want to come in with him?'

'What?' Scaurus shot an amazed glance at the gang leader. 'He offered you a part share in the empire, if you help finance it?'

Petrus laughed.

'And look at you, all offended by the idea. Three months ago you were part of a conspiracy that took the empire from its legal master by force. Using that one' – he nodded to Marcus with a friendly grin – 'to do the dirty work. What's so bad about the idea of settling the succession by the application of a little gold, if it avoids any further loss of life?' He pointed up at the fortress walls. 'That is Pertinax's head they have up there, isn't it?'

Scaurus nodded grimly.

'Yes.'

'There you go then. They've won. They hold the empire in that fortress, nothing less. And they'll sell it to the highest bidder, we've been told. A pair of praetorian tribunes came to Julianus's door during dinner, inviting him to bid for the throne. It seems that they've decided that their best course of action is to go along with what their centurions have done, perhaps for the money, or perhaps just to avoid finding themselves at the wrong end of their men's spears, since that's where the power lies. Anyway, Sulpicianus is already in there, they told us, busily making promises to the men that killed his son-in-law, so he doesn't seem to have lost any time getting his mourning done and getting back to business, does he? We're just here to provide him with a little competition and test just how keen he is to wear the purple. But before we do . . .'

He took off his cloak and draped it around Scaurus's shoulders, calling one of his men forward to do the same for Marcus.

'And take your helmets off, I doubt the bastards will happily negotiate if they realise that you're with us. And now, if you'll excuse me for a minute, I have an empire to buy.'

He walked forward until he was twenty paces from the gate, then raised his voice to shout at the deserted walls.

'Good evening, gentlemen! Didius Julianus is here, at your invitation, to enter negotiations for a rather significant item that you have to sell! A chair, I believe?'

A lone figure with the cross-crested helmet of a praetorian walked down the rampart until he was standing by the spear on which Pertinax's head was affixed.

'We do have such an item to sell!' Scaurus seethed, realising from his voice that the centurion was none other than Tausius. 'But there is already a buyer on the premises, and a generous bid has been submitted! You would have to better his offer to take the item away!'

'And his offer is?'

'Five thousand sesterces a man, on top of the balance of the last emperor's donative!'

Petrus shrugged.

'One moment!'

Petrus turned back to his new sponsor with a knowing smile.

'It's time to choose, Senator. Until now this was a bit of fun, but now it gets real! Do you want to bid for an empire?'

Julianus came forward, nodding distractedly at Scaurus with the look of a man half recognising someone he felt he ought to know.

'I don't suppose that walking away would make us any friends in there, would it?'

'Seems unlikely. By coming up here, you've committed yourself to compete with Sulpicianus, and I suspect the praetorians have high hopes that the battle between you will net them a rich reward. Disappointing them in that respect might not be a wise choice.'

The senator nodded wearily, making Marcus wonder if the initial, flushed enthusiasm he'd felt with the praetorians' invitation had already been replaced by a creeping dread of the trap into which he had voluntarily placed himself.

'As I feared.' He sniffed, steeling himself with a visible effort. 'But as you say, we are committed, so let us see how far my colleague is willing to go. Offer them six . . . no, seven and a half. Surely that ought to do it?'

Petrus looked at him pityingly for a moment, then turned back to the ramparts towering over them.

'The bid here is seven thousand and five hundred!'

Tausius nodded impassively.

'Wait.'

He vanished from sight, and Petrus turned away from the wall.

'That won't be the end of it, not by a long way. What you have to bear in mind, Senator, is that your colleague Sulpicianus is in there with those animals. And he will be shitting himself at the thought they might cut his throat if he is the loser. Aside from which, he is still urban prefect, which gives him the greater auctoritas of the two of you, which makes him more credible as a potential emperor.'

The centurion reappeared above them.

'The bid is now eight thousand!'

'Offer them nine.'

Petrus shrugged.

'It's your money, for the most part. But sometimes in an auction you can end up paying less by paying more, as it were. A big bid can break the other man's spirit, so to speak . . .'

'As you say, the money is mine. I think we'll offer nine thousand, thank you, Petrus.'

The gang leader shrugged and turned back to the walls.

'I suspect he's right.' Scaurus looked up at Tausius with an expression of hatred. 'This bidding by small steps will string the process out longer, and end up costing the winner more than if he'd simply named his best price.'

After a few minutes the praetorian, having consulted with his colleagues inside the fortress, turned back to them.

'Ten thousand is the bid!'

Julianus pushed forward with a determined look.

'Eleven!'

'It looks as if we could be here for a while!' The centurion vanished again, but when he returned, his grin was visible, even with the height of the walls between them.

'Sulpicianus bids twenty thousand sesterces!'

'Gods below!' Julianus took a step back, staring up at the jubilant centurion in disbelief. 'Say that again?'

'Yes, you heard correctly. Twenty thousand sesterces for every man in the guard!'

'Two hundred million sesterces. Even I cannot . . .'

'I warned you, did I not?' Petrus shook his head. 'The man who makes the biggest bid, who doubles the bidding with a single offer, is most often the man who walks away with the lot. But on the other hand, by making such a bid, your rival might have shown us the limit of his ability to promise gold to those animals.

Which presents you with an opportunity, if you have the stones to grasp it. You must either raise the stakes with the same brutality or admit defeat. And hope the praetorians are not vindictive towards you once they have their man on the throne, and enjoy that absolute power. In short, Didius Julianus, either bid this up to the stars or go home.'

'And will you take some share of the pain, if I do?'

'Will *you* reimburse me from the treasury, if I do?'

'Are you both mad?' Scaurus shook his head in disbelief. 'The treasury is empty!'

Both men flashed him pitying looks, Julianus giving voice to what it was they knew, and he didn't.

'Two hundred and fifty million is a sum that I can extract from my senatorial colleagues with the greatest of ease. Ignoring their honking as I pluck their feathers at the point of a praetorian spear. Reversing Pertinax's tax cuts and finding a few new ways to take money from the men who have it won't be beyond the wit of a vengeful bureaucracy, once the freedmen realise that they have absolute authority to fleece the men who treated them so unkindly only weeks ago. Very well then!'

He stepped forward again, raised his hand into the air and spread the fingers wide.

'My last offer, honoured Praetorians! An offer that Flavius Sulpicianus will never match, but an offer that is good for the count of exactly one hundred, after which I am going home to finish my dinner! Twenty-five thousand sesterces for the throne! Two hundred and *fifty* million for your support! But decide quickly, Centurion, because when the count reaches one hundred, I will be gone from here, happy to watch what happens once my rival has his feet under the table and a legion or two at his back! After all, you did behead his son-in-law! Who knows what revenge he might dish up to you . . . ?' He allowed the silence to extend for a moment before throwing his last gambit. 'Not forgetting the fact that you kicked it around the palace in a quite startling show of contempt, did you not?'

He turned away with a hard grin.

'Start counting, Petrus. And make it loud!'

The gang leader drew breath to start the count, but Tausius shouted down at them exultantly.

'There's no need to count! We accept your bid, *Caesar*! Open the gates! We have a purple robe waiting for you, courtesy of our good friend Sporus, and there is a fine ram waiting for your hand on the knife that offers it to the gods.'

The gates opened to reveal the praetorians, equipped in their full battle armour and deployed around the central courtyard in their cohorts, the light of a hundred blazing torches making the polished iron shine like gold.

'Enter, *Imperator* Caesar Marcus Didius Severus Julianus Augustus! Enter, and claim your throne!'

29 March AD 193

'You have three hours, Corvus who is now Aquila.' Petrus grinned at Marcus, gesturing to the ship tied up alongside his warehouse in the city's Emporium district, in the shadow of the Aventine Hill. 'After that this ship must sail, if it is to catch the tide and clear Ostia cleanly. At the stroke of the third hour, and no later, the master of that tub is going to make sacrifice and haul up his sails, after which you'd need to be on a bloody fast horse to catch him before he's past Ostia and away down the coast. And that was your son I saw going aboard a moment ago, right?'

Marcus nodded.

'So whatever this unfinished business is, you'd better get it wrapped up and get back here quickly, or it could be years before you see him again.'

The Roman turned to Julius and Dubnus.

'I have a promise to keep. You two should—'

'Fuck "should", you idiot.' Dubnus's voice was calm, but his resolve clear. 'I've been pulling your chestnuts out of the fire for more than a decade, so if you think I'm going to let you wander off into the city to die with some bastard's knife in your back, you can forget it. I'm coming with you.'

Julius leaned in, jabbing a finger for emphasis.

'And so am I. Because someone needs to watch this oaf's back while he's watching yours. So, where are we going first?'

The three men strode through the half-empty streets, Rome's usual bustle much reduced by the number of people who had chosen to stay at home until the succession to Pertinax was decided, for fear of a praetorian rampage through the city.

'This must be what it's like to be properly feared.' Dubnus grinned at the people shrinking away from their armour and weapons, both of the former centurions carrying axes over their shoulders with a degree of nonchalance that belied their hard-eyed scrutiny of the houses on either side. 'No wonder the bastards have got so used to strutting around like they own the place.'

They reached their destination without incident, brushing aside the private guards set at each end of the exclusive street, intended to keep out anyone without business in the large houses that ran up either side of the wide road, although not without first clarifying which of the generously sized buildings they were looking for. A rap at the door with the knob of Julius's axe handle brought a scowling butler hurrying to open it, the snarl on his lips silenced by the presence of three hard-eyed praetorians.

'This is the house of Quintus Servilius Silanus, don't try to deny it! Bring out your master! If you tell me he's not here, we'll go in there and find him!' Marcus gestured to the two unsmiling axemen behind him. 'And you can only imagine the mess we'll make of the place if we do. Or the blood we might spill.'

'One moment, Centurion.'

Preventing the door from closing with his foot, Marcus listened intently to the raised voices within. After a long moment he shouted a warning into the house.

'Come out now, Silanus, or we're coming in to start breaking things!'

The house's owner appeared at the door, a toga hastily flung about his body to judge from its untidy folds. He pushed his chest forward, closing his eyes in readiness for whatever punishment it was that he was expecting.

'Very well, gentlemen! I can only ask that you make it quick!'

After a moment's silence he opened an eye and looked at the three men.

'You're not . . . ?'

Marcus shook his head in incomprehension.

'Not what?'

'Not here to kill me, for not coming to the senate house.' He shook his head in exasperation. 'For Didius Julianus's acclamation?'

The Roman shrugged, and was about to speak when Julius tapped him on the shoulder.

'If I might?' He stepped forward, placing the head of his axe on the stone lintel and leaning forward to go face to face with the terrified senator. 'Silanus? You were among those shouting for Commodus to be dragged with the hook, were you not? And, from the voices we could hear a moment ago, you're not alone. There are a few more of you rats hiding in there, aren't there?' The senator looked at him in helpless silence. 'I thought so. We don't have to burst in and take our axes to you all, of course. It's really up to you.'

Silanus slumped visibly.

'What do you want?'

'A thousand gold aurei would probably be enough to make the problem go away. Not to seem greedy, but there are men to pay off. Men who know where you live. And divided between a few of you rich senators, it seems a small price to pay.' The big man grinned mercilessly. 'Pop off and get the money, eh? You and your mates can work out whether they're going to pay you their share later.'

The ashen-faced senator vanished back into the house, and the three comrades waited in silence while the sound of frantic argument came distantly to them from within. After a few minutes, he returned with a bag which Julius took from him and hefted in his hand, judging its weight.

'This is nowhere near a thousand. Is it?'

'It's all I have in the house! Nobody else has any money on their persons!'

Julius turned to Marcus.

'This is no more than five hundred. What do you think?'

'I think we should get into them!' Dubnus glared at the shrinking senator, playing the part of an incensed praetorian to perfection. 'They killed Hercules!'

'Perhaps there's another way to pay what you owe us?' Marcus gestured at the house's interior. 'After all, you were at the emperor's auction back in Januarius, were you not? Perhaps you bought something really expensive that would make up for the lack of gold?'

'Yes! Yes, I did!'

He scurried away, returning a moment later with the gold-shelled gladiatorial helmet that had been the auction's first lot.

'This cost the best part of two million sesterces! Almost twenty thousand in gold! Take it!'

Marcus pulled a face at the offer.

'There's no way we'll get that sort of money for it now. Who's going to want to buy Commodus's helmet, and mark himself out as a man who gloried in his death? This is scrap value only, friend!'

'But it's all I have!'

'That's the only thing you bought in the whole auction?'

The Roman raised an interrogatory eyebrow, and the senator's brow creased.

'Well, I did buy a slave, now you mention it. But surely—'

'Fetch him.'

'Him? How did you know what sex—'

Julius leaned forward, putting a finger on Silanus's chest.

'Fetch. The child. Now.'

He withdrew the finger, then pushed the senator hard enough to send him several steps backwards. Knowing he was beaten, Silanus turned and scurried away, returning a moment later with the child Alinus, who looked up at Marcus and nodded with the same preternatural calm he had displayed in the palace. He was dressed in silk, and his face was subtly made up to make him appear more feminine than was already the case.

'Take him!' The sweating senator pushed Alinus over the threshold. 'Just spare me!'

Dubnus picked the boy up effortlessly and turned for the gate, but Marcus leaned forward to speak quietly in the senator's ear, Julius at his shoulder with a murderous scowl.

'That child is now free. *You* freed him when you gave him to us. Do you accept that?'

'Yes! Anything!'

The two men turned and followed Dubnus into the street, where he was waiting for them with an expectant look on his face.

'Where now?'

Titus Menius Caudinus opened the door of his newly purchased house with equal trepidation to that displayed by Silanus, understandably given the previous day's events. His face fell when he saw the three red-tunicked men waiting in his garden, but his dismay became a puzzled frown at the sight of the effeminately dressed child standing at Dubnus's side.

'Gentlemen? How can I—'

'We've no time for explanations, Menius Caudinus.' Marcus looked past the baffled official into the house with a look that combined sorrow and longing. 'I used to live here, with my wife. Does that tell you all you need to know?'

Caudinus composed himself with admirable speed.

'Valerius Aquila. I didn't expect ever to meet you.'

'And you never have.' Julius leaned forward with a forbidding expression. 'Do you understand me?'

The imperial secretary nodded imperturbably.

'Perfectly. And I assume, to judge from your presence here, that I have never met your colleague the Hamian, either?'

'A wise deduction.'

'In which case I can only assume that the child is your reason for being here?'

'Yes.' Marcus shepherded the boy forward with a gentle hand

on his shoulder. 'This is Alinus. He was a slave in the palace, until the last emperor sold him. And now he has been freed by the man who purchased him. Who, as you can tell from his clothing, has been abusing his innocence. And who, seeing the error of his ways, has agreed to free the boy.'

Caudinus nodded in recognition of what was, for the child, a momentous change in his fortunes, and went down on his haunches to look the boy in the face.

'My congratulations, Alinus. You have been blessed with great fortune by these men.' He looked back up at Marcus. 'Am I to assume that this change in the boy's status was unexpected by his former owner?'

'You are.'

'And you've brought him here because . . . ?' The imperial official raised a hand. 'No, I think I can guess. With the change of regime, you will be leaving the city. Soon, I expect, before the guard get around to looking for you. Which means you want me to look after the child?'

Marcus nodded down at him.

'Take him up to the Palatine. Find Sporus, the maior domus, and tell him of the child's revised status. Warn him that I will return to Rome, some day, and that I expect to find the boy alive, and well, working in the imperial secretariat where he can come to no harm. If that is not the case when I eventually come back to the city, then both of you will come to know the meaning of the word vengeance.'

Caudinus smiled wanly at him.

'Have no fear, Marcus Valerius Aquila. A man with your grim record will have no problem inspiring complete obedience, even from the other end of the empire. I wish you a safe journey, and you can be assured that I will regale Sporus with a few of the stories that reached our ears in the secretariat as to the unlikely feats of martial excellence that you pulled off over the years, just to make sure that he considers your threat with the appropriate degree of respect.'

Back at the Emporium's dock, they found the ship's master

sharpening his sacrificial knife, while Petrus handed out small bags to the vessel's oarsmen.

'A little bit of gold to encourage them to take to sea in the closed months. He's getting quite a large quantity of the stuff' – he hooked his thumb over his shoulder at the captain – 'even though I'm told it's perfectly safe if you stick to the coast and only sail on the good days. You can repay me some day, when you're all drawn back here for some more fun and games.'

'There won't be another time. But I thank you, brother.'

Julius embraced the gang leader, who submitted to his bear-like grasp with as much dignity as he could manage.

'Oh, you'll be back. Men like you usually are. And besides, once the dust has settled, it'll all be calm again. Didius Julianus has the look of a man who'll be just malleable enough for us to talk some sense into him.'

The three men took their leave of him, Marcus not looking back at the city as he boarded the ship and joined the group of Scaurus's familia on the forward deck. He took a seat next to his son, putting an arm around Appius and smiling his thanks at Julius's wife Annia for taking care of the child.

'Did you achieve whatever it was you risked missing our departure for?'

He nodded at her with a smile, his heart lighter than it had been for months, despite the disastrous end to their venture that had Scaurus staring out over the river's western bank, clearly mourning the death of his uncle.

'Yes. We rescued a young life, or so it is to be hoped. A child the same age as my Appius, who had been sold into the house of an abuser.'

'Then you are to be congratulated, although the praise would be as much for the fact that you three idiots managed to get back here in time. Much as I love your son like my own, he needs his father.'

Marcus nodded.

'And here I am. Where we're going, I expect we'll never need to be separated again. Look, the master is making his sacrifice.'

He sat the boy Appius on his knee, pointing out the ship's captain as he poured a generous libation of wine onto the Tiber's filthy water, crumbling and scattering a handful of honey cakes that were instantly set upon by the quayside's squabbling gulls. Julius sat down beside his wife, sliding his axe into the heavy bag and leaning back to enjoy the morning's chilly sunlight.

'Well, that's that. A disaster it might have been for the tribune, but at least we all survived. Even the infamous gladiator Aquila.'

Annia snorted derisively.

'The cack-brained idiot Aquila, more like. Telling his son they'll never be separated again, when the gods only know how likely he is to keep that promise.'

'He means it.'

Annia shook her head at her husband.

'I *know* he means it. He meant it last time, before we all upped and followed your precious tribune into this nest of vipers.'

Julius shook his head briskly.

'No, just this once you're wrong. This time it really is different. Which is why we're going as far from Rome as it's possible to go, without ending up knee-deep in Parthians which, trust me, I'm never going to do again.' The big man stretched wearily. 'The tribune knows the man who commands in Syria, and says he's the least likely member of the nobility to try on the purple for size. We'll have warmth, good food and good wine. Everything a retired soldier needs to be happy.' He raised a hand to forestall her rejoinder. 'Apart, that is, from the firm hand of a good woman to keep him retired.'

'Keep you retired?' Julius's woman laughed at him, shaking her head. 'Me? You fools are no more capable of retiring than I am of believing your bullshit. Even if you believe it yourself.'

'And I won't argue with you, my love. Time will tell the truth of my words.'

She looked over the ship's side, raising her eyebrows and shaking her head in implacable disbelief.

'Indeed it will.'

And then Morban and I will have a reckoning, she thought, but didn't add, with him coughing up the two aurei that he's matched to one of mine. You'll be wearing a crested helmet again inside the year, as I have wagered, and I'll be sadder but richer. Which is the way of things, when you love a man who loves the pack of wolves he runs with more than he loves life itself.

She smiled indulgently at her husband as he sat his son and daughter on his knees, and at Marcus as he explained to Appius the various parts of the ship, pointing at each and telling him what their purpose was.

'Let them have a few months of happiness. They've earned it.'

Julius looked over at her curiously.

'What's that, my love?'

She shook her head.

'Just a quiet prayer, Julius. A request to the gods for the most I can hope for. Ah look, here's Lugos come to speak with you.'

Startled, he turned to find the barbarian giant squatting on the deck next to him with a scroll in his hand.

'It will be a long day at sea, I am told. And so this seems like the best opportunity I will have to read you an old story from the age of bronze.'

'Oh no. Gods no! Tell me this isn't happening!'

Shaking his head, he craned his neck to look past his countryman at Morban, who was grinning victoriously at him.

'How much of my gold coin is he paying you?'

'All of it.' Lugos smiled, his huge face beaming with amusement. 'It seemed important to him, for some reason.' He unrolled the scroll. 'So, shall we begin, Centurion?'

'And that's Greek? You haven't got the Latin version hidden—'

'"Sing, O goddess, the anger of Achilles son of Peleus, that brought countless ills upon the Achaeans."' Lugos turned the scroll to show him its close-packed script. 'You know that there are twenty and four of these in Homer's story?'

'And so unless you suffer from the same sickness that afflicts your tutor when he reads at sea, this will be a long day?'

'Indeed.'

'And you want how much to go away and read it to someone else?'

'Two silver will be an adequate reward.'

'Half an aureus?' Julius shrugged. 'Worth it.' He reached into his purse. 'And here's the gold I would otherwise have given Morban.' He raised the coin, showed it to the former standard-bearer and then dropped it onto the giant's extended palm, grinning at Morban's pursed lips and rolled eyes. 'Now go and read to young Lupus, and leave me to lick my wounds.'

Julius winked at Annia, stood and walked down the ship's length between the straining oarsmen to the prow, looking out at Rome with an expression of disdain as the ship pirouetted on its banked oars in the Tiber's stream to face downriver.

'No place for a warrior, is it?'

He turned to find Marcus beside him.

'No. No place at all. But then, we're no longer warriors, brother. When we divest ourselves of this praetorian fancy dress, we'll be free of that life. Forever. Bringing up children and avoiding the ire of a ferocious woman are what lie in my future.'

Marcus nodded.

'Let us both hope that the head of our familia is correct in his judgement, and that Pescennius Niger decides to stay loyal to the throne.'

'In which case I'll add a plea for his loyalty to my prayers for peace, a long life and death in bed at an advanced age.'

Fully rotated to point downriver, the ship began to accelerate away from the quayside, her rowers bending their backs and breaking into a sailors' song at the master's roared command.

'Peace, a long life and death in bed?' Marcus nodded. 'I think we've earned that much.'

Historical Note

Where to start with this historical note? To coin the old cliché, describing the events that led up to and resulted from that fateful night at the end of AD 192 is a bit like trying to provide an informed commentary on a mass brawl. There's just so much going on, and so many characters. My recommendation for readers who wish to immerse themselves in that detail is *The Emperor Commodus: God and Gladiator*, by John S. McHugh. It's a lengthy and complex read, so don't say you weren't warned, but if you want the detail, it's pretty much all in there. For our purposes, looking to lay out what happened in a few pages, we will consider a historical figure who stands out head and shoulders as being the key player in these events.

Our view of Imperator Caesar Lucius Aelius Aurelius Commodus Augustus, the eighteenth emperor of Rome, has been unavoidably and probably irredeemably skewed by Joaquin Phoenix's portrayal of him in the film *Gladiator*. Not that it's the actor's fault, skilful though he was at playing the role written for him. Scriptwriters know what sells, and in this case their decision was pretty obviously to briskly ignore any nuanced version of the received historical version, and to move straight to full on murdering, cheating, all-round bad guy. The sort of crayon-drawn character that sells movie theatre seats, and which provided an easily identifiable enemy for the wronged (and of course democracy-loving) good guy Maximus. Commercially understandable, but historically unhelpful.

So, what to make of the man? Was he a disaster from day one, and the cause of Rome's descent from the glory years of the 'five good emperors'? Or was there perhaps somewhat more to his reign than that simple straight-line equation? Interestingly, it was the contemporary historian Dio Cassius who wrote that 'our history now descends from a kingdom of gold to one of iron and rust', referring to the end of his father Marcus Aurelius's reign. And this is a theme that runs through much of the commentary that followed, from Herodian to Gibbon – all portraying Commodus as an increasingly unstable and power-crazed dictator whose loss of any grip on reality not only doomed the empire to decline, but caused the senate to turn on him. But was it really that simple?

As is usually the case, the first question that the enquiring reader needs to ask is who benefitted from the establishment of that line of historical 'fact'? And the answer is a simple one – his murderers. As I've tried to weave into the story of *Vengeance*, Commodus's assassination – leaving aside the long history of enmity that my fictional character Marcus Valerius Aquila feels for the emperor – was in truth the murder of an emperor whose legitimacy was unquestioned. And whose imperial lineage stretched back to the reign of Nerva. And it was a murder carried out by men who, in Rome's incestuous network of nepotism and back-scratching, actually owed their positions to either Commodus or his father. So what could have driven them to cut off the hand that fed them? The answer, it is believed, lies in an event that had taken place ten years before.

First, let's establish the backdrop. This was far from an 'era of gold'. By AD 180, the empire was already in deep financial trouble. The costs of fifteen years of almost constant war had run headlong into the chaos wrought by the plague that had been brought into the empire at the start of that period, ironically by soldiers returning from Lucius Verus's victories in the east against the Parthians. Faced with high costs and a shrinking revenue base, Marcus Aurelius's refusal to increase taxes on the nobility had created a deep structural problem in imperial finances that made the only answer, in the short term, debasing the coinage (putting in less precious metal and more base material).

And while this maintained political stability, he had also failed to prevent plotting within the imperial family itself. His wife Faustina appears to have been involved in the revolt of Avidius Cassius, despite the death sentence that would have entailed for her son Commodus. And her readiness to intrigue seems to have been passed on to her daughter Lucilla, who by the early 180s was enraged (having once been the wife of the emperor Lucius Verus, and having been raised as an Augusta), first at being married off to the provincial Claudius Pompeianus, and then at being supplanted in the pecking order by Commodus's wife Crispina. And so she set in train events that were to change the course of history.

The initial turning point on the path to AD 193's momentous events – Commodus's assassination, a civil war that decimated the very nobility who had murdered their emperor, and the resulting outright dictatorship under Septimius Severus – seems to have been the attempted assassination which Commodus survived ten years before in AD 182. An attempt on his life that had been inspired and procured by his own sister. A young man called Claudius Pompeianus Quintianus, who was reputed to be her lover (and who seems to have been a boyhood companion of his would-be victim), leapt from the shadows of the amphitheatre, taking emperor and bodyguard by surprise. But rather than using that moment of advantage to strike swiftly, he seems (if we can trust the historical record) to have waved the blade about, shouting that 'this is what the senate have sent you', and generally been long-winded enough to be overpowered by the praetorians without landing a single blow. For a young man barely out of his teens, it must have been a horrific surprise. A purge followed, several senatorial families paying the price for Quintianus's failure.

Commodus had, until that moment, ruled in the same style as his father, giving much respect to the senior members of the senate on whom the imperial partnership rested, other perhaps than bestowing prominent roles upon his favourite freedman Saoterus. But from the moment that a knife was brandished at him in the name of the senate, it wasn't unreasonable for him to have doubted who he could really trust. And although this was the perennial problem for the emperors – how an imperial ruler and a republican nobility could ever truly co-exist in the fullest sense of the word – it was this attempt at assassination by the senate and his own sister that made him turn away from his father's guiding principles. And this is no surprise, when we consider the way that relationship worked, and how it was betrayed in AD 182.

In simple terms, under the Aurelian model (and long before it, ever since the reign of Augustus) the emperor was declared to be the greatest man in the empire, and loaded with honours, titles and powers. The senate recognised their less exalted position, and depended on imperial *beneficia* to make them great patrons of their clients in turn, enabling them to reward their *amici* for their loyalty. Trickle-down economics, of a sort. It is no accident that the most regular feature of an emperor's day was the early morning *salutatio*, held in the great audience chamber of the Flavian Palace, at which the emperor was greeted by his *amici*, the great and the good of Rome, who would then petition him in much the same way their clients would then ask favours of them.

And this was where the massive problem that the attempted assassination caused was at its most acute. An *amicus* who received *beneficia* was expected to demonstrate loyalty and *gratia*. Yet those prominent Romans who had become involved in the plot had broken the bonds of *amicitia*, becoming instead *ingratus*. As a result, Commodus now started to reject the veneer of equality so artfully practised by his father, for the harsh political reality of imperial rule. Not that he lacked for levers with which to control the senate – having control of all posts, promotions, appointments, monetary grants, privileges and symbols of status. But he was very clearly now in a fight to preserve his own life, and will have been quite clear as to the fates of those in the same position who had failed: Caligula, Nero and Domitian.

Paradoxically, the greatest threat to his life had materialised from both the imperial family and the *amici Caesaris,* the so-called friends of the emperor. We can only imagine the shock that a man barely out of his teens must have suffered. And his response was perfectly understandable – to limit access to his person by members of the senatorial aristocracy who could no longer be trusted. In consequence, a new class of *amici Caesaris* quickly rose to prominence – the palace bureaucrats, professional and effective, who were bitterly hated by the senators who were now deprived of their former influence and power. In their own words, the senate saw themselves as 'the slaves to slaves', since most of the palace bureaucracy were either slaves or freedmen. This reversal of the usual way of things was not a humiliation that was easily borne, as aristocrats found themselves forced to approach and bribe social inferiors to gain the favours they needed to secure the loyalty of their own *amici.* Patronage they considered to be theirs as a birthright was being usurped by commoners, and worse, freed slaves.

Freedmen in positions of influence were nothing new, of course. Roman imperial history was littered with examples of their role in government being tolerated and even celebrated by poets like Martial. What was different in the new model Commodus built to protect himself from the *ingrates* of the senate was the way it quite rationally reduced their access to the emperor for the aristocracy. Men like Perennis and Laetus, members of the equestrian order, and Cleander and Eclectus, freedmen, became the controllers of all imperial contact. Not for nothing was the title *cubicularius* – chamberlain – bestowed upon Cleander, because he had been appointed to a position with the ability to control who came into the emperor's most private quarters. The flaw – obvious in hindsight – was that these newly powerful men were more than ready to conspire with those members of the nobility who felt that they, as senators, should be in the position of ultimate power, and 'do things differently, the way it should be' (in other words, for the benefit of themselves and their cronies in the senate). In the ultimate irony, it was the very men who Commodus hoped would protect him from the senate that were to be instrumental in his downfall.

The path from the attempted assassination of AD 182 was not a simple one, of course, as I have tried to illustrate in the first twelve books in the Empire series. First his sister, boyhood friend Claudius Pompeianus Quintianus and several other senior senators tried to kill him, leading him to place his trust in Perennis as the sole praetorian prefect. Following which, Perennis firstly managed to have his beloved *amicus* Saoterus executed, then cunningly engineered the downfall of his co-prefect Paternus by casting him as being responsible for the judicial murder of the emperor's favourite. Then, when Commodus's trust in Perennis was damaged beyond repair by a combination of military incompetence and what looked quite a lot like plotting to remove the emperor (or at least as it was presented by Cleander), Perennis, like Paternus before him, was ousted and executed. Cleander, in his turn, fell victim to a combination of perceived incompetence and palace intrigues, making way for his successor Eclectus who, just like Perennis and Cleander in their time, posed as the emperor's protector.

And while there were still powerful families within the aristocracy who continued their conspiracies to kill the emperor, and hijack imperial power to deliver power and wealth to themselves and their clients, it was Eclectus who actually had the access needed to circumvent the praetorian ring of steel around Commodus and make their ambitions into reality. Allied with Marcia, the emperor's concubine, who was also his lover, and Laetus, the praetorian prefect, he plotted with Pertinax, another of Commodus's long-standing *amici* and the leader of a powerful senatorial faction. Commodus's trust in these close friends and protectors was repaid with treachery, making it hard not to have a little sympathy for him, given the long list of people who he felt had his back then positioning themselves to put the knife in, starting with his own mother.

And therein lies what might be termed the tragedy of

Commodus's time as emperor. Unable to trust the *ingrates* of the senate, he sought to surround himself with men whose humble origins made them seem trustworthy, or at least less likely to grasp after imperial power than the senatorial families whose belief in their superiority and suitability to rule was hardwired into their belief systems from birth. That it was these freedmen who were to plague his rule with the corruption and conspiracy that resulted in his death is perhaps the ultimate irony of his reign. And might go a long way to explain the almost psychotic state of mind to which he seems to have descended towards the end of his rule.

Whether the reader is inclined to believe that Commodus was made mad by genetics and upbringing, or by the ever-deepening spiral of his rule into betrayal that resulted in his death, one thing is clear: his murder on the last day of AD 192 was the cue for a good deal more terror among the aristocratic families that had conspired to kill him than would have been the case had he continued to rule. And the eventual accession of an emperor, after four years of bitter civil war, who was to rule in a very different manner. But Septimius Severus's rise to power is the subject for another day.

The Roman Army
in AD 182

By the late second century, the point at which the *Empire* series begins, the Imperial Roman Army had long since evolved into a stable organisation with a stable *modus operandi*. Thirty or so legions (there's still some debate about the Ninth Legion's fate), each with an official strength of 5,500 legionaries, formed the army's 165,000-man heavy infantry backbone, while 360 or so auxiliary cohorts (each of them the rough equivalent of a 600-man infantry battalion) provided another 217,000 soldiers for the empire's defence.

Positioned mainly in the empire's border provinces, these forces performed two main tasks. Whilst ostensibly providing a strong means of defence against external attack, their role was just as much about maintaining Roman rule in the most challenging of the empire's subject territories. It was no coincidence that the troublesome provinces of Britannia and Dacia were deemed to require 60 and 44 auxiliary cohorts respectively, almost a quarter of the total available. It should be noted, however, that whilst their overall strategic task was the same, the terms under which the two halves of the army served were quite different.

The legions, the primary Roman military unit for conducting warfare at the operational or theatre level, had been in existence since early in the republic, hundreds of years before. They were composed mainly of close-order heavy infantry, well-drilled and highly motivated, recruited on a professional basis and, critically to an understanding of their place in Roman society, manned by soldiers who were Roman citizens. The jobless poor were thus provided with a route to a valuable trade, since service with the legions was as much about construction – fortresses, roads and even major defensive works such as Hadrian's Wall – as destruction. Vitally for the maintenance of the empire's borders, this attractiveness of service made a large standing field army a possibility, and allowed for both the control and defence of the conquered territories.

By this point in Britannia's history three legions were positioned to control the restive peoples both beyond and behind the province's borders. These were the 2nd, based in South Wales, the 20th, watching North Wales, and the 6th, positioned to the east of the Pennine range and ready to respond to any trouble on the northern frontier. Each of these legions was commanded by a legatus, an experienced man of senatorial rank deemed worthy of the responsibility and appointed by the emperor. The command structure beneath the legatus was a delicate balance, combining the requirement for training and advancing Rome's young aristocrats for their future roles with the necessity for the legion to be led into battle by experienced and hardened officers.

Directly beneath the legatus were a half-dozen or so military tribunes, one of them a young man of the senatorial class called the broad stripe tribune after the broad senatorial stripe on his tunic. This relatively inexperienced man – it would have been his first official position – acted as the legion's second-in-command, despite being a relatively tender age when compared with the men around him. The remainder of the military tribunes were narrow stripes, men of the equestrian class who usually already had some command experience under their belts from leading an auxiliary cohort. Intriguingly, since the more experienced narrow-stripe tribunes effectively reported to the broad stripe, such a reversal of the usual military conventions around fitness for command must have made for some interesting man-management situations. The legion's third in command was the camp prefect, an older and more experienced soldier, usually a former centurion deemed worthy of one last role in the legion's service before retirement, usually for one year. He would by necessity have been a steady hand, operating as the voice of experience in advising the legion's senior officers as to the realities of warfare and the management of the legion's soldiers.

Reporting into this command structure were ten cohorts of soldiers, each one composed of a number of eighty-man centuries. Each century was a collection of ten tent parties – eight men who literally shared a tent when out in the field. Nine of the cohorts had six centuries, and an establishment strength of 480 men, whilst the prestigious first cohort, commanded by the legion's senior centurion, was composed of five double-strength centuries and therefore fielded 800 soldiers when fully manned. This organisation provided the legion with its cutting edge: 5,000 or so well-trained heavy infantrymen operating in regiment and company-sized units, and led by battle-hardened officers, the legion's centurions, men whose position was usually achieved by dint of their demonstrated leadership skills.

The rank of centurion was pretty much the peak of achievement for an ambitious soldier, commanding an eighty-man century and paid ten times as much as the men each officer commanded. Whilst the majority of centurions were promoted from the ranks, some were appointed from above as a result of patronage, or as a result of having completed their service in the Praetorian Guard, which had a shorter period of service than the legions. That these externally imposed centurions would have undergone their very own 'sink or swim' moment in dealing with their new colleagues is an unavoidable conclusion, for the role was one that by necessity led from the front, and as a result suffered disproportionate casualties. This makes it highly likely that any such appointee felt unlikely to make the grade in action would have received very short shrift from his brother officers.

A small but necessarily effective team reported to the centurion. The optio, literally 'best' or chosen man, was his second-in-command, and stood behind the century in action with a long brass-knobbed stick, literally pushing the soldiers into the fight should the need arise. This seems to have been a remarkably efficient way of managing a large body of men, given the centurion's place alongside rather than behind his soldiers, and the optio would have been a cool head, paid twice the usual soldier's wage and a candidate for promotion to centurion if he performed well. The century's third-in-command was the tesserarius or watch officer, ostensibly charged with ensuring that sentries were posted and that everyone knew the watch word for the day, but also likely to have been responsible for the profusion of tasks such as checking the soldiers' weapons and equipment, ensuring the maintenance of discipline and so on, that have occupied the lives of junior non-commissioned officers throughout history in delivering a combat-effective unit to their officer. The last member of the centurion's team was the century's signifer, the standard bearer, who both provided a rallying point for the soldiers and helped the centurion by transmitting marching orders to them through movements of his standard. Interestingly, he also functioned as the century's banker, dealing with the soldiers' financial affairs. While a soldier caught in the horror of battle might have thought twice about defending his unit's standard, he might well also have felt a stronger attachment to the man who managed his money for him!

At the shop-floor level were the eight soldiers of the tent party who shared a leather tent and messed together, their tent and cooking gear carried on a mule when the legion was on the march. Each tent party would inevitably have established its own pecking order based upon the time-honoured factors of strength, aggression, intelligence – and the rough humour required to survive in such a harsh world. The men that came to dominate their tent parties would have been the century's unofficial backbone, candidates for promotion to watch officer. They would also have been vital to their tent mates' cohesion under battlefield conditions, when the relatively thin leadership team could not always exert sufficient presence to inspire the individual soldier to stand and fight amid the horrific chaos of combat.

The other element of the legion was a small 120-man detachment of cavalry, used for scouting and the carrying of messages between units. The regular army depended on auxiliary cavalry wings, drawn from those parts of the empire where horsemanship was a way of life, for their mounted combat arm. Which leads us to consider the other side of the army's two-tier system.

The auxiliary cohorts, unlike the legions alongside which they fought, were not Roman citizens, although the completion of a twenty-five-year term of service did grant both the soldier and his children citizenship. The original auxiliary cohorts had often served in their homelands, as a means of controlling the threat of large numbers of freshly conquered barbarian warriors, but this changed after the events of the first century AD. The Batavian revolt in particular – when the 5,000-strong Batavian cohorts rebelled and destroyed two Roman legions after suffering intolerable provocation during a recruiting campaign gone wrong – was the spur for the Flavian policy for these cohorts to be posted away from their home provinces. The last thing any Roman general wanted was to find his legions facing an army equipped and trained to fight in the same way. This is why the reader will find the auxiliary cohorts described in the *Empire* series, true to the historical record, representing a variety of other parts of the empire, including Tungria, which is now part of modern-day Belgium.

Auxiliary infantry was equipped and organised in so close a manner to the legions that the casual observer would have been hard put to spot the differences. Often their armour would be mail, rather than plate, sometimes weapons would have minor differences, but in most respects an auxiliary cohort would be the same proposition to an enemy as a legion cohort. Indeed there are hints from history that the auxiliaries may have presented a greater challenge on the battlefield. At the battle of Mons Graupius in Scotland, Tacitus records that four cohorts of Batavians and two of Tungrians were sent in ahead of the legions and managed to defeat the enemy without requiring any significant assistance. Auxiliary cohorts were also often used on the flanks of the battle line, where reliable and well-drilled troops are essential to handle attempts to outflank the army. And while the legions contained soldiers who were as much tradesmen as fighting men, the auxiliary cohorts were primarily focused on their fighting skills. By the end of the second century there were significantly more auxiliary troops serving the empire than were available from the legions, and it is clear that Hadrian's Wall would have been invalid as a concept without the mass of infantry and mixed infantry/cavalry cohorts that were stationed along its length.

As for horsemen, the importance of the empire's 75,000 or so auxiliary cavalrymen, capable of much faster deployment and manoeuvre than the infantry, and essential for successful scouting, fast communications and the denial of reconnaissance information to the enemy, cannot be overstated. Rome simply did not produce anything like the strength in mounted troops needed to avoid being at a serious disadvantage against those nations which by their nature were cavalry-rich. As a result, as each such nation was conquered their mounted forces were swiftly incorporated into the army until, by the early first century BC, the decision was made to disband what native Roman cavalry as there was altogether, in favour of the auxiliary cavalry wings.

Named for their usual place on the battlefield, on the flanks or 'wings' of the line of battle, the cavalry cohorts were commanded by men of the equestrian class with prior experience as legion military tribunes, and were organised around the basic 32-man turma, or squadron. Each squadron was commanded by a decurion, a position analogous with that of the infantry centurion. This officer was assisted by a pair of junior officers: the duplicarius or double-pay, equivalent to the role of optio, and the sesquiplarius or pay-and-a-half, equal in stature to the infantry watch officer. As befitted the cavalry's more important military role, each of these ranks was paid about 40 per cent more than the infantry equivalent.

Taken together, the legions and their auxiliary support presented a standing army of over 400,000 men by the time of the events described in the *Empire* series. Whilst this was sufficient to both hold down and defend the empire's 6.5 million square kilometres for a long period of history, the strains of defending a 5,000-kilometre-long frontier, beset on all sides by hostile tribes, were also beginning to manifest themselves. The prompt move to raise three new legions undertaken by the new emperor Septimius Severus in AD 197, in readiness for over a decade spent shoring up the empire's crumbling borders, provides clear evidence that there were never enough legions and cohorts for such a monumental task. This is the backdrop for the *Empire* series, which will run from AD 182 well into the early third century, following both the empire's and Marcus Valerius Aquila's travails throughout this fascinatingly brutal period of history.

The Chain of Command
LEGION

LEGATUS —— LEGION CAVALRY (120 HORSEMEN)

BROAD STRIPE TRIBUNE

5 'MILITARY' NARROW STRIPE TRIBUNES

CAMP PREFECT

SENIOR CENTURION

10 COHORTS
(ONE OF 5 CENTURIES OF 160 MEN EACH)
(NINE OF 6 CENTURIES OF 80 MEN EACH)

CENTURION

CHOSEN MAN

WATCH OFFICER   STANDARD BEARER

10 TENT PARTIES OF
8 MEN APIECE

THE CHAIN OF COMMAND
AUXILIARY
INFANTRY COHORT

LEGATUS

PREFECT

(OR A TRIBUNE FOR A LARGER COHORT SUCH AS
THE FIRST TUNGRIAN)

SENIOR CENTURION

6-10 CENTURIES

CENTURION

CHOSEN MAN

WATCH OFFICER   STANDARD BEARER

10 TENT PARTIES OF
8 MEN APIECE